A FATE OF FLAME

PROPHECY OF THE FORGOTTEN FAE BOOK THREE

TESSONJA ODETTE

A FATE OF FLAME

To the women who were underestimated.
To the witches forged by flame.

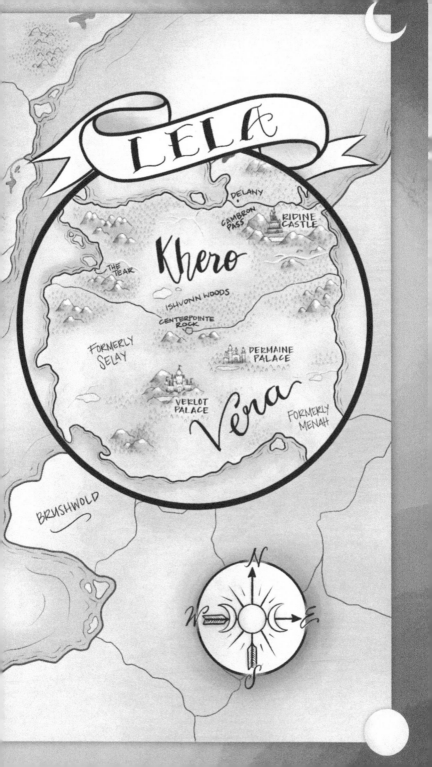

THE BLIGHT

THE VOID

THE VEIL

LE'LANA

BEFORE THE VEIL

PALACE OF THE MORKARA

THE MISSING HEART OF EL'ARA

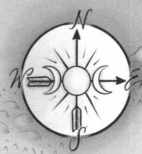

Aveline Corasande Caelan had only one good memory of the dungeon at Ridine Castle. A kiss. It had been delivered with a blend of trickery and desire, and she'd received it with equal parts yearning and rage. It was a strange first kiss between her and Teryn Alante, but it held a special place in her heart.

It was that special place, that steadying warmth, that allowed Cora to keep her nerves from fraying in that same dungeon now. To anchor herself in this moment without letting her mind drift to all the dark memories this place conjured. Cora hated coming to the dungeon, but at least she wasn't a prisoner this time. No, this time she was the captor.

She kept her face impassive as she studied the man tied to the chair at the center of the cell. He was an older man with shaggy gray hair and a build that bordered on frail, but Cora wasn't swayed into sympathy. This man was dangerous.

Captain Alden of Cora's royal guard stepped closer to the captive, one hand on the hilt of her sword. Alden was already an imposing figure with her towering height and scarred left cheek that spoke of her experience in battle, but the way she scowled down at the prisoner, her face lit by the single lantern resting on the ground, made her look downright terrifying. Her golden hair was pulled back in a tight bun that showed off all the hard angles of her face. "Why were you seeking information about Ridine Castle?" she said, voice low and controlled.

To the prisoner's credit, he held Captain Alden's eyes without falter, even though one of his own was nearly swollen shut, and delivered his answer with equal calm. "I was simply doing my job. Every kingdom has its spies. Even yours."

Cora kept her breaths even, her palms open, seeking the truth beneath the prisoner's lies. While her abilities were far from infallible, being a clairsentient witch had its uses. Her magic worked through feeling, both physical sensation and emotion alike. She was familiar enough with her internal nudges to know which sensations meant danger and which meant safety, as well as other varying shades in between. Her emotions fueled her magic and had even allowed her to accomplish strange and unusual feats. The most recent of which was her ability to astral travel. Or, as she'd learned the fae called it, worldwalking.

Now her magic was less focused on her own feelings and more on the prisoner's. Not every clairsentient witch could physically feel the emotions of others, but Cora's magic had always been like this. It was often a burden that required nearly full-time use of mental shields to block outside emotional stimuli, but in this situation her powers were essential.

With her mental wards down, she let the man's emotions flood her. They were dark, heavy, clouded with secrets.

Arrogance tinged these sensations, reflected in his smug expression, the way he grinned despite his split lip. But there was something else there too: a dash of fear. Cora wondered if it had anything to do with the muscular gaoler who leaned against the cell wall behind the prisoner. His arms were folded over his chest, hands curled into fists—fists that had caused the spy's current wounds.

Were Cora kinder and softer she'd have felt bad for the old man's condition. But she was neither kind nor soft where spies from Norun were concerned. Not after the unsettling rumors her own spies had uncovered. According to their intel, the Kingdom of Norun had recently formed an alliance with Syrus—the very kingdom she feared more than any other. For Syrus was home to an enemy she hoped she'd never meet—King Darius Solaria, father of Morkai, seeker of the fae realm. A realm she'd been to, just over seven months ago, and now held valuable secrets about.

Captain Alden spoke again. "Why has Norun taken such an interest in Khero?"

The spy scoffed. "Sudden? I'd hardly call it sudden. Norun isn't easy to forgive, and your kingdom is responsible for the death of Prince Helios."

Cora bristled at the accusation. Retorts roared inside her, but she held them back with a tightening of her jaw. She wasn't here to argue with the prisoner, only to gather information. Still, she was losing patience with Norun's insistence that Khero was to blame for Helios Dorsus' death. The prince may have died in her kingdom last spring after being devoured by Morkai's Roizan, but Cora and her allies had gone to great lengths to refute any association with the former duke and denounce every action he'd taken in the name of Khero. Besides, Helios had hardly been innocent. She'd witnessed his demise firsthand and hadn't been sorry to see him go. Helios had been in the process of trying to kill Teryn when the Roizan attacked, and before that, he'd intended to carve a unicorn's horn from its head while it was still alive.

No, Cora felt no remorse where Prince Helios was concerned. She couldn't even muster a flicker of sympathy for his grieving father, King Isvius of Norun. Yet she wanted none of the blame for what had happened to the prince and resented that she bore all of it. Why Norun was only blaming Khero and not Selay was beyond her. Helios had only come to Khero because of Mareleau's Heart's Hunt. Perhaps it was because Khero was the easier target and closer to Norun's borders. Meanwhile, Selay was no longer just *Selay*. It was now Vera, a kingdom forged from Selay's formal merging with Menah. Compared to Vera, Khero was small and vulnerable, without the support of trade allies across the sea and in other continents.

"Does Norun seek retribution on Khero?" Captain Alden asked.

The prisoner shrugged, the move stunted by his bindings. "Like I said, I'm just a spy. I gather specific information and share it with my masters. I'm not privy to Norun's secrets."

The man's emotions contracted inside Cora, tightening like a fist in her gut. They contradicted the nonchalance on the man's face. "He's lying," she said through her teeth. "He knows so much more than he's saying."

The captive's crooked, half-swollen gaze shot toward her. A corner of his bruised mouth flicked up. "Is this by chance the young queen?"

Cora's breath caught. She stood in shadow near the cell door, the hood of a plain gray cloak pulled low over her forehead, yet the spy had surmised her identity. Had it simply been a reckless guess, or was it obvious?

She was suddenly aware of her poise, the lift of her chin, the way she held her arms easily at her sides. They were habits she'd picked up over the last several months since her coronation. Habits she'd developed as a front, a way to radiate the regality she didn't feel. Yet she'd come to don them with ease now, slipping into them like a second skin.

Alden angled her body to intercept the prisoner's stare. "You forget who's doing the questioning."

"Ah, I see. You'll have to forgive me."

His confidence seeped into Cora, sending chills down her spine. He was the fourth Norunian spy who'd been captured on her lands, yet he was by far the boldest. The others had stayed mute through questioning and had ultimately lost their lives. But how many others might have slipped through the cracks? How many spies were crawling across her kingdom without anyone being the wiser? Cora hardly had enough spies of her own, for Khero was still recovering from all it had lost at Morkai's hands, and that included military and staff. She'd been queen for just seven months, and every day she felt the weight of how much was left to rebuild.

It all fell on her shoulders.

Alone.

No, not alone, she reminded herself. She had allies. Queen Mareleau. King Larylis. And soon she'd have Teryn beside her, sharing her burden as king consort. Her husband.

She'd been engaged to him since last summer, and she'd nearly wed him too, after her brother had been forced to step down as king. Marrying Teryn had been a condition her council had demanded, a formal alliance they'd required before they'd recognize her as Dimetreus' heir. Thankfully, she'd escaped the castle before the marriage had been finalized, for if she'd married Teryn then, she'd have wed a false version of him—Morkai possessing Teryn's body. Not that she'd escaped Morkai's treachery unscathed. No one had. He'd murdered her brother, his councilmen, and Mareleau's father. Three kingdoms had been thrown into chaos after a single night's tragedy.

A tragedy Teryn almost hadn't survived.

Panic laced through her when she remembered how he'd looked when he'd departed home with his brother to be tended to by their kingdom's skilled physicians. The kind of physicians her own kingdom lacked. His cheeks had been so gaunt then, his hair fully white. But she reminded herself he *was* alive. Alive and well, and soon he'd come home to her.

Soon he'd marry her.

Soon she could tell him everything she couldn't say while he'd been healing from his wounds.

Calm warmth seeped into her, lessening some of her dread and anchoring her back in the present moment. She locked that warmth in her chest and poured her focus into her magic, narrowing her attention on the prisoner's emotions.

"I'll ask you again," Captain Alden said. "Does Norun seek retribution on Khero? Is your kingdom planning to invade or attack Khero?"

Cora nearly shuddered at the question.

"I haven't a clue," the spy said, and Cora was struck with another tightening of emotion. Another blanket of heaviness.

More lies. Which meant he knew the answer. And if it was an answer he refused to give, that could only mean one thing.

Norun *was* planning some form of retribution. Everyone on the continent knew Norun was famed for its successful war campaigns. In the last decade, they'd conquered two kingdoms—Haldor and Sparda. Would Khero be next?

Cora's knees threatened to buckle, but she took a steadying breath, fighting past the dank stench of the cell to fill her lungs with air.

The gaoler chuckled from his place against the wall. "Perhaps I can loosen 'is tongue. He's a bit more talkative than 'e was before we had our private chat. Just think how much more 'e might say after our next rendezvous."

A flicker of fear shot through the prisoner's emotions.

"Not yet," Alden said. "I have one more question."

The spy turned a contrived look of boredom on the captain.

"Has Norun formally allied with Syrus?" Alden asked.

Surprise ruptured the captive's emotions, and it briefly colored his expression too. Finally, they'd cracked the spy's smooth façade. His surprise quickly faded, however, and he regained his air of indifference. "How should I know?"

Alden raised her voice. "Is Norun planning an attack on Khero *with* Syrus?"

Another stunted shrug. "I know nothing more than what I've told you."

His emotions grew tighter inside Cora, contracting again, but even without her powers it was obvious he was lying. This man was clever, well-spoken, and knew too much.

Captain Alden cast a questioning glance at her queen. Cora gave her a subtle nod, and Alden tipped her head toward the gaoler. "He's all yours."

The gaoler pushed off the wall with a cruel grin,

cracking his knuckles as he sauntered toward his captive. Cora turned on her heel and exited the cell. As the door closed behind her, the prisoner's fear lanced her gut, but she breathed it away, banishing the no-longer-needed emotions. She strode down the dimly lit dungeon hall, her steps swift, focusing only on the elements around her—the stale air, the stone beneath her feet, the flickering light from the sparse lamps, the moisture dripping down the walls. Air, earth, fire, water. The substances that fueled her magic. Protected her. Guided her. She drew them closer now, imagining them wrapping around her like a cocoon until she could feel her mental shields snapping into place.

The prisoner's fear no longer prodded her, and she was left with only her own emotions.

She reached the end of the dungeon hall when she heard the first strike of flesh against flesh. A grunt of pain. She shuddered, knowing a man was getting beaten on her order, but she could only summon the slightest pity. The spy knew too much and was harboring important information. Information she needed. She wouldn't let herself regret what had to be done.

Cora was a queen to her people.

A witch at her core.

And if it meant protecting her kingdom, she could be a villain to her enemies too.

2

Fatigue weighed heavy on Cora as she ascended the stairwell leading from the dungeon. Taking on another's emotions did that to her, as did thoughts of war. But there was one thing she could count on to clear her head. Or rather one *creature*.

She paused on the next step and closed her eyes, extending her senses outward, seeking a familiar mind. A wordless greeting responded, carrying a warmth as comforting as a hug. Valorre, her unicorn companion and dearest friend, was close enough that she could feel his presence despite the walls between them. She could almost smell the soil of the forest outside the castle, hear the snapping of twigs beneath his hooves, feel the heat of the sun streaming through the canopy of trees. Her lips stretched into a smile. She opened her eyes and raced the rest of the way up the steps. *I'm going to try to sneak out*, she mentally conveyed.

Even though she was often in the presence of her guards or lady's maids, she could find an excuse to be alone and use her worldwalking ability to reach the forest in the blink of an eye. All she needed was strong emotion to drive her and a clear destination.

She expected Valorre to respond with approval, for it had been weeks since Cora had snuck out for a forest ride. Instead, a ripple of hesitation moved through their energetic link. *I don't think you should.*

She frowned as she pushed open the door at the top of the staircase. *Why not?*

Well...because—

"Prince Teryn has arrived." Master Arther, steward of Ridine Castle, practically sprang before the doorway. He wrung his gloved hands as exasperated relief eased the furrow between his brows.

Several emotions shot through Cora one after the other. Shock, panic, excitement. "He...what? He wasn't supposed to be here until tomorrow. When did he arrive?"

"Less than an hour ago, while you were...down *there*." He said the last part in a whisper as he cast a glance at the door Cora had emerged from. Not that there was any reason for secrecy here. No one entered the halls leading to the dungeons aside from Cora, her guards, and approved staff. Now the only other people in the hall besides Cora and Arther were two members of the royal guard who'd stood sentinel outside the door.

Cora shifted her mental focus from her steward to Valorre. *Did you know? Is that what you were about to say?*

Yes, came Valorre's reply.

Why didn't you warn me? He could have. While her guards had been ordered not to interrupt her while she was in the dungeon, Valorre hadn't been given such a restriction.

You were busy, Valorre said. *Didn't want to distract you from scary men in the dark place.*

The dark place was what he called the dungeon. While

their connection was strong enough to give each other impressions of their current locations or environments, Valorre didn't always understand the impressions he received.

Cora returned her attention to Arther as she realized he was speaking again. "—King Larylis and Queen Mareleau will be here in just two hours."

She frowned. "Teryn arrived separately from them?"

"Yes, he said he rode ahead."

Her lungs constricted. "Was something wrong? Was there an emergency?"

"No, it seemed more like he grew tired of his retinue's slow pace."

That was a relief. After everything that had happened last spring and summer, Cora's mind was often quick to go to the darkest places when anything seemed out of the ordinary. But Teryn's actions made sense. Mareleau's retinue was moving slowly due to her pregnancy and the precautions required around travel. She couldn't blame him for taking off on his own. If only he'd sent word ahead of time, she'd have been there to greet him.

"Where is he now?" she asked.

"He said he was tired after his ride, so I escorted him to his guest chamber to rest."

She was about to ask why Arther had taken him to a guest room and not her own chambers, but she stopped herself. Even though she and Teryn would share the royal suite once they were wed, they couldn't be seen sharing quarters before their wedding.

A troubling thought occurred to her.

She took a step closer to Arther. "He said he was tired? Did he seem unwell?"

"He seemed...fine," Arther said, brows knit with confusion.

Just fine? Her lungs tightened all over again. She cast the same question at Valorre.

I didn't see his face, he conveyed. *I saw him riding but he wore a head blanket.*

A cloak, Cora corrected. *Then how did you know it was him?*

Smelled like him.

He has a smell?

Like strength and moonbeams.

Cora nearly snorted a laugh. She could have taken comfort in Valorre's insistence that he smelled like strength, but she couldn't take him seriously with the part about moonbeams. Valorre had always had a bit of a crush on Teryn. Of course he'd smell like strength and moonbeams to him.

She shook her head and pulled her consciousness from Valorre's. This was no laughing matter. If Teryn was fatigued after his ride, that might mean he'd pushed his stamina too far. Mother Goddess, why the hell had he ridden ahead of his retinue? His physicians had given him the go-ahead to travel months ago. In fact, he'd been scheduled to arrive last month but had been delayed when an unexpected envoy had arrived from Brushwold, and Teryn had stayed behind to help his brother host them. An extra month of recovery should have aided his health, but just because Teryn was fit to travel didn't mean he was in peak condition. Cora had seen what Morkai's possession had done to his body. He'd nearly died from it. He'd hardly been able to move or speak when she'd last seen him.

Cora's mind spun to the darkest places all over again.

She lifted her chin. "I must see my fiancé at once."

Arther released a long-suffering sigh and spoke with a

practiced tone. "It wouldn't be proper, Majesty. You must hold a formal audience and greet him before the court. You know this."

She opened her mouth to argue, but he was right. Seven devils, she was loath to admit it, but now that she was queen, she was bound by rules of royal propriety before the public eye. And Ridine Castle was no longer as private as it used to be, especially with her fast-approaching wedding. Her coronation had been a private affair, a somber necessity after a great tragedy, which meant the royal wedding would mark the first public celebration the castle had hosted in years. As a result, eyes were everywhere.

Yet she didn't have the patience to wait hours to see Teryn. She hadn't seen him in seven months. Seven achingly long months with only letters between them. She was dying to see that he was well with her own eyes. To hear his voice. And to tell him all the things she never had the courage to convey by pen and paper.

Arther softened his tone. "Besides, Majesty, he's likely sleeping by now. He asked to rest. We will move your audience with the king and queen to this evening after they arrive, so you may receive Prince Teryn shortly."

Tension unraveled from her shoulders but not entirely. She *had* to see him. Maybe he was sleeping. Maybe they couldn't have the heartfelt conversation she'd been planning for. She could at least rest her eyes upon his face and know he was well. Only then could she fully relax.

She released a calming breath and gathered her composure. Then, steeling her expression, she delivered her lie. "You're right, Master Arther. I am so grateful for your counsel. I shall return to my quarters at once and ready myself for tonight's audience with our royal guests."

"That is the right choice, Majesty. I will clear the way

through the great hall so you may reach the keep without further ado." After a bow, he turned on his heel—but halted midstep. His eyes shot back to her, widening as they took in her ensemble. His nose wrinkled with clear distaste. "Please allow me to take your cloak."

Heat flushed her cheeks. Right. She'd nearly forgotten about the dark cloak she was wearing. Having donned it for secrecy over fashion, it was hardly fit for a queen. And even though Arther would clear the way ahead, courtiers would still see her.

She gave him a thankful grin and undid the clasp at her neck. Underneath the cloak, she wore a mauve brocade gown with a ruffled square neck and an overskirt that parted at the center to reveal layers of ivory lace—a far more regal look. When she passed him a cloak, she added with contrived nonchalance, "Which guest room is my fiancé in?"

Arther's eyes narrowed with suspicion, but he had no reason to hide such information from her. "The Cambron suite, Majesty."

"Thank you, Master Arther."

He bowed once more and strode ahead toward the great hall. Cora hid her smile behind his back.

HER HEART WAS A RACING, RIOTING MESS BY THE TIME SHE entered her bedroom in the royal suite. She'd dismissed her lady's maids, ordering them not to return to ready her for tonight's audience for another hour. She probably didn't need a full hour, considering Teryn was likely dozing by now, but it would ensure no one would enter her chambers and find her missing.

She stood before the mirror, checking her appearance.

Turning her face to one side then the other, she studied her golden-tan skin, her dark eyes rimmed with kohl and powdered cosmetics, her black hair pinned in a coronet. As she patted the neat braid that encircled her head, a stray tendril sprang loose, falling onto her cheek. She was about to reach for a hairpin from her vanity but stopped herself. Teryn's voice rang from memory.

I like when it's a mess, he'd once said about her hair.

A giddy grin tugged her lips as she loosened another strand of hair, then another. With her hair properly mussed, she removed her gloves and brushed her tattooed palms over her skirts, smoothing wrinkles that weren't there. Assessing herself once more, she gave her reflection an approving nod, though she wasn't sure why she was going through all the trouble. Teryn probably wouldn't be awake to see her. Still, on the off chance that he wasn't sleeping, she wanted to look her best.

Anxious excitement flooded her heart, sending it thudding even faster. She needed to steady its raging pulse with at least a sliver of sobriety. While she was satisfied with her appearance, she needed to ready herself for the inevitable changes she'd find in him. He may look different from the man she'd fallen in love with. His hair had been sapped of color during his battle over his body and would likely be brittle and gray. He'd be thinner. Weaker. A far cry from the broad-shouldered man who'd once made her blush while dueling shirtless. It might break her heart to see how much he'd changed. How badly his body had been broken.

But she would love him just the same.

And if he was awake, she'd finally get to tell him that. Finally say the words neither had let past their lips despite feeling them pulse between them, despite almost hearing them in mumbled tones when Teryn was barely conscious, despite reading them between the lines of their letters.

She took a steadying breath, filling her lungs with air. Then, rooting her feet beneath her, she connected to the element of earth. Afternoon sunlight streamed through the open windows of her bedroom, linking her to the fire element. Then the emotions flooding her chest, nourishing her very soul, connected her to water.

Closing her eyes, she thought of Teryn. Felt his proximity, his nearness, his presence, just down the hall. She knew how close his room was. The Cambron suite was just two doors away. If she wanted to, she could sneak down the servants' passage, using her magic to extend her senses, cloak herself in shadow, and evade passersby no matter how busy the secret halls had become. But she wouldn't, for she had faster means. Easier means. Quieter means.

She could cross the distance between them in a single step.

Keeping her emotions fixated on Teryn, she pictured the bedroom in the Cambron suite, imagined him lying on the bed, safe beneath the smooth linen sheets and velvet blankets. She imagined the carpeted floors beneath her feet, the bedroom door behind her, the four-poster bed just ahead. Calm settled over her despite the excitement radiating from her chest. Then she took a single step.

She opened her eyes and found the new destination before her, exactly as she'd imagined it. A cream-and-violet patterned carpet cradled her feet while a mahogany bed stood before her.

But Teryn wasn't on that bed.

He was standing mere feet away, half facing her.

Shirtless.

The top button of his trousers undone.

Her breath caught as she took in the low rise of his waistband, the fingers that had been in the process of loosening the next button down, his muscled forearms. She lifted her gaze, drinking in the sculpted V of his lower abdomen, then his rib cage, marred with the puckered scar he'd earned at Centerpointe Rock. She studied his curving biceps, his wide shoulders, his silver hair that fell in tousled waves just above his collarbone.

Mother Goddess, this was not the frail, weak version of Teryn she'd expected. Sure, he was slightly leaner than he'd been before, but he didn't look unwell at all.

He looked...good.

Really, really good.

Her eyes darted to his face and found his familiar green irises sparkling with mischief. A corner of his lips quirked at one corner. "What a pleasant surprise."

3

Cora had no thoughts. None. Just shock and lust and...what had he just said? He'd spoken, but she'd been too distracted to hear.

"It's a good thing you didn't arrive a second later," he said. "Unless...an eyeful is what you were going for."

Her eyes dipped back down to the open top button of his trousers and she realized what he was referring to. Had she invaded his room any later...

Her cheeks blazed. What the hell had she been thinking? What had she nearly walked in on? Sure, he could have been undressing for bed, but he also could have been preparing to do...other things.

She clenched her teeth as if she could chew through her mortification. How had she not considered the myriad of situations she could have stumbled upon? She'd been expecting a tired, frail figure asleep on the bed, not a virile young man encased in muscle with a teasing smirk on his lips.

What an idiot she'd been. "I should go," she muttered as she whirled abruptly on her heels—

She stumbled as hands framed her shoulders and tugged her back a step. It took her a moment to realize what she'd almost collided with. Straight ahead was the closed bedroom door that she'd nearly slammed into in her haste to get away. Teryn had pulled her back just in time...and now held her against his chest, every inch of his bare torso pressed against her back. His skin was hot against the bare flesh at the nape of her neck—the only exposed skin that touched his.

His voice rumbled low in her ear, his breath warming its shell. "Is that any way to greet your fiancé?"

Her heart slammed against her ribs and she was certain he could feel its rhythm as he held her close from behind. She opened her mouth but she was too dumbfounded to conjure anything like a clever retort. Or *any* retort.

"Or..." He drew out the word as he took a step back, breaking their too-warm contact, and gently turned her to face him. With his hands still on her shoulders—his hold looser now—he asked, "Are you here to break things off with me? Did you have me travel all the way here just to tell me you've changed your mind about us?"

"No," she managed to blurt out. His lips curled in that devious way again and she realized he was teasing. She let herself smile then, let herself focus on all that was familiar about him. His grin, his emerald eyes, his sharp cheekbones. And his voice. The voice she'd yearned to hear every day for the last several months. She blew out a breath, her nerves unraveling.

But her calm was short-lived, for in the next moment, he closed the distance he'd created and moved his hand from her shoulder to her cheek. Her heart racketed once more, and her eyes dipped to his mouth. Was he going to kiss her? She'd been waiting for this moment for so long, yet none of her fantasies had gone like this. She averted her gaze to his neck, taking in the circular scars on both sides of his throat, twins to her own, caused by the magic-suppressing collar they'd both briefly worn. Her eyes flashed back to his, but she couldn't meet his gaze. So instead, she dragged her attention further down. But that only brought her to...

Muscles.

Naked skin.

And...Mother Goddess, why did he look so good?

Her cheeks burned hot as she wrenched her eyes back to his face and found a furrow between his brows.

Slowly, he let his hand slide from her cheek and stepped back again. "What's wrong? Am I making you uncomfortable?" There was no jest in his tone this time, only genuine concern.

That made her heart sink. Squeezing her eyes shut, she delivered an internal scolding. *Get ahold of yourself, Cora!*

As she opened her eyes, she forced herself to hold his gaze without blushing. Or...tried to. "No," she said, voice level. "I just didn't expect you to be so...so..."

Healthy.

Awake.

Handsome.

He arched a teasing brow. "So...?"

She crossed her arms and lifted her chin. "Shirtless."

He smirked at that. "Well, I was about to take a nap. I rode hard to see you." The words *rode hard* conjured the wrong images in her head. "When Master Arther told me you were preoccupied, I figured I'd get some rest."

"Why were you taking off your pants?" As soon as the question left her lips, she regretted asking. Why the hell did she ask that?

"I don't sleep clothed," he said with a chuckle. "You

would have learned that eventually. Sooner rather than later." He winked and sent her stomach flipping.

How the seven devils could he flirt so easily with her, speak to her as if no time had passed, as if a great tragedy hadn't nearly killed him, while she was so flustered? She supposed he'd been prepared to see her exactly as she was. Meanwhile, she'd been picturing a very different version of him.

He squinted, studying her with puzzled amusement. "Why do you seem disappointed?"

"I'm not disappointed. I'm just...I didn't expect..." She waved a hand at his torso. When the gesture failed to deliver her point, she propped her hands on her hips and asked, "Why the hell are you in such good shape?"

"Were you hoping your husband was an invalid?" His tone was teasing again, and it helped ease her nerves.

"No. Just..." Her cheeks blazed like a wildfire. She pursed her lips to hide her embarrassed smile.

"I like seeing you flustered over me for once. It makes me feel like less of an idiot."

She shifted to the side and covered her face in her hands. "I'm being ridiculous, aren't I?"

"What's ridiculous," Teryn said, voice dipped low, "is you haven't let me kiss you yet."

Lifting her face, she glanced at him sidelong, saw the want in his eyes, the serious edge of his jaw. Maybe this wasn't the reunion she'd spent months planning for, but it was the one she'd yearned for. *He* was the one she'd yearned for, no matter what he looked like, no matter his health, his condition, his status. She wanted him. Loved him. And he was finally here. Home.

Steeling her resolve, she fully faced him again. This time she closed the distance between them of her own accord. He was so much taller than her, she had to angle her head back to hold his hungry gaze. When only a few sparse inches separated them, she lifted a hand and rested it over his chest. Her palm thrummed, with magic, with his heartbeat, with the heat of their contact. She rested her other hand at the nape of his neck, beneath his silver-white hair.

"All right," she said, her words trembling. "I'm ready."

Teryn's expression softened, opened, reflecting Cora's vulnerability as he slowly wound his arms around her waist. Then, inch by inch, as if afraid any sudden move might make her flee, he lowered his lips to hers. Their mouths met in a kiss so soft, so tender and sweet, it made Cora want to weep. He kissed her again, the pressure firmer, and all her embarrassment melted away. There was no room for it here, not where their lips met. When he kissed her once more, she pulled him closer, angled her head, and parted her lips. His grip on her waist tightened, and he slid one hand up her spine until it cradled the back of her head. She parted her lips further and his tongue swept against hers, caressing it with needy, probing want.

"Gods, I missed you," he said against her open mouth. The words made her shudder with pleasure. He'd said as much in his letters but hearing those words, as coated as they were in desire, was better than anything she could have imagined.

"Teryn," she whispered.

He stiffened against her, his fingertips digging into the hair at the base of her coronet. His words came out deep, throaty. "Say my name again."

She startled at the demand in his tone, but it was a pleasant kind of shock. Memories blossomed, bringing her back to that dark night last summer, when she'd said his name again and again while he fought to retake his body from Morkai. She expected those memories to dampen her desire, but they didn't. Instead, they reminded her that he'd come back. Time and again, whenever she'd uttered his name, touched his face, he'd come back to her. He'd fought Morkai's possession because of the connection she and Teryn shared.

Her heart opened even more, flooding with warmth. Finally, she gave in to his order and repeated his name. "Teryn."

He devoured the word with another kiss, one hard and unyielding. "Seven devils, I missed the sound of your voice."

She was about to return the sentiment, but before she could, his hands encircled her waist and lifted her with ease. Her bottom hit a hard surface, and she released a grunt of surprise. It took a moment to realize she was now sitting on his dresser. Shock turned to thrill as his lips found hers again, then his hands found her ankles, her calves, her knees. Inch by inch, he lifted her voluminous skirts higher, allowing him to step between her legs. She aided his efforts, dragging her unwanted layers out of the way until she could hook her calves around his waist.

His lips left hers to trail down her neck, then across her collarbone. Slowly, he brushed his mouth over the upper curve of her breast, the flesh raised above the tight bodice of her gown. His hand cupped the other side and she was suddenly desperate to do away with her gown altogether. She arched into him, a fire burning hot in her core. She'd never felt desire so strong, not even when they'd kissed against the tree after Teryn proposed to her. The power of her yearning was terrifying. Addicting. Begging to be quenched.

She pulled him closer, tightening her legs around his waist. His lips left her breast to return to her eager mouth, while his hand slid from her bodice down to her thigh, resting over the hem of her silk stockings. His thumb slowly swept back and forth, and she was desperate to feel his fingers slide beneath her garter, unhook it, and climb higher. Yet his hand did no such thing, remaining on her silk-clad skin. The most delicious frustration surged through her, so she let her hands wander where his did not, sweeping them over his chest, his arms, his back. She slid her palm down the front of his abdomen. His muscles flexed against her palm, and a tremor ran through him.

Mother Goddess, she was drunk on the feel of him and she wanted more. She wanted every inch of his skin, everywhere. She wanted to paint their love with their bodies, their tongues...

The word *love* cooled some of the fire that had taken over her senses.

Right. None of her plans regarding their reunion including lovemaking within the first few minutes of seeing each other. Not that she truly minded, but she'd promised herself she'd express her feelings before they took a single step further in their relationship. Her surprise at seeing him looking so well may have thrown a hitch into some of her preparations, but she was determined to keep the others intact.

With a strangled moan, she pulled her lips from his and leaned slightly back. "Wait," she uttered.

Teryn froze at the word, though his chest heaved with rapid panting.

Silence enveloped them, save for the cadence of their breaths, as Cora cooled her ardor enough to get the next words out. "I need to talk to you about something before we..."

"Before we what?"

"Before we..." She stared down at the nonexistent space between them. "Before we do this."

A corner of his mouth flicked up. "This? What exactly is *this* you speak of?"

She gave him a withering look. "You know what I'm talking about."

His eyes narrowed. "Did you think I was going to take you here and now? That our first time would be on a dresser?"

The way he said that paired with the visuals in her head made her wish she hadn't said a word. She had no qualms about being taken here and now on a dresser.

"You did, didn't you? What a dirty mind you have."

She scoffed. "Me?"

He arched a brow, and she suddenly noticed the placement of her hands. One was still pressed to his chest, but the other...

Her gaze dipped to the thumb and forefinger that were frozen over the button of his trousers. She'd been in the process of loosening it when she'd broken their kiss.

He wasn't the one who'd tried to take things further, *she* was.

She yanked her hand away, but he caught it in his and brought it to his lips. "I'm teasing," he said, then released her, taking a full step back, breaking the circle of her thighs around his waist. "You're right. We should talk first."

She opened her mouth, but how the hell could she speak from the heart and say all the things she wanted to say if her heart wasn't currently in charge?

The flash of heat burning between her thighs reminded her exactly which part of her *was* in charge, and it wasn't interested in conversation. She bit her lip, eyes skating over the sheen of sweat that had just begun to glisten on his chest. Would it really be so bad to just pull him back to her and...save talk for later? She wasn't chaste by any means. She'd enjoyed a few short trysts when she'd lived with the Forest People, experiments devoid of love.

And yet, it was different with Teryn. There *was* love between them, and she needed him to know that. Needed him to know exactly what she wanted from their union. It was more than desire. More than attraction. More than a political alliance for the sake of their kingdoms.

Cora had practiced putting all of this into words, but her lust was chasing it away. She needed to gather her bearings. Reassess. Come back with a clear head.

She swallowed hard and leveled her voice. "Let's talk later."

He grinned. "After dinner then? Come to my room." When she said nothing, he added, "I promise I'll be fully clothed."

A shy smile lifted her lips. "All right. For now, I should go."

With a nod, he held out his hand and helped her down from the dresser. She could barely meet his eyes as she smoothed down her wrinkled skirts. "I'll see you tonight."

"Tonight," he whispered back, his knuckles briefly brushing her forearm.

Everything inside her wanted to fold into his arms with a parting kiss, but she knew better. A parting kiss would turn into so much more. So instead, she turned her back on him. Then, letting her desire fuel her magic, she closed her eyes, pictured her bedroom, and disappeared.

4

The room immediately felt colder after Cora was gone. Teryn stared at the empty space where his fiancée had been just a moment before, awed at how suddenly she'd disappeared. It was the first time she'd used her traveling magic while he was watching her. She'd first used it at the battle at Centerpointe Rock. Then again last summer to escape Morkai's clutches while he'd possessed Teryn's body. Finally, she'd used it to lock a strange magic-suppressing collar around his neck to momentarily free Teryn's body from the mage's control.

It hadn't been until he'd gotten well enough to write to Cora that he'd learned the whole story of what had happened that night. About Cora's newest power. Its strengths and limitations. Where Cora had been before she'd arrived at the meadow. How she'd gotten there. What the collar was and how it had been used against her when she'd unintentionally crossed worlds to enter the fae realm.

Just when he thought she couldn't impress him more, she was always proving just how incredible she was. And now that they'd finally seen each other for the first time in seven months, he was reminded how good she felt. How good she smelled. The sound of her voice. The rhythm of her sighs. Kissing her, touching her, had made him feel so alive. So immersed in his body.

He still had nightmares of what it felt like to be trapped in Morkai's crystal. A disembodied spirit. At night, he often startled awake, panting, shouting into the dark just to hear a voice that was his own, clawing at his skin to ensure he could feel it. During the day, he did whatever he could to feel alive. Walking. Moving. Talking. Writing. Three months ago, he'd been given the go-ahead by his physicians to take up strenuous activity, so he'd thrown himself into training. Sword. Spear. Glaive. Halberd. Anything that would ignite a fire in his muscles and remind him he was the sole operator of his body.

But none of that had made him feel as whole as when his lips had met Cora's, as desire coursed through him like a raging fire when he'd pressed closer to her on that dresser. He smirked at that piece of furniture now. He'd probably come on a touch too strong, but he'd been unable to help himself. He hadn't expected her to show up in his room out of nowhere. It had thrown all his polite, respectful plans out the window. He'd meant to greet her formally, reunite with her softly, and ease them both into the marriage they were about to embark upon.

He barked a laugh. How naive he'd been. There'd been nothing soft, formal, or polite about the way he'd kissed her, nor she him. There certainly hadn't been any of that in the way her hands had roved his chest. The fingertips she'd tucked under his waistband, absently working to free the button of his trousers.

Clenching his jaw, he curled his fists. It was all he could

do to keep from taking himself in hand and releasing the aching tension she'd built inside him. Instead, his only release was a heavy exhale, for now was not the time to act on his baser instincts. Not when he had an audience.

Banishing all thoughts of Cora on the dresser, he secured the top button of his trousers and addressed the woman who stood in the corner of his room. "I'd appreciate it if you didn't spy on intimate moments between me and my future wife, Emylia."

The woman's eyes widened. Her form was semi-transparent and devoid of color, but Teryn had known her when they were both spirits—etheras—and had seen her with brown skin, dark eyes, and black curls.

She brought a hand to her mouth, then dropped it. "You...you can see me?"

"I can." He retrieved his discarded riding tunic from the end of his bed and pulled it over his head. There was no point in trying to nap now. He'd been eager for rest after his hasty ride to Ridine Castle, for the activity had strained him. He hadn't anticipated a need to reacquaint his body with riding, thinking his weapons training had been enough to strengthen him overall. But no, every activity Teryn had once enjoyed now required a period of adaptation. He still had endurance to strengthen. Stamina to increase.

At least his surprise visit from Cora had cleared away his fatigue.

With his tunic on, he turned to face Emylia fully. She shrank away from him, as if suddenly afraid. Then, with a shake of her head, she seemed to remember herself.

"I'm sorry," she said. Her voice was soft and lacked the resonance it would have if she were alive, but he could still make out her words. "I had no idea you could see me."

"That's what you're sorry for? Not that you were spying

on a clearly private moment? How long were you going to watch?" He'd been vaguely aware of her presence—or at least *some* presence, tickling the back of his neck—ever since Cora had entered his room. Strange presences had become common to him over the last several months, so he'd been able to ignore it and give all his attention to Cora.

Emylia shrugged. "I see a lot of things these days that are considered taboo or private. I suppose I've lost that sense of propriety."

"Why are you here?"

"I heard you'd arrived. I wanted to see that you were well."

"No, why are you *here*? In this plane of existence. Why haven't you moved on?"

Her expression turned mournful. "I tried to move on to the otherlife, but I was blocked."

His breath caught. "Is it Morkai?" He hated saying the name out loud. Hated the way it made his skin crawl and made him fear he was merely a visitor in this body and not its owner.

"No," she said, holding up her hands in a placating gesture. "It's nothing like that."

Relief uncoiled his muscles. The last thing he needed was for Morkai to return in any form, even to torment the dead. The mage had already conquered death once. But Morkai was gone for good. Teryn had witnessed the mage's final death last summer, watched as his soul was burned to ash by flames of white light.

Emylia spoke again. "It's more like...I'm the one who's stopping me. There's too much heaviness here." She placed her hand on her chest.

He frowned. Emylia had told him that an ethera without a heart-center would become a wraith. But she still had her heart-center, and she was nothing like the terrifying, mind-less wraiths he'd once fought at Centerpointe Rock, cour-tesy of Morkai's blood magic. So what was she?

"Are you a ghost?" he asked.

She gave him a wry smile. "I'm an ethera with unfin-ished business, so I suppose ghost is an adequate term." When Teryn only nodded, she added, "You're taking this rather well. I would have expected more shock."

Teryn debated keeping quiet about the next part but relented. "You're not the only apparition I've seen lately," he quietly confessed.

She moved closer to him. "What do you mean?"

"Ever since I returned to my body, I've been able to see spirits." His eyes unfocused as he recalled his terror in the early days of regaining consciousness. Every now and then he'd catch sight of floating lights, hazy unaware figures who'd wander in through one wall and out another, or colorless specters who seemed keen enough to witness the present—much like Emylia. At first, the visions had caused great distress, sparking fears that he was one of them, or that they were here to drag him back to the spiritual plane. As months went on and none had interacted with him, much less harmed him, his fears lessened. By now, he was used to it.

Emylia's mouth fell open. "How? Why?"

"I don't know. I would guess it has to do with the fact that I was once an ethera. Or perhaps that I nearly died."

Emylia didn't seem to know what to say to that, and Teryn didn't like the pitying look in her eyes.

"Enough about me," he said. "Where have you been all this time? Are you trapped here? Because your ethera was freed nearby?"

"No, I can wander to any location I've been before, but

I've chosen to stay at Ridine."

"Is this where you have unfinished business?"

"In a way." Her expression turned mournful again. She drifted toward Teryn, then halted in place. She blinked at him a few times, looking as startled as she'd been when he'd first faced her.

"What is it? Why do you keep looking at me like you're afraid?"

She shook her head as if to clear it. "I don't know. Maybe I'm just not used to seeing you like this. You fully alive, while I'm the only one who's a spirit."

That made sense. It was strange seeing her as a colorless being, and not the bright figure he'd known in the crystal.

She settled upon the closed trunk at the foot of Teryn's bed. "I can't shake my guilt over what I've done. Particularly how my actions have hurt Cora. So I've stayed close by and watched over her."

A bittersweet ache pounded in Teryn's chest. He was glad she'd chosen to watch over Cora, but at the same time, she deserved to move on. Even though she'd used her powers as a seer to channel vital information for Morkai—information that had led to countless tragedies at the mage's hands—she was sorry for her role. Love had driven her actions, a blind and reckless love that Teryn could neither condone nor condemn.

Love was madness. Treacherous and beautiful all at once. It could start wars or end them. Could save a life or destroy it.

Emylia had experienced the darkest kind of love. Because of its invisible scars, even the peaceful embrace of the otherlife eluded her.

"How has Cora been?" he asked. "I know what she's conveyed in her letters, but I worry she might be acting like she's fine when she isn't."

"It has been hard for her," Emylia said. "She doesn't let her pain show around others."

He couldn't imagine how painful the last seven months had been for Cora. He'd been nervous to come back to Ridine, terrified over what memories his return might conjure, what new nightmares might await. Yet Cora had stayed the entire time. Stayed in a castle where a blood mage had terrorized her. Stayed in the last place she'd seen her brother alive.

He'd have stayed too, if the choice to leave for Dermaine Palace hadn't been made for him while he'd been unwell. Ridine had still been in the process of being restaffed back then and hadn't had the medical advancements Dermaine offered. Teryn would have suffered less adequate care if he'd been lucid enough to say so, but neither Cora nor Larylis had given him that choice. His healing had been too important to them. So he and Cora had been separated with nothing to connect them but letters. Cora couldn't even use her special ability to visit him, for she needed to be familiar with a place to travel there. He'd worried she'd been suffering on her own, crowned queen in the wake of her brother's death, surrounded by strangers yet again.

The only good that had come from the situation was that Cora had been able to take her crown on her own merit. Lords Kevan and Ulrich were gone, as was King Verdian, leaving no one to diminish Cora's worth as queen, no one to say she couldn't be her brother's heir until after she'd married Teryn. She'd been sent new councilmen from Vera, ones selected by Larylis—and Teryn, once he'd been of sound mind—particularly for their loyalty and open-mindedness.

Still, it had to have been lonely. Painful. Teryn hated that he hadn't been here. Hated that Cora hadn't allowed him to come sooner.

But at least someone had been here to watch over her.

"Thank you," he said, giving Emylia a deep nod. "Thank you for being here when I could not."

Her lips curved in a sad smile. "I haven't found a way to be helpful, but I hope there's something I can do. Something that will allow me to make up for my sins."

"Like what?"

"I don't know, but perhaps the fact that you can see me will matter. I've already told you nearly everything I know about Darius, but perhaps there are other things I can recall. Other things I can discover."

Teryn stiffened. King Darius was a constant source of dread for him, Cora, Larylis, and Mareleau—for everyone who knew the truth. Once Teryn had been well enough to speak and write, he'd conveyed what he'd learned from Emylia while he'd been trapped in the crystal, and Cora had done the same with what she'd learned in El'Ara. Together they'd painted a frightening landscape of possibilities. Only a handful of their most trusted advisors knew what they knew, but they were all of one mind—Darius was not a threat they could ignore.

"He's still alive," Emylia said. "I can't see him, for I can only wander places I've been myself, either as a living being or as a spirit, but I've devoured all the information Cora has learned and tested it with my own knowledge. King Darius has ruled Syrus for five hundred years. Most assume *Darius* is merely a naming convention passed down through heirs, but I know better than to hope that's the truth. The current

King Darius is the same man who sent his son to find information on El'Ara."

Teryn nodded. He and Cora had surmised as much in their correspondence, but anything beyond that was guesswork. "Do you believe Morkai conveyed what he'd learned about Lela? About...Cora?"

Learning what Morkai had done to Cora—cursing her to never bear children during her lifetime—had nearly broken him. Morkai had done it to stop a prophecy from coming to fruition, one that predicted Cora would bear the *true Morkara*, the ruler of the fae realm. Should her child be born, the Veil separating the two worlds would tear, compromising the protective ward that had been forged to keep worldwalkers from entering El'Ara. But somehow, it would also put an end to Darius. According to the memories Emylia had shared with Teryn while they were in the crystal, Morkai had eventually abandoned Darius and had taken his father's mission as his own, long before he uncovered Cora's identity. Was there any hope that Morkai had never shared his later findings with Darius?

"I don't know for certain," Emylia said, "but I assume Morkai told him everything. If not while he was still alive, then upon his death. Even though Morkai abandoned his father after their falling out, I don't think he'd let all his work go to waste."

Teryn couldn't help but agree. Morkai was nothing if not tenacious. If he'd been able to tether his soul to a crystal upon his death, he could have woven a spell that would deliver information to Darius under certain circumstances. And while he and his father sought separate goals—Morkai wanting to utilize fae magic in the human world, Darius aiming to return to El'Ara and rule there—their means were aligned.

Dread sank Teryn's gut. It was too much to hope Darius didn't know about Lela. Syrus' recent dealings with Norun were proof that he was angling to get closer.

His only consolation was something he recalled from Emylia's memories. According to Morkai, Darius was physically weak and couldn't easily leave Syrus. He may be a worldwalker like Cora, but if his magic worked like hers, he couldn't travel to a place he was unfamiliar with. Lela once been part of El'Ara, but after five hundred years, it couldn't possibly resemble the place Darius had once lived. Even if it did, there was another condition Morkai had mentioned in Emylia's memories: Darius was cursed to forget. He hadn't even been capable of recalling the name of the realm he'd come from.

That wasn't enough to make Teryn feel at ease.

"I'm sorry," Emylia said, soundlessly rising to her feet from his trunk. "I shouldn't make you talk about such dire topics."

He shook his head. "It's all right. We need to discuss these things, no matter how dreadful they are. And you will be able to help us. I'm sure of it."

She smiled, and this time it looked genuine. "I must admit, talking to you has reminded me of my humanity. I've gotten too used to being invisible, but now that I know someone can see me, I'll have to mind my manners. I really shouldn't have spied on you and Cora. I won't do it again. Not in...*that* sort of scenario."

"I appreciate that."

"Well, I'll leave you alone for now." Her form began to fade, but not before she gave him a mischievous wink. "I promise to give you ample privacy tonight."

She faded away completely, but her parting words made his stomach tumble as he recalled inviting Cora to return to his room this evening. Though he'd soon see her at the formal audience and at dinner afterward, tonight they'd be alone. Tonight he wouldn't hold back.

Tonight Teryn would bare his heart to the woman he loved.

5

The selfish side of Mareleau Alante resented being back at Ridine Castle. Or perhaps it was her rational side. She had good reasons to dread being here and they had nothing to do with the petty grievances she'd once held against the castle the first time she'd come.

"Gods, what a dreary place," Queen Mother Helena said, glancing around the guest suite. It was a large room, though sparsely furnished. The stone walls were draped with violet tapestries bearing Khero's black mountain sigil. The flagstone floors bore several plush rugs to stave off the late winter chill, and a fire roared in the hearth.

"It's a castle, not a palace, Mother," Mareleau said, irritation lacing her voice as she sat at the edge of the bed, enjoying the relief of rest. Though she'd just left her coach after hours on the road, ascending the stairs of the keep had winded her. She supposed that was normal for a woman three weeks from giving birth.

"I thought the queen would have a better sense for royal decor," Helena muttered.

Mareleau rested a hand on the rounded curve of her

belly and tried to focus on the sweet flutter of movement beneath her palm and not the grating sound of her mother's voice. It was all she could do not to order Helena out. They were alone. Her ladies had gone to fetch their queen chocolate from the kitchen, and her midwives awaited her needs in her suite's sitting room. She'd be happier if Helena were gone too, but she refrained from saying so, partially because she was trying not to give in to her sharper instincts anymore. She'd be a mother soon, and the sooner she figured out how to stop resenting the woman who'd birthed her, the sooner she could trust herself to do better than what had been done to her.

Besides, her mother's criticism was only half sincere. Though Helena tried to hide it, she mourned the loss of her husband and buried it beneath layers of trifling complaints and fussing over Mareleau's pregnancy. And it wasn't that Mareleau didn't understand her mother's gripes about Ridine. Half a year ago, she wouldn't have defended the castle. In fact, she'd hurled her share of insults over its shoddy accommodations. But things were different now. She may not have the best memories of Ridine, but this was her friend's home. Cora was doing her best to be a proper queen, and the evidence was all around her. When Mareleau had last been here, only a small selection of rooms had been refurbished. Now the grandest chambers were fit for royalty. Or...fit enough. She wouldn't have minded if the mattress were plusher or the blankets were softer.

"Such an ugly sigil. And it's everywhere!" Helena wrinkled her nose at the purple tapestries. Then, with a shake of her head, she cast an indulgent smile upon her daughter. "I'm relieved you and your husband kept much of Selay's sigil intact when designing Vera's."

Mareleau wanted to argue that she and Larylis hadn't

had any say in the design of Vera's sigil—an eagle and rose entwined, their silhouettes white on a gold background—nor had they cared to. They'd had much more pressing matters to attend to. Such as merging two kingdoms into one and supporting Cora as their ally, doing whatever they could to ease the chaos that had befallen Khero. New councils had to be forged in both kingdoms. New titles given. Numerous lies to tell. Burdens to bear...

Mareleau blew out a heavy breath.

She didn't expect her mother to understand, for Helena hadn't been here last summer. The queen mother hadn't witnessed the chilling change in Prince Teryn when he'd been possessed by a scheming mage or seen the horrifying monster with four faces, one of which had been King Verdian's. As much as Helena grieved the loss of her husband, their relationship had never been a love match, and all she knew of his death was what the public knew—that a rabid beast had attacked the royal hunting party while they were at rest, and that a fire had broken out as a result. Helena wasn't haunted by the terrors of that night.

But Mareleau was. She knew the truth. And that truth had shaken her world and shifted her priorities. There were more important things than jewels and palaces and luxury. She now knew that relationships were precious, even the ones that were laced with bitterness and conflict. She knew regret for not making up with someone she loved, despite the friction between them. She knew the pain of never getting to say goodbye.

A gentle kick nudged her palm, and a smile warmed her lips, banishing her unpleasant thoughts, even as a far less gentle kick to her ribs followed. Mareleau had numerous reasons for trying not to push others away like she used to, and her unborn child was the greatest one. She still wasn't confident about becoming a mother, but something fierce had sparked inside her months ago, and it grew brighter every day.

Her eyes landed on the opposite wall. It separated her suite from Larylis' and she wished she could tear it down. He was busy changing and readying himself for their audience with Cora, but he'd be far better company than her mother. And she missed him.

Though they'd journeyed to Ridine together, they'd been given separate rooms by the different nobles who'd offered them their homes and hospitality each night, and her accommodations at Ridine were no different. Not only was it proper to offer a king and queen separate chambers if available, but Mareleau required more space at night than she had before. It seemed every evening she added a new pillow to her bed just to feel comfortable enough to sleep. By now she practically slept in a fortress of pillows, stuffed strategically on every side of her. Which, of course, made her a rather difficult bedfellow.

She angled her body to the side and assessed the pillows at the head of the bed, counting four. That certainly wouldn't be enough. She needed at least six—

Another kick prodded her ribs, and she let out a sharp hiss.

"What is it?" came Helena's frantic voice as she darted for Mareleau and planted herself on the bed beside her. "Is it contractions? Has your water broken?"

"Mother," she ground out between her teeth. How often had she heard those same questions over the last few weeks whenever she so much as frowned?

"I'm serious! Are you all right?"

"For the thousandth time, yes."

Helena tutted. "I knew you shouldn't travel so close to your due date."

"I've told you time and again, I'm not that close to my due date."

Helena pursed her lips and a heavy silence fell between them. Neither had broached the subject of the midwives' calculations versus the lie Mareleau had once told. A lie that had won her permission to marry the man she loved but had left her father furious. Mareleau suspected her mother no longer believed her daughter had conceived during the Heart's Hunt like she'd insisted all those months ago, for if that had been the case, she'd be nearly six weeks overdue. Why Helena had never confronted her daughter about her lie, Mareleau knew not, and she wasn't going to confess. She couldn't bear to admit that her lie had widened the chasm between her and her father. Couldn't bear to admit he'd died with so much animosity left between them, save for the olive branch he'd extended in the form of a child's blanket he'd gifted her. A blanket that had burned to ash before she'd even held it more than once.

No, she couldn't bear that pain, that responsibility.

Perhaps Helena knew that.

When Helena next spoke, her tone was no longer edged with worry. Instead, she was back to her halfhearted griping. "I don't understand why you wanted to travel all the way here just to leave again in a matter of days. We'll have traveled more days than we've visited."

Helena was right but Mareleau didn't care. So long as she could attend Cora's wedding and return home by her due date, she was happy. She was hardly in danger of harming her pregnancy due to travel conditions. Their progress was ridiculously slow and careful, taking ten days when it could easily have taken seven. She knew this, because that was how long it had taken to return to Dermaine Palace when she and Larylis left Ridine last summer. And that had been with an injured Teryn in tow. Mareleau had been babied even more than him, her traveling coach the epitome of luxury. It was so large it might as well have been a cottage on wheels, with a built-in divan and ample room for her ladies and midwives to remain at her side.

"What if you go into early labor?" Helena said. "Seven devils, what if you give birth *here*?"

Mareleau rolled her eyes. "We'll be home just in time."

What did it matter where she gave birth? She had several midwives in attendance night and day, and at least one stood outside her door now, awaiting her needs. Even if she were to go into labor on the road, she could handle it. After surviving a monster, a blood mage, and three straight months of morning sickness, there was little that intimidated her anymore.

"I just don't understand why you want to attend your brother-in-law's wedding so desperately. Larylis could have come without you."

"I'm not here for my brother-in-law," she said with a scoff. Though she didn't hate Teryn nearly as much as she used to, it was true that she wasn't here for him. "I'm here for Queen Aveline."

Helena gave her a patronizing smile. "Dearest, you know she only invited you out of formality. You weren't obligated to come."

Mareleau barked a laugh. If only her mother knew that Cora had specifically asked her *not* to come and to stay home and take care of herself instead. If Cora had wanted her to stay home so badly, she shouldn't have ordered her to stay away, for Mareleau was nothing if not stubborn. Just seeing those words penned in Cora's hand made her want to prove her wrong—that she could take care of herself *and* attend her wedding.

"It's not like Aveline had the decency to attend your wedding feast," Helena muttered.

Mareleau shrugged. "We weren't friends then."

Helena pulled her head back and blinked at her a few times. "Does that mean you consider Queen Aveline your friend now?"

"She's not just a friend. She's my *best* friend." Her cheeks flushed at the confession. She hadn't intended to admit her friendship to her mother. Not that she wanted to hide it either. She just wasn't used to being candid with her mother or talking about emotions. Though she tried not to push Helena away as often as she once did, she still harbored a grudge for how her mother had treated her, how she'd ignored the emotions she'd shared, how she'd refused to take Mareleau's love for Larylis seriously, even going so far as intercepting her letters to him and having a scribe forge her heartfelt words into ones that drove them apart for three years. How Helena had failed to show any sympathy or concern when her unwanted suitors had hurt her.

Recalling that now sent waves of fury through her, but she did her best not to turn herself over to the emotion. Mareleau had made mistakes in the past. She could forgive her mother for hers. Or try to at least.

"I didn't realize," Helena said softly.

"Well, now you do," Mareleau said as she rose from the bed and took a few steps away from her mother, "so please stop insulting her home."

A beat of silence followed, then her mother's footsteps slowly approached. "Dearest," Helena said, a hesitant waver in her voice, "I'm glad you told me, and I'm happy you have a friend. I hope you know you can tell me anything."

Mareleau's chest tightened. She couldn't bring herself to meet her mother's eyes. She was too afraid Helena would see the truth and all her secrets would spill out then and there. How could she voice the shadows in her heart, ones that buried her burdens, her guilt over her father's death? That was a level of vulnerability she wasn't ready for, not with her mother.

So she did what she did best. She lied.

Summoning her *magic trick*, she wrapped an air of indifference around her like a protective shroud. "You never know when a friend might become useful," she said, tone cold. "The closer I keep Aveline, the easier she'll be to use later."

Helena's expression hardened in an instant, closing like a shuttered window, but Mareleau was almost certain she saw disappointment in her mother's eyes.

Mareleau had spent a lifetime disappointing Helena, so that was nothing new, and it was far more comfortable to the alternative—opening up, forgiving, and trusting the person who'd once rent scars upon her heart.

6

Cora fought every urge to fidget as she sat upon her throne before an audience of courtiers flanking a carpeted aisle. Any minute now, her royal guests would arrive. She'd have to receive King Larylis, Queen Mareleau, and Prince Teryn with rehearsed formality, all for the sake of their spectators. She'd have to see Teryn, speak to him in a cold and unwavering tone, and try not to blush. After their heated kiss mere hours ago, she feared it would be easier said than done.

Hence her current urge to fidget.

The discomfort of her ensemble certainly didn't help. Her shoulders were heavy with the weight of her ceremonial cape, a mink-lined monstrosity of purple velvet emblazoned with Khero's black mountain at the lapels. Her dress was nearly as smothering with its layers of heavy brocade, silk, and lace, boasting several shades of purple from lilac to violet. Purple wasn't her favorite hue, yet it represented her kingdom. During formal audiences such as this, it was the most appropriate color to wear.

The stares of the courtiers were almost potent enough to

burn, but she kept her gaze fixed on the doorway at the far end of the room, where her guests would soon enter. Her mental shields wavered, threatening to draw in the audience's emotions. To strengthen her wards, she pressed her palms against the smooth, solid arms of her mahogany throne. Her tattooed palms tingled with the strength of the earth element, anchoring her, calming her, smoothing her nerves.

In a small act of boldness, Cora almost always kept her hands and forearms bare, revealing the *insigmora* inked there. The tattoos were a symbol of her magic, geometrical shapes and moon phases that were sacred to the people who had raised her for six years. Her former Head of Council had ordered her not to show off her tattoos, but now that Lord Kevan was dead, she refused to hide them. They were a part of her, as were the Forest People. It didn't matter what rumors circulated about her. If the people surmised she was a witch, so be it. She *was* a witch. While she understood the dangers of outright saying so this early in her tenuous reign, she wouldn't hide it either. Witches—a term hurled at anyone who had uncanny abilities, keen senses, an interest in folk medicine and ancient traditions, or even an overt fondness for nature—would be protected under her rule.

Let them talk. Let them know that ousting such individuals from their towns and homes would not be tolerated. It was the one stance she would not budge on, even if it put her throne at risk. She'd rather lose her crown than ignore the plight of her own kind.

Movement caught her eye from just outside the doorway. Her pulse kicked up, but she kept her expression neutral. The Master of Ceremonies stepped forward and announced the arrival of her royal guests.

"His Majesty Larylis Alante, King of Vera. Her Majesty Mareleau Alante, Queen of Vera."

Two figures crossed the threshold and began their slow procession down the aisle. Cora's eyes met Mareleau's at once, and the other queen gave her a subtle smile. She looked beautiful with her pale blonde hair cascading down her back in neat curls, her silver-blue gown edged with white lace, its high waist sending gathered pleats to cascade down her abdomen, accentuating the curve of her belly.

Gods, Cora wanted to run down the dais and gather the woman in a hug. There were few people Cora felt compelled to greet with such affection, and there'd been a time when she'd vowed that Mareleau would never be one of them. But they'd bonded in an unexpected camaraderie last summer, after Mareleau had shared her vulnerable side and Cora had done the same in turn. Their friendship hadn't ended after Mareleau returned home. They'd struck up a correspondence and sent letters back and forth, almost as often as Cora and Teryn had. Cora had been so fixated on seeing her fiancé for the first time in half a year that she hadn't realized how elated she'd be to see her friend too.

Her gaze left Mareleau to assess the man beside her. She had to smother a laugh at seeing King Larylis, for he looked almost as uncomfortable as Cora felt in his formal garb. He was dressed in a white-and-gold ceremonial coat with a high collar buttoned almost to his chin, and a long gold cape trailing from his shoulders. His dark, copper-brown hair was shorter than she'd last seen it, the sides trimmed while the top was swept away from his brow. Upon his head, a gold crown rested, a simple band compared to Mareleau's silver-and-sapphire tiara.

The pair reached the foot of the dais and dipped their chins in respectful greetings.

Cora returned the gesture and uttered her rehearsed welcome. "Khero gladly receives Your Majesties' presence at Ridine Castle."

Larylis echoed the sentiment back. "Vera is honored by Khero's great welcome."

"We congratulate you on your upcoming nuptials," Mareleau said, her tone melodious and far less stiff than her husband's.

Cora gave a practiced nod. "I accept your congratulations with great thanks."

She clenched her jaw to keep from saying more. So badly Cora wanted to exchange more than dry statements she'd learned by rote, especially with Mareleau. But now wasn't the time. Informal conversation would have to wait until dinner.

Cora's eyes darted back to the doorway, anticipating her next guest. The Master of Ceremonies delivered his announcement.

"Her Majesty, Queen Mother Helena Harvallis. His Royal Highness, Teryn Alante, Prince of Vera, future King Consort of Khero."

Cora gripped her armrests tightly as Teryn escorted Helena through the doorway. Her breath caught at Teryn's warm smile, his gaze immediately locked on hers. She was grateful for their earlier reunion, for if she'd seen him for the first time now—his silver hair tied back from his face, his formal coat in gold and emerald, the latter color bringing out his eyes, the way his trousers hugged his muscled thighs—she might have fallen off her throne.

She could hardly bring herself to cast the queen mother more than a cursory glance, though the woman was dressed almost as elegantly as Mareleau.

Larylis and Mareleau stepped to the side to make room

for the new guests. Teryn held her gaze, eyes twinkling with the same mischief they'd shone with earlier, even as he folded into a formal bow. Her heart kicked up as images invaded her mind, of him hefting her onto her dresser, his lips tasting her skin—

She let out a shaky breath and delivered her formal welcome, an almost-word-for-word echo of the one she'd given Larylis and Mareleau. Her mind was so frazzled she couldn't be sure she hadn't stumbled over her words, but the fact that none of the courtiers snickered was a good sign.

Helena offered her expected congratulations, then Teryn spoke next. "I am humbled and deeply honored by our forthcoming nuptials that will bind our houses in health, sickness, celebration, and solidarity." His formal tone was so at odds with the smile quirking his lips.

Oh, those godsforsaken lips.

She forced her eyes back to his. "Yes," she said before she realized that wasn't the response she'd memorized. Steeling her nerves, she delivered the correct lines. "I too am honored by the strength our union will bring and look forward to our nuptials."

Cold. So cold. So lacking.

His gaze finally left hers as he stepped off to the side to allow Cora to give her attention to her next guests. She wasn't sure who else had arrived today, as she was only expecting a few more noble families to attend. How could she focus on anyone else with Teryn so close?

Against her better judgment, she cast him a quick glance. He winked, and she couldn't fight the smile that curved her lips—

"His Royal Highness, Lexington Quil, Crown Prince of Tomas. Her Highness, Lily Quil, Crown Princess of Tomas."

The Master of Ceremonies' announcement had Cora sitting forward on her throne before she could rein in her surprise. A name left her lips. "Lex?"

She would be mortified by her break in composure if it hadn't been mirrored by Teryn and Larylis. The two whirled to face the doorway just as two figures entered.

A man with dark-blond hair and a plump physique sauntered into the room, a ridiculously smug grin between his ruddy cheeks as he escorted a pretty woman beside him. She was almost as short as Cora with curves that rivaled Mareleau's. Her auburn hair was arranged in a braided updo, displaying a rounded face and a disarmingly pleasant smile.

Cora couldn't believe Lex was here. She'd invited him, but she couldn't recall if she'd been informed of his reply. And the woman beside him was...his wife? He hadn't been married when she'd last seen him, which had been at the battle at Centerpointe Rock. He'd come to Verlot Palace when she'd been taken by Verdian as a temporary hostage, but she hadn't been able to bid him farewell before he'd left. While she and Lex hadn't grown nearly as close as she and Teryn had during their travels last spring, she had fond feelings for the man. To her, he was a hero. He'd outwitted Morkai with a lie, pretending to side with the mage, after which he'd fled to Dermaine Palace to warn King Arlous about the sorcerer's plans. He'd even fought in the battle against Morkai's forces.

I know him! Valorre's exclamation invaded Cora's mind.

When did you get here? She hadn't felt his consciousness connect with hers since earlier when he'd insisted Teryn smelled like strength and moonbeams. He was like that these days, coming and going at will, popping into her mind whenever hers drifted somewhere that interested him. Thank the gods he'd left her alone during her reunion with Teryn.

I know him! he repeated. *One time he didn't share his apple with me. Remember that?* A flicker of resentment wove through the unicorn's words, but his statement was otherwise good-humored.

I remember, Cora said and returned her attention to the approaching couple.

Lex and Lily stopped before the dais and gave Cora an exaggerated bow. Before Cora could deliver her formal welcome, Lex turned to the side and waved at Teryn and Larylis. Not a bow. Not a nod. A casual wave.

Whispers broke out from the courtiers at the fore of the audience, gossiping about his lack of decorum.

Leave it to Lex to breach formalities without a care in the world.

A grin split Teryn's face. Then, with an amused roll of his eyes, he strode forward and crushed Lex in a hug. Cora froze in surprise, flushing as more whispers broke out. Teryn stepped away, and to Cora's surprise, Larylis took his brother's place, hugging Lex with only slightly more restraint.

Mareleau arched a brow at the display while Helena looked scandalized. Cora's gaze flicked to the courtiers, then back to the warm reunion before her. She wasn't sure what to do in this situation. Wait idly by? Call for order? Her palms tingled with a flood of calming energy, and she knew what she needed to do. No, what she *wanted* to do.

She rose from her throne and the audience went silent. Lex separated from Larylis, eyes widening when they fell on Cora. "Oh, right! Majesty, thank you for—"

His words cut off as she marched down the dais, her skirts and cape trailing behind her. Lex's expression faltered, as if he only just now considered that he might have made a blunder. He opened his mouth, stammering for words, but Cora gathered his hands in hers and gave them a firm squeeze. Her lips lifted in an unrestrained smile.

"Lex," she said, tone sincere, "thank you so much for being here. I can't express how much it means to me."

His cheeks reddened and his expression turned bashful.

She released his hands and took up those of the woman beside him. Lily made a startled sound, but her sweet smile remained. "You and I aren't acquainted yet," Cora said, "but I do hope that will change."

"You honor me, Majesty," Lily said, her voice small.

"The two of you honor me." Cora's tone regained some of its formality. She spoke louder, allowing her words to carry to the courtiers. "Lex, you are my kingdom's ally as well as Vera's. You aided us when Duke Morkai tried to destroy us." A collective intake of breath sounded from the audience at the mention of the duke, but Cora continued. "I look forward to furthering our friendship and am grateful for your presence."

Lex bent forward in a bow while Lily dipped in an elegant curtsy.

Cora lowered her voice and adopted a casual tone again as she asked, "You'll join us for dinner, won't you?"

"Of course," Lex said, puffing out his chest.

"Good." With one last smile, Cora left the couple and settled back on her throne with controlled poise. She was pleased to see the courtiers were no longer whispering. Now that their queen had validated what they'd previously deemed unseemly behavior, they had no reason to.

Lex and Lily joined the others and Cora shifted her focus to greet her next guests. Though she continued to deliver her memorized words and welcomed nobles who were no better than strangers, her brief reprieve with her friends was enough to make the rest of the ceremony far more enjoyable.

7

Cora was eager for dinner for more reasons than one. For starters, it would mean the most formal part of her evening was through. Secondly, she was famished. Only now, as she entered the dining hall where aromas of sizzling meats, stews, and fluffy breads infused the air, did she realize she hadn't eaten since breakfast. She'd been too flustered after her kiss with Teryn to take lunch. After the welcoming ceremony, she'd had just enough time to change out of her ceremonial raiment and into a dark blue dinner gown and have her ladies restyle her hair. It now hung over her shoulder in a long braid.

She was grateful that she was the last to arrive—a formality, of course—for it meant the dining hall was loud enough to smother the sounds of her growling stomach. The hall wasn't particularly rowdy, but there was just enough sound from the harpist in the gallery, the shuffling bodies at the tables, and the occasional whisper to keep the room from being dead silent. It didn't stop her from blushing as she climbed the dais at the end of the room and took the empty seat at the head table, between Mareleau and Teryn. Her plate was already laden with the table's ample offerings, eliciting the loudest growl from her stomach yet. She shot a horrified glance at Teryn, but if he heard the sounds roaring out of her, he made no sign of it.

Like her, he'd changed after the ceremony and was now dressed in a dark frock coat over an ivory brocade waistcoat and white silk cravat. She gave him a brief smile but dared not meet his eyes too long, lest she get thoroughly distracted. Dinner may be a less formal affair than the earlier audience she'd held, but she still had duties to perform as queen, and everyone was waiting on her.

Casting a benevolent gaze upon the room at large, she lifted her glass of wine, signaling the start of the meal. The courtiers in attendance raised their glasses, and after the queen took her sip, so did the rest. Relief coursed through her. Now that her guests could begin eating and politely conversing, she and her companions would have some semblance of privacy, for the dais set them apart from the other rows of tables.

Mareleau seemed to have the same train of thought, for she playfully elbowed Cora in the arm. Cora glanced to the side as she took up her fork and met her friend's smile.

"It's really nice to see you again," Mareleau said. Her tone took on a teasing quality. "Your castle isn't nearly as hideous as it was before."

Cora let out a lighthearted scoff. "What high praise."

"You really should have replaced the linens I selected." Mareleau tapped the tablecloth beneath the violet runner. "Don't you recall I selected these with Master Arther out of spite when you wouldn't let me attend the council meeting with you?"

Cora frowned. "What's wrong with the linens? They look fine to me."

Mareleau gave her a patronizing look. One that would have gotten under her skin before they were friends. Now she knew it was cajoling. "Cora, dear, the thread count is offensively low."

Cora rolled her eyes, but the gesture was interrupted by a slight wince from Mareleau. Her hand shot to her belly, a furrow on her brow. Cora opened her mouth to ask if she was all right, but Mareleau gave a subtle shake of her head.

Mareleau leaned in close and whispered, too quiet for anyone else to hear, "I'm fine. I don't want to make either of them fuss over me." She angled her head to the side, and Cora looked down the table. Queen Mother Helena was farther down, engaged in conversation with a visiting marquess. Larylis sat on Mareleau's left, quietly eating his meal. His gaze was so unnaturally fixated on his plate, Cora thought he had to be listening in on their conversation. Then she noticed his attention wasn't on his plate but his lap. More accurately, on the book there, hidden just beneath the edge of the table.

Cora's gaze shot back to Mareleau, eyebrows raised in question. Was reading at the table a usual occurrence for the king? In answer to her silent question, Mareleau mumbled, "Always."

Cora watched her friend for a few beats more, half tempted to extend her senses and ensure she truly was all right. She hadn't wanted Mareleau to travel all the way here in her condition, but of course, she hadn't listened. Still, if Mareleau didn't want people fussing over her, Cora would do her best not to pry.

Instead, she shifted her attention to her plate and brought a bite of almond-crusted lamb to her lips. The meat was so tender, her lashes fluttered shut. It took all her restraint to chew slowly.

A soft touch brushed over the back of her hand. She opened her eyes and found Teryn leaning toward her, his hand propped on the table beside hers, the backs of his fingers caressing the curves of her knuckles, one at a time. It was an oddly sensual touch, and she nearly dropped her fork.

"You're still coming to me tonight, right?" he whispered.

She swallowed her bite of food, her throat suddenly thick. "I am," she said, and a shudder of anticipation tore through her. Mother Goddess, how could she calmly finish her meal knowing she was meeting privately with Teryn afterward? She was looking forward to it with equal parts desire and terror. Would she manage to confess everything she'd been yearning to say? Or would he render her speechless before she got the chance?

Lex's voice cut it on her thoughts. "I'd say I'm surprised, but I'm not."

Cora tore her attention from Teryn's probing stare and faced Lex, who sat on the other side of her fiancé. Lily sat on Lex's right, taking dainty bites of stew.

"About what?" Cora asked before spearing another delectable piece of lamb.

Lex gestured between Cora and Teryn. "About the two of you. It's well past time, if you ask me. And I'm not just talking about the political alliance. I'm talking about...you know." He waggled his brows and gave Teryn a significant look.

Teryn pursed his lips, his expression suddenly abashed.

Cora glanced between the two men, trying to puzzle out what she was missing.

Lex's eyes widened as if Cora and Teryn were daft. "I mean his feelings for you! He's been smitten with you since last spring. You've told her, right?"

Teryn grumbled under his breath, then gave Cora an apologetic look. A strand of silver-white hair fell over his brow, loosened from the leather tie that held the rest back. Cora fought the urge to brush it off his face. "Lex is under the impression that I agreed to rescue unicorns with you because I fancied you."

She nearly barked a laugh but managed to morph it into a soft chuckle. "Is that how you got him to come along on our exploits?" To Lex, she said, "My friend, I'm sorry to say but you've been lied to. His heart was set on a certain bounty, not me."

She gave Teryn a good-humored scowl. She liked that she could joke about the past without resentment. Where once Teryn's betrayal had stung her, now she saw every moment, every circumstance—the good and the bad—that had brought them together as something to be grateful for.

Lex stared open-mouthed as understanding dawned. He uttered an extended, "Oooohh." Then he narrowed his gaze at Teryn. "I don't know why I didn't realize that until now. All this time I thought you were a romantic."

Teryn rubbed his brow. "You weren't entirely wrong."

Lex's expression brightened. "Do say more. Tell me, has this become a love match after all?"

Cora's gaze whipped to Teryn, her cheeks heating furiously. She didn't want him to answer, not here, not publicly. This was the topic of conversation she was hoping to save for tonight. His hand rested over hers, his touch firm yet calming. He gave her a subtle nod, as if to say he understood what she was thinking.

Teryn turned back to Lex. "I'll tell you a secret I've yet to share with my fiancée."

Cora's breath caught and she wondered if she'd misinterpreted the look he'd given her entirely. Maybe he didn't understand her at all. Maybe he was about to confess his feelings for all to hear, when Cora wasn't at all prepared.

"Cora," Teryn said, "was my first crush."

Her mind emptied. That wasn't what she'd expected.

He spoke again. "Princess Aveline Caelan, age six. My first one-sided love. A two-week-long affair, and I daresay she hadn't a clue I existed the entire time."

"What are you talking about?" Cora was halfway between a chuckle and a frown. She couldn't tell if he was making up the story.

He shifted his gaze to hers. "You don't remember at all, do you?"

"Remember what?"

"You visited Dermaine Palace once with your parents. I followed you around like I was your shadow, but tried to evade your notice when you caught sight of me. Whenever you did notice me, you turned your nose up like I was pure scum for existing in your presence."

"I can confirm this is true," Larylis said, leaning forward to speak down the table. "I was quite embarrassed for him."

Something warm and tender flooded her chest. "I don't remember that." It had been so long ago, before the great tragedies that had befallen her—the deaths of her parents, her exile from Ridine. She hadn't even remembered she'd been to Dermaine before.

"I clearly wasn't very memorable," Teryn said.

She realized something else he'd mentioned. That she'd visited with her parents. "So you met my mother and father?"

"I did."

Tears sprang to her eyes. The fact that the man she loved had met her parents—and that they'd met him—meant more to her than she could have imagined. She couldn't bring herself to speak for fear that she'd start sobbing then and there.

"That's a very sweet story," Princess Lily said in her quiet voice.

Cora shook the tender revelations from her mind and poured her attention on the couple next to Teryn. "What about the two of you? How did you come to marry?"

Lex reached beside him and gripped his wife's hand. A proud smile spread across his lips. "Lily is my long-time sweetheart."

Teryn nodded. "I remember you telling me about her during our travels."

Cora opened her mouth, on the verge of asking why Lex had participated in Mareleau's Heart's Hunt if he'd already fancied another woman, but she stopped herself just in time. She couldn't ask such an impertinent question, no matter how her curiosity burned.

Lex leveled a knowing look at her. "I know what you're thinking, and, no, I never had any intention of winning *her* hand," he said with a significant nod toward Mareleau, who in turn nearly choked on her dinner roll. "I only partici- pated in the Heart's Hunt because my father threatened to disinherit me if I didn't at least *try*. I figured I'd give it my worst effort, come home defeated, and then get permission to marry the woman I actually cared for."

"Well, he's a blunt one, isn't he?" Mareleau said under her breath.

Cora's eyes darted to Lily to see if she showed any sign of discomfort at being at the same dinner table as the woman her husband had once been forced to court, but she merely grinned as if thoroughly amused.

Lex went on. "My heart has always been for Lily, and I wouldn't have considered attending that ridiculous Beltane festival if I'd thought I'd had any chance at winning that poetry contest."

"Your poem was terrible," Teryn agreed. *"Your hair is the color of light ale. Your skin a milky pallor."*

Larylis looked up from his hidden book, a distant look on his face. *"You are graceful like a deer and smart like a fox."*

"Ah, yes," Lex said with a grimace. "My prize-winning poetry."

Larylis gave Mareleau a crooked grin. "I'd say your words captured my wife's greatest assets rather accurately."

Mareleau burned him with a glare but it was betrayed by the smile pulling her lips.

Lex cleared his throat and shrank down slightly. "His Majesty isn't uncomfortable about..." He lowered his voice and leaned in, ensuring his words wouldn't carry to the lower tables. "You know...that every man at this end of the table has, in some way, courted your wife?"

Mareleau made an indignant squeak and rounded on Lex. "Does it bother *you* that I'm the one who deemed your poem the winner of my contest?"

Lex pulled his head back. "I don't know why, but I feel like I should be offended by that."

Lily patted his shoulder. "There, there, my love."

Cora's chest rumbled with laughter, and Teryn's mirth was so potent, his eyes were crinkled at the corners. She loved seeing her fiancé so amused, so carefree. This was the most lighthearted royal dinner she'd had since being crowned queen. For the first time since taking the throne, her friends were here. Her beloved was here. There were joys to celebrate, matters to laugh about.

Mother Goddess, she wished it could always be this way.

The darker part of her day—overseeing the prisoner's interrogation—threatened to dampen her joy, reminding her of the threats that might await, but she wouldn't give in. Not yet. Not now.

After Teryn sobered from his amusement, he said to Lex, "You never explained why your father was so against your marriage to Lily, other than the fact that she wasn't a princess. How did you convince him to allow your marriage?"

"Well, you see," Lex said, "my Lilylove is the niece of a Norunian rebel."

Mention of Norun made Cora freeze, her glass of wine halfway to her lips.

"Her uncle, Orik Allgrove, is the former King of Haldor," Lex explained, "and has been stirring unrest against King Isvius for many years now in hopes that he'll build a rebellion large enough to take back Haldor."

Cora listened with rapt attention. Isvius was the King of Norun and Prince Helios' father, while Haldor was one of the kingdoms Norun had conquered several years ago. Lex's mention of unrest and potential rebellion could prove useful if Norun resorted to war with Khero like she feared.

Lex spoke again. "As you can imagine, Tomas is not keen on getting conquered by Norun, and my father has gone to great lengths to avoid drawing attention to our kingdom. Save for building the wall between our borders, of course, which my father stands by as a brilliant necessity. So he feared pairing me with the niece of a known rebel would attract Isvius' scorn."

"What changed his mind?" Teryn asked.

"Aromir wool, of course," Lex said with a flourish of his hand and an exaggerated mock bow. "I can't thank you enough for orchestrating Tomas' inclusion into the trade agreement with Brushwold. When Father learned of it, he was willing to reward me. Hence the only reward I could ever want." He patted Lily's hand, who blushed furiously in turn.

Cora hated shattering the lovely mood with her next question, but she had to ask. "Your father's determination to avoid conflict with Norun must mean he keeps abreast of the kingdom's latest moves and developments. Are you by chance aware of any troubling rumors regarding Norun? Anything about them potentially targeting another kingdom? Preparing for conquest?"

Lex exchanged a weighted look with Lily. Cora extended her senses, desperate to know what lingered beneath that look, but all she could read was...excitement.

"Let's just say," Lex said, a sly smirk turning his lips, "that my rise in esteem and Lily's influence as princess have sparked...certain developments."

Her heart quickened. "Like what?"

Another significant look passed between the couple before Lex leaned in closer. His voice was barely above a whisper. "All the Norunian rebels need for a successful rebellion are weapons. The military confiscated all their weapons long ago and forbids all citizens from bearing arms. Yet it just so happens that someone has a wall. A wall from which certain exports leave. And Tomas' primary export to Norun is manure."

Cora frowned, unsure what he was getting at.

Lily kept her voice as quiet as her husband's. "We're smuggling weapons in shit—" Her hand flew to her mouth, though her lovely face maintained its sweet expression. "Pardon my language, Majesty. In *manure*. Soldiers don't bother auditing the manure merchants' carts. You can imagine why."

It took Cora several moments to understand the brilliance of what they were doing. And the daring. Lex was spurring a rebellion!

Teryn seemed equally as impressed. "Do you know when it will take place?"

"At the end of the month," Lex said. "The rebels almost have enough...manure."

Cora's heart sparked with excitement. If the rebels succeeded, Cora might not have to worry about the hostility the prisoner had hinted at. At least not from Norun. Syrus, of course, remained a mysterious threat...

Teryn placed his palm on her thigh, beside her hand that was fisted around the folds of her skirt. She didn't recall having moved her hand there, but she must have in her anxiety and excitement during all the talk about Norun and rebels. Teryn's fingers smoothed her own until she released the fabric of her skirt. Then he entwined their fingers, a gesture that reminded her they would face this together. They would face whatever came next, side by side.

"Will you keep us apprised of developments?" he asked.

"Of course," Lex said. "Anything for my allies."

8

Cora was ready.

She *was*.

She really, truly was.

At least, she figured if she kept telling herself that, she might be. Dinner had ended an hour ago. Her maids had already been dismissed after assisting with her bath. The evening was creeping toward midnight, and Cora worried that if she waited too much longer, Teryn would give up on her coming at all.

She couldn't dally. What good was pacing around her room doing? She thought she needed to practice what she wanted to say, but she'd been doing that for months, and when it had finally come time to see Teryn, she hadn't been able to convey any of the things she'd intended to.

It was now or never.

Cora brushed her damp palms over the front of her cream velvet robe. Beneath it, she wore an ivory silk chemise trimmed with lace. She tried not to overthink what it meant that she was about to visit her fiancé in her underclothes, for what else could she do? She couldn't have asked her ladies to lace her back into her dinner gown after her bath. Moreover, to say *certain thoughts* weren't on her mind would be a lie. And after their kiss earlier, after the way he'd demanded she say his name, the way he'd propped her on that dresser, she knew those things were on his mind too. But as long as Teryn didn't pounce on her the second she arrived, she'd have a chance to accomplish her mission before being swept up in desire again.

In the meantime, she tugged the neck of her gown a little closer and tied the sash around her waist a tad tighter. Then, closing her eyes, she thought of Teryn.

When her mind raced forward to how their conversation might go, she drew it back and settled her thoughts in the past, at dinner. She recalled the warmth of his fingers laced with hers, his steady, anchoring touch. She imagined the way his skin felt beneath her palm. As her nerves settled, allowing her to fully focus on her magic, she pictured his bedroom. She imagined it much like it had looked earlier, but this time she envisioned it under a blanket of night. Curtains drawn, the lighting dim, the glow of a single lamp warming the walls. She *felt* like she was there. Felt Teryn's presence, his nearness.

Then she took a step.

Felt the distance between their rooms fold until it was merely a hop away.

And planted her feet firmly in her destination.

She opened her eyes to find she'd succeeded in her travels. Only, it wasn't the dimly lit room she'd pictured. Instead, the bedroom was cast beneath a golden glow, the walls flickering with the light of what appeared to be a hundred candles. She was so startled by this unexpected vision, so distracted by the ivory flame-topped pillars that encroached upon nearly every flat surface, from the dresser to the nightstand to the bureau, that she almost didn't notice Teryn.

He leaned against the far wall, one arm propped on a windowsill, ankles crossed. It seemed he'd kept his promise about wearing a shirt and had even managed to keep it mostly buttoned. He was free of his cravat and dinner jacket, the only other articles left of his evening attire being his trousers and open waistcoat. His pale hair was no longer tied back and hung loose like it had when she'd first invaded his bedroom. She was still struck by that moon-white hair, how it was neither thin nor fraying like she'd expected it to be. How it cascaded around his face in lazy waves. How it somehow suited him just as well as his golden-brown tresses had.

"You came," he said, not moving from his place by the window.

She took a few hesitant steps forward, gaze flicking from him to the candles and back again. "You did all this? For me?"

"It wouldn't be the first time." He pushed off the wall and closed just as much distance as she had. Which was a measly three feet. Perhaps he was allowing her to set the pace between them. She nearly sprinted the rest of the way to him, jumped into his arms, and pressed her lips to that deliciously plump mouth of his, but she held back. She absolutely *had* to express herself through words before she turned herself over to her body.

"What do you mean it wouldn't be the first time?" she asked. Then a sound tugged upon her awareness. "And is that...music?"

"It is music." He angled his head toward the windowsill behind him.

Cora saw nothing but a long wooden box. "What is that?"

"Your wedding gift."

Curiosity overtook her. She swept toward the windowsill, her heart racing with every foot of space she closed between herself and Teryn, then brushed past him. The sound was louder now, a sweet yet tinny melody that emanated from the box. The box itself was a long, narrow rectangle of black lacquered wood decorated with red-and-gold cherry blossoms. A jewelry box, perhaps? Teryn stepped beside her, and the scent of soap and pine filled her senses. He leaned in close and whispered, "Open it."

She met his eyes, his smile, and her heart nearly burst from her chest. She was reluctant to tear her gaze away, but she was still so curious about the box. He'd said it was her wedding gift, and the music box was stunning in itself. But if he wanted her to open it, perhaps her actual gift was inside.

Dragging her attention from Teryn to the box, she brought her hands to the lid. As she lifted it, Teryn said, "I know we already chose rings from our royal collections, so I didn't get you wedding jewelry. Besides, I thought this would suit you better."

The music grew slightly clearer as the box opened on a hinge. Inside was a compartment lined with red velvet, and at the very center lay a stunning dagger. Cora's breath caught at the beautiful steel blade, flickering orange from the undulating candlelight, but that was before she noticed the hilt. It was even more breathtaking, with a crossguard engraved in a floral pattern that continued onto the hilt. At its center was the most moving touch of all—a unicorn rearing back on its hind legs, mane rippling and merging into the floral engraving. Tears glazed her eyes as she ran her fingers over the design, marveling in its craftsmanship.

"You like it?" Teryn's voice was edged with uncertainty.

"I love it," she said, and her heart hammered at the word *love*. Slowly, she slid her gaze from the dagger to him.

"I had it made specially for you," he said. "I wanted it to represent you in every way. Your beauty. Your fierceness. Your connection to Valorre. And...to me."

"You?"

He reached for the box and closed the lid again. "Do you remember the first time you held a blade to my throat?"

She nearly barked a laugh that he had to specify *the first time*, but he was right to. He'd been on the other side of her blade more than once. She recalled their first encounter now, when they'd met by a stream. Teryn had almost thrown a spear at Valorre and Cora had stopped him by shooting an arrow at his neck in warning. It had struck a cherry tree behind him, pink blossoms in full bloom. After that, she'd confronted him with her knife and they'd had a brief altercation.

Laughter tore through her chest. "You dedicated my wedding gift to *that* moment between us?"

"The most important moment." His eyes glittered with mirth as he lifted a hand and softly brushed it against her cheek. Her stomach fluttered, and it was all she could do not to angle her face and press her lips to his palm. She would not kiss him until she'd confessed her heart's deepest longings.

But as she opened her mouth to just say it already, the words wouldn't come. Was she supposed to blurt it out? Pair it with some sweet gesture? Sweet words? If only she were as thoughtful as he was. If only she'd had the foresight to have gotten him a gift that would render him speechless. If only—

"May I have this dance?"

Her mind emptied. She'd been so wrapped up in her thoughts, she hadn't noticed Teryn pull his hand from her cheek or step away. He now held the music box in his hand and was winding the brass key at the back. A cranking sound emanated from the box, but as he set it back down, the melody resumed. Cora shook her head to clear it. "Dance?"

He sketched a bow, a sideways grin pulling his lips. As he straightened, he held out his hand. What else could Cora do but take it? Her nerves settled as she placed her hand in his. He pulled her against him, too close for any kind of dance at a public ball. But here, in the privacy of his room, it was perfect. She kept one hand clasped in his and wound the other arm around his back. Then, turning her face, she nestled her head to his chest, the pound of his heart merging with the rhythm of the music box. Slowly they swayed, saying not a word for minutes on end.

Finally, Teryn gently loosened her arm from around his waist and guided her into a slow spin. When he reeled her in, her back was to his chest. They swayed side to side as he brought his lips close to her ear. "I never answered your earlier question."

She shuddered as his breath rustled her hair. "What question?"

He spun her away from him again, then folded her back into his arms, their chests pressed together once more. Holding her eyes, he said, "When you asked about the candles, and I said this wouldn't be the first time, I meant that I've done this for you before. Or something like it. Twice, in fact."

"When?"

He grinned, and there was a bashful quality to it. "The most recent time was for the dinner we never got to have last summer. I had to coerce Mareleau into helping me organize it, but..."

He didn't need to finish. She knew what had happened that night. She'd been an emotional wreck after remembering the curse Morkai had placed upon her, and Teryn had gotten captured in the mage's crystal. Sometimes she wondered what would have happened if she'd never turned him away that night, if she'd gone to dinner with him instead of sitting alone with her pain, but it was folly to wonder. What was done was done.

"The first time, though," Teryn said, "was when I asked you to come see me in the garden at Verlot Palace."

Her heart sank. "The night I left. When I...when I thought you'd married Mareleau."

He nodded, chuckling to himself. "I had the most ridiculous spectacle prepared for you. A candlelit alcove, a harpist, a table set with wine and sweets."

Regret had never pierced her so hard as it did now. She had no clue he'd done that for her. "I'm so sorry—"

"Don't apologize," he said, and there was only gentleness in his tone. "I'm not telling you this, doing this, to make you feel guilty. I'm doing this because I never want to miss anything between us ever again. Never want to miss any chance, any opportunity. Obstacles have drawn us apart, but I will never let them hold me back." His tone turned serious, as did his expression. A fierceness shone on his face, one that told of the hardships they'd endured, the darkness they'd faced and survived.

The song began to slow, the mechanical melody reaching its end. They stopped their dance but neither stepped away. Cora's heart raced, knowing it was time. She could feel the shift in Teryn's mood as well as her own, something as fierce and sharp as lightning crackling in the air between them. Invisible layers fell away, confessions breaching the frail walls they'd both constructed to hold them in place. It was a mutual shedding. A mutual baring of souls. She knew this. Felt this.

Teryn stepped even closer and framed her cheeks in his hands. His eyes locked on hers, blazing with an emerald fire so heated she couldn't look away. "I almost died, Cora. All of us have danced with death, you, me, Larylis, Mareleau. We don't know what lies ahead and our time as living beings isn't guaranteed. I don't want to waste a single second of this life not loving you. Not showing you, in all that I do, that I deeply and steadfastly love you."

Cora nearly sagged against him at the sound of those words. Her lashes fluttered shut as she let them wash over her. She'd known it in her heart, but hearing him say it—*finally* say it—was different.

"You love me?" Her voice quavered.

"Of course I love you." Restraint edged his voice, as if he wanted to shout the words, declare them for the world to hear. "I've said it to you so many times in my mind, in my heart, but you never heard me. I fought to utter the words when my spirit was barely clinging to my body. I've sung it from the depths of my soul. I know you couldn't hear me, but did you never once at least feel its melody?"

"I did," she breathed. "I even sang it back to you. Just... just never aloud."

He released a slow breath, then pressed his forehead to hers. "I'm still waiting to hear it," he said, and this time there was a note of teasing in his voice.

Her heart slammed against her ribs. Yes, now was the time.

She swallowed hard.

"I love you, Teryn. I'm sorry I'm not as romantic as you. I'm sorry I'm not as brave or eloquent with my words—"

"No," he whispered. Placing his forefinger under her chin, he lifted her face, forcing her to meet his eyes. "You're perfect as you are. I want nothing more from you. Let me spoil you. Let me say the things I couldn't put to pen and paper. Let me make a fool of myself before you. You don't have to do anything in return. Just love me."

"I do. I love you. I can't even tell you how much I do."

He sighed, and it seemed to drag years off his visage, making him look boyish and beautiful and carefree. Mischief worked the corner of his mouth. "Does that mean I've good and properly wooed you?"

Cora remembered the promise he'd once made. That even though they were engaged, he'd court her. That before they lived as true husband and wife, he'd win her heart, no matter how long it took.

She realized there was something else she needed to make clear. Placing her hands on his chest, she gathered the collar of his shirt in her fists and tugged him closer. "I don't need you to court me or woo me anymore, Teryn. I don't need us to take our marriage slow, nor do I want to. Do you understand? I'm already yours."

"You're mine?" She'd never seen such a gorgeous smile. His face lit up with it, with pleasure, with pride.

"And you're mine." She pulled him closer again, their bodies flush. The same fierce quality she'd glimpsed on his face earlier now burned inside her, sparking yearning. Now that she'd said all that she'd wanted to say, her body tingled with the desire she'd been holding at bay. It rushed through her arms, filling her palms. It coursed down her legs, gathering at her core. Gods, she loved him. Gods, she wanted him.

A look of surprise crossed his face. Then a question. "When you say you don't want to take our marriage slow..."

She answered him with a kiss.

9

T heir lips met with a reckless fervor, parting at once. Her tongue swept against his, tasting their mutual confession. Cora trembled at the flood of desire pouring through her, so strong it was as if it had broken a dam. She supposed that was expected after she'd pent it up all afternoon and evening. Now she turned herself over to it, let her body take the lead. Her muscles uncoiled as if breathing a collective sigh, one that said *finally*. Every ounce of tension that left her body collected in a pool of heat at her center, warming her lower belly, burning in a ball of hungry heat between her thighs. Meanwhile, her heart opened, expanded, singing with the glorious revelation, the trust, that Teryn loved her. He well and truly loved her.

And he was *hers*.

Teryn's arms wound around her, one hand weaving through her loose tresses, the other pressing into her back, tugging her closer. She arched against him, desperate to feel more of him, all of him. Her palms burned with her yearning, igniting every line of ink that marked them. She released Teryn's collar and let one hand cradle the back of his head, the other slipping beneath his shirt to smooth over his pectoral, his shoulder. He hissed in a breath at her touch, shuddering beneath her palm. A wicked smile curled her lips, and she drew the other hand away from his neck, down his chest, to the hem of his shirt. Lifting it, she slipped her hand underneath and splayed her palm over his muscled abdomen. A stifled groan left his throat and he took her bottom lip between his teeth. She gasped at the slight pressure he applied, thrilled that her touch had sparked such a reaction in him.

He pulled back suddenly, and for a moment she feared he would ask her to stop, tell her *he* was the one who wanted to take things slow. She'd honor that, of course, but as he looked down at her with half-lidded eyes, lips swollen from the ferocity of their kisses, she desperately wished he wouldn't make such a request. Thankfully, he merely reached for the collar of his shirt and pulled the article over his head. Though this was her second time seeing him bare-chested today, this time was different. She felt no apprehension. No fraying nerves. Only fascination and desire.

His chest heaved as he stood before her, making no move to return to her arms. As much as she wanted to feel him against her, she wanted this too—a moment to look him over. Admire him. Drink in the sight of the man she loved without any reservations. She lifted a hand and alighted her fingertips upon his ribs, right over the scar that marred his flesh. He tensed as she touched him, tracing the line of puckered skin. Then she trailed her hand up his torso, over his chest, his collarbone, then up his neck. She smoothed her thumb over the small circular scar there.

Finally, he dared to move, lifting a hand to her neck as well. He brushed his fingers softly over her identical scar, then bent forward and caressed it with his lips. He did the same to the scar on the other side, a slow and tender gesture. They both held these twin marks, a permanent reminder of the collar they'd both worn.

When Teryn pulled back, something dark flashed in his eyes. "If I ever meet the man who did that to you..."

She silenced him with her lips. There was no use making idle threats against the Elvyn male who'd trapped her in that collar, stifling her magic. Fanon was a world away, in the fae realm. Cora may hold the secret to entering the realm—her worldwalking magic paired with Valorre's ability to pierce the Veil that protected El'Ara—but she had no intention of returning.

Besides, she didn't want to think about El'Ara, the Veil, or the prophecy her fate was entwined in. The only thing she wanted to be entwined with right now was Teryn. His lips. His arms. His body. His love.

She pulled back slightly and infused her tone with a taunting lilt. "You may want revenge on the male who put me in that collar, but what about what I did to you? I'm the one who collared you. Do you want to punish me?"

A wry grin quirked his mouth. "Do you want to be punished?"

"I do," she whispered.

"How?" His voice came out like a growl.

It reminded her of how he'd sounded when he'd told her to say his name earlier. The demand in his tone had been so thrilling. She wanted to hear it again.

She gave him a coy smile. "I'll let you make one command of me. Tell me one thing to do to make up for my previous misdeeds, and I'll do it now."

"Anything?"

She stepped closer, angled her head higher. "Anything."

His throat bobbed. Silence stretched between them before he managed to speak. "Undress for me."

That same thrill tore through her. All she could manage in reply was a nod.

Slowly, he backed away from her and sat at the edge of the bed. She stood before him, and a flicker of apprehension moved over his face. "Is this all right?" he asked, voice soft. He reached for her, softly touching her arm as if to tell her she didn't *have* to do this.

His hesitation warmed her heart, but it also filled her with the slightest self-consciousness. Still, she *wanted* to do this. Needed to. Her heart thundered in her chest. "Yes."

With a nod, he pulled his hand away and sat back, his posture easing.

With trembling hands, she undid the tie at her waist and let her robe fall open. She watched his face as his eyes wandered over the length of her chemise. His lips parted as she slowly let the robe fall from her shoulders. Then she dragged the top of her chemise down her shoulders, slipping her arms through and freeing them, before baring her breasts. Her moves weren't elegant or seductive, but it didn't matter. Teryn watched her with such rapt attention, his gaze heavy with desire, that she felt like the most beautiful, alluring figure in the world. She tugged her chemise the rest of the way down and let it fall at her feet.

Teryn bit his bottom lip as he looked her over, then his gaze rested on hers. "Can I touch you?"

She shuddered at the question. "Please."

He reached for her with gentle hands, bracketing her hips with his palms. He pulled her closer to where he sat at the edge of the bed until she was standing between his legs. Their heights weren't so different with him sitting, and for once she stood slightly above him. He lifted his chin and she

tasted his lips, a slow and languorous kiss. When they separated, he brought his mouth to her neck. Then her upper
chest. With his tongue, he explored the arched curve of her
breast. She released a soft cry as his tongue skated over her
sensitive peak. His hands tightened on her hips at the
sound.

Her desire grew tenfold, at the pressure of his palms, the
pleasure he painted with his tongue. It made her knees
weak. Giving in, she dropped herself into his lap, straddling
his hips. Hips that were annoyingly still clothed.

He tensed beneath her, his hands roving along her
upper back then drifting down, down, curving around her
bottom. She pressed her mouth to his again, and he tugged
her tighter to him. Then, in a swift move, he flipped her
onto her back. The soft velvet blankets contrasted Teryn's
hard angles, the stiff fabric of his trousers. Trousers that
were straining against his desire in obvious ways.

"Teryn," she whispered against his mouth. "I want more
of you."

"How much more?"

"All of you. I told you, I don't want to wait."

He pulled back slightly, hovering over her. "Are you
sure?"

"You don't want to waste a single moment between us. I
don't either." With that, she slid her hand down his chest
to the waistband of his trousers, tucking her fingertips just
beneath the fabric. He groaned, then shifted to the side to
undo his trousers' buttons, freeing himself at last. She
didn't think her heart could beat any faster, but it nearly
shot from her chest as she explored him with her palms.
He did the same to her, feeling the parts of her he hadn't
touched yet. They held each other's eyes, coaxing sounds
from each other, testing which touches made the other

shudder, which had them arching into each other for more.

Then finally, when Cora didn't think she could take another second of the beautiful torment they teased each other with, she shifted more firmly beneath him, and let him settle fully over her.

They paused and exchanged a tender kiss. "I love you," Teryn said when their lips parted.

"I love you," Cora echoed back.

Then Teryn seated himself fully inside her. Cora gasped at the fullness, the rightness, the euphoria that thrummed through her as their hips began to move. She'd never felt this before. Sure, she'd taken lovers when she'd lived with the Forest People, but it was nothing like this. Nothing like the connection between her heart and Teryn's. Nothing like the emotion that tore through her as they quickened their pace, reading each other's bodies, movements, signals, as if they were speaking a brand-new language.

Teryn gripped her hand, pressing into the blankets beneath them, an anchor to reality as her euphoria grew. Heat continued to build at her core, growing hotter and hotter, even as the thrust of their hips sated it. She wanted more. More. Again and again.

Finally, she crested the wave of pleasure, feeling it tear through her, coursing through every inch of her body, her soul. Her eyes watered with the force of it. The promise of it.

Teryn pressed his mouth to hers once more. "I love you," he said, voice strangled. "I love you so much, Cora."

The words drove her over the edge, release shuddering through her. Teryn found his next, a wave that chased her own, that danced with it. That rose and calmed with it.

They remained entangled, sweat soaked and spent for minutes on end, neither speaking as they caught their breath, communicating with wordless smiles. Teryn brushed the hair away from her brow. When they finally managed to separate, it was only to rearrange themselves. Teryn reclined on his back while Cora draped herself over him, her head cradled against his chest. She closed her eyes and gave in to a moment of rest, lulled by the sound of his heart.

10

Teryn couldn't stop looking at her, the beautiful woman dozing on his chest, a soft smile on her swollen lips. His body was sated, but his eyes couldn't get enough of her, nor could his hands. He caressed her dark tresses—tangled now, thanks to their activities—and wound his fingers through her hair, memorizing its sheen, its texture. His other hand brushed the dark tan skin of her forearm that was draped across his chest.

How did he get so lucky?

What did he do to deserve this fierce and gorgeous creature?

He studied the side of her face, her bare shoulder, her slender neck. As his eyes settled on her puncture scar, a protective fire burned inside him. He'd felt it when they'd assessed each other's scars earlier. While he felt no bitterness at having worn the collar briefly himself—it had helped him take back his body, after all—seeing hers filled him with rage. In her letters, Cora had told him all that had happened in El'Ara. How she'd been forced to endure that collar for nearly an entire day, how an Elvyn named Fanon had hated her beyond reason, going so far as to pit her against a dragon.

His anger at that Elvyn male was so strong, it overshadowed any sympathy he might feel for those who lived in El'Ara. For the fact that their land was dying, smothered by the Blight that was slowly creeping from the Veil. He was almost glad Cora couldn't fulfill her role as the mother in a prophecy that foretold the fae realm's salvation, if only to spite that single Elvyn. Though he couldn't fully relish it. Not when Cora's inability to birth the prophesied savior had come at such a heartbreaking cost—being cursed by Morkai.

Cora stirred, drawing his mind from his dark thoughts. As she lifted her head from his chest, his stomach sank. He knew what she was going to say before she uttered a word.

A sad smile crept over her mouth. "I should get back to my room."

"Can't you stay?" he asked, running a fingertip over her cheek, her chin.

"I wish I could, but what would my ladies think if they found me missing in the morning?"

She was right. As queen, she granted honors to aristocratic families by appointing their daughters and nieces as her royal lady's maids, or their sisters and wives as ladies-in-waiting. That didn't mean they were women she could trust. As far as Teryn knew from the letters they'd exchanged, she hadn't gotten close to any of them. If they discovered any unsavory gossip about Cora, they could spread it through the castle and beyond in a matter of hours.

He hated that royal women were expected to remain chaste while men were not. He hated that their pure and beautiful love could devolve into a scandal, even though their wedding was a mere few days away. Even so, this wasn't the time to battle such lofty expectations and traditions. Cora's reign was still new.

Yet he couldn't bear to let her go so soon.

"Go back in the morning then, before sunrise," he said.

Her eyes narrowed in consideration. Then suspicion. "I have a feeling we won't get much sleep if I stay the night."

He shifted to the side and rolled her onto her back. Her eyes widened with amused surprise. He nipped at her bottom lip. "Whatever could you mean, Your Formidable Majesty?"

"Hmm, I wonder." She glanced down, arching a brow at the part of him that answered for both of them.

Just when he thought he was sated, his craving for her returned. He angled himself closer to her, let his hand skate up her thigh, her hip, her stomach, until he cupped one of her breasts in his hand. He ran his thumb in a slow circle over her hardened peak, delighting in the way her lashes fluttered shut, the way her lips parted. "What do you say?"

She opened her mouth, either in a gasp or to give her answer, but before he could find out which it was, a rhythmic knock invaded his awareness. It was coming from his sitting room, at his suite's main door. His bedroom door was closed, stifling the sound. He had every intention of ignoring it, even as it sounded again, more insistent this time.

Cora released a heavy sigh. "You should answer that."

Teryn groaned, and it wasn't the pleasurable kind. "Must I?"

She shrugged. "It could be important."

The knock sounded again, an incessant rumble that told him his caller would not relent.

Cora leaned forward and captured his lips in a too-short kiss. "Don't worry. I'll wait until you return before I leave."

His heart fell. That meant she was leaving after all. He wasn't ready to say goodnight, but perhaps if he dealt quickly with their interloper, he could go back to convincing her to stay just a little longer.

With another frustrated groan, he dragged himself away from Cora, donned his shirt and trousers with haste, and marched from his bedroom. He closed the door behind him and strode through the sitting room in darkness, the only light coming from the moon's pale white streaks that shot through the windows. When he reached the door, he flung it open with far more force than necessary.

He opened his mouth, ready to tell his caller to kindly piss off, but held himself back as he saw who was on the other side of his threshold.

Mareleau glowered at him, teeth bared. Without waiting for his permission, she charged inside and closed the door behind her. Crossing her arms, she faced him. "I need to speak with Cora right now."

His mind stuttered before he conjured a reply. "What makes you think she's here?"

She gave him a withering look. "It's five nights before your wedding and you just saw each other for the first time in months. She's not in her room, which means of course she's here. Tell her I need—"

The sound of his bedroom door creeping open silenced her. "Mareleau, what's—"

"Seven devils, Cora," Mareleau said with equal parts relief and frustration. "There you are. I need you."

"Why?" Cora was dressed in her chemise and robe again, though her tangled hair and crooked sash made it obvious what they'd been doing before.

Mareleau glanced from Teryn to Cora, a wild look in her eyes. Finally, her gaze settled on Cora. "Either I've just wet my skirts for the first time in my adult life, or my waters have broken. Gods above." Her voice broke, rippling with a frantic tremor. "I'm going into godsdamned labor."

EVERY INCH OF BRAVADO MARELEAU HAD EVER POSSESSED, ALL her boasting that she could give birth anywhere and it wouldn't matter, fled the instant she admitted she was going into labor. Here. Now. She'd been brave when she'd thought the grand event was still weeks away, and her midwives had indulged her, assuring her she'd more likely deliver late than early. But this...no, this couldn't be happening.

Cora took a step closer. "You're going into labor? Are you sure?"

"I'm pretty sure the water soaking my skirts says I am." She couldn't stop the panicked edge from creeping into her tone, but at least it helped mask her embarrassment. She didn't want to talk about this in front of her brother-in-law, but it couldn't be helped. She needed Cora. For what, she wasn't entirely sure. All she knew was that she couldn't face her mother or her midwives right now. Her mother would fly into hysteria, which would only heighten Mareleau's own, while her midwives would confirm her fears. That this was happening. She was giving birth.

Her abdomen tightened, a strange and foreign feeling that was somehow coming from inside her, against her will. She'd experienced lesser contractions for days now, ones deemed normal by her midwives, but the ones she'd begun feeling this evening were anything but mild. They'd begun at dinner and hadn't stopped.

She closed her eyes, hand to her belly, and waited for

the tightening to pass. When it did, there remained a similar constriction in her chest. "I can't do this."

"Breathe, Mareleau," Cora said, her voice soft and calm. She placed her hands on Mareleau's shoulders. "Tell me slowly. Why are you alone? Where are your ladies?"

"Breah is down the hall." Despite trying her best to speak slowly like Cora had requested, her words still came out rushed and racked with a tremor. "I asked her to keep watch while I came to find you."

"Yes, but why did you come find me? Why not your midwives?"

Mareleau opened her mouth to answer that which she hardly understood herself. She'd awoken after a couple fitful hours of sleep and left her room to pace the halls, choosing Breah to accompany her. Waking up to walk in the middle of the night wasn't unusual for Mareleau, for she often woke due to discomfort and needed to stretch her legs before settling back into her fort of pillows. But tonight, as she'd slowly wandered the corridor outside her suite, waiting for restfulness to settle back in, she'd felt a sudden gush of warm water. She'd frozen in place, her mind whirling. Once she'd been able to form a coherent thought, it had been to find Cora at once.

The reason?

Mareleau shrugged and blurted out the first semi-reasonable thing that came to mind. "I came to you so...so you can stop this."

Cora pulled her head back. "Stop what? Your labor? How the seven devils do you expect me to do that?"

"I don't know. Your...magic."

Cora leveled a look at her that conveyed just how ridiculous Mareleau's words were. Yet she'd already known that as soon as they'd left her mouth. Mareleau had learned many things about Cora over the last few months of their increasing correspondence, particularly about her past, her abilities, and how they related to what had happened that night in the meadow seven months ago. When she thought rationally, she knew Cora could do nothing about her situation.

So why had she come to Cora?

"I just need a friend, all right?" The tightness in her chest eased a little as she settled on this truth. "I need you to be here for me, that's all."

Cora's expression softened. "I'm here. I'll stay by your side through what comes next, but you need to tell your midwives you're going into labor. Your mother and husband too, for that matter."

Teryn voiced his agreement. "Larylis deserves to know."

"I can't tell Larylis," Mareleau said. "Not yet. You know how he gets when he's anxious. He'll start reciting great queens of history who've given birth in unusual situations. If I have to hear about Queen Constantina of Rovana in 56 Year of the Stag one more time, I will scream."

She'd had enough of Queen Constantina, who'd ridden into battle heavily pregnant and gave birth behind a shield wall while arrows rained overhead. Mareleau didn't need that kind of pressure. She wasn't nearly as valiant.

Teryn's jaw shifted back and forth before he released a resigned sigh. "You make a valid point."

"Your mother then," Cora said. "It will be impossible to avoid her anyway. Isn't she staying in your suite with you?"

She was, and Mareleau wouldn't be surprised if her mother was already frantically looking for her. And yet...

"I can't handle her right now. If she finds out I'm going into labor here, she'll only say *I told you so*."

"And I won't?" Cora removed her hands from Mareleau's

shoulders and propped them on her hips. "I told you not to come, Mare. You had to have known this was a possibility."

She had known, and she'd thought she'd been prepared. She'd imagined several scenarios, walked through each one in excruciating detail, per her husband's insistence. So long as she'd agreed to work through the myriad of possibilities they might encounter regarding her pregnancy, he'd support her travels. But in every scenario, she'd been calm. She'd had a plan. She'd dealt with every imagined ordeal with grace.

Reality, however, was proving far different. She hadn't anticipated this all-encompassing shock. This terror. This dreadful feeling that the gods had made a grave mistake in bestowing such a heavy responsibility on her. She wasn't ready. She'd never be ready. Why did she ever have the nerve to consider herself an adult?

Another contraction stuck her abdomen. She closed her eyes and felt a gentle hand smoothing circles over her back.

"I can't do this," Mareleau said, tears leaking from her tightly squeezed eyelids. "I can't be a mother. I'm going to do a terrible job. I'm going to be awful."

"No, you won't," Cora said. "Don't you recall what I said to you, after you first told me about your pregnancy? I said you'll be an okay mother."

The tightness eased, allowing her to scoff. "An okay mother," she echoed. "That's hardly comforting."

"Well, it should be. Because that's all you have to be. You don't need to be perfect. You don't have to do everything right. Was your mother perfect?"

"Hardly."

"Exactly. Look how great you turned out."

Mareleau pried her eyes open but she couldn't see much

through her tears. She coughed on a sob before she managed to say, "You think I'm great?"

"You're at the very least tolerable." The teasing in Cora's voice gave Mareleau a sense of calm to cling to. If Cora was taunting her, refusing to give in to her vanity, things couldn't be too dire, right?

Mareleau blinked the tears from her eyes and found her friend's smiling face. She blew out a shaking breath.

Cora rubbed another circle over her back. "Are you ready? Can we go tell your midwives now?"

Ready wasn't the right word, but she had no other choice. With a shaky nod, she said, "Fine. Let's show Queen Constantina who can give birth in a worse environment."

"Aww, you're insulting my castle again," Cora said in a simpering tone. "You must be feeling better already."

Mareleau gave a humorless laugh, then pinned Teryn with a warning look. "Don't you dare let Larylis in my room until I say so. I don't care if you have to tie him to a chair."

Teryn gave a reluctant nod, then Cora steered Mareleau out the door.

And toward the greatest battlefield she'd ever face.

11

As promised, Cora stayed with Mareleau throughout the entire ordeal. She'd attended numerous births amongst the Forest People and had even assisted with them. But this one was different, for it was her friend on the bed, her friend in pain. She wished she could play a more proactive role in helping her, but between the four midwives, Mareleau's three maids, and Queen Mother Helena, there was little for Cora to do aside from what Mareleau had asked of her: simply being there for her.

Cora held her hand through every contraction. Depending on Mareleau's ever-changing mood, she chanted encouragement or whispered words of soothing. Despite her best efforts, Cora found her mental shields growing weaker as the hours stretched on and on, not a wink of sleep behind her. Delirium took over, and she wasn't sure it belonged more to her or to Mareleau. Their emotions were entwined by morning. Mareleau's pain was Cora's pain. Her fatigue, Cora's fatigue. Her fear, Cora's fear.

There were times the latter emotion grew unbearably

strong, dipping into sorrow and panic when Mareleau would mutter that her baby was too early, that this was too arduous, too long, that surely something was wrong. It almost made Cora wish she had the power of the narcuss.

Morkai's power.

She hated that she even thought of it, but if she had his magic, she could impress calmer thoughts upon Mareleau. A narcuss was the inverse of her power. Where Cora could feel the emotions of others, a narcuss could change what another felt and perceived. Particularly in the minds of the weak or fearful.

Cora banished these thoughts whenever they crept upon her, for what good would they do? She wasn't a narcuss. The only one she'd ever met was Morkai, and he was dead. Cora couldn't force Mareleau's pain and fear away, and even if she could, what right did she have? Those emotions belonged to her friend. All she could do was feel them with her. Help her through to the other side.

The other side finally came.

After twelve hours, a baby boy took his first breath in the world, followed by a tiny, wailing cry. It was just past noon. The room remained dim, the curtains drawn shut. After half a day and no sleep from anyone—save Mareleau's three ladies, who'd left to doze in the sitting room hours ago—the blaring light of day was an unwelcome intruder.

The baby's cry filled the room, such a soft yet sharp sound. Such a signal of joy and relief. It was strange how the cry somehow made everything seem quieter. Calmer. Like the entire world had gone to sleep and now orbited that sweet small sound.

Cora sagged against the edge of the bed, knees on the floor, arms draped over the side of the mattress. Her lungs opened wide, allowing her to breathe easier for the first time in twelve hours, but she still felt the haze of delirium.

Mareleau sobbed as a midwife placed the swaddled babe in her arms, and Cora found her eyes glazing as she watched them, watched her friend's lips widen in a smile, watched as Helena sat beside her daughter on the bed, tears streaming down her cheeks.

"He's so tiny," Mareleau said, a tremor in her voice.

"He is small, Majesty," the midwife agreed, "but he's healthy."

Helena leaned closer to her daughter until their foreheads touched. "He's beautiful."

Mareleau's grin widened. "He is."

Cora smiled, watching Mareleau interact with her mother. Despite Mareleau's worries, Helena hadn't harped on her daughter at all. She'd been stunned silent for most of the ordeal. For the first time, Cora had seen the queen mother as timid, as if the woman was desperate not to upset her daughter and make things harder for her.

"Would you like to try to nurse him?" the midwife asked.

Mareleau nodded, equal parts joy and trepidation on her face.

Cora opened her mouth to ask if she should leave, but before she could utter a word, Mareleau whispered, "Stay. Please."

So instead, she rested her head on her arms, closed her eyes, and gave her friend a moment of privacy.

Cora woke to the sound of song.

She lifted her head and found the room was no longer dim, the curtains parted over the far window to let in the light of an overcast afternoon sky. She wasn't sure how long she'd slept, but the room had been tidied and the midwives were no longer there. Mareleau and Helena were in almost the same positions they'd been before Cora had closed her eyes, nestled side by side. The music Cora had awoken to was coming from Helena. The queen mother sang a lovely, lilting lullaby, her voice a soothing soprano.

Cora straightened, rubbing sleep from her eyes. Though fatigue still weighed down on her, she found much of her delirium had cleared, enough that she could connect to the elements and strengthen her mental wards again. With her shields in place, she met her friend's eyes.

Mareleau brightened. "You're awake," she whispered over her mother's song.

Cora nodded, and Helena finished her lullaby, her final note ringing out long and sweet. Cora cleared her dry throat before she spoke. "I had no idea you sang so well, Helena."

The queen mother beamed at the compliment. "I've always had a talent for music. When I was younger, I was praised for having perfect pitch."

"Oh, don't get her started on her perfect pitch," Mareleau said with a roll of her eyes, a gesture that was tempered by the smile she wore. It seemed the two were still getting along.

"I played harp and piano," Helena said, sitting a little straighter. "I could perfectly recite any song by ear after hearing it only once. I was such a prodigy, my father used to call me his *Little Siren*."

Mareleau said the last two words in unison with her mother, but in a deep and mocking tone.

Cora chuckled, though she was thoroughly impressed, if the queen mother wasn't exaggerating. Musical talents weren't Cora's forte, but she'd always admired musicians.

Especially those amongst the Forest People. She'd known several clairaudient witches who'd expressed their magic through song, using their impressive hearing to compose or replicate beautiful music they would play for the commune. If Helena was as much of a prodigy as she suggested, there was a chance she had a magical gift and didn't even know it. Not every witch came to know their own magic for what it was, for many expressed their abilities in ways that blended seamlessly with societal norms.

Cora held a secret smile. Perhaps she wasn't the only queen who was also a witch.

"Do you want to see him?" Mareleau's question pulled Cora from her thoughts. She angled her head at the empty space beside her, opposite Helena.

"Of course," Cora said with more enthusiasm than she felt. More than anything, she wanted to curl up on a soft surface and go back to sleep. Yet she wanted to enjoy this moment with her friend. Of course she did.

Reluctantly, she dragged herself off the ground, her body aching from her unfortunate sleeping position, and settled in beside Mareleau. She was careful not to get too close lest she wake the sleeping baby in her friend's arms. Perhaps she was a touch anxious too, though she wasn't sure why. She'd been around plenty of infants and children when she'd lived with the Forest People. Even so, she wouldn't call her maternal instincts strong. Maiya, her dear friend and foster sister, had excelled in that regard, scooping up the little ones and swinging them around while Cora kept a modest distance. Then again, Cora had kept nearly everyone in the commune at arm's length.

Mareleau leaned slightly closer to Cora, showing off her bundle. A tiny, wrinkled face was all Cora could see in the swaddling, and though she should say he was beautiful, he looked...less so.

Her maternal instincts were awful indeed.

"He's lovely," Cora said, forcing her voice to sound wistful.

Mareleau furrowed her brow, and for a moment, Cora feared she'd oversold the compliment. But Mareleau's next words held a note of concern. "Is this painful for you? To...to see him? To be in this situation with me?"

Cora's stomach plummeted as she realized what Mareleau was implying. She was concerned for Cora's well-being because of the curse that had been placed upon her. Because this experience was one Cora might never have. To be honest, Cora hadn't given it much thought while she'd been aiding Mareleau through her labor, but now...

The unicorns. The mother. The child. Who do you think you are in that prophecy?

No, she still didn't want to think about it. Didn't want to revisit what Morkai had done to her. Didn't want to reflect on all the information she'd learned from Teryn, pieces of the prophecy that proved, without a doubt, she had been the prophesied mother Morkai had sought.

Blood of the witch, blood of the Elvyn, and blood of the crown. The unicorn will signify her awakening.

More than that, she didn't want to think about what her curse meant for El'Ara. Without their true Morkara, there was no one to command the flow of the *mora*—the fae word for magic—and keep it from seeping out into the human world. No one to stop the Blight that was slowly consuming the realm.

It wasn't sorrow that kept her from these thoughts, nor was it grief.

No, it was something darker.

Something she didn't want to admit.

Apathy.

An emotion that lingered in the wake of her time in El'Ara, when she'd been treated like a criminal by the Elvyn who'd found her. Two of the males, Etrix and Garot, had been kind to her, but Fanon had nearly gotten her killed. Had nearly killed her himself. Even the Faeryn, the race of High Fae the Forest People were descended from, did nothing but eye her with disdain when she'd come across a group of them trying to heal the Blight.

If she looked too close at that apathy, if she recognized even an ounce of truth in it, she'd have to consider that maybe she wasn't such a good person.

Cora forced a smile to her lips. "I'm fine, Mare." Her eyes darted to Helena, who was watching them intently.

Mareleau stiffened, as if only now remembering her mother's presence. She angled her head toward the queen mother, but Helena already seemed to understand. Scooting off the bed, she said, "I should see if your husband is awake yet."

"Thank you, Mother." Mareleau's voice held more gratitude than Cora was used to hearing from her friend. "If he's still asleep, let him stay that way, just a little longer. He was awake all morning."

Helena nodded, then left the bedroom, closing the door softly behind her.

Once they were alone, Mareleau faced Cora again. "I'm sorry. I shouldn't have brought it up in front of Mother. She doesn't know about..."

"My curse," Cora finished for her, voice flat.

Mareleau spoke again. "And I'm sorry that I didn't think of you, that I didn't worry about you until this moment."

Cora let out a long breath, and when she attempted her

smile once more, it was genuine. "I can't possibly condemn you for not thinking of me until now. *I* wasn't thinking of myself either."

"Still, I'll ask you again. Is this painful for you?"

"I'm all right," Cora said, not bothering to hide the weary edge in her voice this time.

"Good." Mareleau cast her eyes back to her baby. A light laugh left her lips. "You know, newborn babies aren't quite as cute as we're led to believe, are they?"

Cora snorted a laugh. "I wasn't going to say anything."

"I mean, he is beautiful in my eyes. Completely and utterly beautiful. And yet...he does look a bit like a wrinkly old man. Don't you, Noah?"

Surprise rippled through Cora. "You named him?"

"It's a name Larylis and I both liked for a boy. I suppose I'll find out if my husband still approves of it once he gets here. Speaking of..." She turned toward Cora with a grimace. "How ugly am I?"

Cora leveled a glare at her. "You're never ugly."

"But my hair must look terrible. What about my eyes? Are they red and swollen from crying? Do I look half dead or more like three-quarters? I'm open to the truth."

Cora rolled her eyes. Her friend's hair was admittedly a tangled mess, but this was hardly the time for vanity.

Mareleau sighed. "No, of course you won't tell me. I'd use my magic trick, but Larylis can probably see right through it."

"Magic trick?"

"Oh, it's not real magic. It's this thing I do where I pretend I can change my outer appearance and influence how another perceives me. I used to do it all the time when I was trying to get out of unwanted engagements. It's just a matter of altering my posture and expression, and it doesn't work on everyone."

"What do you mean? Show me?" Cora was both curious and amused.

"I'll try. But remember, it might not work." Mareleau adjusted her son in her arms and sat a little straighter. Then she held still for a few seconds, staring straight ahead, eyes unfocused. Slowly, a soft smile melted over her lips and she angled her face toward Cora. Her countenance was nearly glowing, her sapphire eyes as bright as the sea, the apples of her cheeks perfectly rosy. She didn't look at all like someone who hadn't slept—

Mareleau shook her head, averting her gaze. "Ah, I'm too tired. I can't do it."

Cora blinked at her, at her profile, at cheeks that had held such a rosy hue for all of a second. At eyes that had momentarily lost their puffiness and the dark circles that hung beneath them.

Had Cora merely hallucinated? Was she so fatigued that her mind had played along with Mareleau's game?

That was when she felt the tingle in her palms, sparking every inked line of her *insigmora*. Was Cora sensing...magic? A heavy warmth settled in her stomach, followed by a lifting sensation in her chest—a medley of clairsentient feeling that said *truth*.

Mareleau...had magic.

Again that feeling in her stomach, her chest.

Truth.

Mareleau could cast a glamour.

Truth.

Mareleau was a witch.

Truth.

12

Maybe it shouldn't have surprised Cora that Mareleau could use magic. She'd entertained the idea that Helena might be clairaudient. Why did it send such a chill down her spine to consider Mareleau might be a witch too?

Another heavy feeling settled in her stomach, but this one was sharper than the one that said *truth*. It said *pay attention*.

She wasn't sure what she was supposed to pay attention to, but she realized she was doing the opposite when Mareleau asked, "Were you listening?"

"No, I'm sorry." Cora shook the thoughts from her head and gave her friend an apologetic smile.

"I said, I'd like to name you Noah's godmother."

Something soft melted in Cora's heart. "You want me to be his godmother?"

"I do." Mareleau's expression turned hesitant. "Is that all right? Do you want that? Or is that incredibly rude of me to even ask, considering your—"

"It's lovely," Cora cut in before Mareleau could mention her curse again. "I'd be honored to be Noah's godmother."

"You know," Mareleau said, drawing the words out slowly, "you could name him your heir." When Cora didn't reply, she rushed to add, "Temporarily if you wanted. Your husband's nephew would make a suitable heir, don't you think?"

Cora glanced down at the sleeping babe. Son of her friend. Nephew of the man she loved. She supposed he would make for a worthy heir. Yet, as the first son of Mareleau and Larylis, he was already heir to Vera. Did that mean...

She shifted her gaze back to her friend, who seemed to already know what was on her mind.

"I promise, I'm not saying this because I want Noah to inherit your kingdom. I don't share my father's obsession with legacy. All I'm saying is that naming him your heir for now could secure Khero's standing even more than your marriage to Teryn will."

Cora huffed a laugh. "When did you become such a persuasive politician?"

"Probably when I was forced to become the queen of two kingdoms before I'd even gotten used to reigning over one."

"Well, you make quite a convincing case."

"Then I'll add one more thing. Merging Menah and Selay into Vera has been beneficial for our kingdoms. Uniting our resources, pooling our assets...I've seen nothing but good come of this. Our kingdoms were small, so merging the two hasn't stretched us thin or made it difficult to serve our people. So if you ended up...you know, keeping Noah as your heir, and Khero merged with Vera at the end of your reign..." Her expression turned hesitant again. "I'm just saying it wouldn't be the worst thing."

Cora pondered her words. While a stubborn, prideful part of her rebelled at the thought of turning her crown over to someone else—someone not of her blood, her family—she recognized this as only a small part of her. The greater part saw wisdom in Mareleau's words. If the curse Morkai placed on Cora never lifted, if she lived the rest of her life without ever bearing her own heirs, Mareleau's suggestion could be the solution she'd been looking for all along. She'd never been overly fond of bloodline politics in the first place, and what she really cared about was the safety of her kingdom. She cared that her people thrived, both during and after her rule. Handing her crown to Noah, to Cora's newly named godson, to a child who might very well come to feel like family soon...

"You're right," Cora said. "It wouldn't be the worst thing."

"See? I knew it was a good idea." Mareleau's expression turned thoughtful. "Three kingdoms united. I wonder why they ever divided Lela in the first place."

A shudder ripped through Cora. Was it relief over having a possible heir? In answer, that earlier feeling returned, sharpening in her gut. *Pay attention.*

To what? Cora wondered.

Then Mareleau's words echoed in her mind, unraveling something...

Something about three kingdoms...

No, three crowns...

And Lela...

He will unite three crowns and return El'Ara's heart.

Cora nearly choked on a sharp intake of breath as the words of Emylia's prophecy invaded her consciousness. Teryn had conveyed everything he'd learned, and she'd done the same with what she'd discovered in El'Ara. Together, in the letters they'd exchanged, they'd merged their knowledge. Even though Cora's place in the prophecy had been thwarted, they'd figured the information might prove useful in dealing with Darius. In understanding him, predicting his aims. Not that it had helped them yet.

So why was this piece of the broken prophecy striking her so fiercely right now? Was she merely being reminded of what might have been? What could have been, were she in Mareleau's place? The promised Morkara in Cora's arms, instead of Noah in Mareleau's?

Or...

Could it be...

Blood of the witch, blood of the Elvyn, and blood of the crown.

Cora stared at Mareleau, assessing her under a chilling new light. After witnessing the glamour Mareleau had cast, she could believe Mareleau was a witch. But did she have Elvyn blood? Cora had never been able to answer that question for herself, ever since she'd learned of this part of the prophecy.

The Elvyn had died long ago. Now that Cora knew of El'Ara's history, she understood that the only fae who had ever lived in Lela were those who'd been trapped outside the Veil. While the Faeryn descendants lived on as the Forest People, there were no records of any Elvyn bloodlines that remained. No way to know if Cora had Elvyn blood in her family tree. Her mother was from the Southern Islands, and the only Elvyn there was Darius. Cora didn't want to consider any blood relation to him. Besides, wouldn't Morkai have known if they were so closely related? Furthermore, it wasn't just *any* Elvyn blood that qualified the prophesied mother. It was Ailan's blood. While Darius and Ailan shared their mother's blood, a descendant of Darius would not be the Blood of Ailan.

That left Cora's father. His ancestry was local to the continent of Risa, so he could have been a descendant of Ailan.

But the same could be said for Mareleau.

When will she be born?

The year of the Great Bear.

Mother Goddess, Cora and Mareleau were the same age. They'd been born the same year. Yet the prophesied mother was supposed to have been born in Khero—

No.

Not the mother.

The true Morkara is the Blood of Ailan, born under the black mountain.

Born *under*, not *to*. Cora pulled back from her friend slightly, heart racing. Mareleau was so enchanted by her sleeping son, whose tiny hand was now curled around her forefinger, that she didn't notice Cora's startled scrutiny. Cora's gaze lifted to the walls, to the purple tapestries lining them, boasting Khero's sigil.

A black mountain over a field of violets.

Cora's breaths grew sharp. Could…Mareleau be the mother? Not Cora? Could Noah be the true Morkara?

There was still one final piece of the prophecy. The line that had been the most convincing of all, proving Cora was the prophesied mother.

The unicorn will signify her awakening.

The unicorn. Valorre. Cora's familiar. After he'd come into her life, everything had changed. She'd awakened to truths she'd never known were missing. Her magic had grown tenfold.

At the thought of him, he entered her consciousness.

You're distressed, he said.

Distress. Was that what she was feeling? She wasn't sure

what to call it, the tremor that had taken over, the thundering of her heart, the tightness in her chest. Perhaps distress was the right word for it, but she was more desperate than anything. Desperate for the truth. For the final piece of the puzzle to click into place, either confirming or dismissing her suspicions.

Valorre, she conveyed, *when we were in El'Ara, you remembered some things. You said you recalled running from dragons—*

I remember everything. Cora felt his surprise as if it were her own. *I...I remember it all now.*

The dragons chased you from El'Ara. Through the Veil.

Yes, they knew my horn would let me leave.

Why did they chase you?

They...they felt her.

Cora swallowed hard. He'd said *her* not *you*.

Who did they feel? she asked.

The Blood of Ailan. They felt her mora.

Magic. They felt the prophesied mother's magic.

"Mare," she said, turning to her friend. Cora could feel the quaver in her voice, but Mareleau didn't seem to notice. She merely cast a questioning glance at her. Cora worked the dryness from her throat before she spoke again. "When did you start using your magic trick?"

Mareleau shrugged. "I've always used it in some form or another. It serves as a sort of protection. A way for me to feel like I'm someone else on the outside."

"Was there ever a time when you felt like...like people started reacting to your magic trick?"

"The suitors I got rid of certainly reacted strongly," she said with a wry grin.

"When was that? When did you first drive away an unwanted suitor with this trick?"

Her expression turned thoughtful. "About a year ago? No, a little longer than that. Maybe a year-and-a-half ago?"

Cora's heart fell. A year-and-a-half ago. When the first unicorn was spotted in the human world.

Mareleau frowned. "Why do you ask?"

Cora couldn't answer. She couldn't form a single word, and thankfully she was saved from needing to as Mareleau's door opened. Larylis and Helena rushed inside. Cora felt detached from her body as she slid from the bed, allowing Larylis to take her place and meet his son for the first time. She wanted to be moved by the tears in Larylis' eyes, by the joy in her friend's face, but she felt none of that. Felt nothing and everything at once as she excused herself and left the room.

Her lungs constricted as she swept from the suite and into the hall. The corridor was blessedly empty, so she let herself lean against the wall, let herself gather in lungfuls of air even as her chest continued to tighten. She tried to root her feet to the floor, to connect with the steadying earth energy, but her mind spun too fast, her thoughts and heart in disharmony as both fought for an anchor.

Mother Goddess, why did she feel this way? Why did she feel like her world had just been upended? Surely this wasn't the right response. Yet she couldn't name her emotions at all.

Was this simply the shock of discovering the prophecy remained?

No, this was more than that.

It was never me, she said to herself.

She waited for relief to follow. Relief was what she should feel. That was what her frail hold on logic told her, anyway. She'd never wanted to be the central figure in some ancient prophecy meant to save a people who didn't even care for her. She didn't want to save or condemn El'Ara. She didn't want any of this. Shouldn't she be glad the burden was no longer hers to bear?

Yet that...

That was the source of her unnamed emotions.

The burden wasn't hers to bear.

It never had been.

But she had already borne the brunt of it. She'd been targeted by a blood mage. Cursed by dark magic. Her childhood destroyed. Her future tampered with.

She'd.

Already.

Suffered.

She named it then, that dark and swirling vortex of emotion that tore through her, growing, releasing, spilling from her eyes in the form of tears.

It was rage.

Rage.

Violent and bottomless, so vast she wanted to scream.

"It was never me," she said through her teeth. A strangled sob caught her voice, and she dropped her face to her hands, her fingers curled, digging into her skin. "It was *never* meant to be me."

All she heard were her sobs. All she felt were the trails of her tears, the heaving of her shoulders.

Then strong arms folded around her, bringing with them the scent of soap and pine. And a voice, deep and mellow, whispering her name, weaving through the chaos of her rage. It was Teryn. Her anchor. She melted into his arms and buried her face in his chest. She cried, screamed, and shouted until the anger left her breath.

Until her fury got its fill.

13

I t tore Teryn up something fierce to find Cora crying like this. His soul felt as if it were being ripped from his body all over again. His first thought upon finding her sobbing in the hall was that some great tragedy had befallen Mareleau or the child. But how? It had only been minutes since he and Larylis had awoken from where they'd haphazardly dozed on the furniture in Teryn's suite to the news that Larylis was officially a father. Larylis had left with Helena and must already be inside. Could something have happened in those few extra minutes he'd given his brother to meet his son in private?

As he wrapped his arms around Cora, he understood that wasn't the case. The way his fiancée trembled in his arms, teeth gritted, hands curled around the fabric of his jacket, told him this was not a shared grief but a personal one. And the way she wailed "It was never me" over and over sent a chill down his spine.

Once she calmed enough to separate from him, he ushered her swiftly down the hall to her quarters. Everything inside him wanted to scoop her up and carry her into her room, but she was the queen of this castle. He would not cause a spectacle if he could avoid it. Where he couldn't draw the line, however, was at being alone with her. Propriety could go to the seven devils, as could the bewildered maid who tried to argue as he ordered her out of Cora's suite.

With the door slammed shut and privacy secured, Teryn led Cora to the wingback chair before the roaring hearth. It was afternoon, but the late winter chill was prevalent. He hoped the heat would ease her tremors, though he knew better than to think they were due to the cold. Regardless, she had to be at least somewhat chilly, as she was still dressed in the same ensemble he'd last seen her in—the same robe and chemise that had graced his bedroom floor last night.

No longer racked with sobs, Cora settled into the chair, eyes unfocused. Teryn's chest tightened at the sight of her, at her empty expression, her red-rimmed eyes. He wanted to comfort her, assure her, hold her, but he didn't know what kind of comfort she needed right now. There was a chance she wanted to be alone. It wouldn't be the first time. The last time he'd found her crying, she'd asked for exactly that, and he'd acquiesced against his every instinct. If she pushed him away now, would he have the strength to grant that request?

Daring neither to get too close nor pull away too far, he settled for kneeling before the chair, his hand softly covering hers. "Cora," he whispered, eyes searching her dark, empty irises. "What happened?"

She said nothing for several long moments, but that was better than her asking him to leave. Finally, her gaze sharpened and focused on Teryn. Her lower lip quivered, sending a spear of pain through his chest.

"I'm not..." She cleared her throat, blinked away fresh

tears, and tried again. "I'm not the mother from Emylia's prophecy."

Silence.

Such agonizing silence.

But he didn't dare speak yet. She wasn't finished with her tale, and she needed the freedom to express her pain on her own terms. In her own time.

Cora's throat bobbed before she spoke again. "Mareleau is. She always was. It was never me."

Questions surged through his mind, but he tightened his jaw to keep them at bay. Not yet. He couldn't hound her with questions yet.

Instead, he gave her hand a soft squeeze. With the other, he slowly lifted his fingertips to her cheek and wiped away the trail of tears glinting in the firelight. Keeping his voice steady, he asked, "Do you want to talk about it?"

Her gaze went distant again, but she eventually gave a nod. "Yes. I need logic right now."

She stood and approached the fireplace. Teryn rose to his feet and followed, leaning against the wall beside the hearth, his arm propped on the mantle. Then she told him. She explained what had happened in Mareleau's room and the revelations she'd had. She told him all the reasons she believed Mareleau to be the true prophesied mother. Mareleau was very likely a witch, and it made sense for her to be the Blood of Ailan too. More sense than Cora, at least.

Teryn could see why she thought that. Cora had been forced to try to bond with a dragon in El'Ara, something only those of the Morkara's bloodline could do. The attempt had failed miserably. Though there had been reasons to explain it—she'd removed the collar too late, her Elvyn blood was too diluted—it made the most sense that she simply wasn't of Ailan's lineage.

"Every time I stated that I was descended from Ailan," Cora said, voice hollow as she watched the dancing flames, "it always felt wrong. It always felt like a lie. I'd thought it was because I wasn't confident in claiming such a significant role in the prophecy, but the truth is that...it wasn't me."

Teryn reached out and brushed his knuckles against hers, a silent reminder that he was here. He was listening.

She spoke again. "As for Valorre, he was chased from El'Ara by the dragons who'd sensed Mareleau's awakening magic. Valorre was able to pierce the Veil with his horn, but when he reached the other side, his memories were compromised."

Something flickered across her expression. Hurt or rage, he wasn't sure, but this had to pain her. Valorre was her best friend and familiar. Meeting him must have felt like fate, the one solace that came from being entangled in the web of prophecy.

Yet now she had no place in that prophecy. She'd only met Valorre because he'd unwittingly been looking for someone else. Worse was that which she'd yet to say.

That she'd been cursed in Mareleau's place.

She, who had no part in the prophecy, had been hurt and abused because of Morkai's misinterpretation of Emylia's words. Not that he could wish Cora's fate on Mareleau. She was his sister-in-law, the woman Larylis loved. She was Cora's friend.

But to say he didn't feel the slightest bit of resentment that she'd been granted the safety of a coddled childhood while Cora had been running for her godsdamned life would be a lie.

"This is my fault." The voice startled him, for it didn't belong to Cora. He straightened and found Emylia beside him, between him and Cora. Her eyes were on his fiancée, her semi-transparent form rippling with tremors. "I did this."

Cora shook her head and faced Teryn, oblivious to the apparition standing beside her. "Valorre has all his memories back. It happened suddenly—"

"I'm so sorry," Emylia's voice cut over Cora's, and Teryn tried to tune it out. He couldn't acknowledge her presence, for Cora didn't know about Teryn's uncanny new ability.

"—which makes me wonder if the Veil has torn."

"This is why I can't move on," Emylia wailed.

"What do you think?" asked Cora.

Teryn opened his mouth, but Emylia spoke first. "This is why I'm plagued with guilt."

"Emylia," he barked, unable to ignore her a second longer.

Both Cora and the spirit stiffened. Cora frowned. "What about Emylia?"

Closing his eyes, he rubbed his brow.

"I'm sorry, Teryn," Emylia whispered. "I didn't mean to intrude. I didn't realize you could see me again."

"Well, I can, and you are intruding. This is a private conversation."

"Wait..." Cora's voice had him opening his eyes with a resigned sigh. "Are you...talking to Emylia *right now*?"

He supposed there was no better time to tell her. "Yes."

"How?"

"Ever since I returned to my body last summer," he explained, "I've been able to see spirits. Emylia is the only one who has communicated with me. She's been watching over you."

Emylia clasped her hands to her chest. "Tell her I'm sorry."

"She says she's sorry."

"Tell her this is all my fault. Tell her I don't know how I'll make up for what I've done. Tell her I—"

"Emylia," he said, a warning in his tone, "I get it." Then to Cora, he said, "She feels incredible guilt for her part in channeling the prophecy. She hasn't been able to move on to the otherlife and hopes she can atone."

Cora's expression hardened, and he didn't miss the way her fingers curled into fists at her sides. Then she averted her gaze to the fire and folded her arms over her chest. "It was a mistake, but I can't hold it against her. Nor can she be blamed for the actions Morkai took based on the conclusions he came to."

Her voice sounded dry and rehearsed but it seemed to appease Emylia. Her form ceased its trembling. "If there's anything I can do to help, please tell me," Emylia said.

"She wants to help," Teryn conveyed.

"Has she learned anything useful as a spirit, now that she's been freed from the crystal?" Cora asked.

"She confirmed that the current King Darius Solaria of Syrus is indeed Morkai's father."

"That's hardly news," Cora countered, though her words lacked bite. "We already guessed as much. Does she know what his plans are? Is he using Norun to wage war on Khero?"

Emylia shook her head. "I don't know about his current plans. All I know is that he sought El'Ara and likely still seeks it. If he's learned what Morkai discovered—that Lela is the Heart of El'Ara—he might seek to invade Khero to gain access to the Veil, with the goal of finding a way to cross it. Since the Veil surrounds the entirety of Lela, he might not stop at targeting Khero either. He might try to conquer Vera too, just to ensure he can freely search every inch of the Veil."

Teryn conveyed Emylia's words, then added to Cora, "At least we know he's physically weak. And that he doesn't know what you know—that unicorns can pierce the Veil and that a worldwalker can use them to enter El'Ara."

"Yes, but there is an additional concern," Cora said. "The prophecy stated that the Veil would tear when the true Morkara was born. The latter has happened, so we must assume the former has too. Valorre suddenly got all his memories back this morning—"

Her words cut off, and Teryn was certain they were thinking the same thing. "Darius might have his memories back too." He looked at Emylia for confirmation.

She shrugged. "Morkai said his father had been cursed to forget El'Ara, but he didn't say how or why. It could have been the Veil that had made him forget."

"Which means a tear in the Veil could return his lost memories," Teryn said. Seven devils, if Darius had his memories back, if he could recall the land he'd once left, the land that had once been a piece of El'Ara, could he world-walk straight here? Cora had told Teryn about the war she'd learned of in El'Ara, and how Darius had used his power to bring in human armies. Did that mean he could worldwalk with multiple people in tow? Did he even need to ally with Norun to accomplish his goals?

Cora took in a sharp breath. "What if the Veil was also the cause of Darius' physical weakness? What if..."

A chill shot through him. She didn't need to finish. If Darius was no longer weak, they might soon face a formidable foe.

"What does this mean for us?" Cora asked. "What's going to happen?"

"I don't know." They locked eyes, and his shoulders grew heavy. There were still so many unanswered questions.

Some Teryn wasn't ready to voice; primarily, if they had to choose between war with Darius or complying with him, would it be better to simply give him access to the Veil? Would it really be so wrong to condemn El'Ara, if it rid the human world of such a great threat? Or was Darius as ambitious as his son? Would he use his power as Morkaius of El'Ara to harm the human world too? Teryn knew one thing; there wouldn't be any easy answers.

"At least we hold intel he doesn't have." Cora kept her voice low as if she feared the very walls would carry her secrets to their enemy. "He doesn't know about Mareleau and Noah. He doesn't know about my and Valorre's ability to cross the Veil."

Teryn nodded. "We should do whatever we can to stop word of Noah's birth from spreading. If Darius finds out a royal child was born *under the black mountain*, that could be all he needs to put the pieces together."

"You're right," Cora said. "We need to keep his birth a secret. Hopefully we can stop rumors from spreading before it's too late." She turned on her heel and marched toward the door.

Teryn caught her hand in his, halting her. "Where are you going?"

"I need to tell Helena not to announce Noah's birth. And...and I need to tell Mareleau the truth."

He took a step closer. "You've been awake for over a day. Rest. I can speak to Helena and Larylis. He can tell Mareleau."

She pursed her lips, and the fatigue tugging at her features made it clear she was at least tempted by his offer. She shook her head. "No, I should be the one to tell Mareleau. I want to be there for her." Her jaw tightened when she said the last part, but he didn't comment on it.

"Let me at least deal with Helena then. Let me bear this burden with you."

Her shoulders dropped and a sad smile worked the corners of her lips. "All right."

He gathered her face in his hands and forced her to hold his eyes. "Sleep as soon as you've spoken to Mareleau. Promise me."

She nodded. Then, with a parting kiss, he let her go.

His chest tightened as she left the room. It had pained him to see Cora cry earlier, but it pained him just as badly to see her so composed. So determined. She must be smothering her grief. Burying it. Yet he could relate. After his father had died, he'd buried his emotions in a flurry of activity and constant motion. How could he tell her not to do the same?

"I'll go home to Zaras," Emylia said, reminding him of her presence. He found her colorless form bent before the fireplace, staring longingly at the undulating flames. He wondered if she yearned to feel their heat. "It's the closest I can get to Syrus. Perhaps I can uncover some useful information about Darius."

"Thank you," Teryn said.

Her face crumpled as she straightened and faced Teryn. "I really am sorry. I've caused her so much pain."

"I know."

With that, Emylia's form rippled and dispersed until nothing of her remained.

Teryn blew out a heavy breath, steeled his nerves, and left Cora's room to nip a rumor in the bud. Hopefully he could cut it down before it had a chance to take root outside these walls.

14

Larylis had read every book he could find about pregnancy, childbirth, and parenting, his sources ranging from medical texts to fiction. He'd been startled to find just how quickly he'd run out of reading material. And it wasn't because he'd read through them so quickly. It was because the royal libraries at both Dermaine and Verlot were severely lacking in the subject. Especially where parenting was concerned or any of the myriad of other facets of becoming a new father.

So when he met his son for the first time, he found not a page of reading had been adequate in preparing him. The emotions welling up inside him at the sight of his wife holding their tiny child were stronger than anything he'd felt before. Stronger than grief or mourning. Stronger than desire or betrayal.

Mareleau's joy mirrored his own as he settled onto the bed beside her. He let that joy wash over him. Let it sweep away the last vestiges of the anxiety he'd carried around all morning. The last twelve hours had been hell on his nerves. Mareleau hadn't wanted him in her room while she labored, and he'd respected that. Respected it yet went half out of his mind pacing Teryn's room. His only comfort was reciting all the great queens of history who'd delivered early babies or experienced surprising births. Teryn had tolerated this madness with stoic calm and had stayed by his side all night and morning until both had fallen into fitful rest.

When a knock had sounded at Teryn's suite door, Larylis had bolted awake at once, shooting to his feet from the divan he'd been dozing on. His heart had nearly leaped from his chest when his mother-in-law announced that Mareleau was ready for him to see her.

He'd rushed down the hall to his wife's room at once, fearing his heart might stop before he made it.

But it hadn't. Instead, his heart had been shattered and soothed all at once.

And now it was calm.

Calm.

A feeling he wished would last forever.

He could hardly tear his eyes from his son—from Noah —but he managed to shift his gaze to his wife. His brave, beautiful wife. She caught him looking at her and gave him a warm yet tired smile.

"You did well," he said.

Her expression faltered a bit at that. "Yes, I secured our heir."

"You know I didn't mean it like that."

She blinked a few times as if realizing she did in fact know. She shook her head. "No, of course you didn't. I suppose I'm already on edge waiting for all the congratulatory sentiments. Congratulating not me for being a mother, and not Noah for being born, but our legacy. That we've finally secured our throne. As if simply being crowned isn't enough. To be honest, I almost wanted him to be born a girl, just to spite their expectations. And yet..." She released a heavy sigh. "Birthing male heirs is what is expected of me as queen, so I better steel myself for all the congratulations."

Larylis draped his arm behind her and hugged her close to his side without disrupting her seated position or the sleeping babe in her arms. "It's not what I expect of you. If we'd had a girl, I'd have been just as pleased. I'd have named her our heir without any reservations. I would have empowered her as she grew up. I wouldn't belittle her or make her feel inferior in my attempts to protect her."

She winced at his words, reminding Larylis of the guilt she harbored over her father's death, particularly over their lack of reconciliation. But it hadn't been her fault, and his tragic death didn't mean they had to overlook his flaws. Verdian had been a great king but an imperfect father, just as Larylis' own father had been a great king yet a flawed husband to Teryn's mother.

Larylis wouldn't be like either of them. He would honor their lives, mourn their deaths, and learn from their mistakes—the same way he learned from textbooks and historical records.

"You are right, though," he said. "We have our first child, a male heir, which means we are going to be inundated with mildly offensive and outdated platitudes."

She smirked at that. "At least we have Cora and Teryn's wedding to overshadow our big news. We'll have some respite before the attention shifts to us."

"We'll be expected to host a grand party," he said with a grimace.

"Does that mean I can coerce you to dance?"

He made an exaggerated look of displeasure. "I suppose I can tolerate a single dance."

Her smile grew brighter, sweeter. She angled her face toward him and lifted her chin. "I love you, Larylis."

His heart stuttered. They'd been married for over eight months now, and he still wasn't used to those words.

"I love you too," he whispered back, then brushed his lips against hers. He didn't dare kiss her any deeper, for she was fatigued. He'd claim her love, not her attention. Not until she was rested and ready to divert any focus from Noah to Larylis. He didn't care if it took weeks. Months. Years, even. He'd gleaned enough from his many hours of reading to expect things to be different between them for a while. They'd find a new rhythm. A new way of life. A new way to love one another, even as their hearts had now split into three.

He pulled his lips from hers, but their eyes remained locked. Gods, she was beautiful. Even more so now, with her hair mussed and her eyes shadowed with dark circles. He was so enchanted by her that he didn't notice they had a visitor until a throat cleared.

He turned his gaze to the door, expecting to find Helena, for she'd stepped out to give them privacy when Larylis had arrived. But it wasn't his mother-in-law standing in the doorway. It was Cora.

The darkness in her eyes, the grief in her expression, should have been enough to warn Larylis that his world was about to be upended.

Cora hated being the bearer of such tidings. It brought her no satisfaction to see her friends' happy faces cloud over. She'd almost lost her nerve and kept quiet but that would have been even more unbearable. Cora was done lying to the people she loved, especially where magic was concerned. She'd seen negative repercussions both from telling the truth and keeping secrets, but the latter had always burdened her more. More than anything, Mareleau deserved to know the truth. As did Larylis.

So she told them.

She sat at the foot of the bed, not wanting to close the distance lest the proximity of her friends' emotions test her mental wards. Halfway through, Teryn joined her, sitting silently at her side, her hand in his. He must have spoken to Helena already. Cora wasn't sure what he'd told her to ensure she kept Mareleau's midwives and maids silent. Helena had been left in the dark about magic and only knew what had been made public. So Teryn had either given her an ominous warning or made something up. Whatever it was, Cora trusted him. He'd asked to share her burden so she would let him.

Silence fell after she relayed what she'd come to say. Mareleau spoke first, her voice trembling. "You think I'm a witch."

Cora nodded.

"That I have Elvyn blood."

Another nod.

"You think Noah is...is..." She stared down at her son, her face twisted either with shock or confusion. "You think he's some prophesied fae king?"

"Yes," Cora said.

Mareleau's shoulders sank. If she hadn't already looked exhausted, she looked practically lifeless now.

Larylis too looked drained, his face pale. His voice was hoarse as he said, "What does this truly mean? In a practical sense."

"We don't know," Teryn said. "All we need to worry

about now is keeping Noah's birth a secret. We'll spread word that Mareleau left. That she was too uneasy being here so close to her due date."

Mareleau scoffed. "I came here for your wedding."

Cora gave her a pitying glance. "You can't be there, Mare. Not unless you can hide that you've given birth."

"So you're telling me," Mareleau said, her tone sharp, "that I came here for a wedding I can't attend. And that my very presence *for* your wedding is what made the prophecy come true. What would have happened if I'd stayed home? Would that have broken the prophecy? And would that have been good or bad? Is this really all on me and my actions?"

A flicker of panic-laced guilt shot through Cora, but it wasn't her own. Mareleau's spike of emotion battered Cora's shields. Cora shifted on the edge of the bed, pressing one of her feet more firmly on the floor to ground her energy and strengthen her wards.

"What exactly is Noah meant to do anyway?" Mareleau said. "He's a godsdamned baby. And what clue do we have from the prophecy? *He will unite three crowns and return El'Ara's heart.* The prophecy said a whole lot about me, but not much about their true Morkara. Are we supposed to fend off King Darius until Noah comes of age and becomes some fated warrior that will destroy him?"

Cora had no answers to give. She glanced at Teryn, wondering if there was more Emylia could tell them. As far as Cora knew, she'd been a seer—a witch with strong clair-voyance—which meant she'd channeled the prophecy from images and put them into words. Had she seen how Noah would unite three crowns? What it meant for him to return El'Ara's heart? There were so many ways those words could be interpreted. Uniting three crowns may already have happened when Cora considered naming him her heir. Or would her marriage to Teryn bring that about, as her husband's nephew would surely link Khero to Vera, regardless of who was named heir? The three crowns themselves could refer to the two kingdoms Mareleau inherited plus Khero. Or it could refer to Vera, Khero, and El'Ara, united by his birth. Returning El'Ara's heart could simply mean reforging Lela into a single kingdom. Or it could mean drawing the land back to El'Ara.

Cora's mind spun with possibilities.

Mareleau spoke again, and this time her voice cracked. "What about the future? Is Noah supposed to grow up just to leave me to rule the fae realm?"

Cora met her friend's tear-glazed eyes. "We don't know, and we can't worry about that now."

"How can I not worry? This is unfair."

Unfair.

The word lanced her chest, and she flinched.

Mareleau spoke again. "I never asked to be part of this prophecy. For my newborn son to be burdened with this responsibility. I never asked—"

Mareleau's voice cut off, her eyes wide as they locked on Cora's. It was then Cora became aware of her own expression. Of the tightness of her jaw. The narrowing of her eyes. She hadn't meant to glare at Mareleau. Hadn't meant to react so sharply to her friend's tirade.

Mareleau averted her gaze from Cora's. "I'm sorry. I didn't ask for this but neither had you."

Cora said nothing, for what could she say to that? To the reminder that Mareleau may bear the true responsibility as the prophesied mother, but Cora had already been punished for it?

Cora hated the flicker of resentment that sparked in her heart. Hated the anger that continued to simmer.

A soft cry shattered the air, and all eyes fell on Noah.

"I need to nurse him," Mareleau said, tone flustered.

"We'll give you privacy," Cora said, and she and Teryn rose from the bed.

Larylis gave his wife a questioning glance, but she whispered, "Stay."

Cora's chest tightened as she and Teryn headed for the door. She couldn't help but feel anxious after that tense exchange she'd had with Mareleau. Desperate to mend the rift, she stopped at the doorway and turned a hopeful look to her friend. "I'll come back later, all right?"

Mareleau met her eyes and gave her a soft yet tired smile. "All right."

Cora let that smooth the edges of her nerves as she and Teryn left the room, his hand clasped comfortingly around hers.

15

Flames simmered around Cora. She could feel them more than see them, their heat scalding her hands, her cheeks. As for where she was, she didn't know. A smoky haze clouded her vision, smothering her senses. Finally, a pinprick of darkness stood stark within her murky surroundings. She darted toward it. It grew with every step she took until it widened around her, forming a hallway. The smoke cleared, but the flames remained. Still, it was just the heat of them. A hint of gold flickering up the walls. No matter how she tried to focus on those flames, all she saw was reflected light.

Sweat beaded her brow and dampened her nightdress. She rushed farther down the hall, turning her attention right and left for any sign of where she was.

Then she felt it. A sickening unease. A deep and hollow knowing that something wasn't right. She'd felt this way before, night after night, haunted by dark hallways. That was when she recognized the walls around her. Walls that had graced countless nightmares. Her dreams of Ridine, of the night she'd been condemned by her brother and banished from the castle by Morkai, had once been so pervasive she'd needed a sleeping tonic. That dream had run its course after she'd returned to Ridine and reclaimed her role as princess. Yet nightmares hadn't ceased plaguing her. After last summer, her mind had gained new fuel for dark tableaus. Her brother's visage fused with the body of a Roizan had visited her darkest dreams regularly.

While her nightmares always wrenched her heart, they no longer terrified her as badly as they once had. She could recognize that she was dreaming far faster, detach herself from her fear.

She halted her steps, acknowledging that this too was just a dream. A new manifestation but a dream nonetheless. Releasing a slow sigh, she closed her eyes and tried to focus on her true body, on the bed she was nestled in. The heat of the flames distracted her, pulling her mind back into the realm of the nightmare.

Then a voice.

"We meet again, Aveline."

Cora clenched her jaw, hatred boiling her blood. She opened her eyes. Duke Morkai stood before her, hands in his pockets, posture at ease despite the light of the flames still dancing up the walls. They turned his dark suit a flickering orange, illuminated the underside of his jaw.

Her fury continued to rise at the sight of him, but she felt no fear. Even here, in the bounds of this nightmare, she knew Morkai was dead. Teryn had witnessed the mage's soul being consumed by light. It had devoured all that was left of him.

This was merely a facet of Cora's mind, nothing more.

This she could face.

"If only we could meet again," she said through her

teeth, "just so I could see your expression when I told you you were wrong."

"Wrong?" He arched his brow.

"You were too confident in your own findings. You didn't even question them when the answer was a kingdom away. You chose the wrong girl. Tormented the wrong girl. You failed in every way."

His lips widened into a cruel grin. "Did I?"

In a flash of movement, Morkai's arm shot out to the side, toward one of the shadowed walls. As he drew the arm back to him, he pulled a figure along with him.

Mareleau.

It was like he'd dragged her from the shadows. He shoved her forward, and she stumbled to the ground at Morkai's feet. As she lifted her head, her eyes found Cora's. She reached for Cora, but the sorcerer's hand closed around her throat from behind. He hauled her roughly toward him until her back slammed into his front. He wound his arm over her middle, caging her against him.

"Did I torment the wrong girl, Aveline?" Morkai taunted. "Perhaps I should remedy that."

Mareleau's eyes were wide and frightened, pleading with Cora. "Help me," she got out before his fingers, impossibly long now, tightened further around her throat.

Cora let out a strangled cry. She may have escaped her fear before, but now it grew tenfold, spiking her pulse at the sight of her friend. She tried to remind herself this was a dream, but this was the first time someone other than her— someone alive, someone she cared for—was in danger in one of her nightmares. It battled reason and logic until all that was left was terror.

"Let her go!" Cora shouted.

"Will you take her place then?" Morkai asked. "Will you

suffer what she suffers? Will you allow me the pleasure of strangling the life from your lungs in her stead?"

Cora opened her mouth but couldn't make a sound. The answer should be yes. The answer should be...

It should be...

"You said I chose the wrong girl." Morkai thrust Mareleau away from him, closer to Cora, but his fingers remained around her throat, ever extending until they took the shape of claws. One pointed tip dug into the flesh at the base of her throat, drawing a line of blood.

"Stop," Cora said.

"Make up your mind, Aveline. Who should I have targeted? Who should I have hurt? Her? Or you?"

"Neither."

"Oh, but you must choose. Which of you shall burn?"

The scent of burning hair flooded her nostrils, and Cora noticed the ends of Mareleau's pale strands blackening. The light of the flames grew higher, their heat almost unbearable, but still she couldn't see them.

Another claw sank into Mareleau's neck. She whimpered, fighting against his hold. "Should it have been her all along?" Morkai said. "Should I have cursed her? Framed her for murder? Drove her into the forest?"

"No!" Cora shouted.

"Would you trade places with her then? Here? Now?"

Again, Cora couldn't bring herself to take Mareleau's place. Why? Why couldn't she do the right thing?

But...was it the right thing?

The dark resentment she'd felt earlier sparked in her chest.

I don't need to suffer in her place.

I never deserved to.

"Say it out loud," Morkai said, his voice a taunting hiss.

"Confess the darkness in your heart or it will burn you from the inside."

"No," she said through her teeth. "That's not me. Those thoughts aren't mine. I would never wish my pain on someone else."

"Then why won't you take her pain away? Why won't you willingly take her place?"

"That's different. This isn't real. You aren't real."

"I am the shadow you won't acknowledge. I am the ember you wish you could smother."

"I don't care what you think you are. Just let her go."

Morkai's gaze darkened into a glare. "I'm disappointed in you." With that he released Mareleau's throat and thrust her into Cora. Cora pulled her friend close, lungs heaving with relief, but as her arms closed around Mareleau, the other woman collapsed into ash. Tremors racked Cora's body as she stared at her soot-covered hands. At the pile of ash that was once her friend.

Finally, she saw the source of the flames.

They were coming from her all along.

CORA WOKE WITH A SHARP CRY BUT STIFLED THE SOUND AS she blinked into darkness. Her chilly room was a balm on her sweat-soaked skin, and for several long moments she simply lay there, listening to the beat of her heart, the pulse of her breaths, until both settled to a more natural rhythm. Once she could rise from her bed without shaking, she crossed the floor to her window. Pulling back the long velvet drape, she found an inky night sky muted by the frost coating the window.

As she stared out at the dark scenery, she willed her

mind to sharpen, to fully separate from the dream. Once it did, she realized what day it was. Or soon would be.

The day of her wedding.

That calmed her down, aided in clearing her mind.

She couldn't have been asleep for long, considering the lack of light on the horizon, paired with how late she'd gone to bed. She should get back to sleep if she wanted to be rested for the grand event. She was already sleep-deprived as it was. Over the last few days, sleep had become second to spending time with Mareleau and Noah. Though her friend had Larylis and Helena to support her and give her chances to rest amidst the chaos of having a newborn, Cora wanted to be there too. Since Mareleau was rumored to have left Ridine, she was forced to remain in her suite, something that drove her half out of her mind. The least Cora could do was spend time with her.

Images from her nightmare shot through her mind. Of Mareleau's horrified expression. Of the blood trailing down her throat as the sorcerer dug claws into her neck.

Are you all right? Valorre's question cut through the memories, dispersing them.

She calmed once more as she connected to her unicorn friend's consciousness. He wasn't as near as he normally was, but he was still within range to communicate. *Yes*, she conveyed back to him.

The blood mage can't hurt you, Valorre reminded her. *He's gone. He'll never come back.*

I know, she said. He was right, yet she hated that Morkai could still haunt her like this. Worse was the dread that was her constant companion—the knowledge that while Morkai may be gone, his father remained. Everything that had happened to Cora, to her friends, to her kingdom, Darius had begun. He may not have asked his son to try to harness fae magic in the human realm, but he'd sent him on a mission to find El'Ara. That mission had led to all the knowledge had Morkai discovered. To Emylia. To the prophecy. To Lela.

To Cora.

Fiery rage burned in her heart. It reminded her too much of her dream, but she wouldn't give in to those terrible visions again. Sleep called to her, but she dreaded returning to the nightmare. And there was one place she could count on to make her feel bold. Brave. Accomplished. To remind her of just how strong she was. With resolve in her heart, she donned her robe and strode from her room. The halls were empty this late at night, save for the guards patrolling them. They acknowledged her with deep bows as she brushed past.

She left the keep and entered the wing of the castle she sought. One that rarely saw visitors. Then up a dim staircase she climbed, to a tower that once held so much darkness. Moonlight greeted her as she entered the North Tower Library, bathing the circular room in a pale glow. It fell upon the clean flagstone floor, the freshly polished tables, the bundles of herbs and flowers that hung to dry from the rafters.

Satisfaction flooded Cora. This room had belonged to Morkai, but no longer held an ounce of his influence. Cleaning the library had taken much of her focus over the last several months, as every item had to be energetically purified before it could be burned or buried. Just weeks ago, her task had been completed at last. The room belonged to her now.

She could have sealed it off and never set foot in it again, but she'd decided to do the opposite, invading it with her own energy. Her own magic. Here she could fully be a witch, honoring the practices the Forest People had instilled in her. Not that she had many chances to truly practice magic these days. Yet taking over this room, using it to dry herbs, to collect stones, leaves, sticks—anything that caught her fancy while out on forest rides with Valorre—was enough. It was proof that she'd bested Morkai, in life, in death, and after.

She breathed in deeply, allowing her pride to grow. "I defeated you," she said to the room, her voice devoid of quaver. "You may haunt my dreams, but you're gone."

No darkness echoed back. No shadows flickered in reply. There was merely peace here.

Her muscles uncoiled and she strolled along the perimeter of the room. She'd had it fully refurbished with a new couch, a single bookcase, and a few small tables and nightstands. She stopped at the nearest nightstand, its surface decorated with an array of crystals she'd found by a stream nearby. They were arranged in a circular pattern around several crisscrossed sticks. Together they formed a talisman for protection. She smiled down at her work, but her grin faltered as her gaze fell just beneath the tabletop, to the narrow drawer there. Gingerly, she slid it open.

Moonlight glinted off a cuff made from two elongated talons, as dark as obsidian. It was the magic-suppressing collar. She hadn't known what to do with it after she'd found it in her pocket upon returning from the meadow last summer. It was a dangerous object, one the Elvyn had used to stifle her magic. Yet it had also saved her and her friends in a couple of ways. When she'd used it on Teryn, he'd been able to temporarily wrest control of his body from Morkai. When she'd used it on the crystal, she'd been able to break the stone, freeing Teryn's ethera. Unlike Morkai's belongings, it didn't hold any dark energy, so she couldn't bear to destroy it.

Instead, she kept it here, hidden yet revered. Hated yet treasured.

Beneath it lay the only thing of Morkai's she hadn't destroyed.

His book of blood weavings.

It was perhaps the most dangerous item of all, yet she'd never found a way to burn it. She'd cleared its residual energy, but the horrific tapestries and spells remained. At least they were only blueprints. The only active blood weaving—the one that had killed Lurel—had already run its course.

There was one more reason she'd kept the book instead of burying it with the other dangerous, undestroyable items: the niggling sense that maybe one day they'd need the information in that book.

It had already come in handy once, when Teryn had glimpsed the blueprint that had rendered Morkai's crystal unbreakable. Teryn had reversed that tapestry, gaining freedom for himself and Emylia. He'd used blood magic, a forbidden Art, but he'd done it for good.

Maybe that was where Cora's most secret motivation lay.

In hopes that someday they might figure out how to reverse the blood weaving Morkai had used to curse her.

Slamming the drawer shut, she lifted her chin and reminded herself all she'd survived. All she'd conquered. And all she still had to look forward to.

Her wedding.

Teryn.

Once the sun rose, it would finally be time to marry the man she loved. She'd been waiting months for their reunion, yet she'd hardly seen her fiancé lately. They'd opened their hearts, shared their love, taken pleasure in each other's bodies for the first time...and then their lives had been interrupted by Noah's birth. They'd slept separately ever since, following the rules of propriety and honoring Cora's own fatigue.

After her wedding, that would change. She'd done enough for Mareleau. Gods, she'd done enough for her kingdom too.

It was time to focus on herself.

She deserved that.

She wouldn't let the prophecy or her nightmares cast shadows upon the day she'd been eagerly awaiting. She wouldn't let guilt or resentment or selflessness keep her from enjoying the one bright spark in her life.

The future may be uncertain, and her foes may be closer than she liked.

But here, now, she'd enjoy the present. The peace, the love, the excitement that awaited her.

For as long as it could last.

16

Teryn didn't have the best memories of the Godskeep at Ridine Castle, but he was hoping to make new ones today. If anything could help him forget what had happened the last time he'd been here, when he'd been helpless as Morkai used his body to undermine King Dimetreus, it was his wedding.

If his bride ever showed up.

He wasn't sure if she was late or if time had slowed to a crawl simply because he was the sole focus of every pair of eyes in the nave. The aging Godspriest stood behind the altar in white robes and seven beaded necklaces, each to represent a different deity, but being the groom, Teryn made for a far more interesting sight.

Most of those in attendance were strangers, esteemed nobles or representatives of Khero's great houses, though there were a few familiar figures in the front row. Larylis sat beside Lex and Lily, a trio of comforting faces. Mareleau and Helena were absent, as they were now rumored to have departed early for the queen's well-being. Thankfully, it seemed they'd fully managed to smother the rumor of

Noah's birth before it had spread beyond Mareleau's bedchamber.

He flicked his gaze up to the rafters and found Berol's telltale silhouette. He wasn't sure how or when his peregrine falcon had snuck into the Godskeep, as she normally kept to the forest surrounding the castle, but it seemed she was determined to attend his wedding. He wondered how Valorre felt about being excluded.

As he lowered his eyes back to the audience, Larylis gave him a reassuring nod while Lex winked at him. It was enough to bolster his nerves, and he focused his attention at the end of the aisle. The closed door. Where soon his bride would enter and she'd fully be his—and he hers—at last.

He hadn't expected to be this nervous. It took great control to resist the urge to fidget, to tug the smothering collar of his ceremonial coat, a burden of white-and-gold brocade with a ridiculously high-buttoned neck, affixed with a golden cape. It was almost identical to the raiment his brother had worn to the formal audience with Cora, and now it was Teryn's turn to represent Vera's sigil and colors. This entire ceremony was more for the benefit of the people than anything else, so Teryn's attire was meant to demonstrate his side of the formal union between Vera and Khero.

The tune from the pipe organ shifted to a more distinct melody, one that had Teryn straightening. He knew what that meant.

It was time.

The doors at the end of the nave slowly opened. His breath caught as Cora filled his vision. She was dressed in an ivory gown with a square neckline, ruffled sleeves that opened at her elbows, and delicate lacework down the front of her skirt. The back trailed behind her with more lace, as did the violet cape that hung from her shoulders. Her neck was adorned with a gold necklace beset with amethyst stones, and her simple gold crown rested upon her head. Her dark tresses had been braided into a complex updo. She wore ivory lace gloves that ended at the wrist so as not to hide her tattooed forearms.

His grin was automatic, but as his eyes met hers, he couldn't help the teasing tilt that angled one corner of his lips. Not when he could see just how uncomfortable she was. She'd already complained by letter about her ostentatious wedding gown, and she had to be wincing at all the attention she was now receiving. Teryn's eyes weren't the only ones on her. The audience had risen to their feet and watched as she made her slow procession down the aisle, trailed by her maids.

Teryn held her eyes with every step, and she did the same with his. The nearer she came, her expression grew more relaxed, her smile wider. As she approached the dais, his attention snagged on her waist. At first he hadn't noticed the ivory silk belt she wore there, but now he did, for upon it hung the dagger he'd gifted her, half hidden in the folds of her skirt.

His heart tumbled and melted all at once, and his smile grew wider yet. "Perfect," he whispered as she took her place beside him. She let out a shaky breath, giving him one more gorgeous smile before facing the altar.

Gods, she was beautiful, just like the blade he'd given her. He was honored she'd paired it with her gown. It suited her more than all the lace and silk and jewels. It suited *them*.

The Godspriest began his speech, which meant Teryn had to wrench his eyes away from his beloved. The inches of space between them were proper yet agonizing. He wanted to reach for her palm and pull her closer. Instead, he clasped his gloved hands at his waist and forced himself to focus on the Godspriest. The man's words were drowned out by the racing of his heart, the anticipation rushing through his blood.

Finally, the Godspriest directed him and Cora to face each other. They did as told, and Teryn was rewarded with the sweetest, most timid smile he'd ever seen grace Cora's lips. He'd seen her naked. He'd touched every bare part of her. He'd felt her tremble with release. Yet this was a new level of intimacy. Vulnerability. And he was glad of it. Glad that this ceremony could still feel so deeply personal, even though they were merely performing a ritual countless others had done before.

Upon the Godspriest's instruction, he and Cora clasped hands. Even through their gloves, he could feel the warmth of her. He held Cora's eyes, lost in them, in her, as the Godspriest performed the next part of the ritual.

One by one, he removed a strand of beads from around his neck and draped them over the couple's clasped hands.

Red beads for the Goddess of War.

Blue for the Goddess of the Sea.

Green for the God of Mercy.

Gold for the God of Justice.

Black for the Goddess of Death.

White for the God of Creation.

And finally, pink for the Goddess of Love.

Then came the ceremonial words. Cora went first, repeating the dry and feelingless statements to Teryn. When it was Teryn's turn, he held her palm tighter, desperate to convey that which was in his heart. Not the words he had to repeat. But the ones in his mind.

Open your senses to me, he silently begged of her as he gently tightened his grip once more in a single, deliberate pulse. *Feel what I truly mean to convey.*

Out loud he said, "I, Teryn Alante, Prince of Vera, take you to be my wedded wife."

I, Teryn, ask you to have me, exactly as I am.

"In doing so, I bind our houses..."

I bind my heart to yours.

"...uniting Vera with Khero."

Uniting our souls.

"I honor you for better or worse, for fairer or fouler, in sickness and health..."

I honor you in all things. I am here for you always.

"...to love and cherish 'til death do we part..."

I love you. I've already loved you beyond death. I fought death for you and I will fight death again if it means coming back to you.

"...in accordance with the law of the seven gods."

This is what I want. What I choose. I choose you. I will always choose you.

Cora's eyes glazed with tears, and he wondered if she'd understood. If she'd opened herself to his emotions to at least feel what he'd woven between his words. She squeezed his hand back in answer. She knew what was in his heart.

The Godspriest removed the beads from their hands, granting blessings from each of the gods. Then, finally, their hands no longer burdened with the strands, the man announced them husband and wife.

Teryn's heart thundered against his ribs as he reached for Cora. He wasn't even certain the Godspriest had stated they could kiss, but he didn't care. He framed her face in his hands, and her arms wound around his waist. Their lips met in a firm yet tender kiss. How badly he wanted to deepen it, to sweep his tongue against hers, to steal her breath and give her his in return, but he settled on a prolonged meeting of their mouths. A silent reiteration of everything he'd conveyed in his vows.

When they eventually pulled apart, he found Cora's cheeks were wet and her smile was wide. "I love you," she whispered, the sound drowned by the audience's applause.

Those words would wreck him until the end of time. He'd never tire of hearing them. He nearly bent in for another kiss when a shadow fell over Cora's face. Cora froze, and the Godskeep fully darkened. The room was already dim enough, lit only by the few narrow windows lining the nave, but it was as if the curtains had been closed over them all at once.

Just as fast as the shadow had fallen, it was gone. Silence echoed in the room, punctuated by startled gasps. Teryn and Cora exchanged a questioning glance. That hadn't seemed like a natural shadow. It had moved too fast to be a cloud covering the sun, and the sky had been overcast when he'd entered the Godskeep earlier. What the seven devils had caused that shadow?

In answer came a piercing screech that shattered the air.

17

Mareleau jolted awake at...something. Had it been a sound? Had Noah cried? A glance at the bassinet beside her bed told her he was still asleep. With a sigh, she rolled back onto her pillows. She hadn't been dozing for long, as she'd only begun her nap after Noah had fallen asleep. Now that she was awake, a plethora of unwelcome feelings settled over her. Unending fatigue. Bitterness at being excluded from her best friend's wedding. Ever-darkening resentment over the prophecy. Anger at not being able to leave her room.

"Did you hear that?" her mother asked as she swept into her bedroom from the sitting room.

"Hear what?"

Brow furrowed, Helena approached one of the windows and peered out. "I thought I heard something. An animal, perhaps."

Now that she thought about it, she had startled awake at something. "It was probably just a bear in the woods."

The words dried on her tongue as soon as she said them. They reminded her too much of when she'd said nearly the same thing before she came face to face with Morkai's monstrous Roizan. A creature that wore her father's face...

"This place isn't suitable for you and Noah," Helena said, scowling at the landscape.

Mareleau said nothing in Ridine's defense. After being stuck in her suite over the last few days, she was starting to regret every kind word she'd said about the castle, every way in which she'd defended it to her mother. It was starting to look much like it had when she'd arrived last summer, dreary and sinister despite its new furnishings. Even her emotions harkened back to how she'd felt then.

Useless.

Helpless.

A pawn on a game board.

This time, instead of her father moving the pieces, it was fate.

Destiny.

Her faceless nemesis.

She clenched her jaw at her own futility. If only she had someone corporeal to rail at, to rebel against, then perhaps she wouldn't feel this crushing weight on her chest—

A soft cry emptied her mind. Tenderness softened her edges as she rose from the bed and greeted her awakening son. Just looking at him reminded her she wasn't useless. She had a purpose. Fate be damned, her purpose was to raise her son.

For what? For whom? some part of her taunted, forcing her to confront the fact that the prophecy wanted Noah to be some destined king of the Elvyn. Their Morkara.

She internally scoffed. If fate wanted her son, it would have to go through her first. It would have to greet her face to face and drag her and Noah onto their destined path.

Mareleau would not be weak. She would not give in to

her darker emotions or the ones that made her feel small. She'd stand tall and proud and remember that she'd gotten everything she'd wanted through her own means, and she'd do it again.

A smile curled her lips as she lifted her son from his bassinet. At the feel of him in her arms, a warm yet tender fire filled every part of her. It was enough to burn away the dregs of jealousy over Larylis attending the wedding without her. At least they could leave once it was over and all the guests had departed.

She bounced Noah in her arms and brought her face close to his. "I can't wait to bring you home," she said in a sing-song voice. A tone she never would have imagined using in the past.

"I still don't understand why we didn't leave with your ladies and midwives," Helena said, eying Mareleau with a questioning glance. "If there's a spy here, wouldn't it be safest if we'd left?"

Mareleau pursed her lips. Teryn had come up with a lie to keep Helena quiet, telling her they suspected a spy from Norun may have infiltrated the castle with one of their guests to attend the ceremony. According to his story, it wouldn't be safe to admit Noah had been born here, in case the spy sought revenge on Vera for the death of Prince Helios. Mareleau had done nothing to refute Teryn's tale, for only the truth would suffice, and she wasn't ready to give it.

"You know why," Mareleau said, keeping her voice level. "The coach with my ladies will serve as a decoy. Once they send word that they've arrived at Dermaine, we'll know Teryn's suspicions were unfounded. It's merely a precaution."

Helena made a flustered sound and turned back to the window. "To think Norun could seek to target us at all."

It was an unsettling thought, and it wasn't far from the truth. She'd learned about the threats Cora had uncovered. Even though Norun's attention seemed fixed more on Khero than Vera, that didn't mean they held Vera blameless. And that was without considering the alliance Norun was forging with Syrus—an island kingdom not too far across the Balma Sea. If King Darius sought to invade, he could do so by sea, and the nearest shore he'd find belonged to her kingdom.

A shudder rippled through her, but she tore her thoughts from such troubling matters and focused all her attention on her son once more. He'd ceased crying and was blinking his tiny eyelids. Her smile grew wide as she watched the little furrow on his brow, one he always seemed to get when he was looking up at her. Or whatever he could see of her. She brought her face closer and kissed his soft forehead. Breathing deep, she inhaled the sweet scent of him, and peaceful joy settled over her.

This was love. This was happiness. This was the culmination of everything she'd fought for, without even knowing it.

"You're so good with him." Helena's voice stole her attention. There was a wistful note to it. Helena's expression was soft and open, something Mareleau rarely got to see, and when Mareleau met her mother's eyes, they were glazed with tears. "You're better than I was with you. You're more attentive. More involved."

Mareleau wasn't sure what to say to that. Helena had tried—and failed—to convince her to employ a wet nurse. She'd pressed the matter for months during Mareleau's pregnancy, insisting it was proper for a queen, that royal women didn't nurse their own children, and some didn't even see their children more than once or twice a day. Mareleau had only grown angrier and angrier, and Helena had eventually given up. It was strange that Helena was now praising the actions she'd once deemed unqueenly.

"I don't know if I've said it out loud," Helena said, "but I think you're going to be a wonderful mother. You're already a wonderful queen and...and a wonderful daughter."

The tenderness in her voice cracked Mareleau's heart. It weakened her, speared her with guilt over the lies she kept. She'd been determined to have a somewhat less volatile relationship with her mother, but they still had many broken bridges to mend before they could have anything like a true mother-daughter bond. Yet her mother's words closed some of that distance, bound some of what had been broken. Helena was taking the first step. Was it time for Mareleau to take the next? There was only one thing she could think to close her end of the chasm.

Tell the truth.

About her lie.

About her guilt in her father's death.

About the prophecy.

It terrified her to state even a word of confession regarding any of these subjects. And yet...

She could start with one small truth, couldn't she?

"Mother, I..."

Helena took a step closer. "Yes, dearest?"

Mareleau took a trembling breath. "I didn't conceive during the Heart's Hunt."

Her mother gave her a sad smile. "I know. I can do math as well as your midwives can. You did what you had to do. I understand that now."

Relief coursed through her. That wasn't so bad. In fact... it was sort of good. Could she confess even more? Put her guilt to words? Tell Helena the truth about how King Verdian had died?

She took another deep breath. "When Father came here for the signing of the peace pact—"

Her words were swallowed by a sharp sound, one that made both women jump. A shadow fell over the room, there one moment and gone the next.

"That's the same sound," Helena said, whirling back to the window. "What in the seven devils was that?"

Mareleau cradled Noah close to her chest and approached the window beside her mother. The sound echoed through her ears, a chilling screech she'd never heard before. It wasn't the roar of a bear. It wasn't even the bellowing cry of the Roizan. It was louder. Sharper. And so very wrong.

A rhythmic sound reached her ears next, a pulsing thud from overhead. It drew closer. Louder. The room seemed to shake with the beat.

Then another shadow darkened the room, and this time they saw its source.

A winged creature soared over the castle, far too large for anything that should be airborne. Far too terrifying to even exist. Its body was long and sinuous, covered in pale, opalescent scales. Its wings were comprised of white feathers. So fast it flew past, becoming a pinprick in the distance in a matter of seconds.

Mareleau swallowed hard, hoping that was the last she'd see of it.

Yet that hope was futile, for the creature drew near once more, from a speck to a distinct shape, soaring straight toward the keep. She saw its face then, a massive scaly thing framed by more white feathers, its terrifying snout trailing long whiskers. It flew by the window, and Mareleau and Helena leaped back.

Helena released a yelp of alarm. "That thing...was that a..."

Mareleau knew the word her mother was trying to find. It seared her throat as she finished for her. "A dragon."

18

Outside the Godskeep, Cora's stomach dropped into a hollow pit as she stared at the creature circling in the sky overhead. Chill after chill shot through her as she took in those white scales, those feathered wings. There was no doubt what this creature was. *Who* this creature was.

It was Ferrah. The white dragon she'd met in El'Ara. Cora couldn't help but remember the heat of Ferrah's flames as she'd chased Cora in a rage.

Even more chilling was her next realization: this was irrefutable proof that Cora had been right, that Noah was indeed the true Morkara. If dragons were in her world, the Veil was torn.

Teryn placed a comforting hand on her lower back, but she could feel the tension radiating from his palm. The same tension etched the lines of his face. His jaw was slack, eyes haunted, as he stared at the creature. He hardly seemed to notice Berol flapping frantically over his shoulder, unable to land for the absence of the leather pad he normally wore when outdoors. Finding no good perch, she flew to the Godskeep roof instead. Teryn let out a shaky breath ending with, "Seven devils."

The sentiment was echoed by those around them, muttered in gasps, whimpers, and startled cries. After the piercing screech had sounded, she, Teryn, and Larylis had left the Godskeep with a handful of guards and ordered their guests to remain inside. But when the second screech had rumbled the entire building, the others came rushing out. Master Arther had tried to calm the guests down, but he now stood silent, his eyes turned to the heavens as Ferrah swooped across the overcast sky and disappeared into the heavy clouds.

"Mareleau," Larylis said, his voice strangled. "Noah." As he rushed into the castle, Cora had her next revelation. Not only was the Veil torn, but Ferrah was here for the same reason she'd chased unicorns through the Veil and into the human world.

She was here for Ailan's heir. The true Morkara. Mareleau and Noah.

The question was, what did she want with them? Was it enough to merely find them? She couldn't imagine the dragon sought to harm them. Dragons were supposedly connected to the Morkara's bloodline. Cora had drawn Ferrah's wrath when Fanon had forced her to try to bond with the dragon, but...she had to believe Ferrah would react far less violently to El'Ara's promised savior.

That was her hope, at least.

"You've got to be godsdamned kidding me," came Lex's voice. He and Lily came up beside them. "Was that a bloody dragon?"

Teryn gave a tight nod.

Lily turned pale as she glanced at her husband. "I

thought your tale of unicorns and wraiths was strange enough."

Captain Alden approached her queen with a bow. "Orders, Majesty?" Her voice held no quaver, but her composure was betrayed by her ashen face, the haunted look in her blue eyes. Cora had appointed Captain Alden to her royal guard for her battle experience. She'd fought for King Arlous at Centerpointe Rock and bore the scar on her cheek to prove it. She'd witnessed the horrors on that battle-field, beheld wraiths, the Roizan, and deadly vines wielded by magic. When Cora had taken the crown and worked with Larylis, Teryn, and Mareleau to staff her castle, Alden had been one of the first to gain a position. Yet even after all the captain had seen, she was clearly shaken.

Cora opened her mouth, but she didn't know what to say.

"Shall I post archers?" Alden asked.

Archers. What the hell could archers do against a dragon? Arrows couldn't combat fire, and she suspected they couldn't pierce dragon scales either. Besides, Ferrah hadn't attacked. Not yet, at least.

Memories of the dragon's searing flames chasing her heels flooded her mind.

"Post them," Cora said, and her voice wasn't nearly as steady as Alden's. "Defensive positions only. Shoot only if she attacks. Do not provoke her."

Alden bowed, then rushed into the castle.

Cora wanted to feel comforted by the protection of the royal guards who remained behind, as well as the archers Alden would post, but her stomach only sank further. Dread filled every inch of her, blaring a warning.

Her mind went to her unicorn friend.

Valorre! She mentally reached out to him. He'd been out of range all morning. She suspected he was sore about being excluded from her wedding and had chosen to entertain himself far away. Still, she had to ensure he was all right. She remembered how frightened he'd been of Ferrah in El'Ara. *Valorre, are you near?*

Fornication! Yes, I'm near.

His mental reply brought her equal parts relief and confusion. The first word was entirely out of place. *Are you all right? Are you safe from her?*

I'm safe. They aren't paying attention to me.

Cora's blood went cold. *They? There's more than one?*

I saw two. Excrement, this is bad.

She frowned at yet another out-of-place word. Fornication. Excrement. Since when did he randomly state such crass words? *Valorre, are you trying to curse?*

I would never place a curse on someone, even if I knew how.

No, I mean...is that your attempt at using expletives?

His only reply was a ripple of puzzlement.

If the situation weren't so dire, she'd be amused, but this situation was far from amusing. According to Valorre, Ferrah wasn't the only dragon here. She rushed to the other side of the courtyard outside the Godskeep, eyes to the sky, seeking any sign of wings among the clouds.

Teryn shadowed her steps, hand protectively on her lower back. Just minutes ago he'd touched her for far more pleasant reasons. The sealing of their marriage, their kiss. Everything had been perfect.

Then it had been shattered.

Resentment tightened her chest.

Teryn sucked in a breath. "Fire."

Cora followed his line of sight to a column of gray smoke wafting into the air in the distance. Mother Goddess, she hoped that wasn't a village. She blinked a few times, orienting herself with nearby geography. Her only solace was that there were no surrounding villages in that direction. There was, however, vast farmland.

The column grew denser, rising higher into the clouds.

Then a dark shape emerged above the trees. Cora made out the distinct silhouette of wings lifting a sinuous body into the sky.

Too fast the dragon approached, crossing the distance in a matter of wingbeats. And it didn't take long for Cora to realize it wasn't Ferrah. This dragon was probably twice as large with midnight-black scales and leathery wings instead of feathered ones. It flew over the courtyard, lower than Ferrah had dared to fly, eliciting cries of terror from the wedding guests.

Cora stepped back, pressing herself into Teryn. She flung out her hand and he grasped it tightly in his. Her heart pounded so hard she feared it would shatter her rib cage.

She held her breath as it flew past the castle, praying it would fully leave. Yet instead of soaring into the distance, the dragon circled around Ridine and made its descent. Its enormous wings pulsed through the air in heavy beats, slowing its momentum until it landed on one of the battlements. A funnel of air rushed over the courtyard, snatching a tendril of hair from Cora's previously perfect updo.

No cries erupted from the battlements. No arrows shot through the sky. Captain Alden would still be readying the archers. Thankfully, the dragon didn't attack. It merely perched upon the battlement like it was its nest. But what would happen once the archers arrived?

"Go. Just go," Cora whispered, wishing she could use her magic to convince the creature to leave Ridine.

Another pair of wingbeats sounded overhead. Ferrah had returned. Following the black dragon's lead, she circled over the castle before descending toward it. To Cora's terror, she landed not on another one of the battlements, but directly upon the keep. And she didn't nestle upon the roof like her companion. Instead, she gripped the crenellations and leaned over the edge, stretching her long neck until her head was level with the top row of windows.

Ferrah was looking for something. No, someone.

Cora knew exactly who. She'd known as soon as Larylis had uttered their names and charged into the castle. Was he with them already? Mareleau must be terrified either way.

A screech shattered the air, louder than anything she'd heard yet. Cora's gaze whipped toward the black dragon. Its head was reared back, its attention locked on the next battlement over. Cora couldn't see it from here, but she guessed Alden's forces had arrived and that the dragon had noticed them. A red glow blazed between the scales on the dragon's throat. Cora's shout was drowned out by those around her as a burst of crimson flame shot from the dragon's mouth.

Urgency propelled Cora toward the castle, though she didn't know what she was doing. What the seven devils could she do? Perhaps the dragons weren't here to harm Mareleau and Noah, but they were a danger to everyone else. To her archers. Her wedding guests. Her castle.

Her guards marched after her, as did Teryn.

"Orders, Majesty?" called the guards.

"Where are you going?" Teryn asked, taking her arm and pulling her to face him.

Panic raked claws down her throat. She didn't know what orders to give. She'd asked Alden to post archers on the battlements and now they...

Mother Goddess, they might all be dead now.

What could she do?

What the bloody hell could *any* of them do?

Teryn gently grasped her shoulders in his hands. "We need to get the dragons away from Ridine," he said, his voice deep and calming, serving as an anchor. Her tether to logic. "Is there anything we can do to aid that? Anything that will lessen the casualties? Anything *you* can do?"

He said the last part in a lower tone, though he needn't have bothered. He was referring to her magic, but the guests in the courtyard were far too frightened to pay them any heed. And those of her royal guard knew of her magic. Or, at the very least, she'd never hidden it from them.

The question cleared some of her panic. She may not have the answers, but perhaps she could find them through her Art. The last thing she wanted to do was relax and turn inward, but she'd long ago learned the value of doing so.

Closing her eyes, she let out a slow exhale and rifled through her flurry of anxious emotions until she found the steady ones lurking beneath. She shifted her stance, feeling solid earth beneath the soles of her silk wedding slippers.

A line from the prophecy wended its way through her consciousness.

The unicorn will signify her awakening.

She frowned, unsure of what that had to do with this situation. Then she remembered. The dragons had sensed Mareleau's awakening magic and had sent unicorns through the Veil to find her. Now that the dragons could enter the human world of their own accord, they could find Ailan's heir themselves. That was why they were here.

She'd already gleaned as much.

Yet there was something she hadn't touched on.

If the reason they could find Mareleau was her magic...

Cora's eyes shot open as the solution dawned on her. It was a risk. There was a chance it might not work.

And she'd have to hurt Mareleau to do it.

19

Mareleau had never seen anything so large or imposing as the black dragon that had passed over the keep moments before. She'd thought the white dragon had been terrifying, but this new one was positively monstrous. Her heart beat a frantic rhythm as she and Helena stood beside the window, alternating between peering out it for any sign of the beast and hiding out of view. There was no sign of either dragon now, just the pillar of smoke in the distance. Mareleau could only pray to the seven gods that Ridine wouldn't soon share the same fate as whatever now burned.

Noah began to whimper in her arms. He was probably hungry, but she couldn't nurse him now. Not when dragons were swarming the sky. She shushed and rocked him, though how could she calm him when she couldn't even calm herself?

The floor rumbled beneath her feet. Or was that the ceiling?

"Oh, gods." Helena clutched her hand to her chest.

"What the hell is happening? How is this possible? How are these creatures..."

The room rumbled again, and there was a distinct tapping that sounded above the ceiling.

Devils below...was one of the dragons on top of the keep?

A shadow darkened the window, and Mareleau leaped back. There was certainly something above the roof. She lowered her voice to a whisper. "Maybe we should get away from the windows—"

"Mare!" Larylis' voice had her jumping out of her skin, but as she whirled to find him charging into her room, her nerves settled by at least half.

She heaved a sob as she ran to him, letting him fold her and Noah into a hug.

"What's happening out there?" Helena asked.

"There are two dragons—"

Larylis' voice was cut off by a screech that pierced the air, the sound far too close and loud for comfort. It was coming from directly above her room. Human shouts followed, though these were more distant.

"The archers must have attacked," Larylis said, then gently loosened Mareleau from his embrace. Placing a hand at her back instead, he ushered her toward the door. "Come, we need to get you—"

Another screech, then a wall-rattling thud. Mareleau looked over her shoulder just in time to see something long, white, and scaled—a dragon's tail—slam against her bedroom wall from outside. The windows shattered from the impact, sending shards of glass surging into the room. Mareleau uttered a cry, ducking her head just as Larylis angled her behind him. Helena clung to her daughter's side, either shielding her or simply cowering.

Together they rushed from the bedroom, heads low to avoid shards of glass to their faces, and entered the sitting room. Thankfully, they'd already been near the door when the windows had shattered, so most of the splinters hadn't reached them. Mareleau's breaths came out in jagged sobs. Her feet didn't stop moving. She was desperate to be out of her suite, out of the keep. There were fewer windows in the sitting room but that didn't mean they were safe.

Was anywhere in Ridine safe when there were two dragons?

They left the suite and entered the hall. It was empty, as all the guests had been at the wedding, yet screams could be heard deeper in the castle. Perhaps from servants.

Larylis led Mareleau down the hall at a swift pace, Helena marching at their side, keeping as close to her daughter as she could. They halted at the next intersection. Larylis looked down one way, then another. Mareleau caught sight of the row of windows that lined one of the halls. Her heart climbed into her throat at the view. Upon one of the battlements the black dragon perched. Shouts rang out, probably from soldiers or archers, and a lick of red flame shot into the sky.

Larylis ushered her down the opposite end of the hall instead. "Seven devils," he said under his breath. "Where do I take you? Where might they be unable to sense you?"

"Sense me?" she echoed.

Larylis said nothing, simply stared ahead, brow furrowed as he frantically guided their party toward the stairs that led out of the keep. That was when Mareleau realized something she hadn't considered until then.

The dragons were here for *her*.

Or perhaps it was Noah.

Either way, this...all of this...

Was her fault.

She rooted her feet in place, her lungs constricting. Noah let out a wail that shattered her heart and clashed against her ever-growing fear.

"Mare," Larylis said, whirling to face her, "we have to keep going. I'll take you somewhere safe."

"Where? Where can you take me that will keep us safe from dragons?"

"I...I don't know. They may only be attacking because they were provoked by the archers, and I doubt they're here to hurt you. Not if what Cora learned in El'Ara is true. If I can at least take you somewhere the dragons can't sense you..." His expression fell, shoulders drooping.

That told her enough to realize where his mind had gone. She voiced it. "The dungeon."

Helena gasped. "You can't take her to the dungeon."

Larylis rubbed his brow. His voice came out laced with fatigue and regret. "Just until the dragons leave. *If* they'll leave. It's the deepest level of Ridine. I'll stay too, I'll—"

"Yes." The word flew from her lips even as it sank her heart. The last place she wanted to be was in a godsdamned dungeon. But if it kept her and Noah safe...if it kept Ridine safe, her friends safe, and everyone else who was here...

She lifted her chin, portraying a queenly aura she didn't feel. "It must be done."

Larylis' expression grew even more tortured. He opened his mouth, but before he could say a word, a figure bounded up the stairs. Mareleau's eyes grew wide at the sight of Cora, her hair spilling from its updo, the delicate lace at the hem of her ivory gown torn and stained, even though she had half of it gathered in her arms to assist her climb. Their eyes met, and Cora's countenance turned apprehensive. Still, she rushed straight for Mareleau.

"I'm sorry," Cora said, voice strained as she reached for Mareleau. Mareleau froze, expecting an embrace. But her friend wasn't here to comfort or hug her.

A sharp pain erupted from the sides of her neck. Then came the weight of something resting against her clavicle.

Cora took a step back, eyes glazed with tears. "I'm so, so sorry, Mare."

Mareleau shifted Noah's weight to one arm and lifted her free hand to her neck. Her fingers met a smooth, hard surface. She realized then what this was.

Cora had collared her.

20

Teryn's first day as king consort had thoroughly gone to shit. Thankfully, Cora's gamble with the collar had paid off. The dragons had disappeared hours ago, but only after leaving a dozen shattered windows, a crumbling keep roof, a charred battlement, and a few casualties in their wake. Teryn hadn't seen what had sparked the fight between the archers and the black dragon, but Captain Alden's report stated the dragon had grown hostile as soon as it had spotted the armed soldiers. Their arrows had done nothing to the creature, and they'd had no defense against its flames, hence the casualties.

Now those lives hung heavy on Teryn's shoulders, if only because they weighed on Cora's. She'd given the order for the archers to take their posts. He wouldn't let her bear that alone.

He eyed her across the council table; she was seated at the head while he occupied the foot. She didn't bother maintaining a regal posture as she sank deep in her chair. It was evening now, and their formal council meeting had ended. They'd come up with very few solutions regarding the dragons, only addressed reports of burned farmland, missing livestock, and the overall terror of the people who'd spotted the dragons in person. The wedding guests had been desperate to leave Ridine at once, and Cora and Teryn had decided to let them. There wasn't much they could do to protect them, whether they were at Ridine, on the road, or in their homes, so if it made them feel safer to flee the castle, so be it. Only those who'd come from north of Khero were cautioned to stay until a scouting party could be sent ahead. Which, thankfully, was just one retinue.

Lex and Lily entered the room with hesitant expressions. A hazy figure swept in along with them, one only Teryn could see. The ghost was female, and from the look of her simple yet dated attire, she must have been a servant who'd died at Ridine decades ago. She swept down the length of the table, hardly noticing its occupants. But as soon as she approached Teryn's end, her eyes locked on him.

She launched a floating step away, muttering to herself. "No, not you. No, no, no, no. Not that one." Then she left almost as quickly as she'd come, disappearing into the nearest wall. That was the fourth spirit Teryn had spotted since entering the council room, but the first that had come so close. Not to mention her strange reaction. It reminded him of Emylia's startled responses when she'd first learned he could see her as a ghost.

Thoughts of Emylia made him wonder if she'd made it to Zaras. If so, had she managed to gather any intel on Syrus? He wasn't sure how fast a spirit could traverse great distances, but now that Emylia was no longer tethered to the crystal, he supposed many things were possible.

Cora brightened somewhat when she saw Lex and Lily, though the look held a fatigued edge. "Come," she said, extending a hand to the empty chairs.

Now that the formal council meeting had ended, only two figures aside from Teryn and Cora occupied places at the table: Captain Alden and Lord Hardingham. The latter was a middle-aged man with neatly trimmed auburn hair, a short beard, and kind brown eyes. He was previously Larylis' councilman—and his father's before that—and was now Cora's Head of Council. After Cora had lost her brother's councilmen to Duke Morkai's slaughter last summer, she'd been left with no one to fill the roles. So Larylis and Mareleau had strategically staffed her council with the most trustworthy men and women they could spare. Hardingham had been at the top of that list.

"Thank you for agreeing to meet with us," Cora said as Lex and Lily claimed seats at Cora's end of the table.

Lex blushed. "Thank you for including us in...whatever this is about. I hope we're talking about those bloody dragons."

"Yes," Teryn said, giving him a halfhearted grin, "we are talking about those bloody dragons."

The council room door opened again, and in walked Larylis and Mareleau. Larylis looked as exhausted as Teryn felt, dark circles shadowing his eyes. Mareleau, on the other hand, walked with her head held high despite the collar piercing both sides of her neck. Her skin was red and inflamed around the punctures, but she wore the object as if it were a necklace. Teryn had been too distracted, too detached from his body, to recall how it had felt to wear the collar. And he hadn't been burdened by it for long. Whereas Cora had been forced to wear it for hours.

Cora paled as soon as her eyes landed on her friend. She rose from her chair and rushed to her. As she reached Mareleau, she fluttered her hands as if she couldn't decide whether to give her a consoling touch or not touch her at all lest she cause pain. "Are you all right? Does it hurt?"

Mareleau waved her off, but there was no malice in the gesture. "Don't baby me, Cora, I'm fine."

Cora bit her lip before forcing a smile. "I'm glad you're all right." She returned to her seat, and Mareleau and Larylis claimed chairs near Teryn's end of the table. Larylis and Lord Hardingham exchanged warm greetings.

"Where's Noah?" Teryn asked.

"He's sleeping," Larylis said. "Helena is with him."

"She won't be attending?"

Mareleau answered with a decisive, "No."

Teryn figured that meant Helena was still in the dark about most things. He and Cora had organized this less formal meeting to discuss the topics they couldn't—or weren't ready to—share with the council.

A dark shape dove from the rafters, eliciting a squeal from Lily. But it was only Berol, so no one else was startled. She hadn't wanted to let Teryn out of her sight after the appearance of the dragons and had followed him inside the castle afterward. Now she alternated between haunting the rafters and crowding his personal space. He'd had the presence of mind to don his shoulder pad, upon which she landed now. Absently, he extracted a strip of duck from his waistcoat pocket and fed it to his falcon.

"If that's all of us," Cora said, "I'll begin. Lex and Lily, I'll address what concerns you first so you needn't feel obligated to remain if you'd rather not linger on the dark topics we're about to discuss."

Lex and Lily exchanged a worried glance, then returned their attention to Cora.

Cora took a deep breath. Teryn wished he was sitting beside her so he could hold her hand. Remind her he was here. She wasn't alone. Her eyes flicked to his as if she'd been of the same mind. With the warmest smile he could muster, he gave her an encouraging nod.

She nodded back and angled herself toward Lex and Lily. "If you're wondering why we've requested that you follow a scouting party home to Tomas, instead of departing at once, it's because the border north of Khero may be unsafe. Now, humor me while I explain the next part, for I know it will come across as fiction. Something called the Veil surrounds the kingdoms of Khero and Vera, the land once known as Lela. The Veil is like a curtain between our world and...well, the fae realm."

She paused, waiting for their reaction.

Lex frowned, his mouth curling halfway toward a grin. But as he met Teryn's gaze and found there was no mirth on his face, he paled. Facing Cora again, he said, "Fae realm. Right. I've seen unicorns, a man-and-unicorn-eating monster, and now dragons. A magic curtain to the fae realm shouldn't be impossible to accept."

Lily gave an awkward laugh but it was tinged with hysteria. "Right," she said in her small voice.

Cora continued. "Until recently, only unicorns had been able to cross the Veil, and only to leave the fae realm—El'Ara—which is why they only recently appeared in our world. The appearance of dragons tells us the Veil has been torn. In other words, there's an opening somewhere in that curtain that separates our worlds. We don't know where the tear is or what would happen if people accidentally crossed it. Nor do we know what other creatures may emerge from it."

"It could be anywhere," Teryn said. "Or everywhere. We don't yet know if the tear is a single location in the Veil, or if it merely means the entire Veil is weakened."

Cora stood from her chair and pointed at a map that had been laid out upon the table from the previous meeting. She tapped the stretch of land between northern Khero and southern Vinias—the kingdom that lay between Khero and Tomas. "Since the Veil surrounds Lela, it exists here too. You can't reach Tomas without crossing it."

"Even if you go by sea," Teryn added, "you'd still have to cross the Veil. You are, of course, welcome to do whatever you choose, but as you are our friends and allies, we suggest you let our scouting party test it first."

"Oh, I very much agree," Lex said. "I'll trust your scouts to assess the border. No questions asked."

Cora turned her attention to Captain Alden. "When will the scouting party be ready to depart?"

"Majesty," the captain said, "Lieutenant Carlson will be ready to depart for the Khero-Vinias border at first light."

"Thank you, Captain Alden," Cora said with a gracious nod. "Any other updates?"

Alden cast a hesitant glance at Lex and Lily before answering. "Yes, Majesty. I have one pressing update that I didn't bring up during the formal meeting, for it is a private matter of state regarding a subject not all council members are apprised of. Do I have your permission to speak on this subject now, Majesty?"

"You do."

"We've gotten more intel from the Norunian spy in our captivity."

Teryn straightened. Cora had told him about the man being held in the dungeon, as well as the overall influx of spies from Norun. "What did the spy say?"

"He admitted to Norun's formal alliance with Syrus and confessed King Darius is in southern Norun at this time, near the Norun-Vinias border. While he wouldn't outright confess that Syrus and Norun seek to wage war on Khero, he admitted that Darius has recently summoned a fleet of warships from Syrus to make landfall in southwestern Vera."

Larylis cursed under his breath.

Cora and Teryn locked eyes across the table. Even though they'd suspected Norun and Syrus were allying to target Khero, this was the first outright confession they'd gotten that it was so. Not only that, but Khero wasn't the only target. If the warships were landing in Vera, King Darius sought Larylis' kingdom too.

If Darius had already launched the warships before the spy had been captured, he'd made the decision long before the appearance of dragons.

Before irrefutable proof that the Veil had been torn.

Before proof that the true Morkara was born.

How would Darius proceed once he learned of today's developments? It would be impossible to keep word of the dragons from spreading. For all they knew, they could have flown over the entire continent of Risa by now, and beyond. Worse was the fact that Darius had already launched his fleet. It didn't take more than two weeks to cross the channel between the Southern Islands and southwest Vera. The fleet could already have made landfall.

Teryn's mind reeled. So badly he wanted to say something comforting. Something hopeful—

"I know nothing about the naval fleet." The voice came unexpectedly from his side. Teryn bit back a curse, nearly leaping out of his skin as he found Emylia occupying one of the vacant seats at his left. His sudden jolt had Berol launching off his shoulder in favor of his chair's backrest.

"Don't do that," he said to Emylia under his breath. Luckily, his voice didn't reach the others at the table, for

Lord Hardingham had everyone else's attention now, reading the report of dragon sightings he'd shared at the council meeting.

"Sorry," Emylia said. "I thought you would have noticed my arrival. Anyhow, like I said, I can't confirm anything about the naval fleet, but I've managed to gather that Darius has been away from Syrus for at least a month, and half his military force is currently out of the kingdom."

Teryn assessed her information. It gave weight to the spy's confession about Darius being physically present in Norun, and potentially accounted for the warships too. If half his military force was gone, they had to be on those ships. He pursed his lips, not daring to share what he'd learned with those at the table. Cora was the only one who knew about his strange new ability to see spirits, and he wasn't in the mood to explain it to anyone else. He'd tell her after the meeting.

Lord Hardingham set down his report and looked to his queen for further discussion.

Cora's eyes were distant, her countenance falling with every second. She looked so empty. So defeated. Teryn curled his hands over his armrests. It took all his restraint not to run to her. He wanted to soothe her, touch her, but he kept his seat. His wife wasn't weak. She was stronger than anyone knew, and he'd never undermine that, even at an informal meeting like this. He'd save comforting caresses and calming words for behind closed doors.

"What do we do?" came Mareleau's voice. Finally, her cool façade cracked. Her voice trembled, with what sounded like fear at first. But as she spoke again, her tone was colored by rage. "What the seven devils do we do? This collar may keep the dragons from Ridine Castle now, but I can't wear it forever. And it won't stop the beasts from burning land and crops and devouring livestock. It won't stop Darius from knowing..." Her throat bobbed and angry tears glazed her eyes. Larylis reached for his wife's hand, gathering it in his. Mareleau's jaw shifted side to side before she finished what she'd been trying to say. "It won't keep him from knowing my son—his prophesied enemy—has been born. What the hell do we do?"

Cora sank deeper into her chair and rubbed her brow. "I...I don't know. There's so little we can do right now. I have one idea. I don't know if it will help, but I think it will be worth trying."

Teryn leaned forward, propping his elbows on the table and steepling his fingers. "What's your idea?"

She blew out a heavy breath. "Mareleau, Noah, and I will go to the Forest People."

21

Cora's suggestion was followed by dull silence. She didn't blame those around her for their shock. Even she found the idea she was about to propose daunting. Locating the Forest People might be impossible. They might not welcome her back, even as a visitor. Not all members of the commune had agreed with the elders' decision to involve themselves with the battle at Centerpointe Rock, and Cora's very existence defied the Forest People's primary rule: never get involved with royals or royal matters.

Still, she could think of no better way to find at least some answers. Solutions too, if they were lucky.

Mareleau finally broke the silence. "What do you mean we'll go to the Forest People?"

"Who..." Lily's soft voice was barely audible, but she cleared her throat and tried again. "Who are the Forest People, if you don't mind me asking? Um...Majesty?"

Cora offered Lily a gentle smile. "Don't worry about calling me Majesty here. To answer your question, the Forest People are a commune of witches and Faeryn descendants. They raised me for six years when I was living in exile from Ridine Castle."

Cora's gaze flashed to Alden and Hardingham, who revealed no discomfort at her explanation. They already knew the truth about her past, about Morkai and magic, but she was still getting used to speaking so freely about such subjects with her closest allies. Part of her expected to be condemned for daring to voice the truth, much like Lords Kevan and Ulrich had done, devils take their souls.

"The Forest People know about the prophecy," Cora said. "I've heard them speak about it before, but I didn't have enough context to understand what they were saying. If anyone could give us a clue about how to deal with the dragons, it's them."

She'd been so shocked when the Forest People elders had spoken about the prophecy. It was the first time she realized the elders held vast knowledge they didn't share with the rest of the commune. If anyone knew the most, it would be Salinda, the commune's Keeper of Histories and Cora's former foster mother.

"You've lost me," Lex said. "I don't know a damn thing about this prophecy."

"I'll fill you in before you leave," Teryn said.

Cora continued. "Furthermore, there's still the mystery of Ailan. Darius and Ailan were trapped outside the Veil together. If Darius is still alive, Ailan might be too. She might be our key to sorting this all out, and the Forest People might have some clue as to how or where we could find her."

"I still don't understand," Mareleau said, an icy edge to her tone. "Why would Noah and I come with you to find them?"

"They may know how to suppress your magic without the collar," Cora said. It was the only reason she sought to bring Mareleau with her. "I know how to draw mental wards around my own magic, but I haven't a clue how to teach you to do it, nor how to do it for you. The Forest People have witches skilled in protective wards."

Larylis spoke next. His voice was slow and controlled, but his rigid posture betrayed his composure. "Couldn't you find the Forest People first and bring someone back to aid her?"

Cora sighed. "I doubt I could convince any of them to leave the commune, much less set foot on royal land. The Forest People take great lengths to stay out of royal matters."

"So they might not help me anyway," Mareleau said.

"I think if we go to them, they will. I know at least some will be open to it. We have to try. You said it yourself, you can't keep that collar on forever."

"I take it you intend to bring Mareleau and Noah alone," Larylis said, and this time his tone was far from controlled, "as you've said nothing about me. Or Teryn. From this, I must surmise you intend for me to be separated from my wife and newborn son."

She swallowed hard and forced herself to meet his eyes. Her fatigue was growing by the minute, which made for weak mental shields. Already the emotions of her companions were invading her senses. Larylis' anxiety slammed into her, tinged with fear, grief, and anger. She wished she could allay those feelings, but she couldn't. She could only add to them. "A naval fleet is heading for Vera's shores. I can't tell you what to do, but I'm certain you already know the necessary course of action."

He cursed under his breath, his hand curling into a fist

over his armrest. "I must ready Vera's defenses," he said through his teeth.

Cora took a fortifying breath before shifting her gaze to Teryn. His eyes were distant. He sat sideways in his seat, elbow on his armrest, jaw propped on his palm. He rubbed his brow with his free hand. "And I must stay here to act as Khero's ruler while you're gone. The queen and her consort can't both be absent at such a tumultuous time."

Cora's heart cracked. He was taking this decision better than she expected, but that was only on the outside. Inside, his emotions were just as frayed and raw as Larylis' were. She hated doing this to him. Hated that this was her idea and that she'd leave him so soon after their wedding. Berol nipped at his cheek from her place on the back of his chair. He gave the falcon a sad smile and scritched her feathered chest.

"Well, it's lovely that everyone else seems resigned to this absolutely ridiculous plan," Mareleau said, not bothering to hide her ire, "but I still have several questions. How the devils are we supposed to find the Forest People?"

Cora winced. She'd told Mareleau about her past in one of the many letters she'd written to her friend over the last several months, which meant she knew the commune was nomadic. They moved camps every season, ensuring they were never in any place long enough to draw local attention, as well as to follow the most favorable weather. Yet Cora knew the general area the commune would be in. As it was still winter, they would be in southwest Khero. Though that wouldn't last for long. The commune would move again by Ostara, which was two weeks away.

That left only one option.

She'd have to locate them with her magic and use her

worldwalking abilities to travel directly to them. She hadn't a clue if she could accomplish the first task—

If you can feel them, we can find them, came Valorre's voice.

She relaxed slightly. He'd checked in with her frequently throughout the day to assure her he was in no danger from the dragons. Knowing he was still safe was enough to smooth the edges of her nerves. Yet his words did little to bolster her confidence.

You said that before and things didn't work out so well, she reminded him. It was how they'd ended up in El'Ara. Cora had been in the process of feeling her way to the Forest People—or trying to, at least—when Valorre had somehow overridden her focus with visions of his own. Of his original home. He'd taken the step that was required to initiate Cora's abilities, and they'd found themselves in the fae realm.

That was my fault, Valorre said. *I won't do that again.*

I still don't know if it's possible.

I think it is. I believe we can do it together. I'm your familiar, remember?

She relaxed even more. Valorre was indeed her familiar. She used to scoff at the concept of familiars, seeing them only as a witch's pet devoid of a magical bond. But now she understood it was more than that. As her familiar, Valorre strengthened her magic. She never could have entered El'Ara without him, without his visions, memories, and his horn's ability to pierce the Veil. But would they be able to find a place neither of them had physically been?

We can find the Forest People. I'm sure of it.

She hoped he was right. She *needed* him to be right. Otherwise, they'd be searching forever.

She voiced her idea aloud and received another long stretch of silence.

Then Mareleau barked a laugh. "You're going to use magic to find them. And you're somehow going to do it with me and Noah in tow."

"That's too dangerous," Larylis said. "Have you ever used your abilities with another person before?"

"With Valorre, but not with another human being. I'll practice first." She didn't bother feigning confidence. She knew this was madness. Yet they had to try. Her one consolation was that she suspected it was possible. The Elvyn had told her how Darius had used his abilities to bring in human armies to attack El'Ara with iron weapons. That meant he'd been able to travel with multiple people at once. Cora hated comparing herself to him, but if it meant her goal was viable...

"I'll practice with Teryn," she said, "if he'll let me."

"Of course," he said at once. "With Berol too."

"Berol?"

He offered the falcon a strip of meat and she hopped from his backrest to his shoulder pad. "You're taking her with you. As soon as you find the Forest People, send her back to me so I know it worked."

It was a risk adding another being to her travels. She'd already have to worldwalk with Valorre, Mareleau, and Noah. Now Berol too. And that was only if she managed to locate the commune. "We'll all do our best to rest tonight, and I'll practice in the morning. As soon as I'm certain I can accomplish this feat, we'll depart."

"You'll depart," Larylis echoed, "as early as tomorrow?"

"Yes. Likewise, I assume you'll want to leave for Vera at once." She hated that every word deepened the agonized look in his eyes. There was only one concession she could offer. "After I find the Forest People and they've helped Mareleau suppress her magic without the collar, I'll bring her and Noah straight to Verlot Palace. I've physically been there, so it won't be a challenge for me to worldwalk there."

That eased some of the pain on his face but he said nothing.

Cora shifted her gaze to Mareleau, awaiting her next objection. She didn't blame her friend for her qualms. No, she fully understood them. If Mareleau decided not to come with Cora to speak to the Forest People, she'd accept her decision. But she was confident they could help mask her magic and render the collar unnecessary. Cora couldn't stand the thought of her wearing it a second longer, and that was only considering her friend's pain. There were other possible complications, like infection.

To her surprise, some of the fire seemed to go out of Mareleau. She shrank down, as if sinking into her own resignation. Her voice came out hollow as she spoke. "You said the Forest People might have answers about the prophecy. They might know more about Noah's role in it. About...my role."

Cora could only nod. A bitter ache flashed through her, a reminder of how she'd been targeted for that very role. A role that was never hers to play.

"And they are firmly against Darius," Mareleau said, "who we know sees us as his enemy."

Another nod.

Her eyes grew distant. "Then they very well may be the only ones who can help."

"I think they're our best chance at understanding the situation we're in," Cora said.

"Fine." Mareleau rose from her chair in a rush. The chair legs screeched against the flagstones as she shoved the piece of furniture back, then promptly swept from the room without another word.

Larylis was much slower to rise, and he lingered at the table for several long moments before he spoke. "I don't like it. I don't like any of this. But I understand the necessity of this plan."

That was all Cora could have hoped for. None of them liked the situation they were in, but if everyone understood and accepted how they must proceed, Cora could be satisfied.

Larylis followed his wife. Alden and Hardingham exited the council room next. That left only Lex and Lily.

Lex gave them a wary grimace. "I only understood a solid half of what we talked about just now, and I sure don't envy you. I almost feel guilty for leaving tomorrow, but this isn't exactly my circus or my monkeys."

Cora frowned. "Did you just call my kingdom a circus?"

Lily placed a hand on her husband's forearm. "What he means is, even though we must return to our own kingdom, we will do whatever we can to help."

"That's exactly what I meant!" Lex beamed. "You can count on us to pass on any intel about the King of Syrus. If he's in southern Norun near Vinias, we'll hear about it while we journey home to Tomas. Vinias is a neutral kingdom, and they aren't known for discretion when it comes to other kingdoms' affairs. Then again, it also makes them a shit ally when they're all that stands between you and a kingdom that seeks to—"

Lily elbowed him. "As promised, we'll keep you apprised of rebel activity in Norun too. The rebels may not be able to keep King Darius at bay, but if they succeed at stirring chaos in Norun—or, as we hope, taking Haldor and Sparda back —he won't be able to depend on Norun's military forces to aid him."

That sparked something like hope in Cora's chest. "Thank you."

Once Lex and Lily exited the room, leaving Cora and Teryn alone at last, Cora swept over to her husband. He was still slumped sideways in his chair, and when she kneeled before his legs, Berol launched from his shoulder to the rafters. Teryn gave her a sorrowful smile. She returned it and scooted closer on the floor, resting her head on his thigh. There was something comforting about sitting like this, with him in the chair, her on the floor, his leg a firm pillow. It made her feel—at least for now—like she didn't have to be the one in charge. The queen responsible for weighty decisions. Like this, she could be small and afraid, soothed by the man she loved.

He extended a hand and ran his fingers over her smooth tresses. She wore a simple day dress beneath her more formal robe, her hair in a long braid. They stayed like that for several quiet and contented moments.

Then Cora angled her face until their eyes locked. "This isn't how I wanted to spend the first day of our marriage."

His hand left her hair to brush her cheek. "Nor I. If someone had told me I'd have my new wife on her knees before me on my wedding night, I'd have had a much different picture in mind."

She was too tired to even blush at his words, though she appreciated his attempt at levity. So badly she wanted to believe their night could be salvaged. She'd been looking forward to an encore of the passion they'd explored the night he'd arrived. But now, with the lost lives of the archers weighing on her heart, as well as her anxiety over what was to come, this wasn't the time for desire.

Teryn knew it too, for he did nothing to take advantage

of their current position, despite his teasing words. Instead, he continued to caress her cheek, her hair, while she nestled against his leg, breathing in the scent of him, letting his stoic calm—however feigned—forge a moment of peace in this godsforsaken day.

22

Larylis had never hated being king more than he did now. He understood what Mareleau needed to do. Understood the importance of his duties in defending Vera's shores. But why did necessity and duty have to stand in such stark contrast with his heart? Why was the best solution to be separated—however briefly—from his wife and child?

He climbed the stairs to the keep, his pace brisk to catch up with Mareleau. Then he found her. Gone was her haughty anger, her fierce demeanor. Instead, she sat slumped on the top step, shoulders hunched, head lowered. He rushed the rest of the way up and crouched on the step below her, bringing them face to face.

"Mare, what's wrong?" He winced at the question, for he knew what was wrong—everything. *Everything* was wrong.

She lifted her face, her cheeks wet with tears. When she spoke, her voice was small. "My neck hurts."

His eyes darted down to the collar. The skin around the puncture was red and inflamed. His heart fissured at the sight of it, but where cracks had formed, tenderness flooded in. It left no room for bitterness or anger. Only love and logic. The two things he treasured most.

"The Forest People will help you," he said, and he hoped it was true. It had to be. He'd seen them wielding vines as weapons at Centerpointe Rock. Stifling Mareleau's magic or teaching her how to build magical wards around her powers had to be possible.

Being separated from Mareleau and Noah no longer seemed like something to rail against. It still tore him up to think of being away from them, of Noah experiencing a single day where his father wasn't present or involved, but he could accept it now. He could let her go, knowing she'd find physical relief from her current pain. He could return to Vera and rally his forces, knowing he was defending their home. Noah's future.

His heart, necessity, and duty were aligned after all.

She sniffled and attempted to dry her eyes. "I hope so."

He shifted onto the step beside her and put his arm around her shoulders. She started to lean toward him but released a hiss of pain.

"I can't even lean into you," she said, and that brought on a renewed flood of tears.

Larylis folded himself around her as best he could without disrupting the collar, caressing her back, stroking her hair. For several long moments, she simply cried. He was grateful for the late hour and the fact that most—if not all—the wedding guests had already departed. Mareleau would be embarrassed if anyone else saw her this way. She always put on such a proud façade around others. She'd even done so with him, acting cold and haughty whenever they'd been forced to interact during their three-year estrangement. He'd witnessed firsthand just how readily she wielded her outer composure as a shield.

But shields could break, and hers had borne its brunt of emotional warfare the last few days. She needed this release of tears, this moment where she could safely crumble. He was determined to give it to her. To make it last as long as she needed. And if anyone dared intrude, if someone so much as stepped foot at the base of the stairs, he'd impale them with a glare so dark they'd leave in an instant.

Luckily, no unwanted interlopers found them, and soon Mareleau had cried her fill. He was about to extend his hand and offer to escort her to her suite when she blurted out a question that had him rooted in place.

"Did I force you to fall in love with me?"

He blinked at her, unable to find any strand of logic or reason in her question. Her cheeks were dry now but her eyes were distant, and she pointedly refused to meet his gaze. "What do you mean?" he asked.

She pursed her lips before answering. "I mean my magic. Did I use my magic on you to make you fall in love with me? Did I...conjure a glamour that made me desirable?"

He remained dumbfounded. How could she consider such a thing?

She spoke again, her words becoming increasingly rushed. "Now that Cora has told me that my...my *magic trick* is real, I can't help but wonder if I've used it in ways I wasn't aware of. I've ended unwanted engagements with it. I've made men think I was ugly, clingy, or annoying—whatever would cast me in an unfavorable light—which I always thought was just me acting. But it wasn't just acting. It was a glamour. And if I can create a glamour to make men dislike me, then I can—"

"Don't you dare finish that sentence," he said, his tone firm. He returned to his previous position, facing her on the step below. He wouldn't make her turn her head just to meet his eyes. Instead, he gave her no other place to look, filling her vision as he crouched before her. Tenderly, he gathered her hands in his. "You didn't cast a glamour to make me fall in love with you."

Tears glazed her eyes. "How do you know?"

"Because," he said, allowing his lips to tilt at one side, "if you recall, I didn't like you at all when we met. We bickered all the time. I insulted you in ways I'm embarrassed to recall all these years later."

She emitted a shaky laugh that was half tangled in a sob. "I insulted you worse."

He returned the laugh. "Yes, the flirtations of fifteen-year-olds leave much to be desired. Yet isn't that proof enough? Our first kiss was in the middle of an argument. Would I have pressed my lips to yours while you were hurling insults at me if I hadn't been completely and utterly smitten with you?"

"That sounds like proof that I *did* use magic on you," she said, yet there was humor in her tone. "Who in their right mind would have kissed a prickly woman like me?"

"Someone who loved you, petals, thorns, and all."

She chuckled. "Of all the men who've ever had the nerve to compare me to a flower, I never expected you to be one of them."

"Honestly, I saw your thorns long before I saw your petals. Before and after that sweet stretch of time when we first fell in love, you only showed me those thorns."

It harkened back to the nickname he and Teryn once gave her: Thorn Princess. Larylis had uttered the moniker disparagingly on many occasions, but in his secret heart of hearts, he'd carried a feeble hope he'd feel even the slightest prick of her ire. If that was all he'd ever get from her, he'd take it.

"I loved those thorns," he whispered.

Her expression softened. She shifted her hands, no longer limp beneath his, and clasped his palms.

"I've only ever seen you," Larylis said. "You, exactly as you are. Wicked and beautiful. Brave and cruel. Sensitive, sweet, and kind. Fierce, fiery, and bold. I've seen what you hide and what you present to the world. I've seen your love and loyalty. Your bitterness and rage. If you've ever cast a glamour, I've never seen it, Mare. Just you."

Her face crumpled, returning to tears. "It's so unfair," she wailed, gesturing to the collar. "I would have kissed you just now, but I can't lean—"

Larylis cut her off with a press of his lips. It was a soft kiss, just a tender brush lest anything firmer make her jostle the collar, but it was what they both needed. A gentle reminder of their love. The sweetness that was forever between them, even on the darkest of days. Their relationship had seen its share of challenges, and they'd come out stronger after each one. They would get through this too.

Mareleau felt empty as she entered her quarters, but it wasn't the bad sort of emptiness. It was a refreshing kind. She'd released so much with her tears, shed layers of frustration, bared doubts that had haunted her these last few days. Larylis' loving words had placed a balm on her soul. She could still feel the warmth of his hands, even though he was no longer holding them.

He'd left after escorting her to her suite, for he now had travel plans to organize for his return to Vera, but he would be back tonight, to spend what may be their final evening together before they had to part ways.

She hated the thought of being away from him, but she hated the collar more. She'd do whatever it took to rid herself of the device. Even if it meant traveling by magic to plead for the aid of strangers. Strangers who had magic. Strangers who might know more about her and Noah's role in the prophecy.

Her confidence flared as she opened the door to her bedroom, and she was able to greet her mother without betraying a hint of the emotions she'd succumbed to in the stairwell. Helena sat in a chair by the window, staring out at the night sky while Noah dozed in his bassinet, set upon a mahogany stand. Mareleau's heart softened further as she approached the bassinet and took in her son's peaceful face. The sight of him swept away the remnants of her woes and replaced them with a tingling warmth. She wanted to gather him in her arms and hug him to her chest, but she resisted, not wanting to wake him. He'd likely wake to nurse shortly anyway.

She approached the window and assessed the inky sky spread above the dark silhouette of mountains. "Any sign of dragons?"

Helena finally tore her gaze from the window. "No, not since they departed earlier." Her eyes drifted down to Mareleau's neck, narrowing on the collar.

Mareleau braced herself for the questions she knew were coming. Her mother had begged her to explain what was going on, why she wore the strange collar, why she no longer needed to stay cooped up in her room. Mareleau had given her only curt answers, mostly consisting of half-hearted promises of *later*, and she'd eventually need to make good on that. Yet all the bracing in the world couldn't prepare her for the words that left her mother's lips.

"Were you present the night your father died?"

Mareleau stiffened, her chest tightening. She swallowed the dryness in her throat and forced a casual tone. "You know I was at the camp for the signing of the peace pact."

"Yet you were not with those who were attacked. You, Larylis, Teryn, Aveline, and your ladies were the only survivors."

"We were the only ones who'd stayed behind while the others went out on the hunt." Despite her attempts to sound nonchalant, a tremor racked her voice.

"So you didn't see the rabid beast that attacked the party."

A shudder tore through her as visions of flame and monstrous flesh entered her mind. She couldn't bring herself to say no. Couldn't carry on with the same story she'd allowed her mother to believe. The same story that had been released to the public. "Why do you ask?"

Helena exhaled a slow sigh, her attention drifting back to the window. "Now that I've witnessed dragons, creatures that shouldn't exist, I can't help but think of the rumors. Ones of wraiths and monsters during the battle at Center-pointe Rock. And it makes me wonder about what happened to your father. Makes me question if it hadn't been a rabid beast at all, but something...something more like..."

Helena trailed off, jaw going slack. She looked so worn, the furrow on her brow deepening all the other lines in her face. Her skin, while normally radiant, was dull and pale. Her gray-brown hair hung long and limp around her shoulders.

Mareleau had been so distracted by Noah, by the

stresses and novelty of being a new mother, by the revelations regarding the prophecy, at the unfairness of being cloistered in her room, that she hadn't given her mother much thought. Now she realized this was one of the first times she'd seen Helena without her signature extravagant state of dress. Ever since Noah was born, she'd stayed with Mareleau, refusing to join the others when Mareleau took to seclusion in her room. She'd donned simple clothing, didn't complain about their lack of maids, and aided Mareleau into her nursing gown each day as if she were the maid. Over the last few days, Helena hadn't acted as the esteemed queen mother. Just...Mareleau's mother.

A pang of guilt struck her heart.

Helena shook her head and faced Mareleau once more. "I know I haven't been the best mother to you, and I know I've given you reasons not to trust me. I betrayed your love when I intercepted your letters with Larylis and had new ones forged. I abandoned you to your suitors and didn't apologize when they hurt you or made unwanted advances. I know I don't deserve your trust, but I'm asking you to try to let me earn it. To please not shut me out. If there's something going on, some burden you're carrying, something you're not telling me...please invite me in."

Her mother's expression was so vulnerable, so sincere, it tore down her defenses.

It was time to tell the truth.

With a sad smile on her lips, she perched upon the bed.

"Come," Mareleau said, patting the spot beside her. "There is much I need to explain."

23

The next morning, Cora and Teryn stood hand in hand, Berol upon her husband's shoulder, in the middle of their bedroom. Should anyone stumble upon them, holding stock still and silent, eyes closed, dressed in their most basic and un-regal daytime attire, they'd have made an odd sight indeed. Thankfully it was early, just after dawn, and all the servants knew better than to disturb a new couple after their wedding night. Not that they'd had one in the newlywed sense.

They'd spent the night in Cora's bedroom—*their* bedroom now—nestled in each other's arms. But they only touched as an extension of the comfort they'd sought in each other in the council room the night before. Their hearts had still been too heavy when they'd gone to bed. That heaviness hadn't dissipated with daybreak, and now that it was morning, there was work to be done.

Cora breathed deeply, filling her lungs with air, inviting the element in and around her. She shifted her stance, feeling the firmness of the floor beneath the soles of her shoes, anchoring herself with the earth element. A squeeze from Teryn's hand did the same, and as she pressed his palm in return, her heart flooded with warmth. She focused on it, letting her love for Teryn grow, to fill her chest, to lift her mood. That was the element of water, which echoed the blood surging through her, the moisture on her lips. She breathed deeply again, and this time she focused on the gentle sunlight kissing her eyelids as it streamed through the windows. It resonated with her strength of will, her determination. The element of fire.

With her connection to the elements secure, she shifted her focus back to Teryn, to the warmth of his hand, to her awareness of his presence. Then to Berol's. She was prepared to test not only her ability to worldwalk with another person but Berol too. Furthermore, she would determine if she needed to be touching both of them, or if it was enough that Teryn and Berol were touching, and that Cora *intended* to bring both along.

She opened her consciousness, allowing her mental wards to come down as she took in the emotions of her two companions. She sensed them, felt a flicker of Teryn's nervousness and Berol's far more neutral curiosity. She sank into those feelings for several breaths until the connection felt effortless. After that, she filled her mind's eye with a vision of a particular place in the woods, not too far from the castle's outer walls. It was where she often met with Valorre for one of their carefree rides whenever she could steal away from her queenly duties, and she'd grown accustomed to worldwalking there.

She envisioned the space, a small clearing with a wide oak tree. Behind it was a large shrub, and Cora knew her bow and quiver of arrows were stashed there. Practicing archery had become another component of her secret rides with Valorre. She could practice in the armory whenever she wanted, but doing so outdoors was more satisfying than shooting in the training room, watched by guards and attendants. Practicing in the forest made her feel so much like her old self—or more like her two selves combined. The witch and the queen. Daughter of the Forest People. Daughter of the crown.

The thought curled the corners of her lips, and her connection to the space strengthened. In turn, her vision of the clearing sharpened. She imagined the scent of earth and frost, pictured the rising sun slowly illuminating the space more and more. Shifting her feet again, she imagined how the earth would feel, hard after a chilly night but just beginning to give way beneath the morning thaw.

She focused on Teryn's hand again and found her connection to him had remained intact. All that was left was to take a step.

With one more deep breath...

She honed her focus on that clearing...

Lifted her foot...

And settled it onto firm soil.

She opened her eyes with a gasp as the chilly morning air brushed her cheeks, her hands. Her gasp was echoed by Teryn, whose eyelids had flown open as well. And there, upon his shoulder, perched Berol. With her hand still clasped around Teryn's, Cora whirled toward him with a wide smile.

"You did it." He shook his head as if he could hardly believe what he was seeing. Berol flapped her wings and launched off his shoulder to one of the oak's lower boughs. Teryn faced Cora and softly laid his free hand on her cheek. "You're godsdamned incredible."

His praise flooded her chest. She had to admit she was impressed with herself too. She'd been fairly confident she could accomplish the feat of traveling with others, but thinking it and doing it were two different things. Now that she'd proven it was possible, her pride swelled. It was enough to help her forget the darkest aspects of their situation, if only for a moment.

She lifted her chin and Teryn met her halfway in a tender kiss. His lips were warm, a welcome thing in their frigid environment, and as he pulled her ever closer, a spark of passion ignited. She angled her head, parting her lips for the sweep of his tongue. Perhaps she was merely riding the high of her accomplishment, but she suddenly wished she'd tried a little harder to enjoy her wedding night. Perhaps it wasn't too late—

I'm here, I'm here!

She froze at Valorre's words. His presence filled her awareness, and she could sense him trotting toward them from not too far away. With a sigh, she reluctantly broke their kiss and gave Teryn an apologetic smile.

His lips curved in a lopsided grin that had her stomach tightening. "Let me guess. Valorre's here?"

"He is. I told him to meet us if he felt my presence enter the woods."

"What stellar timing that unicorn has." He gave her one more kiss, on the cheek this time.

Cora sensed Valorre's excitement growing with every step he drew nearer. He must be excited to see Teryn, for it was a greater level of anticipation than he usually reserved for her. It made sense considering the unicorn hadn't seen Teryn since the battle at Centerpointe Rock. Unless she counted when Valorre had supposedly glimpsed him riding toward Ridine from afar. But he'd smelled him more than seen him, if his talk about the scent of strength and moonbeams was true. Even before that, when Teryn had come to

Ridine last summer, the two hadn't met face to face. By the time Valorre had reunited with Cora after they were separated in El'Ara, Teryn had been unconscious and recovering from his wounds.

Finally, Valorre trotted into the clearing, pulling up short as he saw them. His body stilled, head straightening, ears perking up. His emotions flared inside Cora, and what she first took as joyful surprise shifted into something she didn't fully understand.

"Hi, old pal," Teryn said, offering a wave.

Valorre gave a snort, then skipped back a step. His nostrils flared, his posture stiffening.

Cora frowned. "What's wrong, Valorre?"

He stomped a hoof, snorting again. His emotions flared once more, and this time Cora could make out a distinct thread of indignation. *How...how dare he get more handsome!*

She leveled a glare at him. "That's what you're upset about?"

Teryn glanced between Cora and Valorre, only able to hear one side of the conversation.

That's my *look!* Valorre said, scraping the earth with his front hoof. *I'm the one with a mane like moonlight. Why does* he *have one now? And why does it make his eyes glitter like emeralds? Fornication, I'm so embarrassed. Why didn't you warn me?*

Cora pursed her lips to keep from laughing. This was a serious matter for Valorre.

It's insulting that he must try to look more beautiful than me. I am not pleased. Not pleased at all. With that, Valorre trotted back in the direction he'd come.

Teryn turned to Cora with an arched brow. "What just happened?"

She stepped close to him and reached for one of his silver-white strands. "He likes your hair."

Teryn gave her a wry grin. "That didn't seem like admiration."

"Trust me, it was." Cora shifted her fingers to the pale tresses near his brow and brushed a strand off his forehead. "I don't know if I've mentioned it, but I like it too—"

No, no. Valorre charged back into the clearing and made a beeline straight between Cora and Teryn, forcing them to step apart. He sidled into Cora, herding her away from Teryn. *We have work to do.*

With a roll of her eyes, she mouthed *sorry* at Teryn, who merely chuckled at Valorre's odd behavior.

Come, Valorre said, stopping only once they'd reached the other side of the clearing. *Let's find your Forest People.*

Cora was about to settle in and focus on her next test when Valorre let out yet another snort. Shaking his mane, he said, *I am still much taller than him.*

THE MORNING SUN HAD FULLY RISEN OVER THE CAMBRON Mountains by the time Valorre settled down enough for Cora to concentrate. He'd asked about a dozen times whether Teryn could see him blushing, to which she'd reply that he couldn't blush. To that, Valorre just had to know if she was *certainly sure* he couldn't. She was almost of a mind to find the Forest People without Valorre, but the threat of her not needing his aid was enough to get him to relax.

After reconnecting with all the elements, she placed her hand on Valorre's soft hide. Her palm thrummed in response, sending warmth radiating down every line of her *insigmora*. She glanced briefly at her forearm, where the geometric shapes spanned from her palm to just below her bicep. Her gaze settled upon the spiral that marked the skin above her elbow crease. Beside it, new shapes had taken form, a crescent moon, a few small triangles. She recalled when she'd noticed the spiral. It had been the first tattoo that hadn't been physically marked upon her. Instead, it had formed on its own, something that had surprised her but not Salinda. Ever since, more tattoos had grown, particularly after the tragic night last summer.

Despite being a Faeryn tradition, her *insigmora* had taken on a life of its own. Cora now knew she had no fae blood, neither Elvyn nor Faeryn, yet her tattoos continued to grow with her magic, just like they did for the other Forest People. Even apart from them, Cora's body, her magic, remained entwined with those who'd trained her. They were family. They were a piece of her heart and soul. She could find them.

She let this confidence wash over her as she closed her eyes and settled her attention on her heart, drawing on her love for Salinda and Maiya. She pictured their smiling faces, felt their warm hugs, heard their encouraging words. Doubts shot through these imaginings, bringing questions of whether they'd be happy to see her again or if they'd condemn her for not visiting sooner. Or if they'd be upset that she came back at all, because of their rules about royals.

They are family, Valorre said. *You don't need to doubt them.*

She let his words bolster her confidence, and she breathed her doubts away. Returning to thoughts of Salinda and Maiya, she settled deeper into her affection for them. For the strong guidance of a mother. The love of a sister. The loyalty of family. She lingered here, fueling her magic with emotion. Then she let her mind drift from her foster family to the camp in general. She sought the scents of woodsmoke and herbs, imagined the sounds of those waking from slumber. Memories of whispered voices, hushed steps, and the comforting clatter of cookware flooded her consciousness. The memories were so vivid, it was like she was there. Truly *there*.

Whether it was just a memory or a glimpse at their location, she knew not, but an internal nudge told her she was on the right track. This was how to find them. How to feel them.

She let her memories sharpen yet turn yielding at the same time. She opened herself to alterations, to imagine the camp's surroundings without shaping the location from physical recollection. All the while she kept her heart tethered to her love for the commune that had raised her, for Salinda and Maiya, for her other friends and acquaintances, for how they'd taught her to be the witch she was today.

Something warm and heavy pulsed in her chest, blooming outward and flooding her arms, her palms, tingling her *insigmora*. It pulsed back at her from her connection to Valorre, from his soft flank to her palm, up her forearms, and back to her heart. The circuit continued, a pulse of loving energy.

I can feel them too, Valorre said. *I feel the camp. I hear it. Smell it.*

Excitement rushed through her, but they needed to see something too, if they wanted to travel there. Preferably something outside the camp, so they didn't show up out of nowhere like apparitions.

There's a lake, Valorre said. *My brethren have seen it. They've passed the lake and the camp. The two locations are close.*

Cora's concentration nearly faltered at that. Valorre could sense fellow unicorns when they were nearby, but if the Forest People were in the region of Khero she expected them to be, he was sensing his brethren from a much farther distance than usual. And...communicating with them? But how? Was this a side effect of the tear in the Veil?

Yes, Valorre said. *I remember now. I have always sensed my kin when nearby, like all fae can.*

Cora recalled Etrix saying something similar, that the Elvyn could sense their kin. But for Valorre...

All unicorns are connected. Brethren. Kin. And now I can sense them easier than I could before.

That's...amazing, Cora said.

There would be more time to marvel at such a connection, but for now she pushed her awe aside and settled back into her meditative state. His vision of the lake filled her mind. Frost marked the shore while the lake's glossy surface reflected a cloudless sky. She couldn't be sure how long ago this vision was from, but that didn't matter. The location was important. Keeping her heart wrapped around her warmest emotions, she poured all her attention into that image. She imagined how the earth would feel beneath her feet, how the water would sound as it lapped upon the shore. Valorre did the same, his concentration strengthening her own, until the location felt real enough to touch.

Real enough to step into.

With a deep breath, she took a step...

And rooted herself at the edge of the lake.

Awe fell over her, but it was interrupted by an icy breeze that bit her cheeks, much sharper without the protection of the woods. She glanced at Valorre, who seemed far less surprised as he looked out at their change of location.

"We did it," she said.

Of course we did, came his smug reply. *I am quite talented.*

She couldn't stop the grin from forming on her lips, but there was still one thing left to do to ensure their task had worked as intended. A wave of fatigue swept over her and attempted to fray her concentration, but she breathed deeply, strengthening her connection to the elements once more. Then, extending her senses, she sought familiar strains of consciousness. At first, she got nothing back, felt nothing in her quiet surroundings. She pushed further, extending her reach wider. Valorre sidled into her, as if to remind her to utilize his strength as well. She reached for him again, pressed her palm to his hide...

She felt them.

It was a small spark, but it was there.

Salinda.

Maiya.

She'd found the Forest People.

24

Teryn paced the clearing, feeling as if he were going out of his mind. A chill had crept down his spine when he'd witnessed Cora and Valorre disappear, and it hadn't left since. He stared at the empty space she'd occupied. The plan had been for her to try to find the Forest People, travel there, and return at once.

"Shouldn't she be back already?" he voiced aloud.

Berol gave him no answer. She seemed fully unperturbed as she preened on the oak branch.

He shook his head. Had it been five minutes? Ten? Thirty? Or had it merely been seconds that felt like hours—

Sound and motion filled the clearing. He halted his pacing and found Cora and Valorre in nearly the same place they'd vacated. His heart leaped into his throat, half with relief, half with surprise. Even though he'd been expecting her, he wasn't sure he could ever get used to seeing someone appear from thin air. Berol too had lost her composure and was rapidly flapping her wings, squawking at the newcomers.

Teryn rushed to Cora and framed her face with his hands. She looked slightly pale and unsteady on her feet. "Are you all right? Did something happen?"

Despite her pallor, she grinned, and the sight set him at ease. "I'm a little tired, but everything went fine. I found them. I truly found them. Now Valorre and I both have a clear image of the location. That will greatly aid my efforts when I return with Mareleau and Noah in tow."

"And Berol," he reminded her. It would be even harder waiting for his falcon to return with word that their party had made it and had physically reached the camp, but at least it would be something.

She rolled her eyes. "Yes, and Berol."

He let out a heavy breath and folded his wife in his arms. Perhaps he was being overprotective, but soon they'd part ways and he wouldn't be there to protect her at all. If this was his last chance to fuss over her, he'd take it. He planted a kiss on the top of her head. "You have no idea how tormenting it was to watch you disappear."

"I have some idea," she said, and the serious note in her voice reminded him that she had witnessed similar terrors. Not with him turning fully invisible, but his soul leaving his body. A blood mage taking over. Or when Teryn had nearly died.

They stepped apart and Valorre tossed his mane with a snort.

Cora's smile turned wry. "Valorre wants to know if it was torment watching him disappear too."

He wanted to laugh, but Valorre's earlier tantrum had him steeling his expression. "Oh, very."

Valorre must have been pleased by that because he seemed to stand a little taller as he shook out his mane.

"We should return." Cora strode over to the oak tree and extracted a bow and quiver from behind it. Shouldering her weapons, she said, "I might need these for our travels."

That of course had his protectiveness flaring yet again. The thought of her being in any sort of danger made him want to discard his duties as king consort and insist on coming with her. But he knew better. Not only could his wife protect herself, but with her absent, he was the only one who could protect Khero and Ridine Castle. Staying behind *was* his way of protecting her. His eyes flicked to her waist where the dagger he'd gifted her hung from her belt. That eased his panic even more, for he was fully aware of her skills with a dagger.

"I'll be fine," she said, as if she could read his mind. "Besides, I'm not leaving just yet. We have some time."

He nodded, but his mind lingered on the last word. They hadn't fully set a time for Cora, Mareleau, and Noah to leave. They hadn't even determined if it would be today or if they'd wait for the following morning. He supposed it would depend on the severity of Mareleau's discomfort with the collar as well as how dire the situation with the dragons had become overnight. He hadn't heard a single roar or wingbeat while they'd been in the woods. If they were lucky, the creatures could have fled back through the Veil, unable to sense Mareleau's magic.

Teryn's hope was short-lived. After Cora worldwalked them back to their suite, a missive from Lord Hardingham awaited outside their bedroom door. A council meeting would commence at once to address the latest developments with the dragons. Teryn and Cora rushed to get ready, not even bothering to call upon their servants to aid them, and hurried to the council room.

There they got their answer for how dire the situation

had become.

The first report stated more crops had burned. The second reported dragon sightings all over the kingdom and beyond. The final, however, detailed the burning of a farmhouse. The family of four that lived there. And the father who had died in the flames.

Teryn's stomach dropped to his feet. He and Cora didn't have time after all.

Only for goodbye.

FOUR INNOCUOUS WORDS WERE NOW THE MOST HATED IN Mareleau's vocabulary: *it's time to go.* Cora brought these words to her door, and as much as she wanted to argue, she didn't dare. She'd heard the report too. Larylis had told her after she'd insisted on his honest summary of the council meeting he'd attended with Cora and Teryn. After that, she'd known it was only a matter of time before Cora came to give the official word that they had to leave.

At least Mareleau was—hopefully—closer to comfort. Sleeping in the collar had been even more uncomfortable than sleeping while pregnant. If leaving now meant she could soon forgo the godsforsaken device, then she at least had one bright side to look forward to.

She forced herself to focus on that alone as she prepared for her journey with shaking hands. Larylis was gathering his party for his own travels, and Noah was sleeping in his bassinet. Mareleau was left on her own in her bedroom to pack for a journey she still struggled to reconcile. She'd never traveled without a retinue. Without maids and a coach. What the hell was she supposed to bring for a magical trek to visit a mystical commune in the woods? How the seven devils was she supposed to prepare—

A gentle hand fell over hers, stilling her trembling fingers as she fumbled with the chemise she was stuffing into the leather traveling bag.

Helena spoke in a calm tone. "Allow me."

Right. Mareleau wasn't fully alone. Her mother was here too. She faced Helena, blinking back tears. Helena made no mention of Mareleau's undignified crying nor the sheer number of small, tangled braids that wove through her tresses, courtesy of Mareleau's habit to braid when she was anxious. Instead, she simply smiled and gestured for Mareleau to step aside.

Despite Helena's kind expression, her eyes were shadowed with dark circles. They'd spoken for a long while last night, shedding tears as Mareleau finally confessed all the truths she'd been hiding. Helena now knew how her husband had died. How the last contact Mareleau had had with her father was a gifted blanket that she'd later lost to the fire. Something had changed between them ever since. Something small and fragile existed where there once had been a wall of thorns. It wasn't perfect, and it wasn't exactly warm, but it was open. That was enough.

She stepped back and allowed Helena to take her place before the bag that was perched at the foot of Mareleau's bed.

Helena moved slowly, calmly, extracting everything Mareleau had packed, then sifting through each item. In the past, Mareleau would have railed at her mother for inserting herself into her business, but this didn't feel like nitpicking, nor a way for Helena to demonstrate superiority. This felt like care. This felt like something a mother would do.

"Queen Aveline said you wouldn't need much," Helena

said, "as the people you are visiting will have plenty of resources for you and Noah. Let's pack a spare nursing gown, underclothes, and swaddling. That will be enough."

Mareleau's throat constricted as she watched her mother pack the bag. Something Helena had likely never had to do for herself.

Yes, something had changed between them indeed. Mareleau hoped it would continue to grow when she returned.

Once Helena finished packing the bag and faced her daughter with a proud look, Mareleau did something she rarely felt inclined to do.

She hugged her mother.

AS SOON AS THE SUN HAD SET, LARYLIS WALKED WITH Mareleau to Ridine's stables, his wife's bag slung over his shoulder and his son in his arms. He tried to memorize the precious shape and weight cradled against his chest. Noah was so small. So light, even in the layers of swaddling he was wrapped in. It was agonizing that Larylis even felt the need to treasure this moment, to treat holding his son as a last memory. Yet it would be a final moment, for a short time at least.

The seven gods were cruel to separate them like this. He only hoped that when Cora worldwalked Mareleau and Noah home to Verlot Palace after they accomplished their task with the Forest People, he'd be there too. And not fighting on Vera's shores against King Darius' army.

That gave him an unwanted chill. He'd hardly slept a wink last night and probably wouldn't until he received confirmation about Darius' fleet. He'd received no word that it had been spotted yet. Of course, the ships could already be approaching Vera's shores. The news would be delayed by the rate a messenger horse could travel. It was the worst kind of anticipation, like being poised barefoot on shattered glass, waiting to feel the sting of the cut.

He shook the thoughts from his mind and refocused on Noah in his arms. His son was content, freshly nursed, and awake. The last light of the setting sun painted his chubby cheeks pink, the only part of him visible from his swaddling. Larylis was grateful that the night was decently comfortable for the end of winter, absent of icy wind or torrents of rain. A small consolation.

Too soon they reached the closed doors to the stables. Captain Alden stood outside—the only other person they'd come across on their way here. Cora had arranged things so they could leave privately, without stirring too much gossip or concern. They hadn't refuted the story that Mareleau had already returned to Vera, and the official statement regarding Cora's upcoming absence was that she would lead another scouting party to the Khero-Vinias border. Easy-to-digest lies for the councilmen and allies who weren't privy to the full truth.

Alden nodded and stood aside, granting them entry. As they paused before the doors, Larylis glanced at Mareleau. She lifted her chin and threw back her shoulders, despite that awful device she still wore, then let out a shaky breath.

"Are you ready?" he asked, shifting Noah's weight to one arm so he could brush his fingertips against hers.

Her shoulders dropped and she gave him a sad smile. "No. But...yes.

They found Teryn and Cora already inside. Teryn greeted them with a nod. Berol, perched upon Teryn's shoulder, chirped at seeing Larylis. Exhaustion etched the lines of

Teryn's face, and Larylis knew then that there was one person who felt like he did. Yet even they couldn't find comfort in each other's company for long. Come morning, Larylis would depart with his retinue.

Larylis' gaze shifted to Cora, who was busy saddling a horse.

Only...it wasn't a horse. It was Valorre.

A unicorn.

Getting saddled.

Now he understood another reason why Cora had demanded such secrecy and had wanted to wait until just after nightfall. She'd smuggled a unicorn onto castle grounds. While the existence of unicorns had become somewhat accepted by the greater public over the last several months, most citizens had never seen one. It would certainly cause quite a stir if any of the servants spotted Valorre.

Larylis couldn't help feeling awed at his proximity to the creature. He'd seen the unicorn charging through the battlefield at Centerpointe Rock, but he hadn't met him face to face. If his heart weren't so heavy, he'd be amused at the sight of the majestic fae animal with a saddle on his back.

"There's a unicorn," Mareleau said, pulling up short.

Right. She must be shocked. While Larylis had at least glimpsed Valorre with his own eyes, Mareleau had never seen a unicorn in person.

Cora lifted her gaze from the saddle's buckle. "Mareleau, please meet Valorre." Her words were kind yet edged with impatience or fatigue. Then she added, "Yes, Valorre, you look incredibly fashionable."

Valorre tossed his mane then shifted his head toward Teryn.

Cora rolled her eyes and addressed Teryn. "Valorre wants to know if *you* think he's fashionable."

Teryn extended a hand and patted the side of the creature's neck. "Oh, I think you look incredibly dashing."

Valorre whinnied as if Teryn's praise pleased him, while Berol nipped Teryn's cheek from her place on his shoulder. He idly scritched her feathers to placate her too.

"You're saddling him," Mareleau said. "A unicorn."

Cora tugged on the buckle, testing that it was secure, then straightened and brushed her hands on her gray wool cloak. Beneath it, she wore a simple wool skirt and matching top. Mareleau too had chosen her plainest nursing gown for her travels, though her fur-lined Aromir wool cloak betrayed her status.

"I figured this would be the easiest way to use my abilities with all of us," Cora said, retrieving a quiver of arrows from the stable floor and securing it to the saddle. "You will mount Valorre with Noah, Berol will perch on the pommel, and I'll worldwalk while touching Valorre's side. That should bring us all to our destination."

Mareleau scoffed. "*Should*? That word doesn't inspire my confidence, Cora. And I'm supposed to mount a...unicorn? Sit in a saddle holding my infant son?"

Larylis shared her reservations. Panic flared sharply inside him, but he reminded himself that Queen Constantina of Rovana had led her army to victory with her newborn son in one arm and her sword in the other, dripping with the blood of her enemies. Not that he wanted Mareleau doing anything as reckless as Queen Constantina. At least Cora had cushioned the saddle in blankets and furs.

Cora grimaced. "It's sidesaddle. I figured you'd prefer that."

Mareleau threw her arms in the air. "Yes, well, it doesn't

negate that my lower bits were stretched to oblivion mere days ago."

"It's just while I'm using my abilities," Cora said. "We can walk the rest of the way as soon as we get to our destination. And...if you really don't want to come, you don't have to, Mare."

Larylis' breath snagged on an ember of hope.

Yet did he truly hope she'd stay behind? Remain in that painful collar for even a second longer than necessary? The ember cooled, and he realized it hadn't been hope at all, merely selfishness.

Mareleau finally replied, "Fine, I'll mount the unicorn."

Valorre snorted and scraped a hoof on the floor. Cora released a long-suffering sigh before turning a pleading look at Mareleau. "He wants to know if you think he looks fashionable too."

That seemed to drain Mareleau of her ire. Her expression went slack before a slight smile curved her lips. "I think he's beautiful."

After Cora finished preparing Valorre's saddle with all their belongings, Teryn retrieved a mounting block. Mareleau marched up the block and climbed into the saddle with practiced ease, wincing only slightly as she shifted in her seat. Now it was time for Larylis to release the bundle in his arms.

His eyes burned as he approached his wife. He stared down at Noah's face one last time, studying his eyelids that had fluttered closed, the sweet, furrowed look on his face as he slumbered. Gods, his heart ached. He hated this wordless goodbye. Hated the way his heart was being cleaved in two as he climbed the mounting block and gently transferred Noah into Mareleau's arms. Tears trailed down his wife's cheeks. He leaned forward and met her lips with a brush of his own.

"I love you," he whispered.

"And I you," she replied, voice trembling.

He slowly stepped down from the mounting block, feeling colder with every inch of space he placed between him and the two people he loved most. From the corner of his eye, he saw Cora step out of Teryn's arms, caught Teryn swiping a hand over his cheeks. Berol launched from Teryn's shoulder and landed on the saddle's pommel.

"There's one last thing to do," Cora said, tone wary. "We need to remove the collar. Otherwise, it could interfere with my abilities."

Larylis' heart leaped into his throat. "Is that safe?"

Cora angled her head toward him. "The dragons might sense her magic, but we'll be gone before they can locate her here. And when we get to where we're going, I can put it back on."

Mareleau's expression sagged as if she dreaded both having it removed and replaced. "Do it," she said through her teeth. "Let's get this over with."

Cora climbed the mounting block and reached for the collar with both hands. The cuff opened on its hinge. Larylis' gaze locked on the twin lines of blood that trailed down his wife's neck, but Cora wrapped a strip of gauze loosely around where the collar had been. He had to grit his teeth to keep from interfering, to stop himself from begging her to stay.

He was half in a daze as Cora pocketed the collar, stepped down from the mounting block, and placed her hand on Valorre's flank.

Larylis watched, hardly breathing, not daring to blink.

One second.

Two.

Cora took a subtle step forward.

Then they were gone.

Gone.

And Larylis felt as if all the warmth and light had been leached from the world.

25

Cora planted her feet on the lakeshore. Opening her eyes, she saw the lake blanketed in night, a crescent moon reflected on its surface. She shifted her gaze to Valorre's back and released a slow exhale as she found all her companions intact upon the saddle—Mareleau, Noah, and a mildly flustered Berol, who flapped her wings before readjusting her position on the saddle's pommel.

Mareleau blinked at their new surroundings, though Cora couldn't be sure she wasn't blinking tears from her eyes. This couldn't be easy for her. It wasn't even easy for Cora, and she was somewhat used to the jarring effect of instantaneous travel by now. Neither of them could be expected to get used to leaving the people they loved.

I told you it would be easy to get here. Valorre's boastful voice interrupted her thoughts. *I am incredibly helpful.*

You are, Cora replied. His arrogance wasn't unfounded; because of him, it had been much easier to reach the lake this time than the first, even with her extra travelers. Since both she and Valorre had the image of their destination in mind, she hadn't needed to focus quite as hard. Instead, Valorre had held the image while she'd sensed her companions.

Mareleau sniffled, drawing Cora's attention back to her.

"Are you all right?" Cora asked.

"Fine," she bit out, but her shoulders were visibly shaking. She looked pale too, though it was hard to tell for certain in the moonlight.

Cora glanced at the gauze around Mareleau's throat. There were two dark spots on each side, but the material wasn't soaked through. That gave Cora some semblance of relief. If her friend was pale, at least it wasn't from blood loss. Her relief was short-lived, for she knew what she had to do next. She reached inside her cloak pocket until her fingertips brushed the sleek tines of the collar.

"Don't." Mareleau's voice trembled as she spoke the word, her eyes locked on Cora's pocket. "Please don't replace it just yet. I know it's selfish of me to ask—"

"I understand." Cora withdrew her hand and left the collar where it was. She was half relieved, for she wasn't sure she had the strength of will to exacerbate her friend's wounds if she could help it. "Perhaps we can reach the Forest People and get aid before the dragons sense you."

"Thank you," Mareleau said, her expression easing. "If we hear a single wingbeat...do what must be done."

Cora nodded.

"Where are we?" Mareleau rushed to ask, as if eager to change the subject.

"We're in southwest Khero. I believe this is Lake Sarrolin, which means the nearest village is Brekan. Now I need to find out which direction the Forest People are."

Cora closed her eyes and extended her senses. A wave of fatigue washed over her, much like it had the first time she'd come here. This time, it must be due to the feat of traveling with so many. She was tempted to take a moment to rest, but she didn't want to risk staying in place too long, lest they attract the dragons. Breathing deeply, she pushed past her exhaustion, seeking nearby emotion. Valorre snorted, reminding her to utilize him. She pressed her palm to his neck. Her fatigue lessened and her awareness increased. Familiar energies brightened at the edge of her consciousness. She shifted side to side, seeking direction. Her heart pulsed as she faced the opposite end of the lake.

That was where she would find them. "Let's go."

Salinda was already waiting for her.

Cora felt her proximity before she saw her, half hidden in the shadows of a cedar tree. As they approached, Salinda stepped forward, eyes crinkling at the corners. Moonlight shone on the woman's dark hair, her simple wool dress, the tattooed skin visible on her forearms, chest, and neck. As well as the single tattoo that marked her as an elder: the triple moon at the tip of her chin.

Cora's heart lifted, both at the familiar loving face and the tangible proof that stood before her. She'd already known she'd succeeded in finding the Forest People. She'd been able to *feel* them. But now Salinda was there, serving as irrefutable evidence that Cora had used her clairsentience to worldwalk to a place she'd never physically been.

You had my help, Valorre reminded her.

You're right. She couldn't have done it without him. Without their connection. Without his link to his unicorn brethren and the image of the lake they'd helped him form.

Still, she wanted to take a little credit for herself.

Cora rushed the rest of the way to Salinda, and they met in a tight embrace. The smell of rosemary filled her senses, such a beloved aroma that always reminded her of her foster mother.

"Maiya knew you'd come tonight," Salinda said, squeezing Cora tighter.

When they released each other, Cora scanned the trees around them. "Is Maiya..."

"She stayed back at camp."

Cora's heart sank. She still wasn't sure her party would be permitted to enter the camp, but she hoped she'd at least get to see Maiya. Regardless, it was impressive that her friend's claircognizance had grown so strong. She'd predicted Cora's arrival the last time she'd come too.

"She knew exactly where you'd be this time. South end of camp, toward the lake." Salinda's eyes left Cora to land on the figures lingering slightly behind. Some of the mirth left her expression, and her voice took on a subtle edge. "She also mentioned you'd be bringing friends."

Cora understood the woman's apprehension. Doing what she was doing—bringing strangers to the commune— would have been against the rules when she'd been considered one of them. It was so much worse now that she was an outsider. A royal. "I did," she said, masking her grimace. "Please allow me to introduce you to Mareleau and her son, Noah. Mareleau, this is Salinda. The woman who raised me for six years."

Mareleau tipped her chin in greeting. It must have rankled her pride to be introduced as simply Mareleau and not her full title as queen, but they were all better off if they spoke as little of royal matters as they could. For now, at least.

"And you remember Valorre," Cora said. Some of the

Forest People had met him when they came to fight at Centerpointe Rock, and he'd basked in the reverence they'd shown him. He tossed his mane, eager to draw Salinda's attention. Cora didn't mention Berol, for the falcon had already taken to the skies on their way here. She didn't thrive off meeting people the way Valorre did.

"It's lovely to see you again," Salinda said to Valorre, offering him a respectful nod.

Valorre's emotions flared with pride. *Ask her if she thinks I look fashionable—*

I'm not asking her that right now, Cora mentally conveyed, then spoke to Salinda out loud. "This may sound like a strange request, but we desperately need someone's aid in suppressing Mareleau's magic."

Salinda squinted, studying Mareleau. "Bernice is our most skilled warder now. She took Druchan's place as an elder witch."

Cora's breath caught at the mention of Druchan. He hadn't been fond of Cora after she'd returned to the commune with tidings of war, but he'd fought at Centerpointe Rock anyway. And died. She couldn't help but feel responsible for that.

Salinda continued. "Bernice can create a lasting ward around another's magic, but...I'll need to see if I can convince her to leave Nalia."

A spike of emotion slammed into Cora. She'd kept her mental shields down to sense her proximity to the camp, and now she felt a hollow grief that wasn't her own. She spoke through the secondhand pain. "Is something wrong with the High Elder?"

"She's been unwell for days," Salinda said. "She'll only allow Bernice to tend to her. We think she's..."

Salinda didn't need to finish. High Elder Nalia was dying.

"I'm so sorry," Cora said, and this time her own grief mingled with her foster mother's. Nalia was beloved by everyone in the commune. She'd been one of the few people who'd supported Cora when she'd confessed the truth of her history and identity. She'd always been old, wrinkled, and hunched. Yet fierce too. When Cora had last seen her, she'd seemed as healthy as ever.

"She's had a full and long life," Salinda said, her voice rich with emotion. "There isn't a single person alive who hasn't known her from birth. We knew she'd eventually leave us. Now, come. Let's get you and your friend to my tent without drawing too much attention."

THE WITCH NAMED BERNICE SAT BEFORE MARELEAU IN Salinda's tent, burning a bundle of fragrant herbs in a clay pot. Cora had never been personally acquainted with the witch when she'd lived in the commune, but she recognized her curly red hair and her wide build. Bernice was clairalient and used scents to cast wards. Both Bernice and Mareleau kept their eyes closed while they sat on Salinda's cot. Meanwhile, Salinda rocked Noah in her arms. He'd woken after Mareleau had dismounted Valorre—who was now wandering the woods nearby—and, after being nursed, was content enough to be held by a stranger.

The tent grew hazy with the smoke, but it was a comforting aroma. The blend of sage, rosemary, frankincense, and mugwort was commonly used for wards and protection. Cora could have selected them on her own, but she knew better than to think she could do what Bernice was doing. Cora could protect a physical space with herbs but she had no experience in shielding someone else's magic. And Bernice was doing exactly that. The magic sizzled in the air, thickening around Mareleau as the witch guided the smoke around her. The Forest People called it quiet magic, and it was the kind Cora used to dismiss as unimpressive. Now quiet magic had become ingrained in Cora's soul.

Bernice released a slow exhale. "It is done. It should hold until morning. After sunrise, I'll cast it again if you're still here."

Mareleau opened her eyes. "Thank you," she said, voice tight. Mareleau wasn't used to interacting so freely with strangers, especially with those so far beneath her station. Yet she was being respectful. Or perhaps just quiet. She hadn't said much since they'd arrived.

Salinda returned Noah to his mother's arms and faced Bernice. "How is Nalia?"

Bernice rose from the cot, not meeting Salinda's eyes. "The High Elder has asked me not to speak on her condition, so I won't."

Cora frowned, studying Bernice's pursed lips, her suddenly tense shoulders. She expected to sense the same sorrow Salinda emitted, but Bernice seemed more annoyed than anything. Salinda gave the witch a sympathetic smile but didn't press for more.

Bernice left the tent before Cora could make sense of the exchange.

"Now that we've taken care of your friend," Salinda said, "will you tell me why you're here?" If the edge in her tone wasn't evidence enough of her apprehension, it flowed from her in waves. Gone was the joy of their reunion. Not that Salinda was angry. She was more wary, as she had a right to be. Cora was clearly not here for a casual chat.

Salinda settled on a pile of furs near a makeshift writing desk, upon which quills, ink pots, and dozens of loose papers were messily strewn. She gestured for Cora to take a seat on the cot next to Mareleau.

Cora did so, exchanging a hesitant glance with her friend before saying, "One of the reasons for my visit is as you already know; we need to mask Mareleau's magic. She only recently discovered she's a witch, and there have been...unfortunate consequences. We are grateful for Bernice's help, but we were hoping someone can teach her to ward herself."

"I see. And what are these unfortunate consequences?"

Cora swallowed hard. "That's the second matter we've come here for. Has anyone in the commune reported dragon sightings?"

"So you've seen them too? A pair flew overhead yesterday morning. We could hardly believe what we were seeing." She shook her head, expression bemused. "Though I suppose if unicorns can return from extinction, dragons can too."

Cora pursed her lips. She needed to tell Salinda the truth about where the fae creatures had come from, that they'd emerged not from extinction but a different world. But there was so much more to explain before she could touch on that.

Salinda's eyes narrowed, and her bewildered look turned to concern. "Are you suggesting the dragons are the unfortunate consequences of your friend's magic?"

"In a way," she confessed, and the weight of her tale settled all around her, lacing her bones with another wave of fatigue. She pushed past it and went on to explain what she could, starting with her unintentional visit to El'Ara and all she'd learned there. About Satsara, Darius, and Ailan. About the Veil and the Blight. How and why the unicorns had entered the human world, chased by dragons to find Ailan or her kin. Then—after casting a questioning look at Mareleau and receiving a subtle nod in return—she confessed to her companions' identities. Not only was Mareleau the Queen of Vera, she was also the prophesied mother. The Blood of Ailan. And Noah was the true Morkara of El'Ara.

Salinda leaned back in her pile of furs, eyes distant. "That's a lot to take in. None of us had ever surmised that Lela was a land from another realm. We thought our ancestors were from another time, not another place. We knew about the prophecy and the first Morkaius, but not in such detail. The Blood of Darius is a term known to us, but we've never heard the names Satsara or Ailan. And we hadn't a clue Darius referred to a living king."

Cora's stomach dropped. She'd hoped Salinda would have more to share. That she'd admit that she knew everything Cora knew—and beyond—and that the elders had simply chosen to keep these historical facts a secret. She clung to one last strand of hope. "Are you sure there's nothing else you know? When we spoke about Duke Morkai last spring, the elders seemed to know so much. Do you at least know where any of the Elvyn may have settled after the Veil was formed? The Faeryn became the Forest People, but where did the Elvyn go? If Darius is still alive, his sister might be too. If we can find her..."

"I'm sorry, Cora," Salinda said, lips curled down at the corners. "At this point, it's safe to say you know far more—"

Her words were drowned out by a distant shout.

Then another.

Salinda bolted upright and rushed from the tent. Cora scrambled after her, but she froze in place as she reached the tent flap.

That was when she felt it.

The clairsentient warning ringing through her blood.

That was when she heard it.

The rhythmic beat of wings.

26

The shouts from the camp rose to a crescendo, mingling with wingbeats and a distant, ear-splitting screech. Cora rushed the rest of the way through the tent flap, just as a gust of wind slammed against her, blowing her braided hair back. She turned her face to the sky as an enormous silhouette passed overhead. Then another shape, at the other end of camp near the common area. There, the white dragon—Ferrah—began to descend. Her feathered wings beat the air, extinguishing the cookfires and sending startled diners scrambling back, dropping clay bowls in their haste.

Salinda had stopped several paces ahead. She abruptly whirled toward Cora with accusation in her eyes. It was a look devoid of malice. Only fact.

Cora had brought this upon them.

Her legs nearly gave out at the realization. Bernice had said the ward would last until morning, but it apparently hadn't been strong enough to mask Mareleau's magic from the dragons. Guilt struck her chest, and with her mental shields still down, she felt the fear of the commune. It blanketed her mind, drowning out her sense of self.

Ferrah descended fully to the ground. Archers and spearmen surrounded her. Cora wanted to shout that the weapons wouldn't work against the dragon and would only make her angry, but she couldn't form a word, not with so much secondhand fear clouding her senses. Besides, her voice would never carry over the cacophony. The screams. The wingbeats. A second dragon—the black dragon— began to descend. The archers fell back.

Aimed.

Shot their arrows.

The arrowheads glanced off scales.

A violet glow emanated from the base of Ferrah's throat, illuminated behind her opalescent scales. Then a red glow from the creature still mid-descent.

Cora! Valorre's voice shattered the noise, broke through the outside emotions, and gave her something to cling to. She breathed deeply, steadying her feet, regaining control. With an exhale, she forced the outer emotions away and slammed a makeshift ward in place. It was enough to sharpen her mind and remind her of the solution she carried.

She plunged her hand into her cloak pocket.

"Do it," came Mareleau's voice.

Cora spun around to find her friend outside the tent, Noah in her arms. The gauze was gone, exposing the inflamed wounds on her neck. Cora's stomach churned but they had no other choice. Regardless of their efforts, they'd failed. The Forest People couldn't help them. Not with Mareleau. Not with the prophecy, the dragons, or the threat of Darius.

They'd fully failed.

Gritting her teeth, she extracted the collar from her pocket and charged for Mareleau. "I'm so sorry," she said as she prepared to clamp it around her neck—

"Ferrah!" The female voice rang through the camp, rising above all the other sounds.

Cora was dumbstruck at hearing the dragon's name. Who else would know it but her? She halted, the collar mere inches from Mareleau's neck, and cast a look over her shoulder. Ferrah snapped her maw shut, closing her teeth over a flicker of purple flame, extinguishing it in a puff of smoke.

The voice called out again. "Hold your weapons! Fall back."

The archers and spearmen hesitated.

Cora scanned the crowd, seeking the speaker, but it was too dark to make out a single figure amongst the chaos. Only one cookfire remained burning, the cauldron that had hung over it now toppled on its side, its contents spilling onto the soil.

The black dragon landed beside Ferrah, sending the ground rumbling.

"Fall back!" the voice repeated, and the fighters lowered their weapons and scrambled away from the two creatures.

Finally, Cora could make out the speaker. A tall, slender female strolled toward the clearing, hand outstretched toward the dragons. She made a shushing sound, and the dragons seemed to calm.

Ferrah folded her wings down her back and shuffled a few steps away, head low. The black dragon, however, took a step closer. But not to attack. Instead, it lowered its head, crouched down, and touched its massive snout to the woman's outstretched palm. Its sinuous black neck trembled, and a soft rumbling emanated from its chest. A sound somewhere between a chirp and a cry left its mouth as it nuzzled the woman's hand. The creature was so much larger than the figure, it could have knocked her over with a single breath. Yet all it did was gently nudge her hand, eyes closed.

Cora's feet moved before she knew what she was doing, drawing her closer to the clearing. The dragons. The woman.

"I'm here," the woman said. "I'm here, Uziel."

Silence fell over the camp, though it was punctuated with whispers and muffled cries.

Cora stopped moving once she reached Salinda's side. She was much closer to the clearing now, but she still didn't recognize the woman from behind. Long black hair trailed down her back and her brown skin was unadorned with tattoos. The brown bodice and patchwork petticoats she wore seemed slightly too big in places and too small in others. Her bodice was loose and seemed to ride high on her midriff, while the hem of her skirt was well above her calves. A style inappropriate for winter.

"Who is she?" Cora asked, but Salinda only shook her head.

The woman stepped closer to the dragon and pressed her forehead to the creature's snout. It let out another string of chirps. Then the woman spoke.

The words sent a chill down Cora's spine. Not because she understood them, but because she *couldn't*.

Couldn't, yet she recognized their cadence. The way they rang with a strange sense of familiarity.

She was speaking the language of the ancient fae.

A language the Forest People rarely spoke, aside from sparse words and partial phrases. Yet this woman spoke with ease and clarity...like the Elvyn had in El'Ara. Though their words had been translated by magic, she'd heard them speak before Etrix had woven his translation enchantment.

The dragon named Uziel kept its head lowered and backed away from the woman's hand. Then, extending its leathery wings, it beat the air. Once. Twice. The first gust of wind sent the woman's long black hair blowing away from her face, revealing the pointed tip of an ear. The second gust rushed over the camp, and Cora had to shield her eyes as clouds of dirt funneled into her. By the time the wind subsided, the dragons were no longer on the ground but soaring high overhead.

Then they were gone.

Relief uncoiled inside her, and she realized much of it wasn't her own. She hadn't been able to make out Valorre's voice since he'd called her name, but she felt his proximity, their mental link.

You're all right? he asked, his voice finally cutting through the disorder in her mind.

I am, she said, but she couldn't focus on herself right now, or even Valorre.

Her gaze locked on the woman, still facing away from her. Cora knew who she was. There was only one person she could be.

Finally, the woman turned around.

A pair of familiar eyes met hers, and Cora realized there wasn't only *one* person this figure could be.

She extended her senses beyond the thin walls of her temporary shields. The energy that pulsed back was as familiar as those dark irises. Her body was unrecognizable aside from the shape of her eyes, the kind expression in them. Gone were the crow's feet that once lined them, the wrinkles that had dug deep furrows in the woman's face. Gone was her hunched posture, her aged frame.

Salinda seemed to realize the same thing. She took a step toward the woman. Her voice was strangled as she uttered the name. "Nalia?"

It shouldn't have been possible. Nalia was supposed to be dying. She was supposed to be the oldest woman in the tribe, not the tall and youthful beauty who strode toward them now, drawing the eyes of the frightened and confused spectators. But this woman bore the High Elder's energy. Despite outward appearances, this was her.

The woman stopped before Cora and Salinda. She gave the latter a sad smile, which revealed the ghost of the wrinkles that used to frame her eyes. "Yes," Nalia said. "It's me."

But that wasn't her only moniker. It struck Cora that the answer had been here all along. Hidden in the High Elder's name itself. She spoke it out loud, reversing the letters, and marked this woman as the one she'd needed to find.

"Ailan."

The woman with two names released a heavy sigh and met Cora's eyes. "Yes. I am she."

27

Whispers broke out from those nearby.

"Who is she?"

"Did she say she's Nalia?"

"Did she just speak to the dragons?"

"Is that...Cora?"

"Who is the stranger beside her?"

Cora's skin prickled as several sets of eyes fixed on her and Mareleau. Mareleau edged closer and Noah let out a small cry, drawing more eyes their way.

Ailan—or Nalia, or whatever the hell Cora was supposed to call her—whirled toward them. Voice low, she said, "Go to my wagon. I know the two of you have questions."

"They aren't the only ones with questions," Salinda said, marching up beside Ailan. "You owe us all an explanation. The elders especially."

"I know. And I will give them one. First, let us get our guests some privacy while we set everyone at ease."

"We?" Salinda pulled her head back. Their argument was drawing even more nearby spectators. "You want me to help you put everyone's minds at ease? I don't even know if they *should* be at ease. I don't know who you are—"

"You know me." Her words were firm yet kind and sounded so much like the High Elder. "Please, take my side for now. Once I've spoken with our guests, then with the elders, you can make your own decision."

Salinda's jaw shifted side to side. "Fine."

Ailan gave her a tight smile, then faced Cora and Mareleau again. "Go to my wagon. I'll be with you shortly."

Cora was happy enough to oblige. With her mind still reeling, she could use a few quiet moments to collect her thoughts. Cora led Mareleau to the center of camp toward the High Elder's wagon. In the winter months, Nalia spent her nights in an enclosed living wagon as opposed to a tent like most of the others. Cora kept her head down, and Mareleau shuffled close at her side, but most of the commune was too distracted to pay them much heed, especially under the blanket of night.

Soon they reached the wagon and climbed up the short steps to the ornate door, painted in a green, yellow, and red floral motif. The inside glowed with lantern light, illuminating the rounded ceiling, the brightly painted walls, the ornate blankets, the cramped furniture. The tiny space somehow managed to host a bed built atop a cabinet, a small nightstand, two long benches, and even a stove and countertop. More of Bernice's herbs clouded the air, so it must be true that the witch had been tending to the High Elder. But why? The woman hadn't been dying like everyone thought.

Cora and Mareleau sat on one of the cushioned benches. Noah hadn't stopped fussing since he'd let out his attention-drawing cry, so Mareleau set about undoing the top of her nursing gown to feed him. Cora nestled into the corner of the bench and drew her knees to her chest. That was when she realized she was still clutching the collar. Thanks to whatever Ailan had said to the dragons, she no longer needed to use it on Mareleau. For now, at least. She stuffed it back in her pocket.

"Well, this certainly could have gone better," Mareleau said. Her dry tone gave Cora some sense of normalcy to cling to. "You truly had no idea?"

"That our High Elder, who we all assumed was a Faeryn descendent, was living a double life as a legendary Elvyn royal? Not a clue."

Mareleau huffed a cold laugh. "I can't tell if the whole name reversal is utter brilliance or the stupidest thing I've ever heard."

Cora heartily agreed.

Mareleau's eyes wandered the inside of the wagon as she nursed her son. "So...this is how you lived for six years?"

"No, this is luxury," Cora said. "I lived in a tent."

"A tent? Like the first one we entered, with the messy furs and lack of furniture?"

"Salinda is renowned for her disorderliness. But yes, I lived in a tent like that. With Salinda's daughter, Maiya." Her chest squeezed at the name. She hadn't seen Maiya in the crowd earlier, but it would have been nearly impossible to notice her in the chaos anyway.

"How did you do it? How did you go from being a princess to a runaway living in the woods without losing your mind?"

Cora shook her head. "I didn't have much of a choice. Morkai released me from Ridine's dungeon and sent his Roizan after me. The woods were my only option. I'm lucky the Forest People found me, otherwise..." She shuddered to think of what might have happened. She'd have starved or perhaps been eaten by some wild creature. She'd always been grateful that the Forest People had happened upon her when she'd been aimlessly wandering, but only now did she grasp just how miraculous it was. At twelve, she hadn't known how large her kingdom was, or how vast and unpopulated the forests. She'd had no reason to believe there weren't dozens of communes like the one that had found her.

Yet now she knew there was only one. And it had found her before any dangers had.

Another shudder ripped through her, but this time it carried a feeling that was somehow both heavy and light at the same time. It prickled her skin like a thousand tiny threads brushing over her, radiating with some potent energy—

"Did you like it here?" Mareleau's question pulled Cora from her thoughts.

She shook the strange feeling away. "I did. I loved it. No matter how much I love my kingdom, my castle, and Teryn, the Forest People will always feel like another home to me."

They sat in silence for a while longer. Or something like silence. Outside the camp, voices could still be heard. Footsteps. Commotion. She was glad not to be part of it, not because she didn't want to help, but because it wouldn't be welcomed or needed. The Forest People may be her second home, but very few considered her family anymore.

The door finally opened and Ailan marched up the steps into the wagon, followed by Salinda and Bernice. "Thank you for waiting for me," Ailan said to Cora and Mareleau as she settled upon her bed. Salinda and Bernice claimed the other long bench, both wearing disgruntled expressions.

Mareleau had finished nursing Noah—who was now

awake yet content—and shifted closer to Cora as if she wanted to be as far away from the Elvyn woman as possible.

"I still think this conversation should happen in the presence of the elders," Bernice said.

"And I insist that I speak separately with them," Ailan said. "Otherwise, we'll spend an hour arguing over whether Cora should be here. Besides, we'll have a much fuller picture to share once we address the reason she and her friend have come."

"They came here to find you, *Ailan*." Salinda said the name with no small amount of ire. She shook her head. "I don't even know what to call you."

"Call me Ailan or Nalia. The latter has been my name for five hundred years. Longer than I was called Ailan."

"Why did you choose that name anyway?" Cora said, her voice coming out smaller than she wanted.

"If you know who I am, then I take it you know about my history? The battle with my brother? The Veil my mother wove to lock him out of El'Ara?"

Cora nodded.

"Then you know that Lela was once a piece of El'Ara," Ailan said. "When Satsara sealed off her unfinished Veil, it pushed the remaining, unwarded land into the human world. My brother and I were henceforth trapped here. Darius used his worldwalking abilities to return to his father's island kingdom, Syrus, while I remained here. Yet soon I realized the Veil was affecting my memories. I began to lose them. This was a good thing where my brother was concerned, for it seemed he'd forgotten even sooner than I had, losing even his memory of Lela's existence.

"For me, forgetting was a tragedy. I didn't want to forget lest I was still needed in El'Ara. Lest there was any way I could figure out how to return to my home. Still, the memories slipped away. I forgot the name of the fae realm. I forgot that I'd come from another realm at all. I did my best to record what I did recall, and I passed that on to the Faeryn who'd been trapped outside the Veil, and later to their descendants. After a brief sojourn in human society, I settled with the Forest People for good, and they accepted me as one of their own. By then, I couldn't remember much, but I knew we needed to protect this piece of land called Lela. I chose a moniker that would allow me to keep some semblance of my former self intact."

"Why do you look like this?" Bernice asked, eying Ailan through slitted lids. "You asked me to suppress your magic over the last several days, and each day you've appeared younger. I held my questions upon your order, but if this is a time for answers, I'd like to know why you've had me keeping secrets from the rest of the commune."

"This is my true appearance," Ailan explained. "High Fae cease aging when they reach maturity and can maintain the same appearance until they take Last Breath."

Cora puzzled over the last two words. She stated them like they were a specific title, though the meaning felt like *death*. Was Last Breath the Elvyn term for dying?

Ailan spoke again. "My aging was another effect of the Veil. With only a slight connection to the magic that fuels my immortal life—the magic that seeps from El'Ara—I aged like a human. And yet, the small amount of magic I receive has been enough to allow me to continue living. Then five days ago, I felt a surge of magic. An increase of *mora* pouring through the Veil, unlike anything I've felt since living on this side of the ward."

Cora's muscles stiffened. "The tear in the Veil."

Ailan nodded. "Not only did my memories return, but I

began to age in reverse. I kept to my wagon, unsure how to address what was happening—"

"You hid from us," Salinda said.

"Call it what you like, but I did what I felt was necessary. My whispers told me to wait."

Salinda pulled her head back. "What do you mean by *your whispers*?"

"I'm a truthweaver," Ailan said. "That's my Elvyn ability. Like a witch who's an oracle or seer, I weave threads that seek truth and receive guidance in return. The whispers of my weavings told me to stay. Wait. But then the dragons came."

Cora's eyes darted from Ailan to Bernice. "Is that why you had Bernice suppress your magic? To hide from them?"

"I wasn't ready for them to find me."

Anger heated Cora's blood. She sat forward on the bench and spoke through her teeth. "Instead, you let them find her." She gestured toward Mareleau. "Instead, you let them attack my castle. My people. You let them burn crops and...and let their flames take lives."

Ailan's face fell but she said nothing.

Cora spoke again. "You spoke to them tonight. You made them leave the camp. Does that mean you could have sent them away from the start? Could you have sent them back to El'Ara if you hadn't been hiding from them?"

"I didn't send them back to El'Ara. I ordered them to wait for me until morning. To find a safe place to nest away from people. Uziel is my bonded dragon. Now that he's found me, he won't leave my side. And Ferrah is young and reckless. Neither will return to El'Ara until I do. Which I will soon."

"Why did you wait? If you can return to El'Ara, you

should have done so as soon as you knew the dragons were looking for you."

"I told you," Ailan said. "My whispers said to wait—"

"Your whispers are flawed."

"They never speak without reason."

Cora scoffed. "What reason could your whispers have had for allowing dragons to wreak havoc on my kingdom? Or do they only care for the fae realm?"

Ailan lifted her chin, refusing to be cowed by Cora's growing rage. "I see three reasons sitting before me now. Three people they clearly wanted me to join before my return."

Cora's eyes widened as she realized Ailan was referring to her, Mareleau, and Noah. The latter two she could understand, but why had she included Cora? She'd lost her place in the prophecy—no, she'd never had a place.

"What do my son and I have to do with this?" Mareleau said. "What is his role in this ridiculous prophecy? You do see he's a baby, right? Yet your brother is targeting Khero and Vera *now*. What can Noah do to stop the Blood of Darius, or whatever the prophecy says?"

Ailan's expression softened, as did her tone. "Blood of my blood, I wish I had all the answers. Time and again, I've cast truthweavings, yet my whispers tell me the same things every time. Things I'm sure you already know. I've even shared these whispers—what you call the *prophecy*—with the elders, as it was the one way I could try to protect this land should I perish before my brother. I don't know much more about the prophecy than you likely do, but without a doubt, you are my kin, and he is my heir. He is the true Morkara of El'Ara."

Mareleau pulled Noah closer to her chest. "But what does that mean? What do you expect him to do? The prophecy states that Noah will unite three crowns and return El'Ara's heart. That he will end the Blood of Darius. Does that not refer to him coming of age and inheriting three kingdoms? Facing Darius?"

Ailan furrowed her brow. "Inheriting three kingdoms?"

"Noah is the heir to Vera," Cora explained, "which was merged from two kingdoms already. And I...I considered naming him my heir as well, as he's my husband's nephew." She pursed her lips before she could say a word more. Before she could admit that she couldn't have an heir of her own because of the curse Morkai had placed upon her.

Ailan's eyes went unfocused as she considered. "I can see your reasoning for interpreting it that way, but it could mean many things. Prophecies are never infallible. They are merely whispers of one's weaving, open to interpretation. Their very nature makes them deceptive, which is why they often come to fruition in unexpected ways, even when one tries to stop them."

A flicker of anger ignited in Cora's chest. She knew plenty about that. She was the victim of such misguided interpretation.

Ailan continued. "First of all, my whispers never said Noah would face Darius, only that his birth would tear the Veil and set into motion Darius' end. That has already begun. As for uniting three crowns, it could refer to uniting the three kingdoms of Lela like you've surmised, or it could refer to uniting two human kingdoms with El'Ara. Returning El'Ara's heart...well, that part is both essential and inevitable, but it doesn't mean he'll physically do it himself. You, however," she said, shifting her gaze to Cora. "I'm uncertain of your role."

Cora bristled. "My role? I have no place in this prophecy. Morkai thought I was the mother, and many of his actions revolved around that assumption. But he was wrong. He focused so much on me, he never guessed the true mother was meant to be Mareleau." Every word burned like fire on her tongue, but she kept her expression steady.

"You may not have been named in the prophecy, but you have been drawn in nonetheless. Maybe you were always meant to protect Mareleau. To serve as a decoy for my kin." She smiled indulgently, like she was bestowing some great honor upon Cora.

"Decoy," Cora echoed, voice cold. All the anger she'd tried to hold back now flooded her, sending her fingers curling into her palms. "Do you know what Morkai did to me as a *decoy*?"

Ailan's eyes went wide but she gave no reply.

"Are you saying that I suffered for some grand purpose? That I was cursed in her place by design? That I was toyed with all so I could protect *her*—" The bitter tang that coated the last word silenced her. Fire filled her vision, reminding her of the nightmare she'd had the night before her wedding, when Morkai had taunted her using Mareleau's life.

Should it have been her?

Devils, no, of course it shouldn't have been Mareleau. Morkai shouldn't have cursed either of them.

Flames danced in her mind again, and she saw another flash from that dream, how even though she'd saved her friend from the duke's clutches, Mareleau had burned to ash as soon as Cora had touched her.

I am the shadow you won't acknowledge. I am the ember you wish you could smother.

She forced the echoes from the nightmare away until the tightness in her chest eased. Reluctantly, she met Mareleau's gaze. Her friend had gone a shade paler.

Cora shrank back. "I'm sorry. I didn't mean it like that."

Mareleau gave her a sad smile. "You're allowed to mean it like that. I wouldn't blame you for resenting me for what was done to you."

Tears glazed her eyes. "I don't, Mare. You're my friend. I could never resent you. That...that isn't me."

Salinda leaned forward and patted Cora's knee. While she appreciated the woman's attempt at consolation, the pity that clouded the wagon was potent enough to smother her.

She forced herself to sit taller, burying her unpleasant emotions until she could speak with calm. "I don't have a place in this prophecy."

"You do," Ailan said, not bothering to add to the sympathy that poured from the others. In that moment, Cora was grateful to the woman. Ailan's perspective may enrage Cora, but at least the Elvyn wasn't going to pander to her. "Whether you like it or not, you have become a part of this. I can feel the threads woven around you, linking you to my kin, to me. I never felt them when you lived in the commune before, but maybe I hadn't been looking then. Even so, my whispers drew me to you from the start, long before I knew why."

Cora remembered how she'd shivered at the imagined feeling of threads brushing her skin earlier. She'd been recalling how the Forest People had found her and realizing how miraculous that was. Had Ailan been the reason they'd crossed paths in the first place? Had she been following her whispers the day they'd found her stumbling through the woods?

Another shiver prickled her flesh, along with that strange brush of threads again.

"Maybe you're more than just a decoy," Ailan said, again without warmth. Without pity. "Maybe you have a more proactive role to play. Whatever the case, I don't think we are meant to wait for Noah to come of age and act on his own. The whispers tell me the time is now."

"Now...what?" Mareleau asked.

"Now," Ailan said, "we find the tear in the Veil. Lead the dragons. And return to El'Ara. Together."

28

This was the second time in two days that someone had suggested Mareleau go somewhere she didn't want to go. She stared at the woman with two names. The woman who was a stranger yet somehow also her distant kin. "Why the seven devils would I go to El'Ara with you?"

"Because," Ailan said, "it's the safest place for your son."

"The safest place for him is..." She bit off her words. She was about to say the safest place for Noah was wherever Mareleau and Larylis were, but was that true? Larylis was preparing to face King Darius' navy. War could swarm Vera and Khero any day now. Where *would* the safest place for Noah be?

She stared down at him in her arms, took in his peaceful dozing face. She would do anything to protect him. Anything.

Yet that didn't mean she trusted Ailan. At least she wasn't alone in that. Cora didn't seem any more trusting of the Elvyn, and the other two women in the wagon—Salinda and Bernice—regarded Ailan with unveiled apprehension. Maybe even hostility.

"My brother is coming," Ailan said. "The fact that I have my memories and youth back means the same will be true for him. He will know it means the Veil has torn, that the *mora* is pouring through the tear. And, because of his son's efforts, he will know the reason the Veil has torn—that the true Morkara has been born."

"Morkai knew all about the prophecy," Cora said, sending a spear of betrayal through Mareleau's chest. It wasn't like Cora was necessarily agreeing with Ailan, but she was supporting the woman's case, if only slightly. "He channeled it through a seer named Emylia, and he reported his findings to his father. Darius was the one who had sent Morkai to find information on El'Ara in the first place. There's no doubt Darius knows everything now, as he's already begun targeting our kingdoms—and he did so even before the Veil was torn."

"Then he's even more dangerous now," Ailan said. "He will invade to gain access to the Veil and seek the tear. He's always wanted complete control over El'Ara, and he will stop at nothing to get it."

"Then how," Mareleau said, "do you figure it's safe for Noah to enter the very realm your brother seeks to attack? Wouldn't it make more sense for me and Noah to stay out of El'Ara entirely? If he'll be so fixated on the Veil, he won't have time to consider some prophesied baby that might one day be his doom."

"Noah poses a danger to Darius in the present, simply for being the true Morkara. The *mora* has chosen him, and Darius will be forced to act."

"What do you mean the *mora* has chosen him?" Cora asked. "Isn't the title of Morkara passed down through named heirs? You were named Satsara's heir, which would make you the Morkara."

"Yes, I am Satsara's heir." Ailan frowned as if she was surprised Cora knew that. "Yet there are other ways for a Morkara to name their heir, and there are ways other than death to pass the title on. My mother named me heir, overriding Darius' birthright as eldest, which sparked the war with my brother. He sought to kill both me and my mother, for the *mora* will still recognize bloodline inheritance, if the Morkara and their named heir die before a new heir is named. When he murdered Satsara, I inherited her role as Morkara.

"When Darius realized we were trapped in the human world, he tried to defeat me. If he'd managed to kill me, he would have inherited my newly given title. And he almost did. Before he could land the killing blow, I thwarted him in a similar way my mother had; I relinquished my title. But not to my named heir, for I had no children yet. Instead, I passed the title to my unnamed heir."

"What does that mean?" Cora asked.

"Passing the title of Morkara to one's unnamed heir gives agency to the *mora*, allowing it to choose someone from the Morkara's bloodline. It isn't always the nextborn, either. It can be kin further down the bloodline. Anyone. Unless the Morkara names another, the *mora* is free to choose, however long it takes. This protected me from Darius, for he could no longer end my life without risking his place in bloodline succession. If I'd died before furthering my bloodline, the *mora's* search for my heir would have stalled, and it would have been forced to forge a new path. Yes, there was a chance it would simply have worked in reverse and chosen Darius as my heir, but it also could have chosen a new bloodline entirely.

"He knew the *mora* wouldn't choose him willingly, not unless he was a last resort. It would sooner choose a new bloodline to carry the role of Morkara. Thwarted, he fled to Syrus and left me alive, knowing he wouldn't get another chance at taking the title he so greatly coveted until the next Morkara was chosen from my bloodline.

"Noah has been chosen. He *is* the Morkara. If Darius meets your son face to face, he will know it as well. The Elvyn—even half Elvyn like Darius—can sense their kin when in their immediate proximity. Since Darius and I share Satsara's blood, he will sense that blood in Mareleau and Noah. There will be no fooling him. He will seek to end Noah's life and mine, to follow the reversal of the succession until it's back in his hands."

"Follow the reversal..." Cora tilted her head. "Doesn't that mean he has to kill every person in your bloodline in order to be next in line?"

"No. In the rare cases where the *mora* was given agency to choose an heir, it doesn't consider the generations that lie between the new Morkara and the previous one as contenders for the title. Instead, it considers only the chosen heir, the previous Morkara, the children of the previous Morkara, and so on. I was briefly Morkara, before I passed the title to my unnamed heir, so at one point, my children counted. But as none are still alive, no contenders lie between me and Noah. We are the only living contenders aside from Darius."

Anger simmered in Mareleau's gut. "You drew a target on my son's back. You passed on this burden to some future kin just to prolong your life. Wouldn't it have been better if the title had passed on to a new bloodline? To someone inside the Veil and not in the human world?"

Ailan's face fell. "I considered taking Last Breath and

letting the role of the Morkara leave my bloodline. Had my memories not faded shortly after, I may have eventually done so. But all I had by then were my whispers, and they told me to wait. That the true Morkara would be born from my blood and that Darius would be defeated at last."

"What purpose would your so-called whispers have had for waiting? For passing this burden on to my son?"

"I can't say. There's no way to know what alternate future there could have been. Darius would likely have continued to seek El'Ara despite being thwarted. He'd likely still have fathered Morkai and sent him to find information on the fae realm. Maybe you'd all have been safe from his machinations, but maybe he'd have gotten his way instead. Maybe he'd have succeeded at becoming Morkaius of the human realm without having made an enemy of Cora."

That sent her mind reeling. She hated that Ailan was right. There really was no way to know whether things would be better or worse if Ailan had made a different choice.

She shook her head. "You still haven't given me any reason to believe Noah would be safer in El'Ara than here."

"He's safer on the other side of the Veil because there's still only one way for Darius to enter El'Ara: through the tear, and that is somewhere we can defend, if we can get there first."

Cora spoke. "Does that mean you believe the tear to be a singular location and not a general weakening of the Veil?"

"Yes, the tear represents a single location. One mere split in the Veil. I can feel it like a sliver in the *mora* that flows to me, and it's close. As of now, Darius doesn't know where the tear is. It won't be easy for him to find either, for he's not as strong as he believes. His connection to fae magic is weaker than mine. He relies on his powers as a witch and a worldwalker, but he has no abilities as a weaver. No way to find the tear in the Veil quickly."

Salinda arched her brow. "And you can?"

"Yes, for I have something he doesn't," Ailan said, her lips curling slightly at the corners. "A dragon. Two, actually."

"The dragons can sense the tear?" Cora asked.

Ailan nodded. "Fae creatures have the strongest connection to the *mora*. Uziel and Ferrah will guide us to it. And that includes you, Cora. I need you to come with us."

Cora stiffened. "Why the hell would I come? Why do you keep including me in this?"

"You are Queen of Khero," Ailan said, voice firm. "You speak for your kingdom, and you've already admitted Khero is being targeted by Darius. We're in this situation together whether we like it or not. If we have any hope of defeating my brother, we must stand united and forge an alliance. I want you with me when I return to El'Ara and speak to the tribunal."

"I've already been to El'Ara," Cora said, voice low. "I was neither well received nor well departed."

Salinda and Bernice turned wide eyes to Cora. While Cora had given Salinda a summary of last summer's events, she hadn't gone into much detail.

Ailan's posture went rigid. "You entered El'Ara? Before the Veil was torn?"

Cora thinned her lips, reluctance written across her face. Mareleau knew what she was keeping unsaid. That she was a worldwalker. Salinda had taken the confession in stride, praising Cora for her growing magic, but admitting as much to Ailan was different. The Elvyn viewed her abilities as a threat. Would Ailan see Cora the same way?

"I..." Cora began. "I...apparently...am a worldwalker."

Ailan's eyes widened, her dark irises flashing with something like fear.

Cora spoke again, calmer this time, as if emboldened by Ailan's reaction. "I can use my clairsentience to astral travel to any place I can form a clear image of. I unwittingly did so with Valorre, when he filled my mind with a memory of his home."

Ailan cursed under her breath, shoulders sagging. "The unicorns. It makes sense now. I didn't understand why or how the unicorns first began to appear here, as my memories were compromised. But now...yes, of course their horns can pierce the Veil."

"The unicorns' memories were compromised too, so they weren't able to return to El'Ara," Cora said.

"Now they might remember." Ailan's gaze locked on Cora's. "We must go. We must protect the tear. My brother cannot find out about what the unicorns can do. What *he* could do with them."

"I'm not going back," Cora said. "Your people hate humans. Your consort nearly had me killed."

Ailan sucked in a breath. "You met Fanon?"

"I did. I met Ferrah too, and she tried to burn me alive."

Ailan's throat bobbed. "I'm sorry for how you were treated, Cora. I will not let them treat you like that again. When I return, I will have the authority to keep you safe. I may not be Morkara, but I am something like a regent until Noah comes of age."

"How dare you talk about Noah coming of age, like you have any say in his future," Mareleau hissed through her teeth. It took all her restraint not to shout, lest she wake Noah. "I am his mother."

"In El'Ara you will be respected as Edel Morkara'Elle. That is like a queen mother—"

"I am more than that already. I am a queen in this world. I don't care what I am in your fae realm, or what Noah is."

"It is his birthright, and he's already claimed it just by being born. Unless he chooses to pass the role to someone else when he comes of age, none of us can change that."

"I can refuse. You can't take him from me."

Ailan released a trembling sigh. "No, I won't take him from you, nor will I force you to come. Instead, I will trust that you will do the right thing. That you will put his safety ahead of your personal ambitions."

Mareleau's jaw went slack. The words stung more than Ailan likely intended, for although she hadn't used the word *selfish*, that was all Mareleau had heard. Mareleau had been called selfish numerous times, but only in the last several months did she start to feel it was true. She'd done terrible things to get what she wanted. Lied. Schemed. Hurt people she loved. Was she acting selfishly again? Was refusing to take Noah to El'Ara truly selfish? Would he be safe there?

Her lungs tightened as the weight of this choice squeezed her from every side. She'd made poor choices before. Like when she'd given her cousin Lurel to Cora as her lady's maid—a choice that ultimately resulted in the girl's death. Or when she'd lied to her father about being pregnant, driving a wedge between them. How he'd died before they'd gotten the chance to reconcile.

Ailan's tone softened. "The *mora* chose him, Mareleau. While I believe you and Cora are more important to the prophecy than the whispers have made it seem, there are still reasons it chose him. The *mora* has seen something in him, something El'Ara needs, that no one who has come before him has been able to provide. Fate has seen a future for him in the fae realm, and that same future can be yours. Being the mother of the Morkara is no small thing in El'Ara, and should anything happen to me before Noah comes of age, the *mora* will recognize you as regent over the magic instead.

"I know you love your kingdom, and I understand how much it burns you up to think of leaving it. But El'Ara is vaster than just a kingdom. It's an entire world. A world made up of more than the Elvyn. More than the Faeryn. The Morkara is responsible for redistributing magic to the farthest reaches of the world, over the seas of the Mermyn, down to the fire dunes of the Djyn. There are fae creatures besides unicorns and dragons, homes and communities across the world, innocent beings who depend on El'Ara's magic for survival. They need their Morkara in order to thrive."

Mareleau couldn't help but be moved by the portrait she painted with her words. True, all she'd seen of the fae so far had given her reasons to fear and resent El'Ara. But there was an entire world beyond the Veil that she truly knew nothing about.

A world her son had been chosen to rule.

"Even if you only want to consider your world," Ailan said, "there are additional reasons you must come with me. While I can guide the dragons back to El'Ara, if you and I are separated again, the dragons will sense my blood in you through your magic. They will find you. Stifling your magic with wards may keep them from locating you, but that doesn't mean they won't enter the human world to look."

"Can't you seal the tear in the Veil once you're on the other side?" Cora asked.

"The Veil is more complicated than that. Sealing the tear won't bring El'Ara's heart back. That's a problem we will need to solve after we defeat Darius." She turned her attention back to Mareleau. "You don't have to promise to make

El'Ara your home just yet. We will figure out the future later. Together. For now, we need to defend two worlds. You won't have a kingdom to rule if we don't work together to keep Lela and El'Ara out of Darius' hands. And for now, Noah is safer behind the Veil. Trust me in this."

Her lungs constricted further. She didn't want this burden on her shoulders. She wanted someone else to choose for her, yet at the same time, she railed at the thought of being ordered around or putting her fate in someone else's hands.

She had to make this choice.

For herself.

For Noah.

For whatever consequences awaited.

She was nearly dizzy with the responsibility, yet she managed to form the words, "When will we leave?"

Ailan didn't answer at first. Instead, she closed her eyes, lifted her hands, and linked her forefingers together. Then, angling her palms, she laced the rest of her fingers and pressed the tips of her thumbs to her chest. Mareleau had never seen such a strange gesture. The silence that followed told her Ailan was focusing. Or...listening? She had droned on about her precious whispers.

With a slow exhale, Ailan opened her eyes and slowly unlinked her fingers. "Tomorrow by midday," she said. "We'll take the wagon and find the tear in the Veil before Darius sets foot on this land."

Gods above, she hoped Ailan was right. More than anything, she hoped she was making a choice she wouldn't soon regret.

29

Cora had forgotten the quiet melody of dawn so deep in the forest. It had been too long since she'd experienced the soft hum of awakening activity in the commune, the scent of the morning cookfires, the peaceful silence of those still sleeping. It seemed not even the chaos of last night could disrupt the Forest People's daily routine. The only differences were the extra figures tending to the destroyed common area, lighting new cookfires, raking the earth, and rearranging the stones and logs that served as seats.

She pulled the hood of her cloak lower, hurrying her steps as she passed the bustle of activity. She was determined not to be noticed by the others on her way to find Valorre. Though Ailan had spoken with the elders last night —after offering Cora and Mareleau her wagon to sleep in— she didn't know how that meeting had gone. Cora hadn't seen the High Elder since she'd left with Salinda and Bernice.

Cora still wasn't sure how to feel about Ailan. About all of this. Ailan was so different from the Nalia she'd thought she'd known, yet similar at the same time. She still held the same air of authority. The same kind eyes. At least one thing was certain: Ailan wanted to defeat Darius as much as Cora did.

It was that determination that propelled her feet toward the edge of camp, two sets of letters rolled together and clenched in her fist. She found Valorre not too far away. She hadn't had time to unsaddle him last night, and something was perched upon his pommel—Berol. She paused her preening to eye Cora, then went right back to it.

"I'm glad you were easy to find," Cora said. She hadn't seen the falcon since she'd taken to the skies on their way from the lake.

She's been with me ever since the dragons appeared, Valorre said, tossing his mane in greeting.

"With you?"

We're friends. She came to me for protection. She knows how brave I am.

Cora snorted a laugh. So Berol was a bit of a coward when Teryn wasn't around. Had he been here when the dragons had landed, the falcon would have dove in without hesitation, doing whatever she could to keep them away from Teryn.

"I see where your loyalties lie," Cora said, humor in her tone. "It's obviously not with me. That's all for the better. I suppose it means you'll reach him quickly."

Her heart sank as she approached Valorre's side and extended the hand with the two letters. She hadn't read the second letter, but she could guess at its contents. It had probably been even more painful to write than Cora's. Mareleau's letter would eventually reach Larylis and would convey their newest developments. Particularly the fact that Mareleau would not be returning home after all and would seek refuge in El'Ara. If refuge was truly what they'd find.

Cora's letter was of a similar nature, informing Teryn that she was taking a detour before coming home. At least she had a solid plan *to* come home. Ailan wanted Cora there for the meeting with the tribunal so they could begin negotiating an alliance to face Darius together. Mareleau, on the other hand, only had a vague idea of her stay there. A vague promise of protection.

Cora could at least carry the comfort of a failsafe, one she'd relayed to Mareleau after Ailan and the others had left the wagon: if things in El'Ara took a turn for the worse, if Mareleau and Noah seemed to be in any danger, if they faced even an ounce of scorn from the Elvyn, Cora would take them and worldwalk the hell out of there. She would steal their Morkara and damn them all if it came down to it.

Berol extended her talon at the sight of the scroll.

With a resigned sigh, Cora turned it over to the falcon. "To Teryn."

She expected Berol to fly off at once. Instead, she froze on Valorre's back, beady eyes pinned on Cora. As she released an aggrieved chirp, Cora realized what the falcon was waiting for. "Oh! I...I don't have any treats. I'm sorry."

She is not impressed, Valorre said.

"Teryn will give you extra for me," Cora said with a grimace. Berol abruptly pivoted away from her—a cold shoulder if she'd ever seen one—before launching into the sky with the scroll of letters curled in her talon.

CORA HAD ONE MORE VISIT TO MAKE BEFORE RETURNING TO Ailan's wagon. She wove through the tents, seeking the one that belonged to Maiya. The tents looked similar to one another, especially in the winter season, with their rounded walls and pointed roofs. While the Forest People dressed the reed-and-willow frames of their tents in thinner fabrics in the summer, allowing them to show off bright colors, patterns, and other personal touches, in the winter the tents were comprised of oiled hides and felted wool. As a result, the camp was a sea of brown and tan.

On an exhale, she pried a hole through her mental wards, extended her senses, and searched for a familiar echo. She was struck with a barrage of recognizable energies, so potent they filled her with a bittersweet ache. Of course that would happen; she should have expected it. She may have kept most of the commune at arm's length when she'd lived here, but she'd still been physically close. She'd gotten used to their energies and emotions, and now that she was among them, it was hard to pick out a specific one. Yet there was one set of emotions that tugged on her more than all the rest. She narrowed her focus to it, followed it, and was rewarded with the sight of a figure she'd recognize anywhere.

Maiya stood outside a tent not too far from Salinda's. Her long black hair hung loose down her back. She was dressed in layers of patterned skirts, a long-sleeved top with fur-lined cuffs, and a thick red vest. In her arms was a bundle of firewood.

Cora quickened her pace, desperate to reach her friend before she disappeared into the tent. Maiya paused just as she reached the tent flap and whirled toward Cora. Cora's lips stretched into a wide smile as she closed the remaining distance.

"Cora!" Maiya's grin mirrored hers, though she didn't set down the firewood or embrace her friend. Instead, she cast a furtive glance around the camp and nodded at Cora to follow her inside.

Cora tempered some of her excitement and quietly entered the tent after her friend. She pulled up short at the sight of the interior. The last time she'd been inside Maiya's tent, all of Cora's belongings had remained exactly as she'd left them. They'd always shared a tent since the day Cora had joined the commune. She hadn't expected Maiya to carry around Cora's things and maintain an unused space as if she'd never left, yet seeing proof of her own absence was more startling than she'd anticipated.

That wasn't the only change either. The tent was larger overall with more furnishings, finer rugs, and a much wider bed. This was a married couple's tent.

She faced her friend with wide eyes. "You and Roije..."

Maiya crouched before the small stove and placed one of the logs inside. She grinned over her shoulder. "We were handfasted in the fall."

"I'm so happy for you." The warmth in her heart washed away the bitter ache at having seen her things replaced. Maiya had loved Roije for a long time yet had always been too shy to make a move. When Cora had returned to the Forest People last spring, her friend and Roije had just begun courting. And now they were wed, bound by ritual handfasting. She wished she could have been there, could have seen their ceremony. Maiya must have looked radiant, and Roije—

The blood left Cora's face. Shame replaced her joy as she recalled something about Roije she never should have forgotten.

"Roije...his arm..." Cora swallowed hard, working the words from her throat. "Did he heal well?"

Maiya's expression fell, and she quickly turned back toward the stove, busying her hands with a kettle. "He did."

Cora didn't miss the curt edge to Maiya's words. Did she blame Cora for what had happened to her husband? Roije had fought at Centerpointe Rock and had faced Morkai directly. He'd lost an arm for it. Mother Goddess, she'd thought about his fate several times since then, yet she hadn't considered it since stepping foot into the camp. Not until now.

"I'm sorry," Cora said, voice trembling. "That should have been the first thing I asked—"

"And you?" Maiya faced her again, this time with two mugs of fragrant tea in her hands. "How have you been?"

Cora blinked at her a few times, surprised by Maiya's deliberate change of subject. Her lips were pulled wide but the smile no longer reached her eyes. Cora shook her head, accepting one of the mugs her friend offered. "I...I'm as well as I can be, considering current circumstances."

Maiya sipped her tea. "You're a queen now, if the news from the villages is to be believed."

"I am."

"You still don't mind if I call you Cora and not Highness or Majesty?"

Cora's shoulders slumped. "I always want to be Cora to you. To everyone here."

Maiya's jaw tightened, and Cora was struck with a spear of anger that wasn't her own. Still, her friend's grin remained on her lips and she kept her tone light. "I don't think you can be *just* Cora anymore. Not to the commune at large."

"Why do you say that?"

Maiya gave an easy shrug and took another sip of her tea. "Twice you've returned since leaving us, and twice you've brought terrifying news. Last time, you took some of our people to war. This time, you're taking our High Elder."

"That's not...I don't mean to be a harbinger of doom, but—"

"I'm just telling you how it seems to the commune." Maiya's tone took on a sharper edge. She was so unlike the sweet shy girl she'd been not even a year ago. "I'm explaining why you can't expect to be received as Cora anymore. To the commune, you are Her Majesty Aveline, Queen of Khero."

"And you? You said the commune sees me this way, but how do you see me?"

Maiya let out a long breath, her expression softening. "I see you as a treasured friend whom I'm looking at for the last time."

The weight of that statement pressed hard upon her chest. She wasn't sure how to take those words. Was she saying she never wanted to see Cora again? Warning her to stay away? Or was this a claircognizant *knowing*?

"It doesn't mean I don't wish it were otherwise." Maiya's voice came out soft, strained. "You were my sister, Cora. But...but now you're a queen. You can't just show up when you need something. It makes a mockery of our core principles. The very rule that allows our commune to live in peace."

Mother Goddess, she was right. Cora knew she was right. Fate may have wanted Cora to come here, to meet Ailan, to walk the path her threads had woven, but after this...

She needed to let the Forest People go. Not from her heart. Never from her heart. But she could not use them as her political allies ever again. Even asking them to teach Mareleau magic had been offensive enough. At the time, it had seemed like the only recourse. Yet she couldn't use them as a recourse. A last resort.

"You're right," Cora said, voice trembling. "I can't do this again. I won't do it again. Yet I will keep you and everyone else in my heart. I will protect you in whatever way I can, even if it means never coming to find you again."

Maiya set down her mug of tea and sank onto the foot of her bed. Cora did the same, having no sense of thirst with such a heavy conversation. She kept her distance from the other girl, sitting a few feet away.

"How will you protect us from the newest magic war that's about to clash on our land?"

Cora shook her head. "I don't know yet. Did your mother tell you about it?"

"She told me and Roije late last night. Neither of us could sleep after seeing the dragons, not to mention all the rumors that were circulating camp."

"Ailan—Nalia—is taking us to find the tear in the Veil. We're leaving today, and none of us are asking the Forest People to fight this time."

Maiya stared down at her hands, idly picking her nails. She lowered her voice to just above a whisper. "Have you thought about giving him what he wants?"

"What...who wants?"

"The King of Syrus."

Cora blinked at her. "You mean...give him Noah?"

"No!" Maiya lifted her head and met Cora's eyes. "No, I don't mean giving him the child. What I mean is...as queen, you are in a position to negotiate with him as a fellow monarch. You can give him what he truly wants—access to the Veil. El'Ara. In exchange for leaving Lela alone."

Cora would be lying if she said she hadn't considered it. The Elvyn weren't exactly her friends, and even the Faeryn she'd come across in El'Ara hadn't treated her any better, but that didn't mean they deserved destruction. And what about the other fae? The Djyn, Mermyn, and all the fae creatures like Valorre and the dragons. What would happen to them if Darius took control of El'Ara?

Furthermore, he was a worldwalker. Giving him access to El'Ara wouldn't keep him out of the human world, and she couldn't trust the fae realm was all he wanted. She had to remember Darius was the one to first use the term Morkaius, not his son. He didn't want to simply manage the flow of magic throughout El'Ara like the Morkara was meant to. He wanted to be High King of Magic. He wanted to control and take. If he wasn't content with all he'd gained there, he could take his new powers and turn them against the human world. Even if Cora negotiated an alliance for the safety of her people, could she bear the burden of what else he might do to other kingdoms? Other people?

Darius could never have what he truly wanted unless Noah was dead.

"No," Cora said. "The only way to truly protect our world is to stop Darius entirely."

"What happens after you stop him?" Maiya asked. "Mother said Lela is a piece of El'Ara. That it is the heart of the fae realm. What happens to this land after you defeat Darius? Will the Elvyn seal the tear and leave us alone? Or will they fight to take Lela away from us?"

Cora's breath caught. That was a question she hadn't considered. "I don't know. But I promise you, I will do whatever I can to protect this kingdom and this land."

Maiya held her gaze, but there was no hope in her eyes. Doubt rolled off her in waves. Cora could see herself the way her friend saw her now—young, small, and very much in over her head. Maiya had always believed in her, always encouraged her, but what she was facing went beyond Cora's capabilities. She knew that. But Cora wasn't alone. She had Teryn. Mareleau and Larylis. Even Lex and the Norunian rebels he was supporting. She had alliances she could count on, and she was about to forge a new one with the Elvyn. It was daunting. Maybe even impossible.

But she would give it her all.

Maiya's face crumpled, and her chest heaved with a sob. "I really am happy to see you. You will always be a sister in my heart. Please believe me. I didn't want to have this conversation. I never wanted it to be like this. It's just—"

"I know, Maiya." She reached for her friend and pulled her into an embrace. "I know. You don't have to explain."

She didn't need Maiya to say another word. She understood fully. It was time for a final goodbye. Time to close the door on six years of her life and the people who made her the witch she was today.

Maiya sobbed onto Cora's shoulder, but Cora kept her eyes dry, refusing to add her own emotions to the medley filling the tent. Instead, she opened herself to her friend's grief, her fear, her hopes, and memorized every painful inch of it. That way she could carry it with her. That way she could remember, as she faced the inevitable challenges that lay ahead, what she was fighting for.

30

Mareleau hoped she was at the right tent. She stood before the leather flap that served as a door, Noah cradled in one arm, her free hand raised in a fist, only to realize there was no point in knocking on such a soft material. And she couldn't very well barge in, for there was still the question of whether this *was* the right tent. It should have been easy to find. Not only was it the same tent Salinda had brought them to upon arriving last night, but Cora had pointed it out from the wagon that morning, before she'd left to find Valorre and Berol.

She hated feeling awkward like this, but she was fully out of her element. Here it hindered more than helped that she was queen. Here she couldn't rely on being waited upon. She'd spent the night in a godsforsaken wagon, after all, on a cramped bed. The accommodations had been smaller than the traveling coach she'd ridden to Ridine in, yet Ailan had offered it to her and Cora like it was some high honor.

Mareleau shook the thoughts from her head, reminding herself that if anything would serve her around the Forest People, it was humility.

So she cleared her throat and adopted as pleasant a tone as she could. "Salinda? Are you—"

"Come in," came the woman's voice from inside.

She hesitated. This was normally the part where someone else would open the door for her. But no, of course that wouldn't happen here. She lifted the tent flap and awkwardly shuffled inside.

"Mareleau." Salinda greeted her with a warm smile. It was strange being on a first-name basis with a stranger, but of the few Forest People she'd met, she liked Salinda best. The woman's grin looked tired as she gestured for her to take a seat on her pile of furs. Mareleau accepted the seat, finding it far more comfortable than she expected.

Salinda strolled to the bed where she was packing items into a bag. "I was just getting some things ready for you. Extra swaddling, absorbent moss, a carrying sling, and lactation herbs."

Her mouth fell open. "Oh...that bag is for me?"

"I figured we might have some items you wouldn't have had where you're from."

She was right about that. She hadn't heard of the latter three items. "Thank you. That's...rather kind of you."

Salinda smiled over her shoulder. "You may be a queen and part of some great prophecy, but you are still a mother. And he, whether the heir to a human kingdom or the Morkara of the fae realm, is still just a baby."

For some reason, those words warmed Mareleau's heart. She hadn't realized how badly she needed to be reminded that she was more than the subject of a prophecy. More than a royal. Her identity was her own.

Salinda put the last item in the bag and sat at the edge of her bed. "But that isn't why you came here, is it?"

"No." Mareleau shifted in her seat and Noah began to fuss.

"May I?" Salinda leaned forward, extending her heavily tattooed arms.

Mareleau didn't love when other people held Noah, but she also could use a break. She hadn't had one since Salinda held him last night. Carefully she transferred her son to Salinda, then nestled back into the furs. Salinda began bouncing and speaking to him in a sing-song voice, which halted his mewling protestations.

"I was hoping," Mareleau said, "you could teach me about casting wards with my magic."

Salinda cocked her head. "Now that the dragons are being dealt with, you don't need to learn warding as urgently."

"I may not need to cast wards around my own magic, but I'd like to learn how to cast them in general. I want to protect Noah."

"There is very little I could teach you before you leave. Besides, even though I have both witch and Faeryn blood, my magic favors my Faeryn heritage. Faeryn magic works with the Magic of the Soil. Earth magic. You have Elvyn blood, which utilizes the Magic of the Sky. Weaving, in other words, like Ailan does. You'd have better luck talking to her."

"I don't want to talk to her yet." Mareleau winced at her petulant tone. She simply didn't like or trust Ailan, though that was mostly because Mareleau couldn't help blaming her for everything that was happening now. "I'd at least like to know what kind of witch I might be. Cora uses emotion, and she believes my mother uses sound. I'd like to know which of the six senses my magic favors."

"I suppose I can help with that," she said, tone kind. "So

tell me about your magic. Cora mentioned last night that she discovered you were a witch because you'd cast a glamour."

Mareleau nodded. "I never knew that's what I was doing. I've always called it my magic trick, but I didn't think it was real magic."

"Tell me more about it."

She did, explaining how she'd always had a knack for donning a façade to appear a certain way to others. Most often, she used it to seem composed and regal. To gain respect. Then she explained how she'd honed that talent into something else, to rid herself of unwanted suitors. That was when she'd begun using the term *magic trick*, for it had worked splendidly. Miraculously.

"All I needed to know," Mareleau said, "was what my suitor wanted to see and what they feared to see."

"How did you find out?"

"I just...knew. It didn't take many conversations or encounters with my suitors to figure it out. I knew from what they talked about and what they didn't talk about. I knew from how they acted and reacted."

"That sounds like claircognizance—clear knowing. My daughter has that gift. She's honing her Art for dream divination. Someone will tell her about their dream, and she simply knows its meaning. Other times, she suddenly knows something will or won't happen. Like how she knew Cora would come yesterday."

"I've never done anything nearly as impressive as that."

"Explain more about what you have done then. How have you used what you know to craft a glamour?"

Mareleau shrugged. "In the past, I've simply portrayed the traits my suitors disliked or expressed myself in a way that countered what they did like. I'd make a suitor who wanted a cold and distant wife see me as clingy and smoth-ering. I'd make a suitor who wanted a vapid, easy, and beau-tiful wife see me as cunning, difficult, and ugly."

She'd crafted the latter glamour on the last suitor her parents had tried to pair her with before they'd agreed to let her host the Heart's Hunt. Frederick had nearly won her over. Not her heart, of course, for that had always belonged to Larylis, even when she'd been tricked into thinking he'd abandoned her. Yet Frederick had almost won her hand, a marriage alliance built on common interests. That was before she'd discovered he'd been dallying with her best friend and lady's maid, Katra, and had even promised to make the girl his mistress. She'd delighted in using her magic trick on him then, watching his face turn pale as she'd let her posture sag, let her expression shift into some-thing hideous. Even now, the corners of her lips curled up, vindictive pride igniting in her chest.

Salinda narrowed her eyes. "Have you always cast glam-ours—or used this magic trick, as you call it—for personal gain?"

"I suppose so." Why did she feel like she was admitting to a bad thing? Who wouldn't use whatever was at their disposal for personal gain? Perhaps she delighted a little too much in tormenting the people who'd hurt her, but...well, she certainly wasn't going to admit that.

Salinda's brows knit together as she absently rocked a now-sleeping Noah. "Your mother is likely a clairaudient witch, and we know you inherited Ailan's Elvyn blood from one of your parents. We can assume it was through your father."

"Is that significant?"

"Elvyn-witch hybrids are rare, considering there are no

living Elvyn aside from Ailan. That we know of, at least. It may be possible..."

"What's possible?"

"I believe you're a narcuss. It's a rare Art, so we know very little about it. I've always believed a narcuss to be the shadow of the empath, projecting emotions outward instead of taking others' emotions in. But you seem to utilize claircognizance to project the outcome you want. You change what a person sees and knows about you, forcing an impression."

Mareleau's stomach sank. The way Salinda described a narcuss left little to be desired. Forcing an impression? Projecting an outcome she wanted? Those terms made her seem more like a villain than a witch. "Aren't there other kinds of witches who do something similar, other than... whatever a narcuss is?"

"Somewhat, but the reason I believe you're a narcuss is because the last witch who we know for certain had that power was also an Elvyn-witch hybrid. It could be that the Art of the narcuss is exclusive to that combination."

Mareleau sat forward eagerly. "You know another narcuss?"

"I wouldn't say I ever knew him personally." Her tone held a wary note.

That was enough for Mareleau to put the pieces together. "You're talking about Morkai, aren't you?"

Salinda's nod of confirmation sent Mareleau's stomach roiling.

"I...have the same magic as *Morkai*?"

"It doesn't have to be a bad thing," Salinda said, softening her expression. "I didn't mean to make it seem that way. We just don't have many examples of one using that magic for good. But you can choose how you use it. You may have used it for personal gain before, but there is nothing inherently wrong with that. And as you overcome your personal challenge, you'll find other ways to use your Art, and your magic will grow stronger."

"What do you mean by personal challenge?"

"Every witch grows their magic by overcoming challenges that are personal to them and their Art. Most often, a witch is confronted with the option of doing what feels easiest versus what feels most difficult, what goes against their base instincts. Only you will know what that challenge is, but it very well may be using your Art in a way that feels unnatural. Using it to help others instead of for personal gain."

"Like how I want to learn magic to protect Noah? Isn't that counter to what a narcuss would do?"

"Perhaps," Salinda said. "Yet always question such lines of thinking. As a narcuss, it will be easy to convince yourself that what you do for personal gain is for another's sake. I'm sure Morkai justified all his actions that way."

Her gut turned again. Seven devils, she was right. Teryn had discovered exactly that while trapped in the crystal. How Morkai—Desmond, as he was called before he took on the new name—had originally sought answers for his father, all in the hopes that Darius would resurrect his dead mother. After Emylia died, he'd sought the power of the Morkaius so that he could eventually bring her back. Morkai had believed his dark intentions were selfless.

But...but Mareleau wasn't like that. Was she?

"Am I being selfish for wanting to protect my son? All I want is for him to be safe."

"Why?"

"Why? What do you mean *why*? Because I love him, that's why. Because I want him to live a long, healthy life.

Because I want to see him grow up and experience being his mother—" The words caught in her throat.

"Because *you* want to experience that."

Mareleau thought she might be sick. Even her desire to protect her son ultimately came back to how it served her. Had she always been this way? Had every good feeling, every wish, every hope, been some desire born from her selfish, dark heart—

"There is nothing wrong with wanting those things for yourself." Salinda's voice came out firm. "I didn't say any of that to condemn you, only to demonstrate just how great your challenge might be. Just how subtle the divide between what you do for others and what you do for yourself. Being a narcuss does not make you evil."

Her shoulders sank nonetheless. "What do I do then? How do I ensure I don't end up like...like *him*?"

"Seek the truth inside yourself. Question what you think you know. If you meet darkness, simply bring it to light. Acknowledge it. When you feel those selfish undercurrents running through you, admit them, then let them be. You need not outrun your nature. Just don't let it control you. When you feel a challenge to counter your base instincts, face it. If you fail, forgive yourself and move on."

"You make it sound easy."

"It isn't easy, but you're not alone. A narcuss isn't the only one who faces their darkest side. We all do."

"Even you?"

"Especially me. You saw how quickly I turned my heart against someone I've loved my whole life."

"You mean Ailan? That's understandable. She lied to you. She pretended to be dying to avoid confronting the truth." A cloud of guilt reflected back, reminding her that she could relate to Ailan's actions. She'd pretended to be pregnant, after all.

"Perhaps, perhaps not. What matters is I saw my dark feelings, my hate, my anger, and I called them into the light. I revealed them and released them. I'm still angry and confused. I'm also hopeful that I can forgive her. It is a choice to follow the path of hope and love, even when dark feelings remain. Strength isn't being good or perfect. It's meeting your darkness face to face and moving forward instead of sinking into it. No matter what you find in those shadows, it is important that you love yourself."

Love herself? She'd never had a problem putting herself first, but had she ever truly loved herself? Not especially. She was flawed and had done terrible things in the past, but...could she love those sides of her? Truly love them?

Larylis' voice echoed through her head, warming her heart.

Someone who loved you, petals, thorns, and all.

Well, if he could love her through all her lies, schemes, and manipulations, maybe she could do the same.

She released a slow sigh. "I'll try."

"That's all you ever have to do. Just try."

Mareleau gathered Noah back into her arms and left Salinda's tent. She hadn't gotten the answers she'd wanted. She hadn't learned a stitch of magic.

Yet she'd learned a little more about herself, a side she'd never known. Maybe that side of her—the side she shared with a villain she despised—could somehow prove useful in facing the villain that lay ahead.

31

Teryn hated how quickly relief could turn to dread.

He scanned the letter in his hands three times over, his stomach sinking deeper with each repetition. He'd been so elated to see Berol. She'd caught his eye while he'd been meeting with Master Arther and Ridine's head mason regarding repairs on the keep roof and destroyed battlement. He'd hardly been able to focus on inspecting the parapets and discussing repairs when all he'd wanted was the letter curled in Berol's talon. Yet she'd kept her distance until Teryn's guests had left and he was alone on the battlement.

Now the wind cut his cheeks, threatening to tear the letter from his fingertips, as he read the note once more. Then, with a sigh, he pocketed the letter and leaned over the parapet wall, elbows propped upon the chest-high crenel before him. Berol hopped down from one of the merlons and nipped at his arm. Absently, he fed her a strip of dried venison.

Cora's letter contained good news. They'd found the

Forest People as planned. Mareleau was no longer targeted by the dragons. They'd found a solution to return the dragons to where they'd come from and had even found Ailan.

At least that's what he'd determined from the sparse details her letter contained.

> *We found who we've been looking for. Not just the many I sought, but the one. She has promised to keep her kin safe and has control over the troublesome beasts. I will attend a meeting with her people to form an alliance and will come home as soon as I can.*

Those were the lines that had required the most repetition. From the way she'd avoided stating names and locations, she was being cautious in case Berol was intercepted by the enemy. It was a practical choice yet a maddening one. He wished she'd simply spelled it all out so that he didn't have to guess. But what other conclusion could he come to? They'd found Ailan and would next find the tear and bring the dragons back through it. Mareleau and Noah would be protected behind the Veil, and Cora would try to forge an alliance with the Elvyn.

There was hope in her letter. A miraculous hope at that. Finding Ailan hadn't been part of the plan, only a feeble wish. Yet somehow Cora had found her amongst the Forest People. And an alliance with the Elvyn could be exactly what they needed to defeat Darius. He had two armies, after all—the naval forces he'd launched from Syrus and the forces he'd gained from his alliance with Norun. To defeat him, they needed more soldiers than he had. More strength.

Yet that hope led to dread, for it meant Cora was going farther away. It meant he had even less of an idea where she was, if she was safe, or when she'd return.

I miss you. I love you. I'll return.

That was how the letter ended. He'd trust those words, even if they did nothing to lift the heaviness in his heart.

"You should have gone with Cora."

Berol cocked her head, but Teryn hadn't been talking to her.

A faint figure had formed beside him.

Emylia crossed her arms and leaned against the parapet. "You wanted me to act as your messenger bird as well?"

"Now that I'm reminded how practical and cautious my darling wife can be in writing, I realize you would have served as a better way to glean solid information."

"At least you know she's safe."

Neither of them said what lingered unspoken. That she was safe...*for now*. And now that Berol had left Cora's side, he wasn't sure when he'd get another update.

Berol nipped his arm again. At first he thought she was asking for more treats. While that may be the case, it reminded him of the second letter that had been rolled up with the first. He hadn't dared read it, for it had been addressed to Larylis. That isn't to say he wasn't tempted, for there was a chance Mareleau hadn't been as careful with her words and information as Cora had. She may have shared more details that would give Teryn a clearer idea of their situation. And yet, whatever she wrote was meant for his brother. He wouldn't cross that boundary.

With great reluctance, he turned the scroll over to Berol, along with another strip of meat.

"To Larylis." He didn't mention where to find him, for he was likely still on the road. Berol had demonstrated a remarkable knack for finding those she was familiar with no matter where they were. He trusted she'd find Larylis too.

Berol took the letter and flew off the battlement. He watched as she quickly turned into a speck in the distance.

"Cora will be fine," Emylia said. "You know how strong she is."

He did know, but seven devils, this situation was devolving into unknown territory. Quite literally, in some respects. There was so much they still didn't know. So much they couldn't plan for. Cora's vague details only contributed to that untethered feeling.

His gaze drifted from the sky—Berol no longer in sight —to the landscape. Thankfully it was free of smoke and the shadows of wings and had been since the night before. No wonder he hadn't gotten any new reports of fiery destruction or dragon sightings. If Cora had found Ailan, and Ailan had control over the dragons, that was one less problem he had to address.

Though addressing problems was something he thrived on. Planning for repairs, holding audiences, offering reparations to those who'd lost their homes and crops to dragon fire...he'd been trained for these things his whole life. As troublesome as these matters were, staying busy kept the edge off his restlessness. Moving, acting, problem-solving— serving as king consort while Cora was away—gave him purpose. Robbed him of opportunities to panic.

Something moved far below in his periphery, drawing his gaze to the charred field that marred the castle lawn. There a pale semi-transparent figure wandered across the dead earth. At first he thought Emylia had transported herself there, but no, she was still at his side.

He narrowed his eyes until he could make out the

distinct shape of the wraith, a ghostly sword at its side. Its eyes were hollow holes.

He cast a questioning look at Emylia. "Is that..."

"One of Morkai's warrior wraiths?" She nodded. "I think so."

He didn't like to recall how aggressively the wraiths had fought at Centerpointe Rock. Before that, Morkai had demonstrated his ghastly army's capabilities on the very charred field the wraith wandered over now. Proved how deadly they could be when he forced a servant to face his hoard.

"How did he get the wraiths to follow him?" Teryn asked.

"He did what he'd always done. He used a blood weaving. He burned the castle garden to ash, offering death for life."

"And that's all they needed to fall under his command?"

"No, it was more complicated than that. He shared a connection to those wraiths, through his father. The wraiths he called to him were the souls of those who'd fought in El'Ara for Darius."

Teryn remembered what Morkai had said about the wraiths during his demonstration.

Spirits from a nearly forgotten war.

They died trapped between two realms...

Now they serve me.

"They died in the fae realm," Emylia said, "yet their souls were tethered to the human realm. Their heart-centers were torn from them, leaving them as empty, hollow spirits, unable to cross to the otherlife. Without one's heart-center, they have no attachment to the otherlife, no reason to go home. Yet without a heart-center, they remain forever hungry. Lost. That is where tales of vengeful and violent spirits come from."

So that was why wraiths were so different from ghosts. Ghosts had unfinished business like Emylia or were desperate to cling to the lives they'd had like some of the ones he'd seen in the castle. Wraiths, on the other hand, had lost the very thing that made them want anything. They were hungry but didn't even know what for.

Emylia spoke again. "He used that hunger to his advantage. With his own blood, he wove an attraction enchantment that called the wraiths to Ridine. The wraiths were drawn to his blood because they sensed their former master's in it—Darius, the king they'd served and fought for, the man who'd fueled their sense of purpose when they'd been alive.

"Once Morkai drew the wraiths to the castle grounds, he sacrificed the garden and gave them sentience, and the ability to act as if they were alive, able to wield their weapons and end lives. After that, they chose to follow him. He gave them what every wraith craves—a purpose. He promised them a battle that would help them atone for the mission they'd failed to complete for their former master. Furthermore, he'd end their wandering torment by giving them the peace they couldn't find on their own. Once he had the power of the Morkaius, he would lay their etheras to rest.

"Lay them to rest? How would he do that?"

"Magic can exorcise spirits, though I don't know if Morkai had truly cared enough about their fate to plan that far ahead."

"That's really all it took for him to gain an army of souls? Spill his blood, give them a purpose that harkened back to their former lives, and promise an end to their wandering?"

"No, there was more to it than that. His army was flawed at first. They could only maintain sentience for short stints once they began fighting, and if they were defeated in combat, that would often be enough to end their bloodlust. That was when he forged a connection between them and his Roizan. It allowed them to reanimate again and again, never tiring."

He stared down at the wraith, watching as it wandered aimlessly over the charred field. "Are the wraiths still dangerous? If he sacrificed the garden to give them sentience, do they still have it? Can they still kill, or can they only wander the field that gave them life?"

"Maybe they could be dangerous if they had a purpose again, but that died with Morkai." Emylia frowned, turning narrowed eyes to him. "Why are you so interested?"

Something dark echoed in his chest, and he realized he wasn't questioning Morkai's actions out of idle curiosity. There was a part of him that wanted to figure out what he'd done, to study it from every angle. And a much smaller, quieter part of him that wondered if he could do it too.

He'd already painted with blood. He'd worked blood magic and now knew how simple it was. Not easy, but simple. Just a pattern. A formula.

"Do not lust after blood magic," Emylia said. "There's a reason it's forbidden. There are repercussions."

She was right, and he shuddered at his own thoughts. At how alluring they were, despite knowing he shouldn't have them. Yet something in him had changed last summer, as subtle a change as it was. He'd greeted death. Had danced with it. Defeated it. It didn't repulse him the way it once had, and there was a faint piece of it that stayed with him still, evident in his ability to see spirits. Was that one of the repercussions Emylia was referring to?

He glanced at the warrior wraith again. It walked in slow, hapless circles at the center of the field.

Then it halted.

Turned around.

And lifted its hollow, eyeless gaze to Teryn.

His breath caught as he was struck with a sudden yearning for...

For what?

He didn't know, nor was he sure the yearning was coming from him. It almost felt as if it was coming from the wraith.

Teryn took a step away from the parapet.

The wraith blinked, then averted its gaze. After a few moments of stillness, it proceeded to cross the field and disappeared at the end of it.

Teryn's heart slammed against his ribs. Most spirits avoided him, or at the very least ignored him. But that one...

What was the yearning he'd felt?

"What's happened to me?" he said under his breath. "Why can I see spirits? Why has death chosen to cling to me?"

And if it hadn't chosen to cling to him...then had he chosen to cling to it?

"I don't know." Emylia nibbled her lip. Her wary expression reminded him of when they were locked in the crystal together and she'd hidden information from him.

He fully faced her and took a step closer. She launched a step back, her expression wild with sudden fear.

That wasn't the first time she'd reacted like that.

It reminded him of the ghost in the council room the other day. The one who'd fled after she'd gotten close to him.

He narrowed his eyes. "What aren't you telling me? Why have you been afraid of me?"

She wrung her semi-transparent hands. "It's just...when I get close to you, I feel...I don't know what I feel. It's just this sense that...that I'll cease to exist."

"What does that mean—" His words cut off as approaching footsteps interrupted their unsettling conversation.

"I don't know," Emylia whispered and disappeared before him.

He turned to find Captain Alden striding across the battlement. A small ember of hope ignited in his chest. He'd tasked her with questioning the spy again to see if they could get any more information. If they could just get a little more insight into Darius' plans...

Alden stopped before him with a bow, but when she straightened, her face was pale.

"Report," Teryn said.

"It's...the spy, Majesty."

"Have you gotten more intel from—"

"He's dead. The spy is dead, and it wasn't an accident."

Teryn's mind went blank and he nearly huffed a laugh. He'd been foolish to hope. The last of it drained from his body as Alden finished her report, detailing how they'd found the spy's body in his cell, how his face had been beaten nearly to a pulp.

Teryn replied with a calm he didn't feel, agreed with her conclusion that the spy had been purposefully silenced after revealing information about the naval fleet. When she left, he faced the parapet once more and pounded a fist upon the stone crenel.

He was supposed to solve problems. He was supposed to protect Ridine while Cora was away. Instead, he'd lost their only asset to help them gain intel on the enemy. And worst of all, if the spy had been silenced in the dungeon, that meant something far worse.

There was a traitor somewhere in the castle.

32

For three days, Cora and her companions searched for the tear, traveling mostly at night. This, of course, was to limit the possibility of dragon sightings. There was no way to know if Darius didn't already have eyes in Khero, seeking signs of the tear. He already had spies in her kingdom, or at least his Norunian allies did. And now that a third dragon had joined Ferrah and Uziel—proof that the creatures would continue to pour out of El'Ara in search of Ailan and Mareleau—it was even more imperative that they return them to the Veil.

The road was cloaked in predawn shadows and a faint wash of moonlight as Cora rode beside Ailan's wagon. The wagon was pulled by a pair of the Forest People's horses while Valorre served as Cora's mount—his idea, for he seemed to have taken a liking to his fashionable saddle. Or perhaps he was jealous of the new horses.

When they'd set out for tonight's journey, Ailan had insisted they'd find the tear before sunrise. Cora was surprised that the Veil had torn so close to Ailan and not closer to Ridine where Noah had been born. When Cora had asked her about this, Ailan had explained that even though Noah's birth had caused the surge of *mora* that split the Veil, Ailan was still regent over El'Ara's magic and would be until he came of age. The *mora* was just as desperate to reach her as it was to find its Morkara.

Wings beat the starlit sky overhead, and a dark silhouette rose above the tree line. Cora's hands flinched, one toward the bow at her back, the other toward the quiver of arrows attached to the saddle. She smothered her defensive instincts to draw her weapons and settled for grasping the hilt of her dagger—the beautiful gift Teryn had given her—as she watched the dragon carry off some unfortunate creature in its talons. From the dragon's massive size, it was Uziel. He flew over the road to the other side, where the landscape ended in a steep cliffside. His silhouette dipped beyond the cliff, likely to devour his prey upon the beach far below. Ailan had promised the dragons would cease burning crops and stealing livestock, upon her order, but they still needed to feed. Thankfully, they did so out of sight.

I still don't like them much, Valorre conveyed. *Now that I have my memories, I recall my kind has never gotten along with theirs. Too unrefined.*

Is that so? Cora stifled a laugh and wondered if all unicorns were as arrogant as Valorre.

What the fornication is he even eating? His prey was almost as large as me.

What I'd like to know, Cora said, *is where you got these strange expletives from.*

Strange? How are they strange? The sentinels at the castle walls use them all the time in conversation.

Is that what you do when I'm not around? Wander the perimeter and listen in on the sentinels' private gossip? Cora chuckled. *Regardless, I think you've misunderstood. The words you use aren't quite the same as theirs.*

Yes, well, I could hardly comprehend what the sentinels' words meant at first. Once I gleaned their meaning, I decided to use far more concise variations. I'll have you know that makes me more refined and more creative. I can use better words than shit, crap, devils, and fu—

I get it. You're oh so clever and refined with your foul language.

Thank you. I knew you'd agree.

Cora rolled her eyes.

I'm nothing like these fatherless sons, he said with a huff at the two horses pulling the wagon, Ailan at the reins. *They haven't a thought in their heads. Look how much taller I am! Look how much faster I can trot!*

"No you don't," Cora said out loud, tone sharp. "I know you're faster, larger, and smarter, but you don't need to show off."

Valorre mentally scoffed but resisted his urge to race ahead.

Ailan released a soft chuckle from the box seat. "You have a strong relationship with him, don't you? He's your familiar."

"Yes, he is." Some of her mirth died down. Even after traveling with Ailan for three days, she still hadn't fully warmed to her. The same went for Mareleau, who often treated the woman with downright coldness. She couldn't blame her.

Cora cast a glance down the length of the wagon, finding all the shutters closed with no sign of light behind them. Mareleau and Noah must be asleep.

Ailan spoke again. "I imagine it is like my bond with

Uziel. The Elvyn don't call them familiars, as that term belongs to witches, but the connection is the same."

Cora was caught between curiosity and her steady apprehension of Ailan. She fought past the latter and gave in to the former. "Do Elvyn bond with other creatures besides dragons?"

"No, only dragons, and only the Morkara and their descendants can bond with them. Even so, the dragons can refuse to bond with certain people, regardless of bloodline. That was what happened with Darius. It very well might be what set everything into motion."

Cora nudged Valorre's side to bring him closer to the wagon. The road was plenty wide, but Cora's curiosity made her want to draw nearer. "What do you mean?"

She opened her mouth but didn't utter a word. Maybe she didn't know where to start. When she did manage to speak, her eyes were distant, her gaze hovering over the star-dappled sea that stretched beyond the cliffside. "My brother's jealousy knew no bounds. He hated me from the moment I was born. You know about my brother's father? The prince who worldwalked into El'Ara and stole my mother's heart?"

"Tristaine," Cora said. "I learned about him in El'Ara. How Satsara was sent to weave a ward around him that would banish him from the fae realm, but she fell in love with him instead."

Ailan nodded. "Shortly after Darius was born, she relayed the truth of his parentage to her consort and tribunal."

"Her consort..." Cora was reminded of something she'd yet to mention. "Etrix. He was Satsara's consort and...and your father, right?"

Ailan's gaze sharpened as she whipped her face toward Cora. "Yes. How did you—"

"I met him. He, Fanon, and an Elvyn named Garot were the ones who found me."

"You met my father."

"He and Garot were...relatively kind to me."

Ailan's lips turned down. "I'm sorry Fanon was unkind. I...I can't imagine how the years have felt for him. I've had over five hundred years away from him, but it hasn't been nearly so long for him. More like seventy-five years, based on the discrepancy in the passage of time between here and El'Ara. He must still cling to hope that I'll return, yet at the same time, the truthweavers must have heard the same whispers that have spoken to me. He will know I've furthered my bloodline in the human world. Essentially moving on from him."

"Were the two of you in love?" Maybe it was a silly question. In the human world, political alliances were often loveless, and Satsara's affair with Tristaine suggested her relationship with Etrix may have been the same. But just like Cora had been blessed with a marriage to a man she loved, maybe the same happened in El'Ara.

"We were," Ailan said, her expression turning distant once more. "I didn't expect to love him, but I did, and he loved me fiercely in return. It surprised us both. The Morkara and their heirs are paired strategically with their consorts to grant honors to great Elvyn families, much like human royal marriages. Neither of us expected love."

"What about Satsara and Etrix?"

"Ah, that brings me back to what I'd been trying to explain. Their pairing had been far colder than mine and Fanon's was. They both had lovers, as that is commonplace for many Elvyn.

And unlike human rules of succession, only the Morkara's bloodline counts when passing the role to their heirs. The Morkara's heir can be born from any partner they choose. So when my mother conceived Tristaine's child, the only alarming thing about it was that the child was half human. By then, Satsara and Etrix had begun to form a warm relationship, a love born from friendship and honesty. She admitted to her newborn son's origins and that she'd never banished the human she'd been sent to exile years ago. The tribunal agreed to treat her son with the same respect a pureblood Elvyn heir would receive, so long as she banished Tristaine once and for all. She agreed and raised Darius as her precious prince.

"After several years, Satsara and Etrix grew closer, eventually developing a physical relationship and bringing me into the world. Naturally, the tribunal favored me over Darius, for even though they treated Darius with the reverence required, they remained suspicious at heart. Their misgivings only solidified as he grew older and discovered his ability to worldwalk. What started as simple pranks—startling the servants, sneaking into places he shouldn't go—evolved into dangerous acts. He managed to worldwalk to his father in Syrus somehow, which opened his ability to travel to the human world. From there he'd bring in human captives, sometimes for pleasure, but other times for trickery and torment, abandoning them in the woods and watching how they fared or setting fae creatures upon them."

Cora's stomach turned. All the childhood faerytales that described vicious fae and deadly tricks now seemed chillingly real. But there was something that left her even more unsettled.

"How did Darius worldwalk to Syrus? Had Satsara allowed Tristaine to take him there before she'd banished him, or do his abilities work differently from mine?"

"His abilities work like yours," Ailan said. "He only ever worldwalked to places he'd been before. I never learned how he'd managed to worldwalk to Syrus the first time. Tristaine first found El'Ara unintentionally. Maybe Darius' journey was accidental too."

Ailan was right about Tristaine. He was a clairalient witch who'd first found the fae realm by following a scent. If she remembered Garot's tale correctly, that had been on Samhain, when the veils between worlds were thinnest. Perhaps the same phenomenon had allowed Darius to find his father.

Ailan continued. "As much as my mother doted on her son, not even she could deny how dangerous he was becoming. He'd already reached maturity, and I was approaching it myself. The tribunal urged her to wait to choose her heir until I came of age, just to give us an equal chance at proving our worth. Mother clung to her hope that Darius would change, clung to the child that represented her first love.

"Then came the turning point. I reached maturity and was allowed to try to bond a dragon. Darius had been rejected four times, and the tribunal was beginning to worry Berolla's hatchlings were too wild for bonding. But I was deeply drawn to the eldest and largest of Berolla's progeny —Uziel. We bonded almost as soon as I'd begun the ritual."

Cora couldn't help the grimace that tugged her lips. She'd been forced to attempt that ritual herself with Ferrah and had nearly been burned to a crisp.

Ailan's face fell. "Darius was jealous. He sought to disrupt the ritual by startling my mother's dragon. He worldwalked in front of me and lifted his chin at Berolla—a disrespectful gesture one should never make to a dragon one has not gained the approval of. Berolla swiped out in a rage but Darius disappeared just in time, leaving me to bear the slash of her talons. Uziel swept me aside before the gash turned fatal, but I was still badly wounded.

"Darius wept pitiful tears, begging for my forgiveness, insisting it had only been a prank to test my bond with Uziel. But the tribunal turned firmly against him once and for all. My mother was finally forced to admit that her son was far more treacherous than she wanted to believe. Giving in to the wisdom of everyone around her, and her love for me, she named me heir and prepared to banish her beloved son, the same way she'd exiled Tristaine."

Cora remembered Garot explaining Satsara's attempt. An attempt that failed when Darius realized his mother was trying to weave a ward around him. "He escaped."

"He did," Ailan said. "He used his powers to escape to Syrus before her ward was completed. I'm sure you know the rest. Years later he returned to El'Ara, waging war upon the realm to claim his place as Morkaius of El'Ara. He had Syrus' military strength by then and used his abilities plus the discrepancy of time to constantly barrage our forces. He could worldwalk with entire groups of soldiers at once, then leave and return with more in the blink of an eye. When he needed to retreat and regroup, he could take a week to recover while we had only a day. He was relentless, and his men were armed with iron—the deadliest metal to faekind. Even superficial wounds with iron could be lethal for our fighters, where normally only excessive blood loss, beheading, or voluntary Last Breath could end our lives."

Cora couldn't imagine the terror of constant war, yet it did help her understand—at least somewhat—the disdain Fanon had treated her with. Darius had used his abilities in horrifying ways, even before he'd resorted to war. Playing vicious pranks, taking human captives for his own amusement. He certainly wasn't a glowing endorsement for witches. While she still resented having been treated so cruelly, the Elvyn had no other example to go by. No reason to trust humans or witches when the only ones they'd met had caused harm.

"I'm surprised you don't blame witches like those in El'Ara do," Cora said. "You lived alongside them. Welcomed them into the commune. Appointed them as elders to sit beside you. Or was that only because you'd lost your memories?"

"It is true I forgot many details regarding myself and Darius, but I don't think I could have resented all witches, even if I'd remembered. Witches, fae, non-magical humans...we're all the same. There is good and evil in all of us, and I don't think Darius' heritage as a witch is the reason for his darkness. Maybe my mother was too naive and didn't try to guide him away from his darker instincts. Maybe Tristaine was responsible for filling his head with blood and violence. Whatever the case, I do hope to change the minds of Fanon and those who share his prejudices. They will need to change if we are to ally our peoples and stand against Darius."

"Are you anxious about seeing Fanon again?" Cora asked, only to realize what a personal question that was. She continued to cling to a rebellious fire that kept her from wanting to get too close to Ailan. At the same time, she had loved Nalia, and the more they talked, the more Cora was beginning to merge the two identities in her mind.

"I am," Ailan confessed. "Romantic relationships are hardly my priority, but I can't help wondering if there's a future for us. After our most pressing matters are taken care of."

Cora's heart softened. "Will he really be so angry that you moved on? He knows it's been five hundred years for you."

She shook her head. "He's a stubborn creature, and he's always wanted me all to himself. He never liked the idea of taking lovers or treating our relationship like anything but a committed union between us. I felt the same, of course, but things changed when I was trapped in the human world. Not only were my memories of Fanon disappearing, but I had only the whispers of my weavings to guide me. Once humans discovered the new land that had sprouted from the southern edge of Risa, my whispers urged me to integrate with society and bear heirs. I didn't experience love again, not like I had with Fanon, but I did start a family."

Cora knew Ailan had had children, but Cora hadn't pictured Ailan with a family. A husband. Sons and daughters. "How long did you live in human society before you settled with the Forest People?"

"Once my children and grandchildren died, I felt the whispers calling me away. I met my great-grandchildren, but they didn't cling to me the way my closer kin had, for they had many other relatives. Besides, I couldn't appear to live forever, even with how my appearance had aged."

"Were none of your children immortal, even with the Elvyn blood they'd inherited from you?"

She shook her head. "They aged the same as any human."

"Then how is Darius still alive? Morkai used blood magic to extend his life, but from what you've said about Darius, he's as immortal as you are. Can he even be killed?"

"He can be killed just like the rest of my kind—beheading or excessive blood loss. He heals relatively fast, so a minor wound won't do. Even running him through with a sword won't do much, for he merely disappears, removes the weapon, and heals. But he can be killed so long as he can be outsmarted. And as for your first question, I believe his immortality is due to being born in El'Ara and remaining in the line of succession. If Noah or I perish, Darius still has a chance to claim rule. Until my brother dies, the *mora* will recognize that and fuel his life."

When she put it that way, Cora couldn't help but question Ailan's choices. If she'd died without any heirs, the *mora* could have chosen a new bloodline from someone still behind the Veil in El'Ara. But like Ailan had said then, there was no way to know what the repercussions would have been. Would the new Morkara have been able to fix the Veil and return El'Ara's heart? Would Morkai still have been born to wreak havoc on the human world?

None of them had the answers to *what if*. Yet it did bring to mind a question she'd yet to ask. One Maiya had voiced. Since then, it had clouded Cora's heart.

"What happens to Lela after we defeat Darius? When I asked if you could seal the tear in the Veil, you said it was more complicated than that, because sealing the tear wouldn't bring El'Ara's heart back. So what will you do instead?"

Ailan met Cora's gaze, lips pursed. "I don't know yet, and neither of us may like the answer when we find it."

A chill ran down Cora's spine. She opened her mouth to ask her to elaborate when Ailan tugged the reins and brought her wagon to an abrupt stop. Cora halted Valorre beside it. "What is it?"

Ailan's gaze was fixed at the edge of the cliffside. "It's here," Ailan said, voice breathless. "We've found the tear."

33

Cora dismounted Valorre and watched from the road as Ailan approached the edge of the cliff. The dark sea stretched out toward the horizon while the first blush of dawn slowly crept from behind the mountains in the east. Cora's heart climbed higher into her throat with every step Ailan took toward the cliff's edge. It triggered her instinctual terror to witness something so outwardly dangerous. But according to Ailan, the tear lay at the very edge.

Don't fear for her, Valorre said, nuzzling her shoulder. *She's right. I can feel the tear just ahead.*

Uziel shot up from the other side of the cliff, finished with whatever beast he'd taken to the beach to consume. He landed with a thud down the road. The rustling in the woods behind Cora told her Ferrah and the third dragon were nearby too.

The wagon door swung open and Mareleau emerged with Noah in her arms. Her eyelids were heavy with sleep and her silvery tresses were plaited in a messy braid down her back. "What's happened? Did we—oh, devils."

Mareleau's gaze caught Ailan's figure at the edge of the cliff. The woman stood with her hand outstretched, her patchwork petticoats billowing behind her on the early morning breeze.

Mareleau's shoulders fell. "Don't tell me..."

"Yep. The tear is inconveniently located at the edge of a godsdamned cliff."

Not a fan of cliffs, Valorre added.

Ailan continued to reach into the air before her as she took another step closer to the edge, then to the left. She leaned slightly forward...

Her fingertips disappeared.

She whirled toward them with a wide smile. "It's here. We can step through it."

"Or maybe plummet to our deaths," Mareleau said under her breath.

Valorre conveyed his agreement. *Not a fan of plummeting to my death.*

Ailan faced Uziel, who eagerly padded over to her, head low like an obedient puppy despite his massive size. She whispered something in the fae language to him, then stepped aside. The black dragon took her place at the edge of the cliff and charged forward without a hint of hesitation. His head disappeared first, then his sinuous neck. His enormous belly and hindquarters followed, then finally his tail. Now there was only sky. Ailan continued to watch the space until a black scaled snout protruded from nothingness. Uziel flicked his tongue and disappeared once more.

Ailan gave a satisfied nod. Then, angling her head over her shoulder, she spoke in her ancient language again. Ferrah darted from the forest toward the cliff in a blur of opalescent white, and a slightly smaller green dragon raced after her. Showing the same confidence Uziel had, they sprang off the cliff and disappeared beyond the Veil.

With the dragons gone, Ailan approached the wagon, lips curved in a frown. "There's no way we'll get the horses to step off a cliff. We'll have to hide the wagon somewhere off the road and set the horses free. Considering the difference in the passage of time, it would be inhumane to tether them, not knowing when any of us will be back."

Cora could agree with that, but...

"What about Mareleau?" she said. "We're going to make her walk with Noah through El'Ara?"

There was one solution, of course. Once they were on the other side of the Veil, Cora could try to worldwalk her companions to the meadow she and Valorre had accidentally traveled to last summer. Now that they'd accomplished their goal of locating the tear, it was no longer necessary to travel by traditional means. Still, she resisted bringing the option up. If there was one way to make her return to El'Ara even more unwelcome, it would be to worldwalk there.

"I do have legs, you know," Mareleau said with a withering stare.

Cora returned the look. "You also recently had a baby."

"I can still manage to walk."

I have a saddle. Valorre rippled with indignation. *And I'm quite comfortable to ride. Everyone knows this.*

"We won't need to walk far," Ailan said. "The Elvyn have woven triggers throughout the land that are set off by human intruders. A pathweaver will come straight to us."

That made sense, for that was exactly how the Elvyn had found her and Valorre when they'd entered El'Ara the first time. But Garot had been unable to use his pathweaving in the Blight—

The blood left Cora's face as she realized there was

another thing she hadn't discussed with Ailan. She'd assumed her whispers had told her, but...

"Ailan, do...do you know about the Blight?"

A furrow formed between her brows.

Mother Goddess, she didn't know. Cora desperately did not want to be the one to tell her, and she'd find out for herself soon enough. But didn't Ailan deserve a warning at least?

"The land around the Veil is dying," Cora confessed. "It's a consequence of the *mora* pouring from El'Ara into the human world and being unable to return. Your people call the dying land the Blight. Pathweavers can't use their magic to traverse that part of El'Ara. The triggers may not work there either."

Ailan paled with every word. "I didn't know. Though I should have. Of course there would be consequences to losing El'Ara's heart."

"Having to walk sounds like the least of our worries," Mareleau said in a dry tone that somehow alleviated Cora's guilt. Not that the Blight was in any way Cora's fault, yet she wished she'd have told Ailan sooner. Even Cora had been saddened to see the dead, colorless land of the Blight. She couldn't imagine how much worse it would be for someone who loved that land.

Ailan steeled her expression. "It changes nothing where our plans are concerned. Let's proceed."

THEY LEFT THE WAGON DEEP IN THE WOODS AWAY FROM THE road and set the two horses free. Valorre was rather smug about this, but Cora hoped the horses were intelligent enough to make their way back to the Forest People. The wagon itself would have to remain where it was. Thankfully, it posed little threat as evidence. There was nothing inside that would reveal it was ever home to Ailan, only that it belonged to a nomad. Anyone who stumbled upon it would likely assume the owner had met an ill fate while camped there.

Ailan shouldered Mareleau's bag of belongings while Cora touched each of her weapons in turn—bow, quiver, dagger. A comforting routine in preparation to step off a cliff and return to a realm she wasn't welcome in. Noah was nestled close to his mother's chest in the carrying sling Salinda had gifted Mareleau. Together the party left the woods and approached the road. Dawn was spilling farther over the landscape with every minute, requiring more caution as they crossed over to the cliffside. Cora's gaze darted left and right, her mental shields down, senses extended in case anyone approached. They were still alone. Still safe.

Ailan stepped to the edge and reached into the sky. Her hand disappeared at once. "Cora, do you want to go first?"

Devils, no, but what choice did she have? If Ailan went first, Cora and Mareleau would be left to find the tear on their own. And she wasn't going to make Mareleau go first.

Swallowing her fear, she took a step—

I think not, Valorre said darting in front of her. *I will test the safety of the tear. We can't rely on those inelegant dragons, after all.* With his head held high, he trotted toward Ailan's half-invisible hand. In a matter of heartbeats, he was gone.

Cora had to admit, her arrogant friend had emboldened her. With a fortifying breath, she stepped to the edge of the cliff and extended her hand near Ailan's until it plunged into nothingness. She paused, releasing her breath in a trembling exhale.

Then she stepped off the cliff...

And stepped onto colorless earth. The Blight was blindingly bright after the dim light of dawn, invading her senses with shades of gray. The only color was the cloud-speckled blue sky overhead.

Valorre stood before her, tossing his mane. Despite his earlier confidence, he radiated relief at seeing her hale and whole on this side of the Veil. Cora stepped out of the way to give room to her companions. The Veil was nothing more than a wall of swirling particles of pale mist. Even though it looked like something soft and insubstantial, she knew firsthand that it would feel as firm as a wall should she try to touch it. Aside from the tear, she supposed.

A hand shot through the mist, quickly followed by a body. Mareleau planted both feet before the Veil, her eyes squeezed tight, her arms wrapped protectively around Noah in his sling.

Cora put a hand on her shoulder. "You're all right, Mare. You made it."

Mareleau forced her eyes open and stumbled toward Cora. "That was terrifying."

A second later, Ailan followed, emerging from the mist with far more grace. But as her eyes darted across the landscape, her expression crumpled. Her hand flung to her lips, and she widened her stance as if to keep steady. "This is so much worse than I expected."

All around them was parched soil and the gnarled stumps of long-dead trees. There was no sign of the jewel-toned forests, groves, and meadows Cora had seen on her way to the Blight the first time she'd come here.

Tears glazed Ailan's eyes as she turned back toward the Veil. Extending a hand, she pressed her palm to the swirling particles. Cora watched with rapt attention. Did she know of a way to call the *mora* back? She had claimed to be regent over fae magic until Noah came of age.

With a frustrated groan, Ailan dropped her hand, her fingers curling into a fist. "The *mora* can be called back to the land, but the tear is too thin. It's like pulling it through the finest sieve. The effort to complete such a task...I don't even want to estimate how long it would take."

A shadow fell over them, bringing with it the beat of wings. A gust of wind sent gray soil swirling about as Uziel landed. Cora, Mareleau, and Valorre backed away as the dragon nuzzled Ailan's shoulder. It was similar enough to how Valorre comforted Cora that she could almost find it cute.

Almost.

Ailan's posture relaxed. She turned her gaze to Cora. "Does your magic work here?"

Cora nodded. She'd escaped El'Ara with her abilities before. Her magic hadn't been hampered by the Blight, nor had Fanon's or Etrix's. Fanon had still been able to use his invisible restraints while Etrix's translation weaving had remained. Only Garot seemed unable to weave in the Blight. The only thing that had held Cora back had been the collar she'd been burdened with.

Her skin crawled, remembering its tines piercing her neck, the empty void where her magic had been. She resisted the urge to tuck her hand in her cloak pocket, where the collar remained hidden. She hated carrying it on her person, bringing it to the very place where it had been used against her. But she couldn't have left it in the wagon. Not if she wanted to avoid leaving evidence behind.

"Will you use it?" Ailan said, stepping away from Uziel. "Will you take us somewhere beyond the Blight? Somewhere a pathweaver can reach us quickly?"

Cora's stomach turned. "Are you sure? My magic is hated here. Fanon will be enraged—"

"I don't care." Her voice was so tired. So empty. "I don't want to look at this dying land a second longer than I must. If anyone tries to condemn you for doing what I asked of you, they can take it up with me."

Cora gave a reluctant nod. "I'll try. Gather around me and Valorre."

At a word from Ailan, Uziel launched into the sky. Ailan and Mareleau followed Cora's directions, crowding in close. "We need to make physical contact, and I need to be touching Valorre. Do not break contact, even if I move."

She pressed a palm to Valorre's hide, then clasped Mareleau's palm with her free hand. Ailan settled her hand on Cora's shoulder. Closing her eyes, Cora focused on each point of contact in turn, then envisioned the meadow she and Valorre had traveled to. The image came to mind easily, courtesy of Valorre's clear memory. She shifted her stance, felt the dry earth beneath her shoes, and imagined the plush grass of the meadow. Instead of rot filling her senses, she imagined crisp air and fresh greenery. After acknowledging her companions once more—Mareleau's hand in hers, Noah's sleeping presence in his sling, Ailan's palm on her shoulder, then Valorre's warm hide—she took a small step forward.

She smelled the change of air before she opened her eyes. Heard hollow silence turn to birdsong. As she blinked into warm sunlight, she found the green meadow all around, her companions beside her. They stepped apart and a wave of dizziness washed over her, reminding her of the toll worldwalking with others took on her.

Then they waited.

But it didn't take long.

A swirling vortex of green and brown warped the air at the edge of the meadow until it was as wide as a doorway. Three familiar figures strode through it, one with dark hair, one with copper tresses, and one with honeyed locks and sharp blue eyes. Etrix, Garot, and Fanon. The vortex disappeared as soon as all three were outside it.

Fanon's lips peeled back from his teeth, his eyes widening as they landed on Cora.

Ailan stepped forward, arms spread, commanding the attention of the Elvyn males.

The three pulled up short.

Fanon's chest heaved as if he'd been struck by an invisible blow. He staggered back, but his legs gave out beneath him. He sank to his knees. "Ailan."

With a slow and careful stride, she approached Fanon, then softly laid a hand on his shoulder. "Hello, Fanon dear," she said, voice quavering. "It's been a long time."

34

Mareleau's cheeks heated. The reunion before her was chaste in every way, yet she could see the passion, yearning, and agony that filled the blond Elvyn's eyes. Tears streamed down his cheeks as he tipped his head back and whispered something Mareleau couldn't understand. She'd be more moved by the couple's reunion if she didn't know exactly who the blond was—Fanon, the Elvyn who'd been cruel to Cora.

Her gaze swept to the other two figures. They must be Etrix and Garot, the other two males Cora had told her about. Etrix was the tallest with umber skin and black hair braided with gold and silver thread. Garot was the shortest and widest of the three and had fiery hair, tan skin spattered with bronze freckles, and green eyes. All three appeared no more than ten years her senior, but there was something about them that made them seem ancient and ageless at the same time. Etrix carried himself in a way that made Mareleau think he was the eldest. All had pointed ears like Ailan and were dressed in silk trousers and matching robes belted with a wide sash. She didn't miss the sword each carried at their hips either.

Tightening her hold around Noah in his sling, she sidled closer to Cora and Valorre. She was grateful the attention was fully on Ailan and not them, but it didn't soothe her nerves. All around her was evidence of just how far from home she truly was. The meadow they stood in rippled with blades of grass as high as her calves and as green as the brightest emerald. Willow trees danced in the breeze, their long branches swaying with more motion than a tree should ever have. Butterflies alighted on rainbow-hued dewdrops and carried them away, but their wings were far too vibrant for a regular butterfly. And too plentiful; some had as many wings as a rose had petals. The birdsong that filled the air was melodic but unlike anything she'd heard. It was lovely and terrifying all at once. She wasn't sure whether she wanted to keep looking around the meadow in search of new surprises...or force her eyes to remain only on the familiar.

Ailan stepped away from Fanon. Her fingers lingered on Fanon's cheek for several long moments as she turned to face the other two.

Garot bent in a formal bow and said something in Elvyn. Ailan acknowledged the gesture with a hand to his shoulder. He beamed as he straightened. She approached Etrix next. His dark eyes were turned down at the corners and glazed with tears, yet his posture was stiff. He seemed uncertain how to greet her. Then Ailan folded against his chest, arms around his waist. He in turn wrapped his arms around her and rested his cheek against the top of her head.

Cora leaned in and whispered, "Etrix is Ailan's father."

That caught Fanon's attention. He'd risen to his feet and

now shot cold blue eyes their way. While the snarl he'd first worn was gone, there was no warmth in his expression.

Mareleau's first instinct was to shrink beneath that open hostility, but she wasn't made for shrinking. Instead, she lifted her chin and held his gaze right back with an equally cold stare, eyes narrowing until he finally looked away. She resisted the urge to laugh. That had been too easy. She hadn't even employed her magic trick. Or her Art, as Cora and Salinda called it. Either way, the Elvyn were mistaken if they thought they could beat her at a glaring contest. If anyone could destroy a man with a look alone, it was Mareleau.

Ailan released Etrix from her embrace and asked him something in that same incomprehensible language. With a nod, Etrix took a step back and lifted a hand. Then, crossing two of his fingers, he slid them through the air in a horizontal line.

"Translation enchantment," Cora explained, but she hadn't needed to, for when Fanon spoke next, Mareleau understood him.

"Will you tell us why *they're* here?"

With a smile, Ailan gestured toward Cora. "This is my dear friend and ally, Cora. Formally, she is Aveline Caelan, Queen of Khero."

"So we meet again," Garot said, his face splitting with an easy grin. His gaze shifted to Valorre. "Your friend as well. What a dashing little vest he's wearing. A bit clunky, but—"

"Do you know what she is?" Fanon jutted his chin toward Cora, a motion that carried as much violence as a raised blade. "Do you know she's a witch? A worldwalker? And what in the *mora's* name is that unicorn wearing?"

Mareleau had forgotten how strange it might be to see a unicorn in a saddle, but she was used to the sight by now.

Valorre snorted in response, a derisive sound even to her ears.

"I know exactly what and who she is," Ailan said, ignoring the jibe at Valorre. "I have known her for many years. And based on what she's told me, I am not pleased by how you've treated her in the past."

Fanon paled but said nothing in his defense.

"If you're done making my ally feel unwelcome," Ailan said, "I have someone else I'd like you to meet. Pray you get your salutations right this time around."

She left the three Elvyn to stand at Mareleau's side, then placed a gentle hand on her shoulder. "This is the blood of my blood, Mareleau Alante, Queen of Vera."

"*Khero* and *Vera* mean nothing to us," Etrix said. There was no reproach in his tone, only truth.

"Khero and Vera are the two kingdoms that comprise the land on the other side of the Veil," Ailan said. "The land we once called Le'Lana."

"The land the humans stole," Fanon said with a scoff.

Ailan ignored him. "There's one more I want to introduce you to."

Keeping one hand on Mareleau's shoulder, Ailan rested the other on the outside of the carrying sling. Mareleau resisted the urge to flinch away. She wasn't fond of unwarranted touch, but there was something comforting about Ailan's gesture. She was claiming Mareleau and Noah as her own. In this situation, it was a welcome protection.

"Please meet Noah, blood of my blood and Morkara of El'Ara."

Etrix bent a knee first, folding into a formal display of obeisance. Garot followed.

Only Fanon hesitated. "Our...Morkara. Not *future* Morkara, not merely your heir."

"Yes."

"You relinquished your title to a...a baby."

"I had my reasons." She held his gaze with unwavering authority, much like Mareleau had done, until Fanon bent his knee like the others. For the first time, Mareleau felt a kinship with the woman. Perhaps breaking men with fierce looks had been passed down through bloodline.

"Rise," Ailan said after a few long moments.

The three rose to their feet. Garot spoke with palpable excitement. "We have a Morkara again. This is a moment for future stories! A heroic return to tell for ages, and I'm here to witness it. I can hardly believe my luck."

Etrix spoke with far more sobriety. "Can we stop the Blight? As regent, you can move the *mora* on the Morkara's behalf. You can finish Satsara's Veil—"

"There's much more we must discuss before we take action," Ailan said. "Everything we do will have vast consequences. Calling the *mora* back is no small feat. Even if I called back enough to strengthen a team of our greatest wardweavers, it would take time to untie the edges of my mother's ward and finish where she left off. And that's without considering that Darius will try to invade before we can finish the Veil, or the thousands upon thousands of humans who inhabit Lela."

"What happens to the humans is beneath our concern," Fanon said.

"What happens to the humans is of *my* concern," Ailan said, "which makes it yours. Your duties as steward have been fulfilled. I am here now, so you will heed my word."

There was no room for argument with the edge infusing her tone.

"As you wish, regent." Fanon spoke through his teeth,

but there was a softening around his eyes that harkened back to their bittersweet reunion.

She returned that look, then addressed the others. "The situation may be complex, but I agree it is one we must address at once. Garot, please weave us a path to..."

Etrix finished for her. "Alles'Taria Palace. We kept the name of the original seat of the Morkara, to honor the palace that was lost in El'Ara's heart."

The palace that was lost...

Centerpointe Rock.

Cora had told Mareleau about the rock's origins. While she'd never seen it, only heard about it from Larylis and Cora, the thought that an entire palace could be whittled down to a single ruin like that was chilling.

"To Alles'Taria Palace, then," Ailan said. "Once we reach it, weave a secondary path to take Cora and Mareleau straight to a private room. I don't want anyone gawking at our guests, or even knowing they're here until we've spoken with the tribunal."

Garot strolled to the edge of the meadow and gestured with a complex wave of his fingers. The swirling vortex they'd emerged from opened once more. "Right this way."

Ailan gave an encouraging nod for Cora and Mareleau to follow. Valorre tossed his mane, clearly as reluctant as Mareleau was. Yet she followed nonetheless, stomach turning with every step she took toward the three Elvyn and the strange tunnel. She nearly lost her footing as they entered the Vortex. While the ground remained solid beneath her feet, the swirling colors of green and brown made it impossible to keep her bearings. So she fixed her gaze on Ailan's back instead. The Elvyn closed in behind them.

She cast a squinted look at Cora. Her friend's grimace

told her she was tolerating the nauseating tunnel just as poorly. Mareleau leaned in close. "Yet another situation that could have gone better."

"To be honest," Cora whispered back, "I think it could have gone far, far worse."

An ominous statement, yet Cora would know. The collar she carried was proof enough of just how bad a human could fare in El'Ara. That made the back of her neck prickle as they walked on down the dizzying path with no end in sight. But worse than her fear of what lay ahead was the dread that swelled inside her, growing with every breath, every heartbeat. It reminded her that every minute here was hours back home. Hours were days. A single day was a week.

Being away from Larylis this long was already torment enough.

How much harder would it be for him?

35

It had been four days since Larylis had last seen his wife and held his son in his arms, and every minute was like a spear to the chest. Not even the letter Berol had delivered three nights ago had alleviated the pain. If anything, it had only made it worse. For now, he knew his wife and child were going far beyond his reach.

At least they'd be safe.

He stared out the window in Verlot Palace's Royal Study at the mountains and forest awash with sunset hues. Instead of the pink-kissed green that comprised his view, he wished he could cast his gaze over the Balma Sea and pinpoint the enemy. But not even reports from the southwest lighthouses had caught sight of the fleet.

He'd arrived at Verlot that morning after maintaining a breakneck pace with only the closest members of his retinue. He'd already met with his council and analyzed the updates from the scouts.

No reports of enemy activity. No reports of unexpected ships approaching Vera's shores.

It was too early to expect much as far as his scouts'

efforts were concerned, for he'd only dispatched them by land and sea days ago. Yet shouldn't he have received *something*? Some word that the prisoner's warning was true?

He'd done the calculations a thousand times in his head, and on paper a thousand times more, assessing different routes, different ports, different hidden harbors. No matter how many times he tried to come to a new conclusion, he couldn't. Because if Darius had launched his fleet *before* the prisoner had left to spy in Khero, even if only days before the man had gotten caught and taken into custody, it didn't change that the ships should already be here. They should at least be in sight. If they were staying in the channel, waiting to make the rest of the journey at some later date, merchant ships would have passed, giving scouts some information to glean from talk at the ports.

More troubling was Teryn's newest update, delivered by Berol mere hours ago. Ever since Berol had brought Mareleau's letter, he and Teryn had utilized her to exchange daily updates. Unlike messenger horses, the falcon could fly between the two castles, one direction and back again, in less than a day. So far every update from Teryn had been the same. No news. No updates. Then today…

The prisoner has been killed.

Larylis planted his hands on the windowsill, squinting at the mountain range in the distance but not truly seeing it. He assessed the facts. The prisoner had confessed to Darius being in southern Norun, and that he'd summoned his fleet to make landfall in southwest Vera. Within days, the spy had been found dead in his cell. He'd clearly been punished and silenced, and from someone inside Ridine at that.

And yet…

Larylis pushed off the windowsill and paced before the desk. He couldn't shake the feeling that something was wrong. He may not have emotion magic like Cora, nor was he a seer like Emylia, but the last time he'd had this horrible feeling—when he'd feared his wife was in danger at Ridine last summer—he'd been right. He'd received a warning from Cora back then, and he could have dismissed it, yet his instincts had picked up on a danger he had no explanation for.

And it was happening again.

He knew why. Knew which piece of the puzzle disturbed him the most.

If there was a traitor in the castle, someone who could enter the cell and kill a man without getting caught by the guards or gaoler, they could have silenced the prisoner sooner. Or freed him. Why act only after he'd talked?

The skin at the back of his neck prickled, and he recalled an echo from history. He strode over to one of the many bookshelves lining the study walls. The massive collection of historical records and tales were a new addition after Larylis and Mareleau had inherited Verlot Palace as their secondary residence. Larylis could always think better and clearer when surrounded by books, and with every step he took toward the shelf, the sharper his mind became.

He picked up the book he was looking for and opened it toward the back. Flipping pages, he scanned the text until his gaze landed on the name and date he sought.

King Samuel. The Battle of San Dohrinas. Year 159 of the Eagle.

He read the brief record of the battle, pausing when he found the paragraph he was most interested in.

After days of withstanding torture, the spy in King Samuel's custody revealed where Borfian's forces would invade and gave three locations that they would attack. King Samuel divided his army and sent forces to each location, leaving only a small garrison in San Dohrinas. The city proved to be the true object of Borfian's attack, and the fortress fell in a fortnight.

Larylis closed the book and returned it to the shelf. The case he'd just read about wasn't the first or last of its kind, but it was the most recent he'd studied. The king had done his due diligence to ensure the spy's information was correct. Enemy forces had been spotted in two of the locations, so he'd trusted the third would soon follow. Yet in the end, the two forces had been a bluff and the third hadn't existed at all. The prisoner had gotten captured and tortured on purpose, all to misdirect the king. And even though King Samuel hadn't fully abandoned the city, he'd divided his numbers enough to give Borfian the win.

That was what *this* felt like now. Like they were being toyed with. Divided. On purpose.

The spy had given three pieces of intel: that Syrus and Norun had allied, that Darius was physically present in Norun, and that he'd summoned a fleet from Syrus. The first could be easily confirmed. They'd already suspected the alliance between Syrus and Norun. The second could soon be confirmed as well. As for the last...

Well, the fact that the prisoner had been silenced was proof enough that what he'd said was true.

But what if it wasn't?

Larylis gritted his teeth. The whole situation felt like a mind game. A battle of facts versus instinct. He couldn't call off his scouts. He couldn't ignore the potential that the fleet truly was coming. But he wouldn't sit around and wait to be made a fool of either.

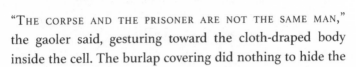

"THE CORPSE AND THE PRISONER ARE NOT THE SAME MAN," the gaoler said, gesturing toward the cloth-draped body inside the cell. The burlap covering did nothing to hide the smell.

Teryn breathed through his mouth, desperate to get this meeting over with so he could leave the dungeon. He'd been in one of these cells before, and his stay had been anything but pleasant. Though at least there hadn't been a rotting corpse back then.

"I'm not supposed to be here," said a frail voice. Teryn did his best to ignore it, for it was coming from the pale apparition that hovered over the dead body. It locked hollow, pleading eyes on Teryn. "Please. I'm not supposed to be here."

Teryn averted his gaze to the gaoler. The man was an inch taller than Teryn, which was saying something, for Teryn was used to being the tallest in most crowds. His arms were roped with muscle and scars, and his deep-set eyes were lined with creases. His lips were thin yet wide and he had a head of shaggy brown hair that reached his shoulders. Though Teryn hadn't interacted with many a gaoler before, he looked exactly like a man who chained and beat people for a living.

He'd also been Teryn's primary suspect for murdering the prisoner. *Had been* being the key, for the gaoler had an alibi. Everyone, it seemed, had a damn alibi, from the guards to the cooks to the dungeon sweepers.

"That's not the same man, Majesty," the gaoler said again. "I've beaten the living piss out of the prisoner. I'd know him if I'd seen 'im. *He* is not the same."

Teryn shifted his gaze from the gaoler to Captain Alden,

who stood off to the side. She shook her head. "He looked like the same man to me. I only saw him with bruises on his face."

The gaoler nodded eagerly. "I put them bruises there. But not those ones. They ain't even in the right places. Whoever put 'em there wanted the bastard unrecognizable."

"I'm not supposed to be here," the ghost lamented, stepping away from the body.

Teryn assessed the semi-transparent figure before asking the gaoler, "What did the prisoner look like before you, uh, beat the living piss out of him?"

"Older man. Gray hair. Slender. A real wily bastard. Bad attitude. Thinks e's cleverer then 'e is."

Teryn's gaze flashed to the ghost. He could only assume the spirit belonged to the corpse, and even though Teryn couldn't be sure the man's hair was gray, for the apparition was colorless, he matched the physical description enough.

"I'm tellin' ye, Majesty." The gaoler crossed his enormous arms over his chest. "Not the same man."

"Thank you for your time," Teryn said. "You may go."

The gaoler gave a clumsy bow and left Teryn and Captain Alden alone before the cell.

Teryn arched a brow and lowered his voice. "We're sure he's not our man?"

"He was off duty at the time the prisoner was murdered," Alden said. "His wife confirmed it, as did the guards. The guards themselves patrolled in pairs, and each soldier has confirmed their partner's presence. None saw any suspicious characters leave or enter the dungeon hall."

Teryn had already been told as much. No one had seen anything strange. No unfamiliar servants. No delayed guard rotations. He had to acknowledge that much of the castle's staff was relatively new and more positions were constantly being filled as the crown regained its wealth and stability. So could he truly trust that there hadn't been a suspicious soul in sight during that time?

"I'm not supposed to be here." The ghost approached the open cell door. Well, Teryn supposed there was one suspicious soul after all.

"Will you give me a moment, Captain?"

Alden's brows knit, but she folded into an obedient bow.

Once alone, Teryn faced the ghost. "Who are you?" he whispered.

"You...you can see me. I knew you could." His voice trembled, as thin and frail as a fallen leaf.

Teryn reworded his question. "What is your name?"

"John McMullighan, sir. Or...Majesty."

That wasn't the name on record for the prisoner. Not that anyone believed the name the spy had given. Vlad Samarus. The surname was one of the most common in Norun and practically screamed *fake*.

"Where are you from?" Teryn asked.

"I'm from northern Khero, Majesty. Greenfair Village."

Teryn pondered the village name. It was north of Ridine Castle. "How did you come to be in this cell?"

The ghost's voice turned pleading again. "I don't know. I was at the tavern after a hard week's work, same as usual. I headed home after a few pints, and then...I have no memories of what happened. Next thing I know, I...I'm looking at my body."

If the ghost's tale was true, perhaps the gaoler was right after all. That was, of course, even more troubling. It meant the prisoner hadn't been murdered for giving away intel. Instead, he'd been freed and replaced with a decoy.

Seven devils...

The prisoner was free. He'd left them with key information about the enemy, but what could he have gleaned in exchange? What had he learned that he could now use against them? And most pressing of all, who the hell had freed the man? Who was the traitor?

Teryn rubbed his jaw. This was bad.

"Take me home." The ghost reached for Teryn's hand, making Teryn launch a step back.

Yearning struck him then, the same he'd felt when the warrior wraith had looked at him from the charred field. "What do you mean, take you home?"

"I don't want to be here. I'm not supposed to be here. I...I want to go back. I have a home, a family. You must take me home."

Pity tightened Teryn's chest. "You can't go home. Your body is dead."

The ghost stepped forward again. "You can take me home. You can make this end."

"I don't know what you mean."

The spirit's tone took on an eerie quality, edged with desperation. The yearning sensation grew, multiplied tenfold. "You are a black flame, burning like the embrace of a cruel mother. As final as death. As comforting as home. Take me home. Take me home. TAKE ME HOME."

"Fine," he rushed to say. He didn't know what he was agreeing to, only that he wanted to stop the specter's frantic wailing. The ghost reached for Teryn's hand again, and this time he didn't flinch away. This time, he extended his palm.

Fingers he couldn't feel closed around his hand. The spirit's expression shifted from agonized to peaceful in the blink of an eye.

Then he was gone.

So was the yearning.

Teryn stared at the place the spirit had been, then down

at his hand. There was nothing to explain what had happened, only the ghost's desperate final words.

Emylia's too.

...if I get too close, I'll cease to exist.

Did Teryn have the ability...to send wandering spirits to the otherlife? Was that yearning coming from the dead, from their craving for oblivion?

His breaths pulsed sharp and shallow as his mind reeled to comprehend what all of this meant. His connection to ghosts wasn't an Art of the six senses, nor was it an earthly power like the Faeryn wielded. He wasn't a witch, an Elvyn weaver, or a Faeryn descendant.

Which left one question.

What am I?

36

Elvyn baths were disturbing. Not that they were unpleasant. Quite the opposite, in fact. Cora reclined in a tub that was nestled in a private, dimly lit room attached to the borrowed bedroom Garot had brought her and Mareleau to via pathweaving. Crystalline sconces lined the walls, lit with a faint luminescence that glowed too unwaveringly to be a flame. The floor was a gold-veined white marble, and the walls were a pale blue crystal, giving the impression that one was walking on clouds. The adjoining bedroom looked the same but with arched windows covered in gold filigree shutters.

The basin she soaked in was larger than anything she'd used at Ridine, twice as wide as her body. It was carved from the same blue crystal as the walls and was perched upon gilded feet. There was no need to wait for servants to haul in buckets of boiled water, for warm liquid poured from a tap at the turn of a handle. It was an impossible magic that Garot had explained as if it were commonplace. That was the disturbing part. For a land that utilized magic that was supposedly weakened by the Veil, this bath was nothing short of a miracle. What greater miracles were the Elvyn capable of when the *mora* was at full strength?

These were Cora's musings as she soaked in the tub, submerged to her neck in lilac-scented water. Her muscles uncoiled with every breath, though she couldn't fully relinquish her anxiety. At the back of her mind remained the constant chiming of an imaginary clock, one that ticked the hours that were passing in the human world. Hours where anything could be happening. Hours she'd never get back. There was nothing she could do, of course. Until the tribunal meeting was over and she had some form of an alliance to bring back to her people, all she could do was wait.

And there were, admittedly, more unbearable ways to wait than in a comfortable bath.

Ah, so you aren't being tortured, came Valorre's mental voice. *That is good to know.*

Another layer of relief unraveled at the feel of his not-too-distant presence. *It seems you aren't either.*

They'd parted in the woods outside the palace before Garot had taken her and Mareleau to their room. She hadn't wanted to separate from him, especially when he still wore the saddle laden with Cora's belongings—her bow and quiver, especially, which Ailan had requested she not bring inside the palace. She feared Valorre may be subjected to the same disdain Fanon had shown. Perhaps even from his own kind, should he cross paths with other unicorns. Yet now, as she connected with her unicorn companion, she got the distinct sense of carefree frolicking.

You must be having fun, she said.

I'm only tolerating my surroundings. There just so happens to be a rather nice meadow outside the palace.

She chuckled. *And I'm only tolerating this bath.*

You see, we are of the same mind.

She wanted to tell him it was all right if he liked this place. El'Ara was once his home, after all. But she held her tongue, for it would only offend him. He was feigning dislike of El'Ara out of solidarity, and if she wanted to confront that, she might have to confront something far more unpleasant.

That maybe this was where he belonged.

Cora soaked until the water began to cool. Only then did she force herself from the tub. She felt bad for having left Mareleau alone for so long, but her friend had been curt and pensive after Garot had departed, and the tangled emotions that seeped into Cora made her think Mareleau might have wanted some time alone. Cora had felt the same. They had so many uncertainties and very few answers. There was much to process and little that could be helped with sympathy or discussion. Not until after the meeting. Which would—hopefully—commence soon.

Outside the tub, she found a bath sheet so plush it almost felt criminal to dry herself off on it. Yet dry herself she did, marveling all the while at its softness and absorbency. Next, she turned her attention to the clothing Garot had left behind along with his suggestion that she dress in traditional Elvyn attire for the meeting. She inspected each article, finding flowing silk trousers, a matching robe, and a gold sash. The silk was the finest quality and a shade of indigo so deep it was almost black. Gold lace and delicate embroidery lined the robe's hems while stars and moon phases decorated the skirt and bodice. She could tell at a glance that the robe was not meant to be worn with a corset. That was all for the better, as the clothing and undergarments she'd arrived in were in grave need of laundering.

Despite the ensemble's simplistic design, once she was dressed, she felt as elegant as she'd be in a ballgown. More than that, she was supremely comfortable. She hated to admit it, but the Elvyn may be onto something in terms of fashion.

She strode to her pile of clothing and extracted two items hidden beneath—the magic-suppressing collar and her beautiful dagger. The first item she tucked into one of her robe's pockets. The latter, she hid behind her back in the folds of her sash. That filled her with a sense of calm. Control. A reminder that she wasn't defenseless in this place where most considered her an enemy.

As she left the bathroom, voices reached her ears. She entered the bedroom and found Mareleau wasn't alone. Her friend sat at the edge of the massive four-poster bed, dressed in a pale blue version of Cora's new attire, bouncing a silk-swaddled Noah in her arms. An anxious expression twisted her features, and several messy braids hung from her freshly brushed tresses. Beside her stood Ailan and Garot.

Garot greeted Cora with a grin. His presence suggested he would take them directly to the meeting and not through the halls of the palace. That made Cora's anxiety flare with a sharp pinch. She'd hardly glimpsed more than a few towering white spires over the treetops before Garot had whisked her and Mareleau directly to their room. The view outside the arched windows in the bedroom revealed sky, forest, distant mountains, and a dizzying view of the land-scape far below. Not having a clearer visual of the palace itself made her feel like a prisoner. It reminded her too much of when she'd been stuck in her beautiful room at Verlot Palace while King Verdian questioned her identity for weeks on end.

She swallowed her panic and brushed her fingertips

over the back of her sash, taking comfort in the firm lines of her hidden dagger. "Is it time?" she asked as she approached the others.

Ailan nodded. She too had bathed and changed since they'd parted ways outside the palace. The bottom half of her long black hair flowed freely around her shoulders while the top was arranged in several intertwining braids around the crown of her head. Her robe was even more stunning than Cora's, in shades of crimson, saffron, and persimmon, patterned with botanicals Cora had no name for. Her sleeves trailed nearly to the floor while her sash glittered with multihued jewels. She looked every inch a royal.

"We've gathered the tribunal," Ailan said. "I've spoken to them on my own and discussed all that can be discussed without you present."

Cora hadn't been aware that any portion of the meeting would be held without them, but she wasn't disappointed to have missed anything. She was here to forge an alliance and nothing more.

Ailan spoke again. "I've secured a binding vow from every member on the tribunal that they accept, honor, and protect Noah as their Morkara, despite his human blood. There was very little they could do to contest it, but it didn't stop them from arguing over his origins for the better part of an hour."

Cora winced. She was indeed glad to have missed that in favor of her overlong soak in the tub. But something snagged her attention. "What do you mean by a binding vow?"

"The High Fae are bound by vows, bargains, and promises when stated with certain words. Breaking them results in immediate Last Breath."

Cora's eyes widened. Faerytales often spoke of fae

bargains but this was the first time she'd heard confirmation of the tales' validity. The same tales also claimed fae couldn't lie, which Valorre had demonstrated to be false numerous times. And Ailan had convinced the Forest People she was dying.

Mareleau narrowed her eyes. "You said you discussed all you can without us present. What exactly are we needed there for? Will we only be talking about the alliance?"

Ailan's expression turned wary. "There are certain formalities we need to proceed with. I may have final say as regent, but the tribunal ensures the Elvyn people get a voice in every decision we make. They would like to discuss...you and Cora. Your human heritage forbids you from being here, which means we need to establish new rules regarding your presence."

Her words had Cora's muscles tensing. "You're putting us on trial."

"I'm not going to lie," Ailan said. "It may feel like that. But they *will* accept you. They may request a demonstration of trust. From Cora in particular. A guarantee that you won't use your magic against them."

Her blood went cold. The collar tucked in the pocket of her robe suddenly felt heavier. She could guess what a guarantee of protection would look like to the Elvyn.

Ailan sighed. "I know it sounds offensive. You've done nothing wrong. Yet our people establish trust through binding vows, and those with human blood cannot make them. The Elvyn people learned the hard way with Darius."

The edges of Cora's indignation softened slightly. Tristaine and Darius were the only humans the Elvyn had ever dealt with, and neither painted a pleasant picture for her kind. As much as she hated bearing such cold suspicion, she could almost understand it.

Even as it boiled her blood.

"Fine," she bit out. "I'll establish trust however I can."

It was for the alliance. Her people *needed* this alliance. They needed any advantage they could get to face Darius when he inevitably came. Yet as Garot opened his swirling tunnel and ushered Cora and her companions inside, she was left to ponder: how could she establish trust with people who saw her as a villain?

37

T he tunnel ceased its spinning in a matter of seconds. The whirling colors of ivory, blue, and gold melted outward to form a hallway featuring the same gold-veined marble floors as the bedroom and bathroom, the same blue crystalline walls. At the end of the hall was a pair of white doors painted with intricate gold vines. Etrix stood before them and greeted his daughter with a formal bow.

"We're ready, regent," he said as he straightened. The fact that Cora understood his words told her he'd already woven his translation enchantment.

However, Cora wasn't sure *she* was ready, and from the way Mareleau edged closer to her, arms cradling her son tightly to her chest, her friend was equally as apprehensive. Cora had been to plenty of council meetings now that she was queen, but was an Elvyn tribunal the same as a council?

They weren't given long to ponder, for Etrix pushed open the doors and led the way inside. The room beyond was a wide, circular shape and darker than the hall had been. The sconces that lined the walls offered only a faint glow. The rest of the light came from overhead, where dazzling flashes of illumination darted beneath a domed ceiling. Cora blinked up at the lights; they came from glowing wings. Were they...butterflies? They cast the room in shades of blue and green. But as she stepped farther into the room, their wings glowed brighter, shifting to yellow and orange. Some deepened to a fiery red.

"Hold out your hand," Etrix said. Cora stopped in place and dragged her eyes from the ceiling to find her companions had halted too. Ailan stood beside Etrix. A butterfly hovered over each of their heads; Etrix's was blue while Ailan's flickered between green and yellow. She didn't see Garot until she noticed him settling into a chair nearby, a blue butterfly over his head. That drew her attention to the circular perimeter of the room and the three tiers of seating that lined the walls, the highest tier being the closest to the walls while the lowest circled the floor at the very center of the room. An Elvyn figure occupied almost every chair, leaving a few empty at the innermost tier.

Remembering what Etrix had said, she turned her gaze back to him and lifted her hand. A butterfly fluttered down from the ceiling and alighted on the back of her hand. Up close, she saw it had a total of eight delicate wings, all of which glowed a cloudy yellow-green. Just as quickly as it had touched down, it launched back into the air. This time, it hovered over her head and remained there, much like the ones floating above Etrix, Ailan, and Garot. Another glance at the dome showed most of the butterflies had dispersed and now fluttered above individual Elvyn figures. The light from their wings illuminated harsh stares as well as some curious expressions like Garot wore. Her eyes fell on another familiar face—Fanon—flickering orange beneath the glow of his butterfly. His eyes narrowed slightly as he met Cora's gaze, and she turned her attention to Mareleau.

It was her turn to claim a butterfly. Mareleau's eyes danced, expression enchanted, as the winged creature perched upon her hand shifted to a blue glow before hovering above her head.

"Their colors match our moods and emotions," Ailan explained, voice low. "They ensure no one hides their true feelings from the rest of the tribunal. They also allow us to wordlessly demonstrate our choices when voting on a decision."

That drained the pleasant aspects of Cora's fascination. Now she felt naked. She was used to experiencing others' emotions, but to have hers bared for others...

The light above her head shifted to orange. If the Elvyn associated color with emotions the same way the Forest People did—especially the more artistically inclined—blue would represent baseline calm, progressing into deeper emotions with teal, green, and yellow, then ending with more heated emotions represented by orange and red. White and violet were often used to express pure or spiritual aspects of magic.

The orange wings overhead made her annoyance clear for all to see. She gritted her teeth.

"Come," Etrix said, gesturing toward the empty chairs at the innermost tier, "take a seat."

Cora and Mareleau exchanged a wary glance before following him to the center of the room, then to the velvet-upholstered wingback chairs. They were about to sit down when shuffling movement had them halting in place. The Elvyn rose from their seats to kneel beside their chairs, heads bowed low. A murmur of *Morkara* rumbled through the room. Cora's eyes darted from the bowed heads to Ailan, only to find her kneeling beside Etrix.

Right. Ailan wasn't Morkara. Noah was.

Mareleau noticed at the same time, her cheeks flushing at the attention her son was receiving. Finally, the figures rose and returned to their seats. Cora and Mareleau did the same.

Ailan sat between Mareleau and Fanon, while Etrix stood at the center of the room. Cora recalled from her first time in El'Ara that Etrix was Head of Tribunal. "Now that we've had our brief recess, we can discuss the last of our topics."

"We should address the criminal offense first," one of the Elvyn seated on the second tier said. A red butterfly cast his cold expression, his pursed lips, his angled ears beneath short dark hair, in a crimson glow.

Cora bristled, knowing she was the so-called criminal in question.

"No," Ailan said, "I already have our first topic prepared. I want a binding vow stated before Queen Mareleau, mother of our Morkara, that you welcome, accept, and protect her, same as her son whom you've already sworn to honor."

A rumble of disagreement spread throughout the room. As more voices added their dissent, Etrix's translation enchantment lost its effectiveness. Too many Elvyn spoke out, and thanks to the butterflies' orange and red hues, Cora didn't need to understand what they were saying to glean the gist of it. They didn't want Mareleau here.

Fury burned in Mareleau's eyes, matched by the red butterfly overhead. Cora reached across her armrest to lay a comforting hand on her friend's shoulder. She hoped it conveyed her wordless promise—that if worst came to worst, she'd worldwalk her and Noah out of there at once.

Mareleau gave Cora a knowing nod, and her butterfly cooled to orange.

Etrix raised a hand, and the arguing ceased. When he spoke, his words were clear, his translation weaving back in place. "We are not here to discuss all humans or witches. Just the two human queens in question. Only one is up for discussion now."

"Mareleau is the blood of my blood," Ailan said. "Should I die before Noah comes of age, the *mora* will recognize her as regent, and there is nothing you can do about that. She must be allowed to stay here with him, even if only for the sake of the flow and control of *mora*."

"Allowed," Mareleau muttered through her teeth, quiet enough so only Cora could hear. "As if they can keep him from me. As if he belongs to *them* and not me."

Cora wasn't sure if the rage she felt was Mareleau's or her own. She was angry on her friend's behalf. On Noah's. Mareleau had only agreed to come to El'Ara for her son's protection, and to keep the dragons from seeking her in the human world. She hadn't even begun to discuss whether she and Noah would live here. Ailan had promised her time to save such choices for later, that they'd figure out the future together after they'd defeated Darius.

Ailan continued. "She brought her son here to honor his position as Morkara of El'Ara. In return, you must honor her as Edel Morkara'Elle."

The last few words remained untranslated, but they were vaguely familiar. Ailan had once said they meant something like a queen mother.

"You've already accepted the *mora's* choice to deem Noah your Morkara," Ailan said. "You've accepted him despite his human blood."

"If we accept her," said the same dark-haired Elvyn from

the second tier, "are we to simply accept all other humans in the future? What if she bears other children? What of the Morkara's children? Are we to accept a diminishing bloodline, accept that our people may one day cease to be should the humans proliferate faster?"

A few Elvyn voiced their agreement, but Etrix spoke. "I've already stated that we are not discussing all humans. Nor are we discussing the distant future. Your fears are valid, and they will be addressed in due time, but today we discuss only the most pressing topics. Do you vow to honor, protect, and accept our Morkara's human mother, Mareleau, as Edel Morkara'Elle?"

Another murmur of dissent hummed around the room, but the voices ceased when Etrix bent his knee.

"Then I shall be the first," he said. His butterfly adopted a violet glow. "Edel Morkara'Elle Mareleau, I state my binding vow that I honor, protect, and accept you as the mother of my Morkara and a citizen of El'Ara."

Garot quickly followed suit, kneeling beside his chair like everyone had done for Noah earlier. Ailan followed next, then—to Cora's surprise—Fanon. After that, the other Elvyn bent their knees in turn until every head was bowed. Beneath the violet hue of their ever-fluttering butterflies, they stated their vows.

When they rose and returned to their seats, the colors shifted mostly back to shades of orange, though some had cooled to green or blue.

Mareleau released a slow exhale. Her relief was so palpable, it made it past Cora's wards. Cora offered her a reassuring smile, but it left her face at Etrix's next words.

"We will now discuss the other human queen, Aveline Caelan."

Cora's heart kicked up, and her butterfly flashed red

before she forced her breaths to even out, her emotions to calm. Everything had turned out well for Mareleau. Perhaps it would go well for her too.

Of course it was easy for Mareleau, sniped some dark part of her mind. *Everything is easy for Mareleau. You're just her decoy, remember?*

Resentment speared her chest. It was so sudden, so violent, she nearly gasped out loud. What the hell was that about? Those hadn't been her thoughts. She could never think that about Mareleau! Yet...they'd come from inside her, not outside. No, that was impossible.

"She was condemned by our former steward," said one of the Elvyn, tone brimming with disgust. Cora was grateful for the distraction. The resentment faded from her heart as she found a new target for bitter feelings. "Fanon sentenced her to death—"

"A sentence that was supported neither by me nor the rest of the tribunal, mind you," Etrix said. "Furthermore, Queen Aveline has been pardoned by our regent. She is a close ally of our regent, our Morkara, and our Edel Morkara'Elle. Her guilt or innocence in breaking our laws is not up for debate. We are here to establish new rules to accommodate the alliance our regent would like to propose to the humans."

"She's a worldwalker," the same Elvyn said. "She entered our world with her magic and left the same way. She should be punished before we can even consider allying with her."

Etrix's butterfly darkened to a shade of teal, the only sign he was growing impatient. "It remains impossible for a worldwalker to utilize their magic to cross the Veil *into* El'Ara. As Ailan already explained, the human queen's actions were accidental. It was only her connection to a unicorn—and his horn's ability to pierce the Veil—that allowed her to enter our world last month."

Last month! Mother Goddess, that's right. To the Elvyn, it had only been a month since last summer's events.

Etrix went on. "Preventing a worldwalker from exiting El'Ara through magical means was never woven into Satsara's wardweaving. She left El'Ara for fear of her life after being targeted by the dragon Ferrah."

"She has crucial information," said another Elvyn, this one seated on the third tier. He gestured toward Cora. "Should she give this information to Darius, share how he could utilize a unicorn to cross the Veil, we'll be done for."

"Which is why we're forging an alliance," Ailan said, her butterfly flickering between orange and red.

"How can we trust her?" said another voice.

Then another. "She's human! She can't make a binding vow."

And another. "I still say she should be punished."

The voices overlapped, compromising Etrix's translation magic once more.

Anger simmered in Cora's gut, melding with the enraged emotions clawing their way past her shields. It sent a piercing ache to her temples.

"I want to hear what Fanon has to say," said Garot.

Cora shot him a glare across the room. Of all the people to make such a suggestion! And she'd thought he was on her side. Was he simply obtuse?

Fanon's jaw shifted side to side. His butterfly glowed a deep orange, and he slouched in his chair like he wanted to be anywhere else. Cora braced herself for whatever hatred he was about to spew.

His voice came out tight. "Whatever I have said or done as steward is no longer relevant. We have our Morkara now, and our regent. I condemned the human queen as I saw fit when the authority was mine, but our regent has condemned those actions in turn. We have Ailan's judgment now. You need not mine."

Cora blinked a few times, surprised by his words. She wasn't the only one. While his statement moved some to silence, it outraged others.

"We still can't trust her!"

"How can we trust an alliance with a worldwalker?"

"She must demonstrate her worth as our ally."

"She could use her magic at any time."

Another ache pierced Cora's temples as the arguments dissolved back into chaos. Devils below, she felt like she was in the council room with Lords Kevan and Ulrich, the target of their ire and suspicion. She never had managed to earn their trust or respect before they'd met their demise, but she had gotten her way a few times with a blend of truth and lies. She tried to think of some way to utilize those same lessons now, but she had just one idea. One that weighed heavy against her thigh and sent a memory of pain through her neck.

Breathing out a slow exhale, she rose to her feet. "Can I speak?"

The arguing voices went silent.

Ailan sat up straighter, brow furrowed. Etrix turned to her, head tilted slightly to the side. His butterfly flickered a deep green, then softened back to blue. "Yes, Queen Aveline. You may speak."

"Your regent has already spoken on my behalf," Cora said to the room at large, not bothering to hide the irritation in her voice, "so I will not repeat what has already been said. No, I cannot make a binding vow, and I know a human's promise means nothing to you without one. All I can offer you is this."

Cora extracted the collar from inside her robe. Her stomach turned just to hold it. She lifted it for all to see. "If you can't trust my magic, then collar me until it's time for me to return to my people. That's all I can offer you."

She held her breath, waiting for more arguments, or for one of the Elvyn to act and snap the device around her neck.

But Ailan spoke first. "Where...where did you get that? Why do you have it?"

Cora faced the regent as Ailan rose from her chair to stand beside Cora. The Elvyn woman's eyes were wide as they locked on the item in Cora's hand.

Cora was surprised by her reaction. While it was true she hadn't mentioned the collar when she'd talked about her time in El'Ara, she'd had no reason to believe Ailan would be so shocked by it. "Fanon used this on me. It suppressed my magic."

Ailan shot a fiery gaze at Fanon, her butterfly darkening to blood-red. She pointed at the device. "That was made for one individual."

Fanon shifted uncomfortably in his seat. "It was made for a worldwalker. I brought it with us to investigate the trigger that had alerted us of an unwelcome intruder."

"You shouldn't have used it on her."

He opened his mouth but quickly snapped it shut. His butterfly was almost as deep-red as hers now. "As you say, regent."

Ailan marched up to Cora and snatched the collar from her hands. "No one will use this on her, or any of my human allies. This was reserved for Darius, and for him alone it will remain."

Disgruntled murmurs sounded throughout the room, but Ailan spoke over them.

"Don't you see now? The human queen has demonstrated trust in the only way she can. She offered to let us collar her, and we will let that be enough. She returned a priceless, irreplaceable item to where it belongs. It is perhaps the only thing that will give us a chance to defeat Darius."

Another ripple of surprise moved through her. Cora had assumed the collar was a common piece of Elvyn technology, not a one-of-a-kind artifact.

"It didn't work before," one of the Elvyn said. Her expression was neutral beneath the glow of her yellow-green butterfly.

"That doesn't mean it isn't an advantage," Ailan said. "Now, enough with this back and forth about Queen Aveline. She is my ally, and she has demonstrated trust like you demanded."

When no one stated a word of reproach, Ailan returned to her chair. Cora did the same and was relieved to feel somewhat lighter. She hadn't realized how much she'd dreaded wearing the collar again until it was taken from her hands. Ailan now held it in her lap, gingerly, as if it were precious.

Cora couldn't help but wonder about it. Why was it so irreplaceable? What had the Elvyn female meant when she'd said it hadn't worked before? Had they tried to use it on Darius? Had it been part of Satsara's attempted ward-weaving?

There was a story there, and Cora needed to know more.

"Now," Etrix said, drawing her attention away from the collar, "let us discuss the alliance."

38

The meeting was tedious. Mareleau was willing to bet the tribunal spoke less about the alliance itself and more about placing restrictions on Cora. She could leave El'Ara via worldwalking, but only with express permission, and in the presence of at least two witnesses from the tribunal. She could not use her connection to Valorre to cross the Veil ever again. She could enter through the tear to report back about her side of the alliance, but there were layers of protocol she'd have to endure.

Mareleau would have felt more indignation on her friend's behalf if her mind weren't swarming with a thousand unanswered questions. They burned her tongue as she and Cora followed Ailan and Fanon out of the meeting room and into another one of Garot's swirling tunnels. Now that the meeting was over, Cora was eager to return to Ridine Castle. Their party was on their way to reconvene with Valorre in preparation for Cora to worldwalk home.

Home. Such a lovely word.

So badly Mareleau wished she and Noah were going home too.

Mareleau hurried to Ailan's side, unable to hold her questions back any longer. "What about my husband?"

Ailan met her gaze with a furrowed brow. Fanon's expression flashed with annoyance before he marched on ahead. Ailan fell back to keep pace at Mareleau's side. "Your husband?"

Mareleau did everything she could to keep her voice steady despite the suppressed rage that tightened her lungs. "You've already made plans for me and Noah under the assumption that we'll be citizens here. That I'll relinquish my kingdom and my role as queen in the human realm and live in El'Ara instead. Need I remind you I've agreed to nothing of the sort?"

Ailan gave her a tired smile. "I know, blood of my blood. I spoke as I did for the tribunal's sake, for I needed to secure their binding vow. But I haven't forgotten what I said to you before. I meant it when I told you we'd figure out the future together. Defeating Darius takes precedence before all else, as does protecting you and Noah."

The swirling colors of the tunnel shifted from the pale hues of the palace to the greens and browns of the outdoors.

"What about my husband?" she said again, her tone edged with impatience. "I want the same protection for him. The same guarantee that he'll be granted respect and citizenship should we decide..."

She couldn't bring herself to finish. She wasn't ready to imagine a future in El'Ara. Noah was a prince of Vera, and she was its queen. Yet Noah's connection to El'Ara transcended bloodline politics and involved an entire world, not just a kingdom. It was a matter of magic and fate. Something she wasn't sure she could fight.

"She's right to ask," Cora said.

Ailan stopped in place just as the blues and greens went

still and spread outward to form a moonlit forest. Garot lowered his hands, his pathweaving complete. Fanon leaned lazily against a nearby tree trunk. Mareleau glanced overhead where dark trees stretched toward an inky starlit sky. Were Mareleau in a better mood, she may have found the quiet woods charming, but now they felt sinister.

Cora spoke again. "I want to know the answer too. Not just about Larylis, but all the citizens of Lela. You may not want to discuss the future with your tribunal just yet, but we deserve to know what's in store for us. I've agreed to forge an alliance between our people so we can fight Darius together, but what exactly are my people fighting for? What future awaits when Darius is gone and all that remains is sealing the tear? What happens to the people of Lela when you reclaim El'Ara's heart?"

"I already told you. I don't know the answer yet."

"Give us something," Mareleau said, voice quavering. "Give us some idea of what our futures could look like. Give me a reason to believe your protection is worth a damn."

Ailan's posture tensed, and she heaved a sigh. "I...I have some ideas for how we could work together. I know you value your kingdom. Perhaps...perhaps we can wait to seal the tear and complete the Veil until you and your husband have lived full lives. Once we defeat Darius, we'll need only worry about healing the Blight. Fifty years in the human world is just over seven in El'Ara. We can hold off the Blight that long, and it will give us time to prepare for what happens next."

The edges of Mareleau's anxiety began to smooth. That didn't sound terrible. She and Larylis could continue to rule Vera and live full lives with their son. Noah could be a prince of two worlds until then.

"If we wait to complete the Veil," Ailan said, "that will

give your people time to prepare for Lela's return to El'Ara. They will have time to find new homes, new kingdoms—"

"Exile," Cora said. "The future you see for my people is exile."

Mareleau's blood went cold at the word.

"Or citizenship of El'Ara," Ailan rushed to say. "I know both options are unthinkable right now, but we *can* work together. That's what our alliance is about. Defeating Darius and forging a future beyond that."

Fanon snorted a laugh.

Mareleau furrowed her brow. Etrix wasn't there to weave his translation magic, so Fanon shouldn't have been able to understand Ailan's words.

He pushed off the tree he'd been leaning on and strode closer to them. With a shake of his head, he said something in the Elvyn language.

"Fanon," Ailan hissed through her teeth.

He spoke again, his tone barbed. Garot nodded in agreement, though his words were lost to lack of translation as well.

"What are they saying?" Mareleau asked.

Fanon sauntered up to her, extending a closed fist. She flinched back, arms going protectively around Noah's sling. He said something with a nod at his fist, and when she made no move, he wrested one of her hands away from Noah and forced something into her palm.

She nearly dropped it before she noticed a delicate silver chain, just long enough to be a bracelet, strung with a small onyx orb.

"Gift from Etrix and one of our charmweavers," Fanon said with no small amount of irritation. Her eyes widened as she realized she could understand him. "And what I said is that my lovely consort is too optimistic."

Ailan glared daggers at him as he moved to Cora next, dropping a bracelet in her hand. Ailan hissed his name again, but he paid her no heed.

"The tribunal will never agree to let humans live in El'Ara," he said. "Nor will they agree to wait a year, much less seven, to seal the tear and complete the Veil."

"You don't know that," Ailan said, then turned her gaze to Mareleau and Cora. "He doesn't know that. I'll do everything in my power to get them to agree to a solution that benefits everyone. Don't listen to him."

"Why not?" Fanon said with a scoff. "I'm the only one telling them the truth. And here's a truth for you, my love. The tear has increased the Blight's growth tenfold."

She paled, her jaw slack. Then she spoke under her breath. "Do you want this alliance or not?"

Fanon said nothing but Garot raised his hand. "I do, but Fanon is right. The tribunal will never agree to let humans live in El'Ara. Well, aside from the Edel Morkara'Elle, but we saw how well that discussion went."

"So, exile," Cora said, tone empty. Movement rustled the underbrush, and moonlight caught on white fur. Valorre emerged from between the trees and gently nudged Cora's shoulder with his muzzle. "I'm forging an alliance for the eventual exile of my people."

Ailan's shoulders fell. "I'll give you time. That I can promise you. As regent, I can hold off the Blight long enough to sort everything out."

Mareleau's heart sank to her feet. The promise of time was meaningless when she couldn't guarantee exactly how much they'd be given. She met Cora's gaze and they exchanged a defeated look.

"I need to get back," Cora said, absently stroking Valorre's neck.

Mareleau didn't want Cora to leave. She was her only friend in this strange place. The only person here who was truly on her side. Once she left, it would just be her and Noah.

Alone.

The future uncertain.

She swallowed the tightness in her throat and reached into the pocket of her robe. She extracted a wrinkled piece of parchment and held it out for Cora. "See that this gets to Lare." She hated that her only communication with her husband could be a one-way letter. For now. She wouldn't give up on getting what she wanted. What she needed.

Cora clasped her fingers around the paper, but she didn't pull away. She gave Mareleau a weighted look, one that spoke of last resorts. Mareleau glanced at Cora's hands, one connected to the paper they both held, the other pressed to Valorre's neck. Realization dawned. All Mareleau needed to do was give the slightest sign, the subtlest nod, and Cora could worldwalk them away. Mareleau would be free of this place where she might as well be a prisoner. She could see her husband again. She could go home.

Home.

Home.

It was a tantalizing offer that sparked every selfish instinct she harbored. But on the other side were the repercussions of that choice. Should she run away like that, they'd forfeit the alliance and make an enemy of the Elvyn people. The dragons would return to the human world to seek her out. Even if she learned to ward her magic, the dragons would likely still search for her and destroy crops, homes, and lives in the process. And she wouldn't put it past the Elvyn to hunt her down themselves and take their Morkara back by force.

Mareleau may be determined to get her way, but her decisions carried weight. Consequences. Ones that could become burdens she might never fully shrug off.

She'd find a better way to fight for what she wanted.

For now...she could only let go.

With a slow sigh, she released her hold on the letter and took a step back.

Cora gave her a relieved nod, as if she was of the same mind. Then she turned her back on Mareleau and fully faced Valorre.

In the blink of an eye, her friend was gone.

Leaving Mareleau and Noah behind, an entire world away.

39

E vening greeted Cora as she planted her feet in the forest outside Ridine. After removing Valorre's saddle and stashing it in the underbrush for the time being, she bid him farewell and worldwalked straight to her bedroom. The room was blessedly empty of servants, but it was empty of Teryn too. A wave of vertigo washed over her, and she sank onto the edge of her bed. She had half a mind to curl up under the covers and sleep, but she shook the thought from her head. How many hours had it been since she'd last slept? The time discrepancy between the two realms made it impossible to calculate.

Whatever the case, she reasoned her fatigue was mostly due to worldwalking to different locations in such quick succession. At least that's what she told herself. In truth, she hadn't expected to feel so exhausted now that she was no longer traveling with multiple companions in tow. Maybe moving between worlds took an additional toll.

Then how had Darius been able to worldwalk so frequently with multiple soldiers during his attack on El'Ara? Had he rested in between? Or were her abilities weaker than his? True, she'd only learned of her traveling magic last year. Yet the fatigue that weighed down her muscles now begged the question—was her magic growing weaker in general?

Her magic had weakened before, when she'd been trapped in the dungeon with Teryn. She'd been convinced Morkai had suppressed her magic, leaving her connection to it frail. But when she'd searched for the source that had stifled her, she'd found it inside herself. It had stemmed from resentment she'd been carrying over Teryn's betrayal.

Something pulsed in her heart.

A feeling that said *truth*.

She placed a hand to her chest, and her palms thrummed in echo of her heartbeat. Did that mean...was she stifling her own magic again?

A leaden weight filled her stomach, and it spoke of her resistance to investigate the source. But why was she resisting? If another challenge was trying to present itself, she had to face it. It was how witches grew their magic, and she needed to be at her strongest. Yet as soon as she tried to soften and yield to look into the dark pull, she saw only flames. Felt only a burning resentment that made her skin crawl, blistering beneath that imagined fire.

She rose to her feet, detaching herself from those thoughts. Investigations into her magic could wait.

Right now, she needed to find her husband.

TERYN THRUST HIS SPEAR, RELISHING THE STRETCH OF HIS limbs, the burn of his muscles. He pivoted, evading his imaginary opponent's attack, and slashed down to parry. Another pivot. A longer thrust of his spear. His entire body moved in concert, his stance shifting in precise yet fluid motions, his spear an extension of his arm. He repeated the drill again and again, his only witnesses being the empty suits of armor and racks of weapons that lined the perimeter of the armory.

Ridine's armory was a windowless hall of mahogany and flagstone with a training floor at its center. This was the only place he could think to go after the latest missive he'd received. The only place he could think to release the anxiety and rage crawling through his body.

King Darius had made his first direct contact with Khero, and it had come in a written demand for surrender. In three weeks, Darius and five thousand men would arrive at a specified location on the Khero-Vinias border. If Khero refused to surrender, they would then proceed to discuss terms for war.

It reminded Teryn too much of Morkai.

The mage's demands for surrender.

The meeting at Centerpointe Rock.

King Arlous' resulting death.

Teryn repeated his drill—thrust, slash, thrust—taking pleasure in how it felt to move. To be alive. To not be a hostage this time.

Yet that solace was short-lived. King Darius was now a concrete enemy, not just a man from myth and rumor. There was no denying that he was coming or what he wanted. There was no taking comfort in doubt, in the sliver of possibility that Darius wasn't a threat like Morkai was, that his alliance with Norun had nothing to do with Khero.

That was the most terrifying part—Darius' threat didn't involve him alone. Half his force of five thousand men belonged to Norun. Furthermore, a legion of twelve thousand Norunian soldiers were already marching from the capital and would join Darius should Khero refuse to surrender. Meanwhile, Khero had only four thousand soldiers.

Seven devils, those odds were terrible.

There had been no mention of Darius' naval fleet, but that was a matter for Vera, not Khero. Teryn was starting to suspect his brother was right. Larylis had posed a theory in a letter he'd sent back with Berol a few days ago. That the prisoner's words had been a bluff meant to draw Vera's attention toward a threat that would never come and leave Khero vulnerable.

Not that it mattered much. Even with their combined armies, they would still be outnumbered. Even if Vera supported the fight against Darius, Larylis couldn't fully dismiss what the prisoner had said. It could have been a lesser misdirection—that the fleet was still coming, but not making landfall in southwest Vera. Which meant Larylis needed to keep some of his soldiers ready in the south.

There was hope in the alliance Cora was forging, but she'd been gone from Ridine for ten days now. It had been nine days since he'd received her letter about going to El'Ara.

Was she still there? Had they found the tear yet?

At least he had some additional intel. He'd been right about Mareleau's letter to Larylis; she hadn't been nearly as sparse with details as Cora had been. Larylis had relayed what her letter had included—that the Forest People's camp had been outside Lake Sarrolin near the village of Brekan. And that they would begin their search for the tear on the western coast.

Teryn would have been livid that she'd divulged so much information during such tumultuous times if it hadn't provided him such relief. Just knowing vaguely where Cora was had carved leagues of stress from his bones. Besides, he couldn't give in to the fear that Berol's letters could be intercepted. That would only lead to madness.

Sweat prickled his forehead as he continued his drill, his mind reeling to come up with countermeasures. Surrender was out of the question, and if Cora didn't come home soon, he couldn't count on Elvyn reinforcements.

No, the best scenario was to face Darius' smaller force. And there was a chance for that. Darius' letter wasn't the only one he'd received today. A messenger had also arrived with a brief note from Lex.

It begins on the thirtieth day. Those who've been robbed will take back what they've lost.

That was all the note had said. It was so carefully yet cleverly worded, Teryn suspected Lily had penned it for her husband. Those two sentences told him everything he needed to know: the Norunian rebels would launch their rebellion on the thirtieth of this month—less than two weeks from now. They would fight to take back Haldor and Sparda, the two kingdoms Norun had conquered. The rebellion would wreak havoc on Norun and delay the progress of Darius' reinforcements. The King of Syrus would be isolated with only his five thousand men.

With some additional men from Vera, they could be evenly matched.

But Teryn didn't want even.

He wanted—needed—to win.

Dark thoughts clouded his mind, taking him back to Centerpointe Rock. To Morkai's dishonorable actions during the meeting. How he'd signaled battle without giving them a chance to negotiate the terms for war. What he'd done made Teryn sick with rage.

Yet as he thrust his spear and imagined his faceless enemy on the other side, he didn't feel nearly as sick when he considered doing something similar himself.

Darius' threat was a matter of power, magic, and desperation.

Maybe only equal measures of power, magic, and desperation could lead to victory.

And Teryn had one idea that might allow him to catch Darius unawares. To end the battle before it had begun.

He wasn't sure he could even do it.

It might damn him to the seven hells.

But if it saved Khero's future, he'd risk the stain on his soul.

40

Cora found Teryn in the armory. The shuffling of his feet and the sound of his heavy breaths reached her ears just before she rounded the corner. He didn't notice her approach. She kept her feet silent so as not to disturb his practice and leaned against the wall just past the threshold.

His pale hair was tied back, revealing a determined look on his face. He wore only trousers, his nightshirt draped over a rack of polearms. Sweat glistened over his taut muscles, a sight that wasn't at all unpleasant. She studied the contraction of his abdomen as he pivoted and slashed, the bulge of his biceps as he thrusted. She'd seen him train with a sword and hunt with a spear, but she hadn't watched him train quite like this—with focus and zeal and a deadly skill that was a bit terrifying yet...strangely erotic.

She folded her arms and leaned her head against the wall, her gaze sweeping over the length of him. Mother Goddess, she was lucky this man was hers. Not that she'd gotten a chance to enjoy her husband quite yet. They'd had their night of passion before their wedding, but they still hadn't had a true wedding night. As she watched him move gracefully over the training floor, she realized just how unfair that was. Here Teryn was practicing for a battle they couldn't avoid while she'd spent...however long she'd been gone establishing an alliance. They should have been wrapped in each other's arms, enjoying the life of newly-weds, not facing war.

"Are you going to keep staring?" Teryn said, startling her. His gaze was fixed on his imaginary enemy as he side-stepped, then thrust. After a final slash and thrust, he angled his body to face her and planted the butt of his spear on the ground. A corner of his mouth lifted. "Or are you going to kiss me?"

A thrilling warmth ignited in her chest at the challenge in his eyes, the taunting in his voice. If he could still make her feel like that amidst everything that was going on, maybe there was hope for them yet. For them to enjoy some semblance of newlywed life.

She raced over to him and he met her halfway, grasping her around the waist with his free arm and pressing his lips to hers. Her palm rested over the slick skin of his pectoral. Just as quickly as he'd kissed her, he pulled away.

His expression turned bashful, but he held her eyes. "Sorry. I'm sweaty, aren't I?"

"I don't entirely mind," she said with a coy look, though she had to admit, her lips tasted like salt.

He released her waist and strode to the rack of polearms, exchanging his spear for the shirt he'd hung there. She was almost disappointed until she realized he was simply drying off. A wicked smile curved her lips. She wanted to look at him like this a little longer. Extend the playful mood he'd begun.

She swept closer to him, evading his detection while he

was drying his face with his shirt. As he brought the linen article down and found her standing so close, his eyes went wide. She blinked up at him, an innocent expression as she reached for the hilt hidden behind her back.

He opened his mouth to speak, but she pulled the dagger from her golden sash and flicked it to his neck. He flinched only slightly but otherwise held perfectly still.

"Don't let me interrupt your training, love of mine," she said.

His eyes simmered, whether with challenge or desire she knew not. All she knew was how it tightened her belly. His lips tugged into a wry grin and he dropped his shirt to the floor. Then, in a flash of movement, he whirled away and retrieved a wooden training dagger from a nearby stand.

They circled each other, and Cora considered whether she should dive for a training blade too. But they were both skilled enough to defend themselves and know when to hold back. She made the first move, striking with her dagger, and he parried her blade with ease. Swiveling to the side, she aimed for his ribs. He caught her wrist in his hand, angled her arm behind her, and twisted her around until her back was to his chest, her knife hand between them. He pressed his practice blade beneath her chin.

"There's something familiar about this position," Teryn said, bringing his lips close to her ear.

She shuddered at the sound and recalled a moment from their first meeting. He'd wrenched her arm behind her that time too, pulling her against his chest, and asked her to stop trying to stab him. The closeness of his voice had caught her off guard then, but now it made her want to get even closer.

She tried to get free the same way she had then, by

striking his instep with her heel. Predicting her move, he widened his stance, but he loosened his hold enough to allow her to wrench her knife hand from his grip. She whirled to face him again, striking. He parried, shifted, parried again. At her next strike, he caught her wrist and pulled her to him once more. This time, her dagger wasn't between them, leaving her back flush to his chest. He held her wrist in place while securing his forearm over her middle. His grip was firm enough to hold her still yet soft enough to feel more like an embrace.

She didn't struggle as he brought his lips to the lobe of her ear. Instead, she angled her head, daring him to land a blow with either his mouth or his wooden blade. Instead, he whispered, "What are you wearing, by the way?"

"You only now noticed?" To be honest, she'd only remembered her state of dress when she'd neared the hall leading to the armory. By then, she'd sensed Teryn's proximity and hadn't felt like changing. It was after midnight now, and Cora hadn't come across any servants on her way to find Teryn, only her husband's guards, who were posted outside the hall.

"Oh, I noticed. Also..." His forearm froze against her midsection. Then, angling the hand that held her wrist, he spun her away from him, and for a moment it felt more like they were dancing. He didn't release her wrist. Instead, he angled her arm overhead, bent at the elbow, and stepped in close. His eyes swept over her form, lingering on the deep V-shaped neck of her robe. His throat bobbed. "You aren't wearing a corset."

She lifted her chin, her chest, letting the lay of the thin silk and the peaks it accentuated speak volumes. "I'm not."

That surprised him enough to allow her to catch him off guard. She freed her wrist and darted a step back.

"How about this?" she said. "For every blow you land, I'll remove an article of clothing."

He bit his bottom lip. When he spoke, his voice came out thick. "And what if you land a—"

Before he could finish, she lunged forward and slapped his thigh with the flat of her blade. Just as quickly, she leaped back, a victorious grin on her lips. "If I land a blow, you have to do the same."

His mouth fell open. "Did that one count?"

"It counted." She dropped her gaze to his waistband, then fluttered her lashes at him. "So go on."

With exaggerated reluctance, he brought the fingers of his free hand to the top button of his fly.

Cora watched with greedy anticipation—

Before she knew what was happening, he lunged forward and slapped her lightly with his wooden dagger, in the same place she'd struck him.

She squeaked in surprise, her defenses thoroughly shaken. She debated striking back, but he was already retreating.

"Looks like we've both landed a blow," he said as he worked his buttons in earnest this time. Then, in a taunting tone, he echoed her earlier words. "So go on."

With a huff, she reached under the skirt of her robe with one hand, not daring to drop her dagger, and slid her trousers down. Teryn stepped out of his bottoms, and she was disappointed to see he wore linen undershorts. Devils take those undershorts. Meanwhile, she had no underclothes at all, for Garot had only left her the robe, sash, and trousers. At least the plentiful folds of her robe's skirt hid her bottom half, which meant she still had the more exciting view.

She charged forward, thrusting her dagger, but he

parried it. She charged again. Again. His defenses had grown sharper, fiercer. It seemed he was determined to get her out of another article of clothing. Well, she wouldn't go easy on him. She was equally as—

With a yelp, she tumbled back. She'd been so focused on striking Teryn's wrist with the edge of her free hand, she hadn't anticipated him sweeping out her feet. While she'd managed to force him to release his weapon, she'd lost her chance to land a blow with hers.

He caught her before she could fully lose her balance and guided her fall to the floor. Pinning her hands over her head, he lowered his body over hers, careful not to crush her with his full weight.

Heat burned deep in her core, tingling at the thrill of him being on top of her. Yet they were at an impasse. His training dagger was off to the side, but she still held hers. As soon as he released her arms, she could land a winning blow. Now all she needed to do was get him to release her.

With a wicked grin, she wiggled her hips slightly. "This brings back memories too."

"I woke you up from a nightmare much like this."

She spread her legs slightly, letting him settle more firmly against her. She hooked a leg around his hip, making his eyes widen. "I seem to recall you promising me pleasure."

"Is that how you remember it?"

She arched her brow. "Am I wrong?"

"What I said back then was if I took pleasure in touching you, you would experience pleasure too."

"And are you, Teryn? Are you taking pleasure in touching me?"

He rocked his hips slightly, and she could feel proof that

he was, in fact, taking great pleasure from this. His grip slackened.

That was all she needed.

Clamping her legs around his hips, she shifted her weight and rolled him onto his back, she on top now. He lost hold of her wrists but flung his hand out toward his wooden dagger. Just as he touched it to her side, she brought her very real blade to his throat.

"I win," she said through panting breaths.

"We both landed a blow," he said.

"Yes, but you only have one more item to take off."

"Don't you too?"

Holding his eyes with a triumphant smile, she reached with her free hand for the sash around her waist. She tugged the tie, and it fell from around her robe.

His expression fell. "Damn that sash."

"Now you know how I felt when I saw your undershorts. Which you will now remove. With both hands. I've won, so drop your dagger and take them off."

Desire darkened his irises at the demand in her tone. He did as told, releasing the dagger and reaching for his waist-band. She rose to her knees, still straddling him, and kept her blade to his throat. She accommodated his moves, easing her blade away to allow him to fully slide his shorts down. He held her eyes all the while, which only made the heat between her legs grow to an insatiable, pulsing throb.

Fully nude, he reclined back down, and she lowered herself onto him once more, spreading the folds of her skirt around her so nothing lay between their bare flesh. His hardness dug against her thigh, even as she continued to hold her knife's edge to his throat. She wasn't sure why she kept it there, only that it deepened the thrill, the desire that coursed through her. And from the way he watched her, jaw slack, eyes roving the sliver of naked skin her robe revealed, he felt the same.

"Do you want me like this?" she asked, voice barely above a whisper.

"You mean with murder in your eyes and a knife between us? Gods, Cora." He uttered her name through his teeth. "I want you in every way you'll have me."

She shifted her hips, rocked them, and he moaned with want. His hands caged her hips, fingers clamped around the silk folds of her skirt with an intensity that spoke of either pleasure or frustration. Her dagger's position left him with little range of motion.

He spoke again, echoing her question back to her. "Do you want me like this?"

In answer, she slid over him, holding his gaze as she guided him inside her. She seated herself fully over him and gasped at the feeling, the fullness. Teryn cursed, his eyes fluttering shut.

She tapped the underside of his chin with the flat of her blade. "Keep your eyes open and watch me."

"Devils," he groaned as his eyes locked on hers again, lips quirked in a devious smile. She moved then, sliding up and down his length, igniting pleasurable sensations that burned hotter with every thrust. Just when she thought she could quench that need, her desire only grew. Teryn's expression, the clear yearning in his eyes, the sounds he made, the way he made no move to make her drop her blade, the way he watched her just like she'd demanded, only increased that feeling.

She never imagined she'd want something like this, that she'd take pleasure with a blade in her hand. But gods, it was a thrill. And yet, even as her passion burned, the thrill gave way to more want, and she couldn't take another moment without his hands on her. She tossed her blade to the side.

Teryn moved at once, lifting his upper body to meet her in a crushing kiss, a violent dance of teeth and tongues. His hands roved everywhere he hadn't been able to touch before, tangling in her hair, caressing the column of her neck, then down the length of skin visible through her open robe. He pulled back slightly and parted the robe further, baring her breasts, her stomach, and the meeting of their bodies.

They watched the way they moved together for several beats, then his mouth closed over her breast. She threw her head back at the caress of his tongue over her hardened peak, and let her robe slip fully from her shoulders. Moans left her lips, ones she didn't care enough to stifle. The guards weren't close enough to hear them, and even if they were, she didn't care. There was a boldness to what they were doing that made her euphoric and a roughness between them that hadn't been there the first night they'd made love. Through it all wove a softness in her heart that made her feel safe. Loved. Cherished. Even as Teryn's teeth grazed her skin. Even as she dug her nails into his back.

Release began to unravel inside her, and she rode that cresting wave. Teryn aided it with his fingertips, circling over her most sensitive spot as he continued to move inside her. Then finally, the sweetest, fiercest pleasure erupted from her, one that sent stars to her eyes and whimpers from her lips. Teryn found his release next, and he guided her hips through every wave and valley until they both were thoroughly sated.

As they fell back, out of breath, and stared at the armory ceiling, Teryn spoke through trembling breaths. "Say whatever you want, but I think I won that battle."

41

As Cora and Teryn left the armory, their clothing haphazardly replaced, Cora wondered if maybe they had been too loud after all. Not that the guards gave any indication as the king and queen emerged from the armory hall, but they were well-trained in keeping their composure. It was the silence of the sleeping castle that brought heat to Cora's cheeks, strikingly still and quiet as they strode up the steps to the keep. Even their footsteps were too loud.

That was also when the mood between Cora and Teryn began to change. It wasn't awkwardness. Teryn held her hand with the same warmth and attention he'd given her body in the armory, and his posture was easy. Instead, the strain came from an inevitable fall back to reality in the wake of their euphoria.

Teryn was the first to voice it, leaning in close and lowering his voice to the quietest of whispers. "King Darius made his first direct contact with us today."

She nearly stumbled up the next step, but Teryn's grip on her hand helped her regain her balance. "He did?"

"He issued a demand for our surrender and detailed the forces that await us should we decline." He relayed those numbers now, told her about the meeting Darius had set at the Khero-Vinias border, and the legion of reinforcements already heading their way.

Cora's head swam at those numbers, but before her dread could grow, Teryn handed her a slip of paper. They reached the top of the staircase, and she read the sparse words scrawled across the paper, illuminated by the dim lamps lining the halls of the keep. It was a short, coded message, but...

"Does this mean what I think it means?"

Teryn gave a nod, and she returned the paper to him. Hope filled her chest as she analyzed the words in her head again and again. It could only mean one thing. The rebellion in Norun was set to strike soon. Darius wouldn't likely get those reinforcements.

Teryn's secrecy made her wonder who else knew. Perhaps no one.

Good. That meant it was truly an advantage.

"There's a traitor in the castle," Teryn whispered. "The Norunian spy you'd imprisoned was murdered after he divulged the information about the naval fleet. At least, that's how it was supposed to seem. In truth, the dead man that was left in the cell was someone else entirely. I know because...because I spoke to the corpse's spirit."

"You *spoke* to a spirit?" She went to great lengths to keep her voice down despite her shock. She knew about his ability to see spirits and that he could communicate with Emylia, but speaking to the ghost of a dead stranger...well, that was only half as alarming as what he said next.

"I learned that I can aid a spirit's progression to the otherlife through touch." Teryn's expression turned wary, as if he hadn't fully come to terms with this new information either. "I spoke to the spirit. He remembered nothing after heading home from a tavern in Greenfair Village. After he told me what he could, he grew hysterical. He begged me to send him on, so I did."

Her mind reeled. And not just over Teryn's strange new power. Setting that shocking revelation aside, she pored over what he'd said before that. The prisoner was found dead in his cell after making his confession. But the body—and its spirit—had belonged to a stranger.

Her pulse quickened. "Someone helped the prisoner escape and left a decoy corpse in his place?"

"Yes. It was supposed to look like he'd been silenced on purpose as punishment for divulging key information. Larylis believes it was all a ruse to get us to separate our forces."

Damn. If he was right, they'd played right into that scheme.

They turned down the hall toward their suite.

"Any leads on who may have helped the prisoner escape?" Cora asked.

Teryn shook his head. "None."

She cast her gaze around the dark halls with fresh eyes, seeing sinister shadows and imagining hidden enemies. Even so, this was probably the safest place to talk—while walking, when there was no one close enough to hear their words, no way for someone to lie in wait and overhear their secrets. Even the guards trailed too far behind to hear them. That was some comfort at least.

They reached their suite, and the guards took their posts on each side of the door. The sitting room held a chill as they entered, but their bedroom boasted the embers of the hearth fire. Teryn retrieved a fresh nightshirt from his dresser and pulled it over his head before he went to stoke the flames. Cora freshened up with the ewer of wash water —cold, unfortunately—and changed into a chemise and thick velvet robe.

With the fire roaring and the room growing toasty, Cora wanted nothing more than to crawl into bed. She was about to do just that when Teryn's snort of laughter had her gaze flying to him.

His eyes crinkled at the corners. "Your hair, my love. Bring me your brush."

Her cheeks heated. After their time in the armory, her hair was probably a disaster. She did as asked, and when she returned to the bed, she found him seated upon it, his back propped against the pillows. His hair had come loose from its tie during their...activities...and now hung around his jaw, a few wayward strands strewn over his forehead. How the hell did he look so dashing with mussed hair?

He patted the space on the bed before him, and she crawled upon the mattress and settled between his legs. She handed him the brush.

"Tell me if this hurts," he said, bringing the bristles to the ends of her hair. His tone and hands were so gentle, a contrast to the firm grip he'd had on her hips, the way he'd palmed her body as she'd ridden him.

That sent a tingle of heat low in her belly, and it took no small amount of self-control not to turn around and initiate an encore. Instead, she kept perfectly still. There was pleasure enough in simply feeling him run the brush through her hair. It was a strangely intimate situation, even though maids brushed her hair daily. Having Teryn do it while they were alone in their shared bed was entirely different.

"What about you?" he asked, his voice deep and

rumbling. "What happened in El'Ara? Do we have an alliance with the Elvyn?"

"The beginnings of one. They haven't offered anything concrete, but by now they will have stationed soldiers within the tear on the fae side of the Veil. They want us to provide two thousand soldiers to guard the human side. We would have to be discreet, otherwise we'll draw attention straight to the tear's location."

"We could close the roads on either side," Teryn said. "Feign a landslide and guard a wide perimeter around the area."

"The tear is at the edge of a cliff, so a landslide would stand to reason. And we could hide our forces in the woods. Still...two thousand men. They've said nothing about how they intend to help us in exchange."

"And that's half our military. We need those soldiers with us when we meet Darius in three weeks. If we can gain Elvyn soldiers to bolster our numbers and face him with just his force of five thousand, we have a chance at winning."

Cora agreed. So long as the rebellion began as planned, they could isolate Darius with his current soldiers.

"It would benefit the Elvyn too," Teryn said. "If we defeat Darius at the Khero-Vinias border, we won't need to guard the tear. Keeping Darius from setting foot in Lela should be our priority."

"I'm supposed to return soon with our requests for the terms of the alliance," Cora said. "I can demand they provide forces for our confrontation with Darius. We can make a plan with the Elvyn to defeat him." She remembered the collar, how Ailan had called it their one chance to defeat her brother. "In the meantime, I can offer a smaller force to guard the human side of the tear, as a show of good faith until the terms have been finalized."

"Larylis can do that," Teryn said. "He's on a ship patrolling Khero's west coast now."

Cora angled her head to meet his eyes. "He's on a ship? Not in Vera?"

Teryn paused brushing. "After he suspected that the naval fleet threat was a ruse, he left on an unmarked schooner with fifty soldiers to investigate by sea. More than that, I think he wanted to be close to Mareleau. She wasn't quite as discreet as you were in her letter."

With a roll of her eyes, she faced forward again. "Of course she wasn't." She meant to say it in good humor, but it came out with a bitter edge. What was wrong with her lately?

"He and I communicate daily through Berol," Teryn said as he resumed brushing. "He left his generals in charge of watching Vera's shores in case the naval fleet threat was real, but he'll come to our aid in allying with El'Ara. I'm certain he'd prefer to oversee the soldiers stationed there."

Cora pursed her lips. It was a bit reckless of Larylis to leave Vera at a time like this, but she understood too. He'd never truly wanted to be king. He'd only wanted to be with Mareleau.

Of course he did. Everyone loves Mareleau. Your own husband wanted to be with her at one time. Remember?

Her hands curled into fists at the bitter words. The last part wasn't even true. *Stop it! Stop thinking like that. Mareleau is my friend. These feelings aren't mine.*

"When will you need to return?" Teryn asked. "If we're going to march Elvyn soldiers from where I imagine the tear is..."

Cora still hadn't dared state its location out loud. She

would save that for the council meeting they'd have tomorrow. When they could post guards around the room and destroy evidence afterward. Even though they continued to whisper, Cora couldn't shake the fear of having a traitor in the castle.

"I'll need to leave soon," she said. "It will take at least two weeks to march soldiers to the border."

There was still so much more to discuss. Most could wait for the council meeting, but there was something she wanted to get off her chest. Something that filled her with a hollow dread. She wasn't sure she could share it with anyone but Teryn.

As if sensing her turmoil, Teryn paused his ministrations and set the brush on the bed beside them.

She angled herself around to face him. "The worst part about allying with the Elvyn..." The words dried on her tongue. She swallowed hard and tried again. "Is that we'll be fighting for our eventual exile from Lela."

Teryn paled. He opened his mouth, but it wasn't he who spoke next.

"Not if you ally with me."

42

Cora's heart shot into her throat as she whirled to face the stranger in their room. Teryn leaped off the bed at once, pulling Cora with him and positioning her behind him. She reached for her waist, but her hands met only air. Seven devils, she'd left her dagger in the armory. Teryn at least had the good sense to lunge for the fireplace poker and brandished it toward the intruder.

The man made no move aside from tilting his lips in an amused grin.

He was on the late end of middle-aged, tall and slender, his posture somehow dignified as he leaned against the far wall, ankles crossed. His salt-and-pepper hair was swept away from his brow to reveal a strong nose and silver-blue eyes that bore an unmistakable intensity. He was dressed in all black from his trousers to the military-style coat he wore. There was nothing familiar about the coat's design to distinguish which military he represented.

Everything about his presence screamed *wrong*, even before she noticed the knife he toyed with.

"I'm glad to see you've finished," the man said. There

was something familiar about his voice. "The stamina you young people have."

Stamina. What was he talking about? Had he...

"Who are you?" Teryn asked, voice deadly calm.

"I'm not surprised you don't recognize me, but surely Her Majesty would. No? Ah, it's the absence of bruises, isn't it? You should pay better attention to the people you have beaten at your command."

Understanding clicked into place. "You're...the Norunian spy."

It shouldn't have been possible. Even without the bruises, there was little to link them by appearances alone. He seemed taller, and far less rough around the edges. But that voice. It held a more distinguished quality, but he was just as well-spoken as the man she'd interrogated in the dungeon. With a deep breath, she opened her senses.

His energy was one and the same.

This was the prisoner who'd faked his own death. Freed by someone in the castle and replaced with a decoy body. And from what he'd said...

The stamina you young people have.

Nausea turned her stomach. Had he been...watching them? Their most private moment? It was one thing to enjoy the thrill of getting caught by people she trusted. Enemies were different. There was nothing thrilling about that. It was simply violating.

Had he been inside her castle all this time, lurking in the shadows?

Teryn shifted to the side, deepening his defensive stance. He opened his mouth and gathered in a sharp breath, as if prepared to shout, but the spy spoke first.

"Don't call for your guards." He flipped his knife and caught the hilt with ease. "I can cross the space between us in a heartbeat and shove this through your throat before you've had a chance to blink."

His words pulsed in her mind.

He could...cross the space between them.

In a heartbeat.

She assessed the floor, the bed between them, the wardrobe he'd have to skirt around. The answer was so crushing, she almost couldn't voice it.

"You're Darius," she managed to say.

"Majesty, I wasn't aware we were on a first-name basis," he said, tone mocking.

That was when she noticed something about his eyes; they were so like Morkai's had been, with that same pale blue color. She tried to find similarities to Ailan, but there were none. His complexion was tan but much paler than Ailan's. His hair was gray where hers was black. But as her eyes fell upon his ears, she saw their subtly pointed tips. They weren't as angled as Ailan's but were more so than Morkai's. Surely she or the gaoler would have noticed pointed ears on their prisoner...wouldn't they? His hair had been shaggy enough to cover them, but—

Another realization formed in her mind.

The only time she'd seen him had been before the Veil had torn.

Any differences in his appearance could be attributed to that. Though his aging hadn't reversed nearly as drastically as Ailan's had, it had darkened his hair, straightened his posture, and elongated his ears.

Terror tore through her. Darius...her enemy...was in her castle.

He was *here*.

Standing before her.

Teryn shifted his stance again, teeth bared in a sneer.

Darius raised his empty palm while sheathing the knife at his waist. When both hands were empty, he said, "I'm not here for violence. I'm here to talk."

"Then talk," Teryn said through his teeth.

"Lower your weapon and I will."

Teryn held still for a long beat, then lowered the poker to his side. He kept it firmly in his grip, however, his posture defensive, still half blocking Cora.

"Right," Darius said. "Now, I'm sure you have questions—"

"It was you all along," Cora said, her mind still reeling. With every breath, more of the pieces were clicking into place. "You were never a spy. You got caught on purpose."

And the prisoner hadn't been freed by a traitor. Sure, he could have had an accomplice, but it wouldn't have been necessary. Because if this was Darius Solaria, King of Syrus, all he'd needed to do was worldwalk out of the cell.

Then worldwalk back with a decoy corpse.

Gods, what a fool she'd been. All this time, she'd thought her best defense against him was to keep him from ever stepping foot in Khero, preventing him from familiarizing himself with key locations and securing places to worldwalk to.

Yet he'd been here all along. He'd waltzed straight into her kingdom and into her castle as if he'd been invited.

He arched a brow. "Was that a question?"

"Why did you do it?"

"I wanted to meet you, and getting captured as a Norunian spy was my best bet."

Teryn scoffed. "You could have sent a formal request for an audience. Or negotiated a meeting on neutral ground."

"Yes, but would you have faced me with an open mind? That's what I came to discover. I wanted to gauge my chances at peaceful relations between us, or see if your preconceived notions were too strong."

"You make it sound like you came for tea," Cora said, "but what you really did was invade my castle under a false pretense and a false name and lie to us. If you wanted peaceful relations, you should have tried something else. Pretending to be a prisoner, feeding us false information, and faking your death was a sure way to turn us against you."

"No, you were already turned against me." His voice took on a cold edge. "Thanks to my idiot son. Foolish Desmond, parading around as Duke Morkai. What a ridiculous moniker. As if calling himself *King of Magic* in the fae language would help him become Morkaius."

Cora stiffened at the mention of Morkai. Or Desmond, as was his birth name. Did Darius know his son was dead? Did he blame Cora for his death? Was he here for revenge? Questions burned Cora's mind, but she didn't want to give anything away by asking the wrong one. She couldn't be sure what Darius did or didn't know already, or what Morkai may have told him.

She shifted her feet, rooting herself to the stone floor, and sought logic over fear. His presence was terrifying and didn't bode well for the safety of her castle. Yet she could learn what she could, starting with the facts they'd already exchanged. "When you pretended to be a Norunian spy, you claimed Norun was targeting us over the death of Prince Helios. Was any of that true?"

"Oh, it was true. Before Desmond met his end at Centerpointe Rock, he detailed the prince's death to King Isvius, attempting to paint Selay as the enemy and potentially gain an ally. But when Desmond couldn't follow up to fan the flames of hatred and control their direction, the King of

Norun turned his ire upon Khero instead. Norun made for an easy ally when I began correspondence with Isvius and mentioned my plans to invade Khero."

So Darius did know about Morkai's death. And his alliance with Norun was real.

"Why are you targeting Khero?"

He gave her a pointed look. "You know why. I know all about the Veil and Lela and the prophecy. Even before I got my memories back, I knew. Desmond was useful in one thing at least, and that was dying. His death triggered an enchantment he'd forged as a safeguard, ensuring his hard work wouldn't be lost if he failed. The enchantment materialized in a veritable tome of information that landed on my study desk in Syrus. Despite our many decades of estrangement, he'd continued to detail his discoveries and actions. The report told me everything he'd hidden from me after our falling out. It was quite illuminating."

Mother Goddess, was there anything he didn't know?

"I hope you see what's at stake now," he said. "The missive you received from me this morning spoke only truth. In three weeks, we will meet at the Khero-Vinias border, and I will demand Khero's surrender. If you refuse, my Norunian reinforcements will follow and lay waste to your kingdom. Moreover, if I wanted to act sooner, I could. Ever since I left your dungeon, I've spent time orienting myself with certain locations in the castle. It would be easy to claim Ridine. I could have control of it by morning."

Tremors racked Cora's body at his words. At the very real picture they painted. She couldn't keep the quaver from her voice, but at least she had enough rage to hide her fear. "Then why are you here chatting with us?"

"Unlike my son, who used war negotiations as bait for battle, I truly want to avoid war. I'll resort to it if I must, plan for it, but I don't want you to be my enemy." He stepped away from the wall, hands clasped behind his back. "Besides, there is an alternative to surrender."

Cora remembered what he'd said when he'd first arrived.

"You want us to ally with you," Teryn said.

"Yes, but instead of talking in circles about it, I want to extend a personal invitation for Queen Aveline to speak with me in private. And no, the invitation is for one, not two. Aveline will come with me alone."

"Come with you...to where?" Cora asked.

"To Syrus."

She barked a disbelieving laugh. "You want me to go to Syrus with you."

"I can walk us there and back in no more than an hour."

He used the term *walk*, but he didn't mean by foot. "Why do you want to meet with me in Syrus?"

"To show you what the kingdom of an *evil immortal tyrant* looks like." He said it with such jest, but there was nothing funny about this situation.

Cora and Teryn said nothing, which made Darius' expression darken.

"I've called it an invitation, but—" He stepped forward again and disappeared at once.

"—it's not—" he said, appearing on the opposite side of the bed.

"—really—" Now by the wardrobe.

"—a request." He reappeared where he'd first stood. He'd moved so fast, they'd hardly had time to react beyond a flinch. He'd worldwalked with ease, as if he'd been taking a leisurely stroll, hopping from one location to the next with each step he'd taken.

Cora wasn't that powerful. She couldn't activate her abilities that fast.

"I don't want to take you by force," Darius said, "but I can. I can cross this space and take your hand before either of you can react."

"Is that how you intend to get us to trust you?" Teryn said, edging closer to Cora, his poker raised once more. "With threats?"

"What else do you want from me?" Darius said with a sneer. "We're enemies until we agree otherwise. I can't make unbreakable vows like pureblood Elvyn can, but I will still state it out loud. I swear not to harm Queen Aveline Caelan at any time while she is in Syrus."

Cora shook her head. "Your word means nothing."

"What matters to you, then? Blood? Well, then let me tell you this. I have a vested interest in you. A reason why I'd rather not kill you, and it has to do with your bloodline."

"What...what do you mean?"

His lips curved in a cruel grin. "You, Aveline, are my kin."

43

Darius' words rattled around in her mind, but she couldn't make sense of them. "What do you mean I'm your kin?"

"You share my blood," Darius said. "Well, not *my* blood exactly. We both share my father's blood, the blood of King Tristaine Solaria. Your relation to him is diluted over many generations, but I can still sense it when I stand before you. The same way my son thought he sensed the weight of prophecy on you. That's what his report had said. That the moment he saw you as a child, he felt a connection and knew you were the prophesied mother. Can you imagine how embarrassed he'd be to discover just how wrong he was? What he felt wasn't the magical tug of prophecy, but the connection fae feel to their kin. Had he been humble enough to harbor at least a shred of doubt, he'd have done his due diligence to follow your family tree. He'd have followed your mother's ancestry to the Southern Islands, then several generations back to King Tristaine of Syrus, his grandfather."

Cora didn't know what to think. What to feel. She was

distantly related to Morkai. He'd targeted her, hurt her, cursed her all because of a prophecy and a sense of connection he hadn't understood.

He'd been wrong.

So recklessly and foolishly wrong.

Every conclusion he'd come to about Cora had been the result of his mistakes.

Everything she'd suffered.

Every loss she'd been forced to bear.

Rage boiled inside her, curling her fingers into fists. Flames filled her mind's eye as a dark weight fell over her, smothering her.

Then a whispered voice. *Should it have been her?*

A thorn of guilt shattered her anger. She forced the dark thoughts from her mind, forced her fury to cool enough to maintain her tether to the present.

Darius spoke again. "I truly mean it when I say I don't want us to be enemies. All I ask is for one hour of your time. Just see what Syrus is like. See what kind of king I truly am. Hear me out, and I'll answer any questions you have."

She breathed deeply, opening her senses to him, to his energy.

"I will not hurt you," he said, "nor will I demand an answer about our alliance today. I will give you time to decide."

She tested the flow of his energy, its lack of constriction. His words didn't feel like a lie.

While she couldn't imagine anything that could convince her to ally with him, this could give her a chance to learn more. And she had one advantage.

She could worldwalk.

Darius had made no mention of her abilities yet, and he couldn't have learned about them from his son's report.

Morkai would have relayed details about Cora's clairsentience, but he'd never learned about her worldwalking
powers while he'd been alive. It was possible Darius
suspected she was a worldwalker based on their shared
bloodline with Tristaine, but the ability obviously wasn't
gifted to all his descendants. Morkai hadn't been able to
worldwalk. Cora's mother hadn't shown even the slightest
inclination toward magic.

As far as Darius knew, she was just a clairsentient witch,
still learning her magic.

Her abilities may not be as impressive as Darius' were,
but if she sensed danger, she could disappear in a heartbeat,
just like him. And maybe, if she could catch him unaware, if
she could get hold of a weapon, even just a knife...

She could end his life.

But what had Ailan said about killing him?

*He can be killed just like the rest of my kind—beheading or
excessive blood loss.*

He can be killed so long as he can be outsmarted.

She wasn't sure she could behead or force excessive
blood loss while outsmarting him, but there was at least a
chance.

And if he could take her away by force anyway...

She sidled closer to Teryn. They kept their gazes on
Darius for several long beats before exchanging a quick
glance. Cora gave him a subtle nod, which made his jaw
tighten. Just as quickly, they returned their attention to
Darius.

Cora opened her mouth to accept his terms, but Teryn
spoke first.

"I want a blood oath. That's how humans secured vows
in ancient times, predating written contracts."

Darius smirked. "Yes, I know how history books work."

"Then cut your palm and state the promise you made earlier. That you will escort Queen Aveline safely to and from Syrus, and that you will take her from Ridine for no longer than an hour, and that neither you nor anyone else will cause her harm."

Darius narrowed his eyes. "When I asked if blood mattered to you, this wasn't what I'd had in mind. Are you like my son, then? Dabbling in blood magic because you're not strong enough to do anything else?"

Cora couldn't help the furrow that formed between her brows. Why *did* Teryn want a blood pact from Darius? She'd never known him to value such old-fashioned traditions.

Teryn shrugged. "You're about to abduct my wife. If you fear I'll use your blood for nefarious purposes, then I'd say it makes the terms of our agreement almost even."

"Only almost?"

"My wife's safety is priceless. There's nothing you could give me but your life that could balance the scales. So I'll ask for your blood."

Darius continued to eye Teryn, but he drew his knife nevertheless. "Very well," he said with clear reluctance. Holding out his hand, he sliced the blade across his palm. A red line appeared, and as he squeezed his fingers into a fist, a drop of blood fell to the stones. Then another. "I, Darius Solaria, hereby promise that I will escort Queen Aveline, by way of worldwalking, safely to and from Syrus, and that we will stray to no other kingdom. I vow that I will return her to Ridine by the end of an hour *or* allow her to leave on her own at any time. Furthermore, I vow that neither I nor anyone else will cause her harm at any time during the course of our agreement."

Cora analyzed his words, seeking loopholes. Not that it mattered. Like he'd already admitted, this wasn't a magically binding vow, just an old tradition based on superstition. Maybe what Teryn had said was the important part. Instilling a hint of fear in Darius could make him keep his word.

She breathed deeply, connecting to all the elements and sought any sign that this was wrong. Dread pulsed back, as did anxiety, but she felt no clairsentient warning. No inkling that this might be a trap.

"All right," she said, voice thick. On trembling legs, she strode out from behind Teryn. He grasped her hand as she passed him, squeezing it. She squeezed it back in wordless reassurance. Her lungs tightened as she released his palm, felt his fingers slip from hers. She took another step. "I'm ready."

In the next breath, Darius stood before her. He placed a hand on her shoulder, then—

Cora was gone. Teryn hadn't been prepared. Hadn't even seen Darius move. He and Cora had come to the same conclusion—that they didn't have much of a choice but to humor him. Not when Darius held Ridine at his mercy. Not when he could come back at any time, fill their castle with countless soldiers, and claim victory by morning.

Either Darius was less capable than he'd made himself seem or he truly was desperate for an alliance with them.

They needed to find out which was true.

And how to exploit it.

That didn't lessen his terror at having witnessed him taking her like that. His rage at knowing he'd agreed to *let* him take her.

Hatred burned hot in his chest as he narrowed his eyes

at the three spots of blood on the stones. Without a second thought, he marched into his sitting room, extracted a piece of parchment from the bureau, and placed the paper over the blood until crimson bloomed over it.

"What are you doing?" Emylia's voice came from beside him. She was as semi-transparent as always, outfitted in an equally hazy loose dress that billowed on a nonexistent breeze.

"Were you here the whole time?" he asked, his tone low and controlled. If she'd been there before, he hadn't noticed her. He'd been too focused on Darius and Cora. "Did you enjoy the show? Did you just stand there mute and watch him take her?"

"What could I have done?"

He was being unfair in taking his frustration out on her, but she'd been avoiding him ever since their last conversation on the battlement. When she'd refused to explain what she'd meant about feeling like she'd disappear if she came too close to him. He understood exactly why now. Because touching her ethera would force her to move on to the otherlife. To claim the peace she'd said she'd wanted but hadn't been able to receive. Peace she'd only find after taking care of her unfinished business.

He knew the truth.

She didn't *want* to move on yet.

And he didn't want her hypocrisy right now.

Teryn finished soaking the blood into the paper and folded it. As he rose, he met Emylia's accusing gaze.

"Don't tell me you're going to do what I think you are," she said.

"What is it you think I'm doing?"

Her lower lip wobbled as her fingers curled into fists. "Let me ask you a question. Why have you been going to that tower room? Why have you been reading that book? You know it's dangerous. You know what that book has done."

He did know, but it didn't shake his resolve, even though she was right in every way. He had no right going into the North Tower Library, reading the book Cora had left stashed inside a nightstand drawer. Seeking answers to the question that had plagued his mind over the past week.

In truth, he hadn't learned anything new, but he had confirmed what Emylia had told him when they'd last spoken. It had all been there, just like she'd described.

"Why, Teryn? Why are you doing this?"

"Because I want Morkai's army of souls."

Her disappointment in him was plain, written in the downward curve of her mouth, the slump of her shoulders.

He shared some of that disappointment too. He'd wanted to wait until he could talk to Cora about it, but now he didn't have time. He needed to act. If Darius returned to attack the castle, he'd be ready. He wouldn't let him win. Whether now, later, or at the meeting at the border, he'd use this advantage.

"There must be a reason why I have this ability," he said. "This connection to death."

"Reason?" She released an angry huff. "What are you talking about? Do you think you're part of the prophecy? You're not. There is no special reason for what has happened to you, just a logical one. Blood magic comes with consequences, just like I've told you. You completed a blood weaving while you straddled the line between life and death. You forged a magical connection *with* death. It's as simple as that."

"Why, though? Why *this* consequence? Why does my touch send etheras to the otherlife?"

She flinched back at his words, demonstrating just how afraid she was of that very power. Then she shook her head. "We might never know. Maybe it's because you succeeded at severing another ethera's ties to your body—Morkai's tie to the mortal world. Now you're gifted and burdened with the ability to do the same for other spirits. To sever the chains that bind them here and free them."

He clenched his jaw. "Then why can't I use it for good?"

"*Are* you trying to use it for good? Or are you lusting after blood magic for revenge?" When he said nothing, she closed her eyes. Finally, her expression softened. She turned a pleading look to him. "Just...take a moment, Teryn, please. Breathe. Connect to your heart. Don't work blood magic on an impulse."

He wasn't acting on impulse. He'd been considering this for a week, weighing possibilities. Still, she was right about blood magic and its consequences. She knew better than anyone that what he wanted to do was wrong. Dark. Forbidden.

Reluctantly, he gave in and closed his eyes. Just like when he'd been trapped as a disembodied ethera, he connected to his breaths, his heartbeat, the rush of his blood, the pound of his pulse. Slowly, he began to relax. His muscles uncoiled, his heartbeat slowed, and the most delicious euphoria struck him. The euphoria of being alive. In his body. In control. It wasn't an impassioned or impulsive feeling. It was real and steady.

He shifted his thoughts to what he'd been considering.

No doubts stood in his way. No guilt. No fear. No remorse.

"I'm doing it, Emylia."

~

Teryn didn't wait to see if she followed him out of the castle to the charred field, the folded piece of paper stained with Darius' blood in his hand. Maintaining the same calm he'd felt after sinking into his bodily sensations, he crouched at the edge of the dead field, just like he'd witnessed Morkai doing the day he demonstrated the abilities of his wraiths. He'd been summoning his Roizan then, but Teryn did it for a different reason now.

He unfolded the bloodstained paper and pressed it against the charred soil. Then he watched and waited. There was, of course, a chance that this wouldn't work. He couldn't perform Morkai's ritual exactly, only use it to inform his own actions. He didn't have any leftover vials of Morkai's blood, just this crimson parchment.

Yet soon a rippling fog crept over the field, much like it had when Teryn had first met the wraiths. Body parts began to materialize—arms, legs, heads, torsos—until the field was filled with hazy soldiers with empty pits for eyes.

Slowly, Teryn rose to his feet and faced the army. Their forms undulated, as if they struggled to maintain their hold on sentience. There was no ferocity in them, none of the violence they'd shown when Morkai had ordered them to fight.

Teryn would have to stir that ferocity himself.

"You lost your lives fighting for King Darius," he said, his voice carrying over the field. He internally winced, hoping none of the castle residents or staff woke up to his voice only to find him talking to himself. Or would they be able to see the wraiths too?

He continued. "You died trapped between worlds, and because of that, you lost your heart-centers. Your connection to life and the otherlife. Morkai gave you a second chance at your lives as great warriors and promised peace when he'd accomplished his goals. Yet he too left you behind."

Some of the wraiths' forms ceased wavering and began to sharpen. Their empty eye sockets seemed to lock onto him, craving more of his words.

"Your former masters may have abandoned you, but I will not. Unlike those you served before, I can make good on a promise of peace. You feel it, don't you? That yearning."

Even more of their forms sharpened, and he tasted their yearning in turn. It grew ravenous. Palpable. The entire field radiated with it.

He was suddenly aware of the danger he was in and how quickly this situation could turn. Should the wraiths want, they could swarm him. They could claim their own oblivion or cut him with their blades.

Clearing his throat, he spoke again. "I can give you purpose and peace. I can give you revenge for being so cruelly abandoned."

His words were manipulative, he knew that. Neither master had meant to abandon them, but soft words wouldn't instill purpose in an undead warrior.

"I won't force you to fight again and again, driving your reanimation through blood magic." The truth was, he couldn't make them reanimate. Not without a blood weaving, and Teryn wasn't willing to do that. And based on what Emylia had said on the battlement, Morkai had been able to secure the wraiths' loyalty through promises alone, but being defeated in battle would end their bloodlust. Which meant Teryn was limited to how long he could use them. And he only intended to use them once. Whether it ended up being in defense of the castle or to defeat Darius at the border meeting, he'd only do this one time.

He continued. "I won't make you wait for some far-off

goal before I make good on what I offer you. All I ask is for one final battle. One last act of noble violence."

He reached for the letter opener he'd taken from the bureau before coming to the field. Digging its tip into his forearm, he made a shallow cut. He held out his arm and let his blood drip onto the black soil. "This is my blood. This is the blood you will follow when next I call for you, to fight one last time. This is the blood that will end your hunger and lay your souls to rest."

His heart hammered against his ribs as he waited for their reaction.

Then, as one, the wraiths bent to the earth on one knee and bowed their heads.

Seven devils, it worked. He'd earned their loyalty, just like Morkai.

He heaved a relieved breath.

"That wasn't truly blood magic." Emylia appeared beside him. Or had she been there all along?

"No," he said, "just a blood vow. A promise I can fulfill."

44

Oppressive heat filled Cora's lungs, pressing in all around her, as if the air itself had grown heavy. With a gasp, she tore away from Darius. He released her, and she launched a few steps back. She hadn't been prepared for him to take her so quickly, and the surprise sent shock waves through her legs.

She kept her eyes locked on Darius, who merely straightened the sleeves of his coat.

"Don't look at me with such suspicion," he said. "I've done nothing but take you to Syrus like we agreed."

Her breaths began to calm, and she dared to look away from him. They stood on a cobblestone walkway on a quiet street. Sleeping storefronts lined one side while a stone wall rose waist high on the other. A soft breeze blew across her cheeks, carrying with it more of that smothering heat.

It wasn't an unnatural kind.

It was merely the temperature of her surroundings.

The Southern Islands were known for their balmy climates, even in the winter. Which must mean they truly were in Syrus. She hazarded a glance at Darius again, but he kept his distance, posture straight, hands clasped at his waist.

"Welcome to my hellish domain," he said. "Please, look around. See what a dark and miserable prison I've subjected my citizens to."

His mocking tone grated on her nerves, but she studied her surroundings. They were dark indeed, but that was only because it was evening. The Southern Islands were a few hours behind Khero, so it was sometime before midnight. As for miserable, there was nothing to suggest an ounce of misery. Strains of conversation and laughter floated on the air, while light streamed from homes, terraces, and nearby buildings.

She stepped closer to the stone wall and found a sloping, layered hillside beyond it, edged with streets like the one they stood on, and tall blocky buildings made from colorful stucco. It was too dark to see the hues clearly, but she caught hints of orange, tan, blue, and pink. Some of the rooftops were flat while others boasted terracotta shingles. She even spotted an ornate domed building far below.

The bottom of the hill cut off in a steep cliff, where the first rows of houses appeared to be carved straight from the stone. Beneath that stretched an endless sea dancing with starlight and the lamps of fishing boats.

Gods, she hated to admit it, but her enemy's island kingdom was beautiful.

She did her best to mask her awe as she faced Darius again.

"Come along," he said, starting off down the street.

"To where?"

"I want to give you a closer look at my people."

"Meaning..."

He paused and glanced over his shoulder at her. "We're going to a public house. Having a few drinks."

She pulled her head back. "A public house?"

"What, surprised a king would deign to interact with his own people? Don't think too highly of me. My people haven't seen me looking this healthy before. No one will recognize me as their beloved monarch. To them, I'll be just an old soldier out for a drink."

Annoyance prickled her skin. "I wasn't thinking about you at all. I was more concerned with the fact that I'm dressed in a night robe."

He wrinkled his nose as he studied her, as if he hadn't truly looked at her until now. "Worry not. You'll do. People from all around come to Syrus, either to visit or take up residence. I offer my citizens a way of life not often found elsewhere—but you'll see for yourself. The point is there are no standards of fashion here, with so many outside influences. No one will look twice at your clothes."

With that, he proceeded again.

Gritting her teeth, she followed him. She was barefoot too, but the streets were surprisingly clean, and the cobblestones were well-maintained. Besides, being barefoot outside wasn't an oddity for her. The Forest People valued physical connections with nature and relished any opportunity to set their shoeless soles on soil.

As they navigated the narrow, winding street that lined the sloping cliff, Cora cast her attention up the hill this time, taking in the ever-climbing incline. More rows of buildings stretched above her, and at the very top stood a bell tower beside a crenellated wall. Behind that rose an enormous white dome. The entire structure was illuminated with lanterns, making it a beacon of beauty. She wondered if that was Darius' palace.

She looked from the bell tower above to the sea below and determined they were only midway up the hill. She couldn't imagine how breathtaking the view might be from the top. As much as she craved such a sight, she was grateful they kept to the outer street that ran horizontally across the hill and not one of the streets that led to the higher levels. She was in no mood for a hike.

Sounds of raucous laughter and the clink of plates and glasses grew louder, as did the frequency of light streaming from the windows. Crowds filled the streets ahead, either from groups of men chatting or couples dining at the small tables set beside the wall. Cora hadn't had many experiences in cities, as she'd often stayed behind with the commune when the Forest People had gone to trade in nearby villages. To see so many figures gathered around so late at night, so animated, so energetic...it was a bit overwhelming.

That reminded her to reconnect with the elements and strengthen her mental shields. She wanted to keep a close read on Darius' energy, but that could wait until they'd settled in at their destination.

She wove through the crowded sidewalk. He was right about no one noticing him as their king. In fact, the people barely noticed either of them. Finally, Darius paused outside a building of pink stucco. More sounds of chatter and laughter echoed from behind the heavy wooden door, above which hung a sign.

The Dragon's Arms Public House.

"Here we are." Darius pushed open the door and strode inside.

Cora followed, anxiety fraying the edges of her mental wards. The pub was packed with patrons filling nearly every table in the room. Ale and smoke infused the air, making the dimly lit room seem even darker. The walls were a cream plaster, recessed with small alcoves that held decorative bottles or oil lamps. The red tile floor was sticky beneath her bare feet.

Darius swept through the crowd with ease, while Cora shuffled in his wake, her heart racing as she skirted around the busy tables. A trio of men rose from their table at the same time, chatting as they closed in toward her, paying her not a lick of heed. She was forced to go around and lost sight of Darius. She shuffled this way and that, then finally spotted him at a small table at the back of the room.

With a weighted glare, she rushed the rest of the way there and planted herself in the empty seat, making an effort to pull it as far away from him as space allowed. She fought to catch her breath, seething at being put in such a position.

Darius leaned back in his chair, as if the pub were his home and not a loud room filled with inebriated strangers. His ease mocked her, making her want to hide her discomfort. If she admitted how flustered she was, she'd have to confess she'd never done this before. Never entered a public house or dined with commoners.

She'd never considered herself a sheltered person. Her early hardships had matured her in many ways, while life with the Forest People had given her the sense that she was self-sufficient and well-traveled. Only now did she realize how few of life's mundane experiences she'd had. How truly sheltered she was. How little she could relate to the average citizen.

She was a terrible queen.

True, she'd only been queen for a matter of months, and before that, she'd lived with a secretive commune. Guilt plagued her nonetheless.

A willowy serving woman approached their table, dressed in a floral-patterned skirt and white top that hung off her shoulders. A red kerchief tied back auburn hair to display a sun-browned face adorned with freckles. Her eyes dipped to Darius' black coat, with its high collar and stiff shoulders. Now that Cora was closer, she noted the gold pins at his lapels, showcasing a dragon in a circle of flame. That must be Syrus' sigil. A strange sigil for a king who was rejected by every dragon he'd tried to bond. Did he still hold out hope he'd gain their approval after he became Morkaius?

Something brightened in the serving woman's expression. "Welcome, esteemed soldier. You honor us with your great presence. What can I get for you this evening?"

"Zaran wine, 170 Year of the Eagle," he answered with a charming grin.

The woman arched a brow at Cora.

"Nothing for me."

"Ale for her," Darius said.

The woman flounced off, slapping a patron upside the head when he pinched her backside.

"Lively, happy, healthy." Darius gestured toward the nearby tables. "No one has been beheaded in the streets or drawn and quartered by moonlight. Who would have thought?"

She maintained a stony expression at his continued attempt at sarcasm. "Just because I don't trust you doesn't mean I assumed you were a bloodthirsty king."

Though she had imagined something like it. How could she not when he'd produced such progeny as Morkai? The mage's takeover of Ridine had resulted in an understaffed castle, dusty halls, and countless soldiers who'd been compelled to obey him by blood magic. She'd imagined

Syrus would be like that too. Unkempt. Lifeless. Filled with cowed citizens with glazed eyes.

Nothing suggested the pub patrons were enjoying themselves by force. They drank. They laughed. Some even sang bawdy tunes. There was an array of people in different states of dress, different fashions, though all shared an aura of informality.

The serving woman returned with their drinks. Darius accepted his glass of wine with one hand and passed a couple of coins to the woman with the other. Cora's eyes locked on his palm as he withdrew it. All she could see of the cut he'd made the blood promise with was a smear of dried blood. Not a gash or scar to be found. So he truly did have rapid healing.

She leaned back in her chair, arms crossed, not daring to drink the ale before her. "So, you've shown me Syrus. Why else are we here?"

"Yes, I've shown you Syrus, but you'll look at neither me nor my kingdom with unclouded eyes until you have good reason to discard your prejudices. You have questions for me. Ask them. I'll answer with honesty." He took a long pull of his wine.

She did have questions, though she still needed to be careful how she asked them so as not to give too much away. Regardless, she'd take advantage of his offer.

Breathing deep, she pried the smallest hole in her mental shields and focused on his energy as she asked, "How long were you in Khero before you got caught as a pretend spy?"

"Not long," he said, and his energy remained steady. "I'd learned about the spies from Norun who'd been caught in your kingdom so I made the same mistakes they did. Spoke to the same traitorous informants. Asked too many obvious questions. I was caught within a week. But I know what you're really asking, and no, I didn't tour all over your kingdom to secure key locations to worldwalk to. I only did that at your castle."

"How long were you wandering around Ridine? Did you worldwalk out of your cell from the start? Where have you been hiding since you faked your death?"

"I haven't been hiding in your castle, cousin."

She bristled at the nickname. They may be distantly related, but they weren't cousins. Allied monarchs often called each other *cousin*, but she and Darius weren't allies either.

He continued. "First of all, I stayed in my cell like a good little prisoner until I was ready to leave. I only left to retrieve a replacement body, and after I planted the decoy, I returned to my soldiers in Norun. I've hardly set foot in Ridine since, aside from the last few days when I was getting the lay of the castle and trying my luck to meet with you."

His energy continued to pulse with the steady hum of truth, but the last part tingled with something sharp and jagged. Maybe there was a lie hidden there, or more to what he was saying. She hoped it didn't mean he suspected where she'd been on the nights he hadn't been able to find her.

"I was lucky to finally find you this evening," he said.

She gave him a pointed look. "In the middle of the night."

"Yes, well, I prefer to avoid witnesses."

"As do I," she said through her teeth.

"Are you embarrassed about my *stamina* comment? Ah, I see you are." He took an annoyingly long sip of wine, an obvious test of her patience. "I didn't lurk and watch, if that's what you're wondering. Yes, I first worldwalked to your castle this evening at an inopportune time and chose to attempt my visit later when I thought you'd be more amenable to a chat. I made my presence known almost as soon as I appeared in your bedroom, so don't paint me as a pervert." He said the last part with a chuckle.

She thinned her lips to show just how little amusement she found in this. "Pervert or no, the fact that you world-walked straight to my bedroom proves you've been there before. Maybe you didn't spend weeks wandering my castle, but you spent enough time there to orient yourself, as you've already admitted, and one of those locations was my most private space."

With a cold grin, he leaned forward, elbows propped on the table, and laced his fingers. "You really are a world-walker. You know exactly how my magic works."

She sucked in a breath but tried to keep her expression even. Damn, even with her precautions, she'd given too much away. "Just because I know how your magic works doesn't mean I'm the same as you."

He perched his chin on his laced hands and stared at her with unblinking silver-blue eyes. "Then why is your heart beating so fast?"

What...

What the hell did that mean? Sounds of the busy pub continued to blare around them. There was no way he could hear her heartbeat in such a loud room. Unless...

Was he...clairaudient?

He was half witch, which meant he had a sensory affinity of some sort. Could it be that while she'd been sensing truth and lies from his energy fluctuations, he was doing the same, but with her pulse?

Darius leaned back from the table and swirled his glass. "How is Ailan?"

Cora's heart lurched before she could steel herself.

He snorted a laugh. "That reaction tells me you have met my sister indeed. I won't ask where she'd been hiding, for I haven't given you enough reasons to trust me yet. And I assume she is behind the Veil by now. Does she look younger than me? I imagine aging has been far gentler on her than it has on me, if she's stayed in Lela this whole time."

She refused to address Ailan. Refused to admit any affiliation with her. Instead, she trained her voice to speak with level curiosity. "You aged poorly because you lived in Syrus?"

"Yes," he said, making no comment on her change of subject. "Living in Syrus, so far from El'Ara's heart, aged me horribly, yet my body refused to die. As soon as I set foot across the Khero-Vinias border, though, I felt healthier than I had in centuries. I didn't fully understand what was happening, but I'd learned enough from Desmond's report to understand that the *mora*—my birthright—was healing me. Then the Veil tore and my aging began to reverse—just the slightest bit—and pieces of memories slowly snapped into place. My magic grew stronger. I believe I'll regain the rest of my youth once I become Morkaius."

Cora couldn't keep the glare from her eyes.

"Ah, of course. You still don't believe I deserve to be Morkaius. To you I'm still an evil Elvyn overlord who murdered his mother and seeks vengeance on his sister. So let's face these misbeliefs head-on and start with where it all began. Let's talk about my darling mother."

45

As much as Cora wanted to avoid listening to Darius drone on about his mother issues, she couldn't deny her curiosity. She'd heard Ailan's side of what had happened, as well as Garot's tale. But how did Darius see those same events? The fact that he used a dragon as his kingdom's sigil, despite never succeeding in bonding with one, suggested his perspective may be far different.

Perhaps the perspective of her enemy could give her an advantage.

Cora released a bored sigh so as not to appear too eager. "Fine, justify your actions. Let's hear it."

He smirked, and his expression held something like admiration. "I'm confident you'll feel differently once you've heard my side."

"Do tell."

He swirled his glass, drained its dregs, then lifted the empty cup. Yet another test of her patience as he waited for the serving woman to return. Cora still hadn't sipped her ale and had no intention of doing so. Her arms remained folded over her chest, her jaw tight.

Finally, the serving woman filled his glass and Darius took a sip, a satisfied look on his face. "The Dragon's Arms is the highest value public house in Syrus under the principles of leisure, liberation, and inebriation. Should the pub stand for other values, such as quietude, relaxation, and propriety, The Dragon's Arms would be a low-value establishment. Whereas the Golden Shore Inn, a few streets down, exemplifies those values to the highest standard."

Cora frowned, unsure of what this had to do with his mother.

He continued. "When stripped of principle, neither establishment is better or worse than the other, just different. You can see that, right? Take your personal preferences away and simply see each of those public houses for what they are. Under its own set of principles, each establishment is considered high value. Given the opportunity to demonstrate those principles to clientele who seek the same, each business is allowed to thrive. That is what the Kingdom of Syrus stands for. No one is limited by birth, bloodline, or social class. Instead, everyone is judged by merit and how they serve certain values."

"Syrus is a meritocracy?"

He nodded. "That was all I ever wanted for El'Ara. And the first person who ever put that idea in my head was my mother, Satsara. From as early as I can remember, she'd whisper stories about my father, who was no longer a prince but the King of Syrus by then. She told me I was a prince of two worlds, and an heir to two kinds of magic. She marveled over my abilities as a worldwalker and filled my mind with visions of the future. One day I would be Morkara, and the most unique one El'Ara had ever had—one with the blood of human royalty and the power of a witch, as well as all the powers that came with directing the *mora*. I could bring advancement to the fae realm, find ways to utilize my witch magic to blend with the *mora*.

"Satsara was the first person to use the term Morkaius. *My little Morkaius*, she'd call me. It was supposed to be a secret name, one I'd never speak aloud, but it filled me with so much pride. I wanted to be High King of Magic. I wanted to fulfill the vision she had for me, be the grand king she said my father was. She supported me. Continued to whisper stories about my father, telling me how much she missed him despite having woven the ward that had banished him from El'Ara for good. 'At least I have you,' she'd say. Her pride and joy. Her little High King of Magic."

His expression turned to a grimace and he took a long swallow of wine. "Then my sister was born. She told stories about my father less and less and turned more of her attention to her consort and pureblood child. By then, I was old enough to understand the prejudices the Elvyn held against me. Etrix, the tribunal, and everyone but my mother eyed me with disgust, even as they bowed. Soon my mother's eyes began to dull when she looked at me too."

"Did you give her any reason to doubt you?" She remembered what Ailan had said about the pranks he'd pulled, the way he'd snuck humans into El'Ara for pleasure and amusement, often to their demise.

He huffed a cold laugh. "Mother was easily swayed by those around her. Once the tribunal no longer had to pretend to pin their hopes for the future on me, they shifted their glowing approval to Ailan. The perfect pureblood they'd wanted all along. They urged her to name Ailan heir, or at least wait until she came of age before making her final decision. I was patient. I waited, confident that when Ailan reached maturity, Mother and the tribunal would see that she could offer only a fraction of the value that I could. Mother's words still rang in my head, after all. I knew how much I could do for El'Ara. Knew I could be a Morkara unlike any other.

"Yet it didn't turn out the way I expected. Ailan was named heir and I was set aside. I was crushed, enraged, heartbroken. Then the unthinkable happened. Mother tried to banish me from El'Ara. Do you want to know how it happened?"

She said nothing, for he'd surely tell her anyway. It didn't escape her that he'd avoided mentioning anything about the prank he'd pulled on Berolla and the injury that had almost killed Ailan. A convenient omission.

After another long sip, his eyes grew distant. His voice fell, and she had to lean forward to hear what he said next over the noise of the pub. "She hugged me. Mother took me to the grove she'd once kept as a sanctuary to meet my father in. She showed me the trees, recounted her fond memories. Then she faced me, told me she loved me, how proud of me she was, and hugged me. It was the first time in a long while that I felt loved by her, and it softened the hurt I'd felt after she'd chosen Ailan as her heir. I hugged her back, reveling in the warmth, in the hope that maybe Mother would change her mind. Then I heard it."

His expression darkened.

Cora was still leaning forward, unable to hide her curiosity. "Heard what?"

"The sound of magic weaving around me."

She arched her brow. Wait, did that mean...

"I'm clairaudient," he said, confirming her earlier suspicions. "My magic is fueled by sound, just like my father's was fueled by scent. That's how I worldwalk. I can travel to any place I can visualize, either from memory or physical sight. I activate my magic by forging a sound connection and control the distance by imagining the sound of my destination as near or far. Just like Father, the first time I worldwalked was by accident. I traveled to him the same way he accidentally stumbled upon El'Ara."

His demeanor eased a little at that, a sad smile forming on his lips.

"Did you travel on Samhain too?" Too late she realized she'd given something away, admitting that she knew about his history.

He didn't seem surprised, however, and just continued to grin at his memory. "No, it wasn't the thinning of the veils between worlds that brought me to him, but a memory of waves. Before Mother banished Tristaine, she let him take me to Syrus. I didn't consciously remember being there, but one day, when I was still just a boy, I unexpectedly recalled the sound of waves, ones so different from the lakes and oceans in El'Ara. Suddenly, I could visualize where I'd been when I'd heard those waves. I was so startled, so overwhelmed, that my magic took over. The next thing I knew, I was standing before an old man in a palace on a sunny hillside, the sound of waves crashing far below."

Cora was relieved at his explanation, for it further confirmed that their magic worked the same way. She too had worldwalked unexpectedly the first time, her magic taking over before she knew what had happened. His magic may be more powerful than hers, but at least she understood its strengths and limitations.

He shook his head, the mirth fading from his face. "I always thought my similarities to my father were what endeared me to my mother, but just like him, I lost her admiration. As soon as I heard the telltale sound of Mother's magic wrapping around me in that grove, I knew what was happening. She was trying to banish me from El'Ara. Not just that, but she was attempting it in the exact same place she'd banished my father in, and in the exact same way. With a hug."

A bitter ache struck her, and for a single breath, his pain was hers. She could almost feel the shock of betrayal he must have felt when his mother hugged him, made him feel loved...and then wove magic to expel him from his home.

Yet she knew the other side. She knew what he'd done. The dangers he'd posed to not only Ailan, but El'Ara as a whole. Cora may not know Satsara, but both Darius' and Ailan's descriptions made it seem like she loved him deeply. Perhaps too much. It must have killed her inside to banish her son, no matter how dangerous he was.

But of course Darius didn't see it that way. To him, he was the sole victim.

He continued. "I worldwalked to Syrus before she could finish her ward, but by then, my father had died. There was no home for me there, and I soon learned that the human realm was just as flawed as El'Ara. It was yet another domain ruled by blood, not merit. Yet another place where I was considered impure. The new King of Syrus—one of my half brothers—called me a bastard. A monster. An abomination. Had either realm judged me for my merit, they would have seen that *I* was the most capable. I could bring the most value as a ruler. I could do more, be more, create more."

"Under the assumption that their values were wrong and yours were right," Cora said flatly.

He narrowed his eyes. "Don't pretend you can't relate. Have you ever questioned the values of your kingdom? Its principles? Its expectations?"

She couldn't deny that. Time and again she'd faced outdated notions. Prejudice. Scorn. Much of a queen's value lay in her husband and—even more importantly—her ability to bear heirs. Even as the monarch of her kingdom, Cora bore the skepticism of certain nobles who'd rather see a man on the throne.

The mere thought boiled her blood.

Yet just because Darius claimed to be better didn't mean he was. His kingdom seemed idyllic, but there were always shadows lurking behind the brightest corners. Even now, she sensed an undercurrent of unrest weaving through the boisterous atmosphere of the public house. As narrow as a splinter, yet strong enough to feel as if it were buried in her side. She hadn't been conscious of it until now, as she'd been more focused on Darius' tale. With every breath, it was growing. Deepening. Creating fissures in the too-perfect cheer filling the room.

The fissure widened. Cracked.

Cora angled her head toward the source of the anomaly.

"Don't you dare report me!" A panicked male voice contrasted the joyful strains of conversation. Cora couldn't see the speaker through the crowd, but she sensed him strongly now. He lowered his voice, but she could still make out his muttered words. "I can't take another demerit this month. You know this."

A deeper tension constricted the energy of the room—a dark and scornful glee at the man's plight. It was coming from those closest to the man and spread farther and farther, from patron to patron, even cutting off some of the conversations—

Darius rose from his chair and set his empty wine glass on the table. "Come, I grow weary of this place. You make for a poor drinking companion."

She opened her mouth, but before she could speak, he grasped her shoulder. Vertigo seized her, and she found herself stumbling over her feet. Sound cut off, as did the stench of smoke and ale. Darius released her, and she managed to regain her balance, but as the dizziness cleared from her eyes, she found their surroundings had changed.

Her bare feet rested on the smooth white marble of a long rectangular balcony. Behind her was an enormous open-air space with several seating areas, potted plants, and ornate rugs. Before her was an elegant balustrade interrupted by thick marble columns.

Darius stood before the rail, as unflustered as ever, gathering lungfuls of air. Cora glanced beyond the balustrade and found they were high above the sloping hillside, with a full view of the multi-layered city beneath them. She must have been right about the opulent building she'd glimpsed on their way to the pub; this must be Darius' palace. There were no guards or servants near the balcony, no nearby strains of emotion to suggest anyone was close by. It made sense that his palace would be so quiet at present, considering the king was supposed to be in Norun.

"Look around," Darius said. "My kingdom is beautiful. What I've created is fair. Syrus flourishes even when its king is not at home. You can see that with your own eyes."

She scoffed. "If it's so beautiful, why didn't you want me to hear more of what that man was saying?"

"He's none of my concern. His peers and the principles of his chosen establishment determine his value. If he's so worried about being reported for a demerit, he should have worked harder to prove his worth."

"You let your people police each other?"

"I give them the authority all citizens should have."

"You encourage a mob mentality. What happens to those

who receive demerits? What happens to those you and your society deem of low value? What happens to those born without able bodies or minds?"

"And you're back to clinging to your prejudices. Look with your eyes, Aveline. Look at this peaceful city. *This* is all I wanted to bring to El'Ara." He gestured toward the sloping hillside. "I succeeded in Syrus, after I won the throne from my brother, and this is all I wanted for the fae realm too. Yet the elite—the Elvyn—wouldn't see reason. Just like you refuse to see reason."

"The Elvyn refused to see reason, as you call it, because you invaded their realm." Wind blew over her cheeks, colder than it had been farther down the hill.

"Such is the way of war and progress," he said. "It is a dark and treacherous thing, and not something to take lightly. You don't want war, do you?"

"Of course I don't."

"Nor do I. I value the lives of my people. I want to see a bright future for all of them. As monarchs, we should do whatever we can to ensure the least number of casualties, don't you think?"

"This is where you propose an alliance between us, isn't it?"

He turned away from the balustrade and faced her fully. "I'm not coming to you empty-handed. I will offer you the very thing the Elvyn want to take away."

"What's that?"

A confident grin stretched his lips. "Lela."

She blinked a few times. "What are you saying?"

"You, Aveline Corasande Caelan, will be Queen of Lela."

46

H er mind emptied.
Queen of Lela.
She...she didn't want that.

Did she?

"El'Ara needs its heart before it can be whole again," Darius said. "The *mora* seeping into this world must hold terrible consequences for the fae realm. Before the Veil, the *mora* traveled through the veins of magic that wove through the land and met at the heart of the world, at the Morkara's palace in the Elvyn city of Le'Lana. The Morkara would direct the flow of *mora* from there to wherever they sought to send it. But the Veil must have compromised that.

"First, there was no Morkara in either world to direct the magic, thanks to Ailan's idiotic plan to pass on her legacy to an unnamed heir." His tone took on a sardonic quality. "Yes, I remember all of that now that I have my memories again. But now the Veil has torn, which, according to Desmond's report, means we have a Morkara again. Goody. Yet still, the *mora* cannot flow like it could before, for the Veil blocks its return. Not even the tear can allow enough magic to bring the *mora* back into balance. No, there are only two solutions: either the Veil must come down completely, or it must be completed to incorporate Lela. The Elvyn will obviously choose the latter, for who knows what repercussions could arise should the Veil be fully erased while the fae and human realms are connected through Lela. Our worlds could collide. Yet as a result of completing the Veil, Lela will return to El'Ara and every human on this land will cease to have a home."

She hated that he was voicing her greatest fear—that everything she was preparing to fight for would result in her people's exile. Ailan had all but confirmed it.

He continued. "The Elvyn will never agree to let humans live in El'Ara. Even if they did, the humans would be considered low-value members of society due to their blood. Because—as I've already stated—the Elvyn cling to principles that only benefit themselves. Yet there is another option that will require neither exile nor subjugation. The answer is written in the prophecy. And that is where you come in."

Impatience tightened her chest. Or was it curiosity? Excitement, even? Whatever the case, she needed to know what the hell he was getting at. It took no small effort to maintain an air of nonchalance. "You mean as Queen of Lela?"

"Exactly. My son abandoned his mission to find El'Ara for me and sought to become Morkaius of the human world instead. I never would have approved, for his success would have meant the end of the fae realm. Drawing on that much magic—claiming it, using it in the human world—would have drained El'Ara. As much as I resent the Elvyn for their closed-minded ways, I treasure the fae realm. So believe me when I say I don't condone anything my son did in his efforts to control fae magic for his own selfish aims."

"And that matters to me why?"

He smirked. "It matters because it will allow you to give me the benefit of the doubt when I say this next part. You will take on a role similar to the Morkaius of Lela. No, hear me out. Your husband remains in the line of succession for Vera, and should he inherit the kingdom, the two of you could reforge Lela and rule the land as a whole."

Cora's pulse kicked up, but she hoped he was too busy talking to notice. It was true that Teryn remained in the line of succession for Vera. As Larylis' brother, Teryn had a claim to the throne. A weaker one compared to Noah, but a claim nonetheless. But Darius hadn't mentioned Noah. Or Mareleau, for that matter. Had he not learned their significance? He knew the Morkara had been born, but had he not figured out who that was?

Hope sparked inside her. They'd kept Noah's birth a secret and had spread the rumor that Mareleau had returned home before Cora's wedding. In truth, Darius, Mareleau, and Noah had all been under the same roof for a handful of days. Did he not know?

Of course he didn't.

If he'd known, her friend would be dead, and her newborn son too.

Unless...

Unless Darius wasn't the monster he'd been painted as.

A heavy weight settled over her chest—a clairsentient warning not to give in to that line of reasoning just yet.

Darius spoke again. "You will fulfill every condition to become the Morkaius, the very conditions my son had tried to fulfill. You'll rule over Lela, a crown given not taken. As monarch of El'Ara's heart, the *mora* will flow to you. Should you want, you could harness it."

She barked a cold laugh. "Are you trying to get me

killed? I know what the prophecy said about becoming Morkaius of this world. *He who harnesses the magic will be destroyed by it."*

His face split with a wide smile, too maniacal to be comforting. "Yes, but you won't harness the *mora.* You are going to push it back into El'Ara. And I, as Morkaius of El'Ara, will tear down the Veil, but only after you've returned the *mora* to El'Ara. Without the forced connection between our worlds caused by the *mora* and the Veil, our worlds will separate once more. Do you see? It isn't the land itself that is El'Ara's heart; it's the *mora.* The convergence of those magic veins. Once inside the Veil, they will collide once more and forge a new heart."

She tried to imagine it, tried to picture what he was explaining. If the true Heart of El'Ara was the magic and not simply the land, the fae realm would have a new heart should the lines of *mora* be forced to recede behind the Veil.

And yet...

"I don't understand," she said. "If I don't harness the *mora,* then how will I have the ability to push it back?"

"Like I said, it's written in the prophecy itself. By becoming Lela's monarch, you become *Morkai,* King of Magic. You will have access to the *mora,* and it will flow to you. Yet you aren't going to keep it or harness it or do anything that will make you the Morkaius."

Was he correct?

She fought to recall everything Emylia had channeled. Everything Teryn had learned from her.

To gain the power of the Morkaius, one must first become King of Magic, a crown given, not taken, and reign over El'Ara's abandoned heart.

To become Morkaius of El'Ara's heart, harness the magic that seeps from its center.

Mother Goddess, it really was hidden in the lines of the prophecy. One didn't become Morkaius unless they tried to harness the magic. The prophecy didn't say what one could do with the *mora* simply by being King of Magic—or Queen of Lela, in her case—but what he was saying might be possible.

"You see?" His voice quavered with fervor. "We'll work together, and we'll both get what we want. You'll protect your people and keep the land that has become their home. I'll rule El'Ara and make it a better place."

A better place...by his standards.

Cora hated how prejudiced the Elvyn were toward humans, but did that give Darius the right to change them? Just because he decided their morals were wrong? Did anyone have the right to override another society's values, just because they thought they knew better? To conquer them, change them, all for that people's supposed *own good*? It was a question that had plagued humanity for centuries. Those who answered yes often used such convictions to justify the subjugation of people under the banner of *civilization*. She'd seen hints of it in her own kingdom when her former council members had wanted to hunt down the Forest People and force them to integrate with society.

She couldn't condone that.

She could *never* condone that.

Darius stepped closer. "What I've created in Syrus—a fair kingdom that values one's merit, not their bloodline—can happen in El'Ara too."

"And what of Syrus?" she asked. "Will you just abandon it for El'Ara?"

"Of course not. After I tear down the Veil, I will once again be able to walk between worlds. The human and fae realms will no longer be conjoined, but that doesn't mean we can't continue to benefit one another. Just think what the future could hold. What advancements we could see on both sides. Humans and fae have so much they can learn from one another."

She breathed deeply, sensing his energy. It radiated with hope, with joy, with excitement, almost too potent for her to bear. He truly believed in what he was saying. Even she could see the potential he imagined. The possibilities of sharing resources with another realm.

Yet there remained that steady sinking in her gut. One that told her this wasn't quite right. Just because someone believed in their own principles didn't mean they weren't flawed.

"You want an alliance with me," Cora said, keeping her tone neutral so as not to reveal that she'd already made up her mind, "and you've shown me how we can help each other once you've conquered El'Ara. Yet what would you have me do *before* you've won? How do you expect me to aid you during your campaign?"

He sobered from his excitement, adopting as level a tone as hers. "I will ask only what is fair. Soldiers, access to your lands, and the location of the tear."

Her pulse jumped, and from his nod, she knew he'd heard it.

"Yes, you know where it is, but I won't try to get the information from you now. I will demonstrate my trust-worthiness and allow you to consider your options. Alliance, surrender, or war. Either way, this can only end in my success. I will find the tear with or without you, and I will find my sister too. I won't ask you to take any lives for me. Ailan, Mareleau, and Noah will die by my hand only."

Cora couldn't keep her reaction at bay, couldn't hold in

her gasp as she heard him speak Mareleau and Noah's names.

"I know about them too," he said, "though I regret that I learned about them too late. If I can claim one flaw, it's that I didn't value the prophecy Desmond was so invested in, aside from what it said about El'Ara. I used logic to test my son's conclusion about you and found it flawed. Since I knew you weren't the prophesied mother, I deduced she simply hadn't been born yet, and so long as she didn't exist, I didn't care about her.

"Before my memories returned, I had no interest in the mother, only reaching the Veil and finding a way inside. Then it tore while I was imprisoned. My mind was befuddled for days as I struggled to process all these new memories, comparing them to the assumptions I'd made, some of which had been incorrect. By the time my mind cleared and I realized the full truth of what had happened—that Ailan's heir had been born *under the black mountain*, in the very castle I'd been imprisoned in—it was too late. Queen Mareleau was gone. As were you."

The pointed look he gave her chilled her to the bone. Did he suspect she and Mareleau had left Ridine together? Even more chilling was the realization of just how close Darius had been to getting his way. For three days, he'd been imprisoned at Ridine while Mareleau and Noah were just floors overhead.

Thank the Mother Goddess his mind hadn't cleared a moment too soon.

"My promises aren't empty," Darius said, "but neither are my threats. My soldiers are in Vinias. Reinforcements from Norun are already on their way from the capital. Only I can stop them. If you're ready to forge an alliance with me, I can end the conflict between Khero and Norun. All they want is Prince Helios' body. I can convince them I've retrieved it. I can halt Norun's progress and stop them from setting foot on your kingdom's soil. Otherwise, they will come for blood and you will be outnumbered."

Breathe in. Breathe out. Don't react.

He didn't know about the rebels. He had no clue that between now and the meeting at the border, his promised reinforcements would get caught in the rebellion. Without them, Darius only had five thousand men. With Khero's forces allied with soldiers from Vera and El'Ara, they could face him with better odds.

"I need more time," she said. "I can't take this alliance lightly. If you want me to trust you, I need more proof. Give me the full three weeks to determine if you're worth my trust and I will meet you at the border as planned with my answer."

His eyes narrowed to a squint. Did he see through her ruse? Did he suspect what she kept hidden? The tic deepened in his jaw and his fingers curled tightly at his sides. Then he whirled back toward the balustrade and propped his elbows upon the rail. His energy flared with frustration.

"Is it the other queen?" he asked, voice low. "Is she the reason you hesitate?"

"You seek to end her life." Emotion crept into her voice, but she didn't bother masking it. "What kind of person would I be if I didn't hesitate?"

"She and her son are two people. *Two.* In exchange for their deaths, thousands of lives could be saved. Are those two lives more valuable than those that would be lost during war? Is it not your duty to put the lives of your people first?" Slamming his fist on the balustrade, he faced her again. "You should *hate* her."

She sucked in a sharp breath.

"My son mistook you for her." He took a forbidding step closer, temples pulsing. "He cursed you to die childless. Destroyed your brother's mind. Tried to start a war in your kingdom's name. You were banished from your own castle, forced to flee, all because you were the wrong girl."

Memories of flames flashed in her mind's eye, the terror of her nightmare echoing in the beat of her heart.

"You've borne the brunt of torment that had been meant for her all along. Does that make you feel noble? Do you fancy yourself a hero, Queen Aveline?" He closed in another step.

She launched back, her knees quavering.

Should it have been her? asked the taunting voice from her nightmare.

Darius continued, tone edged with malice. "Do you take pride in the protection you've provided? Do you enjoy watching her with her newborn baby, flaunting the joy of motherhood that you'll never have? Are you glad you gave up your youth so that she could be coddled? Have you never wondered what your life would have been like had Desmond targeted her instead of you? Have you never wished for it?"

Darkness flared inside her, a dangerous pulse. She tried to smother it down, but it begged her to look at it. Begged to swarm around her. But she couldn't. No, she couldn't. That wasn't her. That darkness didn't belong to her.

He stepped closer once more, towering over her. "Do you deserve the punishment you've been given? Do you delight in the sacrifices you made? Or...do you wish the burden had been given to the one who'd deserved it all along?"

"Stop," she bit out, shoulders trembling. The flames of memory grew brighter. The darkness in her chest grew tighter. It screamed at her, clawed at her, fought to emerge from the prison that was her heart.

Darius lowered his voice to a whispered hiss. "Should that curse truly have been placed upon you, an innocent child? Born in the wrong place at the wrong time? Or should it have been her? Do you wish it had been *her*?"

"Yes!"

Silence echoed in the wake of that word.

She'd meant to stay *stop*.

Meant to refuse.

Meant to say anything but that horrible, condemning word.

Her body shuddered with a sob. Something wet splashed on her collarbone, soaking the neck of her robe. Only then did she realize tears were streaming from her cheeks.

Her chest squeezed...

Then released.

The sob turned into a breath of relief.

And the darkness inside her left its cage.

47

A witch's challenge was a beautiful and treacherous thing. Beautiful in how much it could grow one's magic. Treacherous in how the means of one's challenge only seemed obvious in hindsight. If Cora had acknowledged the darkness in her heart for what it was the first time it had begged her to look at it, she could have grown her magic days ago.

But that was the nature of challenges.

The way of the witch.

It wasn't meant to be easy.

Now that she'd broken that dam inside her, there was no stifling the darkness. She whispered the lullaby of truth it had wanted to hear all along. "It should have been her."

Anger rose inside her, and she didn't tamp it down. She let it strengthen her voice to a shout. Let her fury pour out of her and burst from her lungs, her heart, her lips. "It never should have been me! I hate that I suffered in her place!"

Darius nodded. "As you should."

More and more of the darkness leaked from her chest, eased from her soul. Her mind spun with the euphoria of its release. How long had she been carrying it? How had it burrowed so deeply—yet so subtly—inside her that she hadn't noticed its unbearable weight? Now that she'd given it freedom, she felt lighter than ever. Her mind too felt clearer. Sharper.

And her magic...

Mother Goddess, her magic felt stronger.

It surged through her body, filling every crevice the darkness had occupied. Her magic tingled the lines of her *insigmora*, burning her palms, radiating through her blood.

The blockage was finally gone—the fatigue that had overtaken her when she'd worldwalked. The solution had been there all along, buried in the darkness she wouldn't confront.

But she confronted it now, watching it, acknowledging it, even as it broke her heart again and again, even as it healed each jagged cut it made.

What a cruel and lovely thing it was.

"I knew you were like me," Darius said, voice quavering with fervor once more. "I knew we were of the same mind. You've felt what it's like when someone undervalues you. Or misplaces your value. You feel the same rage that I do. The same sense of justice."

Gods, she wanted to laugh.

She and Darius weren't the same.

He was a fool to think bringing her darkness to light meant she agreed with him.

Everything she'd confessed was true. Every word she'd shouted had come from her heart. But truth wasn't always one-dimensional. Hers was multifaceted.

She wished Mareleau had been cursed in her stead.

She was glad Mareleau hadn't suffered the way she had.

She hated that she'd borne a punishment meant for someone else.

She wouldn't wish the terrors of her past on anyone else, least of all Mareleau.

Yes, that darkness belonged to Cora, a small and vulnerable side of her that she'd tried to ignore. Tried to smother and bury. But that wasn't all Cora possessed. There was a bigger, brighter part of her that could exist beside the darkness. A side that understood her tiny, scared, bitter counterpart for what it was. Not something to be ignored but to be held. Listened to. Freed. Only then could the brighter side truly shine.

Darius remained oblivious and continued to grin at her in triumph. "Now do you see—"

"I still need more time." Her words came out calm. "I will not ally with you until you've proven your merit. That's what you stand for, isn't it? You're asking me to compromise on my principles and allow you to take innocent lives—"

"One of those lives belongs to someone you resent. Taking it would save thousands more. It would end a war before it can begin."

"Yet it's a life nonetheless. I don't take that lightly. Give me the full three weeks, and you'll have your answer when we meet at the border. In the meantime, stay out of Khero, stay out of Ridine, and prove you're someone worth trusting."

Irritation flared in his eyes, but he made no argument. His fingers curled and uncurled at his sides until he released an aggrieved sigh. "As you wish. Just don't forget what I told you. You will be outnumbered at the border, should you refuse to either surrender or ally with me."

"I'll have to take that risk."

He extended a stiff hand. "Shall I escort you back—"

"There's no need." She took a step to the side, a vision of the moonlit forest just outside Ridine in her mind, and planted her feet on cold grass. Icy air filled her lungs where mild heat had been before. Darius' palace was gone, replaced with dense forest and a glimpse of the castle walls just ahead.

She took a moment to breathe, to marvel at how easy it had been to worldwalk here compared to all her recent attempts. She hadn't needed minutes to sink into her destination. Just a vision. Intent. A feeling. And here she was. She may not be as strong of a worldwalker as Darius was, but it was enough that her magic had grown.

Where the purgatory have you been? Valorre's frantic voice filled her mind. He was close enough that she heard the pound of his hooves on the forest floor. In a matter of heartbeats, he reached her. *You disappeared. You disappeared!*

"I'm all right," she assured him as she caressed his silky neck.

His panic lessened only the slightest bit. *I kept my distance and gave you privacy while you were mashing bodies with Teryn, and then...and then you were gone. You were just gone.*

If her poor familiar wasn't so upset, she'd be more amused by his *mashing bodies* comment. Or perhaps more embarrassed.

"I know. I'm sorry to have worried you. That's why I came here first."

Although Valorre's worry was great, there was someone else who was probably equally as frantic.

Valorre's emotions flared with jealousy, which he demonstrated by scraping his hoof in the soil. He nuzzled her shoulder several more times, a tad more aggressively than usual, before he finally relented. *Go on, then. You should tell him you're not dead. He...was doing something strange earlier.*

She pulled back. "What do you mean something strange?"

Valorre gave the emotional equivalent of a shrug. *Something with dead people.*

That was enough to leave her equal parts perplexed and concerned. She gave Valorre a final conciliatory pat before worldwalking straight to her bedroom.

She caught Teryn pacing before their bed, his thumbnail between his teeth. He jumped upon seeing her, blinking several times as if he wasn't sure she was real. His eyes were wild, his hair more mussed than before.

"I'm safe," she said.

Her words broke the spell on his surprise, and his expression eased. He rushed to her and folded her against his chest. "Thank the gods. I was about six seconds away from waging war on Syrus myself."

The comfort of his arms, the scent of his skin, the cadence of his heartbeat against her ear, soothed all the fraying edges of Cora's anxiety. She wished the moment could last. Wished they didn't have to talk about what had happened or what would come next.

But she couldn't put it off.

They didn't have time for that.

She pulled slightly away and locked her eyes with his. His energy constricted. The furrow between his brow hinted at a worry he was desperate to voice. Did it have something to do with what Valorre had mentioned?

"What is it?" she asked.

He framed her face with his hands as if he couldn't bear to release her. His throat bobbed. Once. Twice. His voice came out strained. "I...I need to tell you something. Something I've done. My means were questionable, but I think it can help us."

"I'll listen," she whispered back. "Afterward, I have something to tell you too. I have a plan. Or...the beginnings of one. It might make the Elvyn hate me, but it's the only way to truly protect the people of Lela."

Conviction flared in her chest. She knew what she had to do.

Darius may have been wrong about her in many ways. They were nothing alike. Freeing her darkness hadn't filled her with hatred. Bitterness didn't compromise her ability to love.

But he'd been right about one thing.

Lela belonged to her.

48

For the first time in Mareleau's life, there was such a thing as too many sweets. And too many gifts. They filled nearly every surface of her bedroom, from the dressing table to the nightstand and a good portion of the floor. Two marble dress forms boasted bejeweled robes in the Elvyn fashion, which were so heavy and ornate they had to be hauled in by a trio of servants. Decanters of wine, kettles of tea, and plates upon plates of desserts and confections in bold flavors unlike anything she'd tasted were clustered upon the tea table.

After the tribunal's begrudging acceptance of her, she hadn't expected much from her interactions with the Elvyn people, but within an hour, visitors had begun to call. It turned out not everyone was as curmudgeonly as those who'd attended the meeting. Thanks to the translation charm on the bracelet Fanon had given her and Cora, she could easily communicate with them. Her servants and palace staff rarely said much other than to pay their respects, but they always bowed at the waist or bent at the knee in her presence.

Edel Morkara'Elle.

She'd heard that title so many times since the meeting ended.

Perhaps being the mother of the Morkara wasn't too much of a step down from being queen. It certainly came with perks.

And a very full belly.

Yet as full as she was, she was completely unsatisfied. How could she be content when the future was so unclear? Would Ailan keep the tear open long enough to allow Mareleau and Larylis to live out their lives in the human world with their son? And if not, would Mareleau learn to consider this place her home? Would the Elvyn accept Larylis? What would happen to Vera? Who would take care of her kingdom?

She hated those questions, and she likely wouldn't get answers any time soon. They had a war to win, an enemy to kill.

Meanwhile, all she could do was sit in her pretty room and gorge herself on Elvyn sweets.

That and protect her son, of course.

She stared down at Noah with a grin. He lay beside her at the center of a cushioned velvet mat on the floor, staring at the glittering, swaying mobile—a gift from one of his new Elvyn admirers, of course. He was starting to look less like a wrinkled old man and more like a chubby baby. How old was he now? Just over two weeks? It had been so hard to keep track of time, especially when trying to track the passage of days in the human world too. Were she at home without war on the horizon, she'd have celebrated each week since his birth, marked each milestone with gifts and cake.

Gifts and cake were all around them now, but it wasn't for quite the same reason.

Bitterness sank her chest, edged with impatience. She hated feeling useless. Hated waiting. Hated being surrounded by luxury yet impoverished at heart.

Maybe...

If she could only...

She scooted closer to Noah and extended her hands, palms toward him. Closing her eyes, she tried to sense a tingling buzz of magic, tried to feel a ripple of some hidden strength. Instead, she felt nothing. Yet...wasn't she going about this wrong in the first place? She was—*supposedly*—claircognizant, not clairsentient. Her sensory affinity was keen knowing, but here she was trying to *feel* like Cora could.

How could she truly protect her son and make her magic count if she didn't know how to make proper use of her abilities? Clenching her jaw, she opened her eyes. Noah's gaze was on her hands now as he gummed his tiny fist.

Her heart melted at the sight, taking the edge off her annoyance. "I just wish I could protect you."

If she could at least cast a protective ward around him, she'd feel useful. Salinda had helped her understand her magic when they'd spoken in her tent, but she hadn't taught her how to use that understanding for what Mareleau wanted to do most. It was hard to take her magic seriously when she hadn't a clue how to accomplish her goals.

She adopted a playful tone and wiggled her fingers. "You, little Noah, are hereby protected. No? Nothing? Huh."

A soft knock came from the other side of her bedroom door. Ailan swept in.

Mareleau angled her head to face her. "Has Cora returned?"

"Not yet," Ailan said.

It had only been a matter of hours since Cora left El'Ara, but in the human world, more than a full day had passed. Would it take several days to sort out her side of the terms for the alliance? Weeks? Mareleau would lose her mind if that ended up being the case. The sooner Cora returned, the sooner she might have a chance of getting another letter to or from Larylis.

Ailan approached her and Noah. "What are you doing there?"

Mareleau frowned, unsure of what she was inquiring about until she glanced at her hands. They were still extended over Noah. She snatched them back. "Oh, that. I was..."

Why was she embarrassed to admit it? She had no reason to feel ashamed.

She lifted her chin and feigned confidence. "I was practicing casting a protective ward around Noah."

Ailan settled on the floor beside them. "Did it work?"

"Not yet." She didn't mean to sound so defensive. "That's why I'm practicing."

"Is that what kind of magic you hope to have? Wardweaving?"

"Is that an option?" Mareleau hadn't considered whether she might have access to Elvyn magic.

"Perhaps. I know Salinda helped you understand your witch magic, but exploring your Elvyn side may help too. Your magic is a combination of both. And while a weaver's *mora* doesn't always manifest in the ways we want, it's possible you're drawn to wardweaving because it's your specialty. I'm a truthweaver through and through, without a stitch of talent for wardweaving. My wards are weak when I attempt them. Still, I can teach you the gesture for casting them."

Excitement bubbled in her chest. Was she about to learn how to do something useful with magic at last?

"Even if wardweaving isn't your talent," Ailan said, "a gesture may help guide your witch magic. Sometimes external action can aid its flow, for it gives you something outside yourself to trust in."

Ailan extended her palms, and Mareleau mirrored her. She touched her thumbs to her ring fingers, angled her hands, and then linked the pairs of touching fingers together. Angling her hands again, she touched her pinkies, then her middle fingers, then her index. The motions stretched Mareleau's digits in strange and unfamiliar ways, but the challenge made her feel accomplished. Ailan moved her hands again, this time lacing all five fingers together before separating them.

"You end by encompassing the subject you'd like to ward with your hands," Ailan explained. "It may help to imagine an invisible blanket between your fingers, settling over your subject. For large subjects, you may need to repeat the gesture several times and in several different areas until it's completely covered."

Following her instruction, Mareleau envisioned a protective blanket falling from her hands over Noah.

And then...

She cast a hopeful look at Ailan. "Did that work?"

Ailan chuckled. "The Forest People call it quiet magic, and Elvyn magic operates in a similarly quiet way. Wards are particularly hard to test, for that would require an attempt to break through them. But don't be discouraged.

With or without this gesture, you're still a witch. You still have a sensory affinity you can work with."

"Claircognizance."

Ailan nodded. "Since knowing is your strength, you must build your trust in your abilities. When you cast your ward, you must *know* it works."

Her heart sank. How could she know when she...didn't? How could she have confidence in something she couldn't see or feel? It had been easy to trust her glamours because she hadn't taken them seriously. She'd brushed them off as a logic-based skill, something she'd assumed anyone could do if they'd tried.

"You've tried warding Noah," Ailan said, "but have you tried warding yourself?"

"I don't care about warding myself." It was an immediate response, but it wasn't fully true. "Or...it's more that Salinda said witch magic grows through challenge. So I'm trying to do the opposite of what my instincts want. It's easy to be selfish, so I'm trying not to focus on myself at all."

Ailan frowned. "Is it easy to be selfish? To me, it looks like your resistance to focusing on yourself is stronger."

"Yes because of the challenge—"

"That's not quite how it works." Ailan shook her head. "I may be Elvyn, but I lived with the Forest People for centuries. I've watched witches flourish and grow. You can't challenge your magic; you must wait for it to challenge you. In the meantime, you grow it by working within your nature. Keep performing feats of magic the way you always have—"

"Casting glamours over myself isn't going to keep Noah safe. I want to create a shield around him or make him invisible to any who would cause him harm."

Ailan released a weighted sigh. "I remember those feelings. That need to protect the fragile being you brought into this world. It's been so long since I've felt that."

"Then you understand why I need to protect him. You claim he's safe behind the Veil, but if your brother finds his way here..."

"I know." Ailan set a comforting hand on her shoulder. Mareleau was surprised that she felt no instinct to flinch away. When had she begun to grow used to this woman? Ailan spoke again. "Why don't you try holding Noah and casting magic around the two of you? See if you can evade the notice of the servants who bring you dinner. Or perhaps convince them you have pointed ears, some feature you can get outside confirmation on. Start with a glamour before you try warding. Start with yourself before you try shifting your magic to others."

Her shoulders fell. That sounded like a tediously slow process, but if it gave her something to work on, she supposed she should be grateful. "All right."

Ailan must have heard the dejected note in her voice, for she rose to her feet with a warm smile. "Come, there's someone I want you to formally meet."

49

Mareleau couldn't imagine who Ailan was referring to, but curiosity got the better of her. Ailan headed for the door while Mareleau rose to her feet and gathered Noah from his playmat. She retrieved her carrying sling from the end of her bed and tucked Noah into it as she strode out of her room. Ailan was waiting in the hall.

"Who am I meeting?"

Ailan gave her a sly grin. "You'll see. I'm not sure you'd come if I told you."

That wasn't at all comforting.

Yet her interest was thoroughly piqued as Ailan led her through the palace halls. She was so distracted with trying to puzzle out their destination that she forgot to marvel at her surroundings until they were three floors down. Mareleau hadn't left her room much since arriving at the palace, save for the tribunal meeting. Now that she'd earned the tribunal's binding vow of respect and protection, she was allowed to explore the palace, but it was an unfamiliar place filled with strange people. She'd felt safest in her room.

They reached the bottom floor of the palace, where the ceilings rose four times as high as the ones in the upper halls. Elegant chandeliers sparkled with pale blue and white crystals that caught rays of sunlight and sent shards of glittering illumination upon the walls. Guards dressed in silver armor over white silk robes lined the hall ahead. They bowed as the trio passed. A pair of Elvyn footmen in blue-and-ivory robes opened the ornate double doors ahead.

Sunlight streamed through the doorway as Ailan led the way. A white marble staircase stretched out before them, leading to a large courtyard. Once they reached the bottom of the stairs, Mareleau glanced behind her, taking in the exterior of the palace for the first time. Her jaw hung on its hinge as she assessed the towering ivory turrets, the gilded balconies, and the pale blue crystalline walls that comprised the lower portions of the structure. She hadn't been able to see much of the castle from her bedroom or any of the halls she'd walked through, but this...

This made her realize just how massive Alles'Taria Palace truly was. It was twice as large as Verlot.

"It's beautiful, isn't it?" Ailan's voice startled her from her awe. She stood beside Mareleau, a wistful expression in her eyes as she admired the structure. There was something almost sad about the look. "Alles'Taria was named and modeled after the original seat of the Morkara, the palace that had been built over El'Ara's heart."

"What happened?" Mareleau asked. "I know five hundred years is a long time, but all that's left of the palace is a rock. At least, that's what I've heard."

"Centerpointe Rock," Ailan said with a nod. "I've seen it once, during the battle last spring. With my memories compromised, I didn't recognize it for what it was. I knew it marked an invisible well of fae magic, but I didn't understand how or why. Now I remember."

Ailan's expression darkened. She turned her gaze away from the spires and started off toward one of the many gardens that surrounded the courtyard. This garden contained tiny trees in myriad shapes and varieties, stone gardens marked with impossibly high cairns, as well as several ponds. Mareleau could only half focus on the beauty. The rest of her attention lingered on the subject they'd left behind.

She knew roughly how Ailan's battle with Darius had ended—he'd killed his mother before Satsara had managed to finish her ward. Then he and Ailan were trapped in the human world. But what had their plan been, and how had Darius thwarted it?

"I was supposed to lure Darius far from the palace," Ailan said as they wove through a grove of waist-high trees with vibrant needle-like leaves and twisting, twining trunks. "My army was meant to keep his attention off what my mother was doing. Her dragon was with my forces too, to convince him Satsara was among us. It was imperative that we keep him fighting until my mother's wardweaving was finished. That meant we couldn't overwhelm his army, for that would only make him worldwalk back to the human world for reinforcements. Upon his return, if he tried to worldwalk to any location already covered by the Veil, he'd find himself blocked and know what my mother was up to.

"So we held back, sacrificing our soldiers so he'd keep fighting us, keep thinking he was seconds away from victory. Only once the Veil was complete would we give it our all and either kill him or obliterate his army enough that he'd worldwalk away. If the Veil was finished, he'd never be able to reenter El'Ara again.

"But he was smarter than that. Or, at the very least, he suspected we were holding back. He and I were fighting one-on-one when the truth dawned on him. He hissed our mother's name, and I knew it was over. I reached for him, latched onto his arm right as he worldwalked away, forcing him to take me with him. Next thing I knew, we were in the forest north of the palace. In another heartbeat, he was gone. He'd left me behind on purpose. Either he'd anticipated I'd try to grab him or he realized it as soon as I touched him and altered his destination.

"I ran to the palace as fast as I could, but Mother was already dead and the palace was destroyed. It may have been the force of Satsara tying off the edges of her Veil so suddenly, or the pressure of forcing El'Ara into the human world, but Alles'Taria Palace was obliterated when I got there. The guards were dead, crushed in the rubble or murdered by my brother. He was killing those who remained as I arrived, popping in and out of thin air to behead the survivors before they even had a chance to defend themselves.

"He came for me next, taunting me about how he'd ended our mother's life while hugging her. While telling her he loved her. He'd slit her throat right after she'd smiled up at him and said she loved him too. He didn't yet know that she'd also tied off her wardweaving, blocking him from El'Ara thereafter, but once he did, he tried to kill me in earnest. No more taunting. No more games. So I did what I thought I should in that split second before he tried to behead me; I relinquished my title as Morkara to my unnamed heir."

Mareleau's stomach sank with guilt. She'd condemned Ailan for having made such a reckless choice back then, but could she blame her? She hadn't had much time for rational thought when her enemy could appear from thin air to surprise her with a blade through her neck at any moment.

They reached the far end of the garden where an arch in a tall hedge wall opened to a sloping hillside behind the palace. Rocky steps led down to where the crystalline palace walls gave way to natural stone. There daylight melted to shadow, the sunlight obscured by the turrets.

"Where are we going?" Mareleau asked, her curiosity now tinged with apprehension.

"To the dragon caves beneath the palace," Ailan said. "Ferrah, Uziel, and the hatchlings live there."

"Wait...don't tell me..."

"I want you to meet the dragons."

The blood left her face and she hugged Noah close to her, though he was already as close as he could be in his sling. She glanced down at his sleeping face, then back at Ailan. "Why?"

"You want an asset that will make you feel safe? If you earn the dragons' respect, they will listen to you."

Mareleau blinked at her. "Safe? You think being around a dragon will make me feel safe? You do realize Ferrah shattered the windows of my bedroom at Ridine Castle and nearly had me skewered with glass. And now you want me to take Noah into a cave full of the creatures?"

"They will not harm him."

"Are you certain?"

"Yes." There was no hesitation in Ailan's voice, only warmth. "He is their Morkara. They would no sooner hurt him than me. Besides, Ferrah didn't mean to hurt or alarm you at Ridine. She'd been looking for you. According to Uziel, he and Ferrah acted against the archers in your defense. They saw a threat to you, not them."

"According to Uziel," she echoed. "As in...you can talk to him?"

"I can communicate with him. It's almost like talking. Should you ever grow close enough to one of the dragons to bond with one, you'll learn what I mean."

Mareleau pulled her head back. "That...that's an option for me? To bond with a dragon?"

"Maybe not today, but someday, perhaps. For now, I am confident you can earn enough of their respect to get them to listen to you, the same way they listen to my consort. That way, even if I am not here, you can take comfort in commanding them to protect you."

This was madness. Mareleau should refuse to take a step further. She should run.

But she didn't.

Instead, a strange thrill buzzed through her. Whether it was out of a need to protect her son or simply her ego wanting to be important enough to command a dragon, she knew not. All she knew was that as Ailan continued to descend farther and farther down the hill, toward the craggy base of the castle, her feet followed. Even as her heart raced. Even as sweat pooled beneath her armpits.

They reached the base of the palace where a dark maw split the stone. There really were caves beneath the palace. Dragons lurking floors beneath her bedroom. Who would have thought?

"Being formally introduced to a dragon...is it dangerous?" she asked. It had almost been deadly for Cora, after all.

"It won't be dangerous for you, I promise." Ailan led the way inside the cave opening. Darkness enveloped them at once, and Mareleau threw out her hands for guidance. One palm met a stony wall. She was about to call out for Ailan to wait when a spark of light blinked just ahead. Then another.

Mareleau took a few hesitant steps. Each one sparked more and more tiny pinpricks of blue-green light. After a few more steps, the walls and ceiling lit up like starlight, casting her, Noah, and Ailan in an aqua glow.

"Dragon flame reacts with the minerals in these caves and leaves these residuals. They get denser and denser the deeper we go."

Ailan was right. As they wove deeper into the tunnels, more of the light painted the walls until she could see everything from the ground to the curving, rocky walls, to the towering ceilings dripping glowing stalactites. It was one of the most beautiful yet eerie sights she'd ever seen. If only Larylis were here. If only Noah was awake and old enough to appreciate such splendor.

If this were your home...

Longing and guilt clashed in her heart. What a traitorous thought that was, when she was already Queen of Vera.

But El'Ara is an entire world. A world like this. *A world with magic and miracles I've yet to see.*

She shook the thoughts from her head.

"My bonding ritual with Uziel ended in danger," Ailan said, "but that was only because of my brother. He disrespected my mother's dragon, and Berolla meant to punish him, not me. Two of her talons raked through my chest, nearly puncturing my heart, but Uziel intervened just in time. Berolla was so distraught over what she'd been tricked into doing that she atoned by sacrificing the two very talons that had cut me."

"What do you mean she sacrificed her talons?"

"She voluntarily severed two claws from her toes. That collar Cora had was made from those talons. It took us months to understand the magic Berolla had infused them with. No, that isn't accurate. My mother knew, for Berolla had told her, but Satsara had hidden the talons' true purpose from us. It wasn't until we were close to losing the fight with my brother that Mother finally told us what we could do with the claws. That we could stop Darius from worldwalking by puncturing his flesh with them."

"The war with Darius raged for multiple *months*?" Shame sank her stomach as soon as the naive words left her mouth. Of course they'd fought for months. War could last years. Decades, even. Some queen she was. She changed the subject. "You said Berolla infused the talons with magic. Do all dragon talons contain different kinds of magic?"

Ailan shook her head. "Talon magic is rare. Like unicorn horns, talons disappear into ash after the dragon dies. Only a talon gifted from a live dragon contains magic, and it is up to that dragon to decide how to infuse it. No Elvyn would ever ask of such a sacrifice from a dragon. We're lucky Darius never learned of this ability, or he would have found a way to exploit this gift from them."

Nausea turned her gut, along with another pang of guilt. She'd once ordered three princes to hunt unicorns and bring her a pelt, a pet, and a magical horn. Little had she known, the process for taking a horn was nothing short of torture. Yet another choice she regretted making.

The illumination painting the cave walls brightened, drawing Mareleau's eyes to the view ahead. An enormous cavern spread before them, the ceiling twice as tall as it had been before. Tiny pools of flame flickered over the cavern floor in a multitude of colors—red, green, orange, purple. A hulking shape rested at the center of the floor, its silhouette rising and falling like a breathing mountain. Then, with a grumble that shook the ground beneath Mareleau's feet, the shape moved, stretched, lengthened, until it unraveled as Uziel. His enormous dark head lifted from beside his body. His tail swished across the floor as he flicked his tongue toward Ailan.

Another shape stirred behind Uziel, which launched a swarm of tiny, winged creatures—baby dragons?—into the air. They flew off to perch on stalactites and stalagmites, circling the structures with wary looks at the intruders.

Mareleau shrank back. The baby dragons were only the size of a small dog, but they moved so quickly, stared so suspiciously.

Her eyes darted back to Uziel as the creature behind him fully awakened. The aqua glow of the walls glinted off opalescent scales and white feathered wings. After a stretch like Uziel had made, Ferrah bounded over the black dragon, as agile as a cat, and sat back on her haunches. Her sinuous back curved in an arch while her tail lazily coiled and uncoiled beside her. Long white whiskers draped from her maw—a rather toothy maw that was on full display as she yawned.

Uziel slithered over to Ailan, something like a purr rumbling in his throat. Ailan absently stroked his enormous snout as she spoke. "Uziel has agreed to listen to you. The others don't seem interested in meeting you at this time, but Ferrah seems curious enough."

"Others—" Just then, Mareleau noticed the other hulking shapes that she'd first taken for boulders. There were at least half a dozen other dragons asleep in the cave, though all were slightly smaller than Ferrah.

Mareleau's gaze moved to the white dragon, who watched Mareleau like she was a fascinating jewel.

Or a snack.

She tightened her arms around Noah's sleeping form.

"Would you like to introduce yourself to her?" Ailan's expression was so hopeful, contrasting the churning in Mareleau's gut.

She wanted to say no, to flee, to never look back, but beneath her anxiety, that bold thrill remained.

Not waiting for Mareleau's answer, Ailan stepped closer to Ferrah, gesturing for Mareleau to follow.

Her legs trembled, but she found herself moving before she could think better of it.

Ferrah's tongue flicked out but she didn't startle, didn't hiss, didn't do any of the things Mareleau feared she'd do.

"Bow to her," Ailan instructed. "Keep your moves slow and steady."

Mareleau could barely hear her through the blood roaring in her ears. Her heart hammered so hard it felt as if it would climb from her throat. Yet bow she did, as smoothly as she dared. As she straightened, Ailan instructed her in what to do with her hands. She kept one loose and open at her side—which meant she had to fully turn Noah's weight over to his sling—while she extended the other toward the dragon.

Seven devils, a dragon. I'm greeting a godsforsaken dragon. What if she eats my hand? What if she eats my baby? What if she eats me?

Her panic rose to a crescendo, but she managed to perform the correct movements. Palm toward Ferrah. Hold still. Then breathe.

Breathe.

Breathe.

Ferrah rose from her haunches and took a step toward her.

Mareleau nearly lost her nerve and leaped back, but Ailan warned her to hold her position.

Ferrah stepped closer again. Then again. Her tongue flicked in and out with every step until it glanced over Mareleau's palm. She shuddered as it tickled her skin.

Gods, those teeth were close.

Too close.

Ferrah held her gaze for several uncomfortable moments.

Then, with a ground-shaking huff, Ferrah bounded off, feathered wings pressed close to her sides.

Mareleau's gaze whipped to Ailan. She expected to see disappointment on the other woman's face, but instead she wore a wide grin.

"You see?" Ailan said with a chuckle as Uziel sniffed the side of her head, his breath blowing Ailan's black hair in messy streams. "You've earned her respect."

"*That* was earning her respect?"

"That was more than my brother ever managed. She'll listen to you now. Somewhat."

She couldn't help but feel a pang of disappointment. A secret side of her had hoped she'd earn more than just Ferrah's respect. She'd hoped maybe she'd bond with the creature too. Succeed at what Darius had failed.

"You'll have plenty of chances to bond with a dragon in the future," Ailan said, as if she could read Mareleau's thoughts.

Mareleau opened her mouth to deny such hopes when movement rippled at the mouth of the cavern. The telltale swirl of color warping the air foretold Garot's arrival. He stepped out of his vortex and folded into a bow at once, hands open at his sides. "Forgive my intrusion, most honored ones."

Mareleau thought the gesture was for her, Ailan, and Noah, but when he stood, his gaze darted from Uziel to the little beasts who hissed at him from their perches.

Finally, he faced Ailan. "I have an urgent update. Cora has returned, and she's asked to speak to you at once."

50

Cora waited in the empty tribunal room, where Garot had brought her. The room was even darker than it had been the last time she was here, as the brightly hued butterflies were nowhere to be seen. The only light came from the dim sconces that lined the curved walls. She wandered the circular floor, her muscles tense. Every minute she was here were several lost in the human world, and she'd already lost close to an hour.

She'd followed the agreed-upon protocol, entering El'Ara discreetly through the tear. There she'd been greeted by the drawn blades of the soldiers who now patrolled the fae side of the tear. After that, she argued over the urgency of her visit, which had been a headache even with the translation charm on the bracelet Fanon had given her. In the end, she'd worldwalked straight to the woods outside the palace, where Garot intercepted her.

She still didn't know exactly how Garot could locate her so easily. The first time she'd come to El'Ara, he'd told her about the triggers that were woven throughout the land, explaining that was how Satsara had come to meet Tristaine. Yet Cora hadn't learned more details than that. How did the triggers alert the Elvyn? How did they know the exact location where the trigger had been set off? It was yet more confusing fae technology, much like the impressive bathtub with its drains and faucets.

The door opened to reveal Ailan. And then...

"Mareleau." Cora hadn't expected Ailan to bring her, for she'd requested to speak with Ailan alone. Nightmare flames emerged from her memory at the sight of her friend, along with a burning well of guilt, shame, and bitter rage. Her confession echoed in her head.

It should have been her.

She breathed deeply, neither burying the emotions nor trying to push them away. Instead, she let all those feelings move through her without judgment.

When they passed, her body felt lighter.

Mareleau's expression brightened with a grin, and she met Cora in a one-armed hug. The other arm cradled Noah's sling. Cora sank into the embrace.

She may harbor resentment for Mareleau, but their friendship was stronger. So much stronger. She hoped Mareleau understood that. Hoped she wouldn't hate her for what she needed to do next.

"Come," Ailan said with a gentle squeeze to Cora's shoulder. She proceeded to the other side of the meeting room and opened an almost imperceptible door. Light flooded from behind it, and Ailan beckoned them to follow her inside.

As soon as Cora crossed the threshold, humid air filled her lungs, much like it had in Syrus. The scent of unfamiliar flowers flooded her nostrils. Glass walls comprised three sides of the small room, inviting in the glow of the setting sun. Potted plants and flowers in every color imaginable cluttered the floor and tables while vines crawled up trellises.

Among all the greenery fluttered the glowing butterflies from the tribunal meeting. They emitted a calming blue light.

"They're beautiful," Mareleau said, tone brimming with awe. She strolled to one of the long walls of windows and stared out at the scenery.

Cora, meanwhile, kept close to Ailan, posture stiff. She wasn't here for a leisurely chat, and a part of her dreaded disappointing Ailan. The woman may look different now, but deep inside Cora still recognized her as Nalia, the High Elder she'd looked up to for six years. A figure whose approval she'd sought.

But Ailan's approval was not her priority.

Her people were.

A butterfly flew over Cora's head, its color flashing a yellow-green.

Ailan frowned at the butterfly until it flew away from Cora, its hue returning to blue. She picked up a glass bottle fitted with a pump and nozzle and began to spray the leaves of a climbing vine bedecked with violet flowers. "Did you have any trouble entering the tear? Or getting to the palace?"

"No." It wasn't entirely true, but it wasn't what she'd come to discuss.

"You saw how many guards I've posted at the tear? I have more soldiers stationed throughout the Blight. Did you bring your soldiers to guard the human side?"

Cora's eyes flashed toward Mareleau. "King Larylis is in a ship nearby with fifty soldiers. I'll send word to him to discreetly patrol the area around the tear."

Mareleau whirled away from the window, eyes bright. "Larylis is close by? Can you get a letter to him?"

Cora opened her mouth to answer, but Ailan spoke first.

"Fifty soldiers," she said, brows furrowed. "That's not what we agreed to. I asked for—"

"We didn't agree to anything yet. The situation has changed. I'm taking charge of our alliance. The Elvyn will agree to all my terms or they will forfeit the alliance altogether."

Ailan paused spraying. "What happened?"

"I met your brother. He took me to Syrus and offered me something I can't refuse."

"You're allying with *him*?"

"No. He's given me the options of war, surrender, or alliance, and I am choosing none of those. Instead, you and I are going to make a plan to work against him, and you are going to give me what Darius offered."

Ailan's throat bobbed, and the butterflies closest to her flickered orange. She resumed spraying the plant. "What did he offer you?"

She swallowed hard. "Lela."

Another pause. Another flicker of orange. "Lela? You want me to...what? Leave El'Ara's heart in the human world?"

"Yes." Anxiety bubbled inside her, reflected in the spike of yellow on the nearest butterflies' wings. To calm herself, she turned her attention to the plant life around her. She circled a potted tree, its base consisting of five slender, intertwining trunks. Its leaves were wide, flat, and bright pink.

"You know I can't give you that," Ailan said. "El'Ara needs its heart."

Cora continued to circle the plant, steeling herself to explain the next part. "I know El'Ara needs its heart, and you will have it. The heart isn't the land itself but the *mora*. As Queen of Lela—"

"What do you mean Queen of Lela?" Mareleau marched toward Cora. "Are you...stealing my kingdom?"

Cora couldn't bring herself to meet her friend's eyes. "I'm not stealing your kingdom. I'm inheriting it. You and Larylis are going to abdicate. Teryn will inherit Vera, and we'll merge our kingdoms into one. Furthermore, I demand Larylis and Queen Mother Helena live in El'Ara."

Silence echoed back.

Finally, Cora forced herself to meet Mareleau's gaze. She expected to find red butterflies all around her in a halo of rage, but instead, they only flashed yellow. With a deep breath, Cora opened herself to her friend's emotions, sensing shock, confusion, and...

The emotions lifted.

Dispersed.

The butterflies deepened to a bold shade of green.

A bark of laughter escaped Mareleau's lips. "You're claiming Vera as your own and demanding that the Elvyn accept my husband and mother as citizens."

"I am, and I will brook no debate on the matter. No one can remain in the human world who can contest my rule. Lela is mine."

Mareleau blinked at her a few times. Then her lips curled into a trembling smile, and her emotions swelled with an unexpected warmth. Cora knew then that Mareleau had seen through her demand to her true intentions. Although Cora would be making this choice even if Mareleau hated her for it, she was determined that Mareleau and Noah wouldn't be separated from Larylis and Helena.

Ailan wasn't quite so moved. "You aren't giving your

friend a say in the matter? She hasn't decided if she wants to live here yet."

Cora lifted her chin. "No, I'm not giving her a choice, or you, and I have my reasons."

"Explain them then."

"As Queen of Lela," Cora said, "I will have access to the magic that seeps from Centerpointe Rock into the human world. I'm going to utilize it."

Ailan's nostrils flared. "You can't harness the magic."

"I won't. I'll push it back." She shared what Darius had told her, about the loophole he'd found in the prophecy. "One only becomes Morkaius after they harness the magic. So I won't. I'll go to Centerpointe Rock and use whatever temporary power I'm granted as Queen of Magic and push the *mora* back through the tear. With the veins of magic on this side of the Veil where they belong, you—or your strongest wardweavers—will seal the tear. Once it's sealed, a new heart will be forged, and your mother's wardweaving will no longer be incomplete."

Ailan's expression went blank, demonstrating her awe-laced shock. Then she shook her head. "I can see that as a possibility, but my people will never agree. You're asking us to position you as Morkaius of the human world. Someone who could take everything from El'Ara."

"I can't take everything without harnessing the magic, which would destroy me. Pushing the *mora* back to El'Ara is my only choice if I want to survive."

"My people won't—"

"They will," Cora said, tone firm. "You will make them agree. Tell them anything, I don't care what it is. Tell them I'm exactly what they fear me to be, an evil witch bent on taking Lela for her own. Tell them I'm a bloodthirsty worldwalker, and the only way to keep the peace with me and defeat your brother is to give me what I want."

Ailan set down the spray bottle and folded her arms. She paced before the climbing vines before she spoke again. "I can get the tribunal to agree if you proceed with your plan to push the *mora* back to us at once. You will secure Mareleau and Larylis' word of abdication—"

"So soon?" Mareleau straightened. "That's all it would take? Just a word of abdication, no formal process? No coronation? Just like that, she's Queen of Lela?" There was no ire in her tone, only curiosity.

"This is a matter of the *mora*," Ailan said. "Fae magic. While it will likely take more work to formalize Cora's position in terms of human politics, the magic will recognize her role once you and your husband state your abdication, just like the role of the Morkara can be relinquished upon a single verbal statement."

"That may be true," Cora said, drawing Ailan's attention back to her, "but I am not going to push the *mora* to El'Ara while Darius still lives. That would trap him in the human world and leave us to deal with him."

Ailan arched a brow. "Then what exactly are you proposing?"

"You said we need to outsmart Darius to defeat him, so we will. All he truly wants from me is the location of the tear. So I'll give him a false location. I'll lead him to a predetermined place where we will ambush him."

"You're forgetting he has no reason to stay and fight once he discovers he's being ambushed. He can worldwalk away before anyone can lay a finger on him."

"He will have a reason to stay if you're there."

Ailan's eyes widened. "You want me to serve as bait."

"I'm acting as bait myself by bringing him to the ambush

site. The least you can do is face him. You have the one thing that can stop him, don't you?"

Ailan thinned her lips as she reached into the folds of her flowing robe and extracted the magic-suppressing collar. "Yes, though I failed the last time I tried to trap him with it. I got only a single talon hooked into his skin, but he merely tore it out, tossed it aside, and worldwalked away."

"Then you'll have to try harder this time. Unless...there's more of those?"

"No, this collar is one of a kind. Berolla sacrificed two talons to create it, and it can't be replicated, even if she were still alive." At Cora's questioning look, she went on to explain. "She was trapped on this side of the Veil when my mother died. According to Fanon, she took Last Breath shortly after."

Damn. There went the possibility for more magic-suppressing weapons.

"This," Ailan said, holding up the collar, "is our best hope. Our best chance at preventing Darius from world-walking while I land a killing blow. And you're right; he won't resist the opportunity to face me if I confront him. But that doesn't mean he won't first worldwalk away to bring an army."

"So we'll station troops from our human and Elvyn forces that will be ready to fight," Cora said. "How many soldiers can Darius travel with?"

"During the war, he often brought in upwards of two dozen men at a time."

Cora's mouth fell open. "*Two dozen*? At once?"

Ailan nodded.

She couldn't imagine worldwalking with that many people in tow. Still, even with those numbers, it would take far too long to bring his entire army. "He'll be eager enough to face you that he won't risk your retreat. He'll only bring in enough soldiers to even the odds."

"Perhaps." Ailan rubbed her brow. "When do you expect this confrontation to take place?"

"He agreed to wait three weeks to hear my answer to his offer of alliance. I can pretend to agree to his terms and take him to a false tear location. But we can't rely on that time-line or that circumstance. In less than two weeks, a rebellion in Norun will cut off his reinforcements, leaving him with fewer soldiers to face Khero with. He might grow desperate to act, or suspect Khero's involvement with the rebellion. If that happens, he may revoke his offer of alliance and use threats against me until I take him to the tear. Our plan will remain the same."

"Based on the passage of time in El'Ara, we have at most three days," Ailan said, voice tinged with panic. She resumed pacing, the butterflies fluttering over her head flashing between yellow and orange. "There's still so much more to figure out. We'll need to establish a location, a way to communicate while we secure our plans, and a signal to alert my people that the ambush must begin..."

Cora had ideas for the latter. Berol had already been passing letters between Larylis and Teryn over the last couple of weeks. The falcon was small enough to fly through the tear without attracting the attention of potential spies. Moreover, Cora suspected the Elvyn would have less qualms about using an animal to relay communications as opposed to a human.

Ailan halted and faced Cora once more. "I have one final condition. I will convince the tribunal to accept your terms to keep Lela in the human world, but you must proceed with pushing the *mora* through the tear as soon as the ambush begins. I'll station wardweavers inside the tear who can get to work sealing it as soon as they feel the return of *mora*. That way you have our aid in fighting Darius, but we can take comfort in sealing him out while he's distracted."

"And if you fail," Cora said, leveling a pointed look at her, "the human world will be left to clean up your mess."

"If I fail, it means I'm either dead or he's made his way inside the Veil. Either way, you and I will have done our parts."

"Darius...inside the Veil," Mareleau echoed, shaking her head. "No, that can't be an option. You said El'Ara was the safest place for Noah."

"It is," Ailan said. "I will do everything I can to stop Darius. However, if he does make it inside the tear, the triggers will warn Garot, and you must get to the dragon caves at once. Darius may be fast enough to evade the swing of a sword, and he may heal quickly from most wounds. But there's only so much dragon fire he can withstand, even with his fae healing. Ferrah and the other dragons will defend you. Uziel will face Darius with me. If I can collar my brother, Uziel can burn him. I'll burn with him if I must. If that's what it takes to keep him from worldwalking away."

Cora's stomach turned at that. At the resignation darkening Ailan's tone. She seemed very un-Nalia-like in that moment, and every inch the Elvyn warrior.

Mareleau's throat bobbed. "What about my husband and mother? If the wardweavers seal the tear before—" She snapped her mouth shut and shifted her gaze to Cora. "Oh, right. You can still worldwalk through the Veil, so long as you have Valorre."

"It may take some time," Cora said, "but I can return everyone to their proper places once the tear has been sealed."

"So...this isn't goodbye between us yet?"

Cora gave her a sad smile. "Not yet."

"Does that mean you agree?" Ailan asked. She certainly wasn't keen on sentiment.

Cora had been determined not to budge on her terms, but Ailan's proposed condition was fair. The humans and Elvyn would work together to ambush Darius. If Cora succeeded in pushing the *mora* back, and the wardweavers sealed the tear while Darius was fighting Ailan, at the very least Mareleau and Noah would be safe. Forever. Darius would never be able to cross the Veil.

All she had to do was trust Ailan to end him.

Her muscles tensed at the thought of leaving the ambush in the hands of others while she played her role at Centerpointe Rock. But this battle wasn't hers. It was Ailan's to finish.

And Lela was Cora's to protect.

She blew out a shaky breath. "I agree."

51

With a slash of ink on paper and the press of his royal seal, Larylis was no longer King of Vera. His latest correspondence from Teryn had demanded his abdication, and Larylis hadn't balked. He obeyed his brother's wishes, rolled up his formal decree of abdication, and handed it to Berol.

With his palms planted on the bulwark of his ship, he lifted his gaze to follow her flight path high overhead, the warm hues of the setting sun gilding her feathers. Not a pang of regret plagued him as he watched his last ties to the throne disappear from sight.

Why should he regret relinquishing his crown? He'd never wanted it anyway. He'd only ever wanted *her*.

His wife's recent letter, also delivered by Berol, had explained everything, so he'd been prepared. How badly he wished he could see Mareleau now. To soothe her fears and beg her to revoke her apologies.

I'm so sorry to ask this of you, her letter had said, *after everything you've fought for. I'm sorry you have to give it all up now.*

He released a sigh. How did she not understand? Rising from bastard to king was nothing compared to earning her love. If abdicating was what it took to be with his wife and child, so be it. There was no sacrifice he wouldn't make for them.

A crown and kingdom were small in comparison.

With Berol no longer in sight, he lowered his gaze to the sunlit cove straight ahead. Upon one of those bluffs lay the entrance to El'Ara. As much as Larylis wanted to be there, to guard the exact location of the tear, this was as close as he dared get by sea. After nightfall, he and his men would disembark and take up posts surrounding the bluff.

Watching.

Waiting.

Preparing.

Protecting.

There was still much to plan for. Much to organize with Teryn and Cora. There were still so many uncertainties and risks. But for the first time since Larylis' world had been shaken by prophecy, dragons, and threats of war, he was certain of his role, even as his title had been stripped away. He knew with all his heart that he was in the right place at the right time.

Soon an ambush would begin.

And Larylis would stake his life on protecting the two people he loved most.

~

LEXINGTON QUIL, CROWN PRINCE OF TOMAS WAS A GENUINE, certified revolutionary.

A godsdamned hero, if you will.

And not just to the rebels in Norun but his friends in

Khero too. Today the final shipment of weapons had been smuggled to the rebel forces in the southeastern cities of Norun, and tomorrow the battle would begin. Lex's spies had relayed that King Darius' reinforcements were just north of where the rebels would attack, which meant they'd never make it to Khero.

In one fell swoop, Lex would practically save the whole damn world. He wouldn't be surprised if his portrait ended up in one of those fancy textbooks Larylis was always reading. If so, he'd be sure to send him one, just to boast.

He puffed his chest as he grinned at the small crowd gathered on the battlement atop the wall that marked the border between Norun and Tomas. He used to hate this bloody wall. Not because it wasn't effective; it was. Up until now, his kingdom had avoided all conflict with Norun. Tomas was known as a kingdom of cowards, ruled by a monarch who'd rather hide behind a wall than engage in any form of violence. Lex's kingdom was so unremarkable that Isvius Dorsus, King of Norun, hadn't shown an ounce of interest in conquering it.

Which meant he wouldn't expect what was coming for him tomorrow.

Lex's father, Carrington Quil, the renowned coward king himself, had agreed to send a battalion to aid the fights closest to the border. See? Not so much a coward now, thanks to Lex being utterly bloody brilliant. So what if all Lex had done was secure a trade agreement for Aromir wool? It had been enough to get Carrington to stop fawning over Lex's crybaby brother, who only fed their father's fear of conflict. That little slip of paper promising Tomas inclusion into one of the most coveted trade agreements on the continent was exactly what Carrington had needed to bolster his confidence and convince him to finally aid the rebellion of his former neighbors.

Now those soldiers stared up at the person giving them their pre-battle pep talk, moved to tears by the speaker's words.

That speaker was not Lex.

It was his wife.

His tiny spitfire. His sweet little hellion. His beautiful demon with the voice of an angel. The true hero of the rebellion and savior of the world.

Yeah, Lex couldn't take any of that credit. It belonged fully to her.

Lily wore partial armor and a billowing white gown, the epitome of a warrior angel. Her auburn hair was curled in an elegant updo that put her round cheeks on full display. The softness of her form and the sweetness of her looks paired with her vicious words were an oddly alluring contrast.

"Tomorrow, we will fight to take back the kingdoms of Haldor and Sparda," she shouted. She may be quiet most of the time, but gods above, she could project when she wanted. Her uncle, the former King of Sparda, stood beside her and proudly nodded. Lex, standing on her other side, nodded even prouder. "We will punish Norun for underestimating those they perceive as weak. We will show them that even the smallest rodents bear formidable teeth."

A cheer went through the crowd of soldiers, and Lex tried his best not to swoon. Gods, his wife was adorable. She looked so much like she had when they'd reunited after the Heart's Hunt. Lily hadn't wanted to speak to him back then, for there was that whole bit about him competing for another woman's hand, but he'd had a valid explanation. He'd just needed to find her first. Which he had. Standing behind a podium at a secret rally, giving a speech much like this one, encouraging the rebels to maintain hope. That their time would soon come. All they'd needed were weapons.

Lex had fallen in love with her thrice over while he'd listened to her speech, and after he'd managed to convince her he wasn't pure swine for having participated in the Heart's Hunt, he'd promised to bring her vision to life.

He was honored that the time had come.

She raised her voice and pounded a fist against her breastplate. "Tomorrow, we will stand upon the corpses of our enemies and bathe in their blood!"

Another cheer rose from the crowd, its pitch near deafening.

Lily blushed and grinned from ear to ear like the wicked little cherub she was.

Seven devils, he'd never loved her more.

52

Cora greeted the North Tower Library not with the affection of a friend but the respect of an old enemy. She stepped inside the circular space and found it just as impotent as ever. It was merely a dim, moonlit room, clean enough to prove it was well maintained but with a staleness that spoke of having very few visitors.

She slowly stalked the perimeter of the room with her head held high, not bothering to skirt away from the shadows that gathered in the darkest corners. She swept past pools of moonlight and shadow, as if they were one and the same, and remembered how far she'd come. Just like she'd done the night before her wedding, when she'd awoken from that fiery nightmare, she was here to remind herself of the enemy she'd already defeated. Of the dark energy she'd banished from every object in this room.

Morkai was gone.

Soon Darius would be too.

She'd returned from El'Ara ten days ago, her alliance with the Elvyn secured along with a plan for their ambush. By now, all the pieces should be in place. Larylis and his soldiers were posted in the woods, some near the ambush location, others ready to defend the real tear. Ailan should have sent some of her Elvyn soldiers to join them. Ailan herself would be waiting in the Blight near the tear for the signal that it was time for her to face Darius. The rebellion in Norun should have begun. Cora and Teryn had sent a battalion north to defend the border, should Darius' forces suddenly invade. In two days, Cora and Teryn would ride to join them and prepare for the meeting with Darius. Meanwhile, Ridine's garrison was prepared to defend the castle should Darius appear at any time.

Her mind reeled to keep all the plans organized in her mind, as well as to measure the time discrepancy between the human world and El'Ara. She wasn't sure whether it was a blessing or a curse that time went by so much slower here. For Ailan and Mareleau, just over a day had passed since Cora had left. They would experience a flurry of activity from dawn to dusk until the battle began.

Even Valorre had a job to do. For the last week, he'd been seeking out all his remaining unicorn brethren, and perhaps any other fae creatures who may have come through the Veil. Most of the unicorns had figured out how to return through the Veil on their own after they'd gotten their memories back. But there were still some who hadn't left, and she didn't want them trapped here when she pushed the *mora* back. Cora ached at the silence that had once been filled by Valorre's presence, and it was only made worse knowing she wouldn't see him again until they reconvened at Centerpointe Rock. He may be there already, but she wouldn't know until she arrived.

In the meantime, Cora could only wait. Prepare. Plan for numerous scenarios.

She blew out an anxious breath and circled the room

once more. This time, she paused at the nightstand upon which her talisman of twigs and crystals rested. This was the only surface that gathered dust in the room, for the servants knew better than to disrupt this design. Only Cora tended to it.

With tender care, she removed each twig, each crystal, with careful reverence, then dusted the table with a silk handkerchief she'd tucked into the front of her chemise. Once clean, she replaced the items one at a time, crossing each stick with precision until it formed something like a star, then arranged the crystals around it. With her protection talisman back in place, she gave the nightstand an approving nod. She stepped away, but not before her eyes fell on the nightstand drawer. That was where she'd previously stashed the talon collar, right next to Morkai's book of blood weaving blueprints.

A book Cora now knew Teryn had read.

He'd told her all about what he'd done with the blood Darius had left behind before he'd taken Cora to Syrus. Told her how he'd made a bond with Morkai's warrior wraiths, earning their loyalty for one final battle, before he'd give them eternal rest. All Teryn had to do to summon them was offer his blood.

She'd been chilled to learn of what he'd done, yet she hadn't felt an ounce of fear. It was more...awe. Relief. They now had a way to bolster their numbers without their enemy being any the wiser.

As for their enemy...

He could act at any time.

Cora sensed Teryn's approach before his footsteps sounded on the stairs. She glanced over her shoulder to greet him with a tired grin.

He was dressed down to his shirtsleeves and trousers, his

silver hair hanging in waves around his face. In a few slow strides, he came up behind her and wrapped his arms around her waist. He nestled his face into the crook of her neck. "Couldn't sleep?"

"No," she said. "Besides, I wanted to wait for you."

He'd been in the study all evening, arranging correspondences with the trusted few who knew about Larylis' formal abdication. They were keeping it a secret for now, so as not to alert Darius of their intentions, but they still needed to set some things in motion so as not to throw Lela into chaos once all was said and done.

They stayed like that for several long, quiet moments. These were the moments Cora treasured lately. The calm before the storm.

Too soon, Teryn pulled away. She turned to face him, lacing her hands behind his neck. He frowned, then ran a hand down her bare arm. "Aren't you cold?"

She hadn't noticed the cold until now, but dressed in only her chemise so late in the evening, and in a room without a fire, she had to admit she was chilly. "A little."

He smiled down at her and rubbed both of her goose-flesh-covered arms, pausing as one of his hands brushed over her bicep. He stroked the skin with his thumb, eliciting a shiver from her. "Your tattoos have grown again."

Brow furrowed, she slid her hands from behind his neck, resting one palm on his chest while she inspected the other arm. Sure enough, on the inside of her bicep were more geometric shapes that hadn't been inked with a needle. "Oh, you're right."

She hadn't noticed before now, as it wasn't a part of her body she regularly inspected, nor was it an area that drew her attention in the mirror. Yet as surprised as she was to see the new designs, she'd experienced a similar phenomenon last year, when a spiral appeared on her inner elbow. Salinda had explained that Cora wasn't the only one whose *insigmora* had taken on a life of their own. The tattoos themselves were a Faeryn tradition, passed down to the Forest People—Faeryn descendants and witches alike. Now that she knew more about Lela's history, she wondered if it was the influence of *mora* that made the tattoos grow on their own.

Furthermore...what would it be like once fae magic was properly sealed behind the Veil?

Would her *insigmora* cease growing without the aid of ink and needle?

Would the Faeryn descendants who lived among the Forest People cease being able to use the Magic of the Soil? Would they never again wield roots and vines like they had during the battle at Centerpointe Rock? Would only witch magic be left in the world?

Her questions left her with a pang of guilt, for she hated to think she might be condemning some of the Forest People to a magicless life. Yet it was impossible to know the answers, and she'd already made her choice. She knew what she had to do. She'd deal with the consequences after the *mora* was sealed and Lela was safely hers.

Teryn ran his hand over her arm again from bicep to wrist, then lifted the back of her hand to his lips. "We should get to bed."

She stepped closer to him and heaved a sigh. "Must we?" She'd spoken out of anxiety, for she dreaded sleep these days, fearing all the ways things could go wrong during slumber. But the way his eyes dipped to her mouth made her reconsider her motivations behind the statement.

Teryn lifted his eyes back to hers, holding them with passionate intensity. Her palm was still pressed to his chest, her other hand still resting in his. Slowly, he lowered his lips to hers and caressed them with the softest, sweetest kiss. It was a balm on her soul, a blanket for all her frayed nerves. She melted against him, angled her head, and let him deepen the kiss.

Mother Goddess, she loved him so much. Loved how a single kiss could make her forget her fears. Her worries. The risks they'd soon face.

Yet Teryn's kisses could only do so much.

They couldn't drown out the clamor of bells that shattered the night.

CORA'S HEART HAMMERED AGAINST HER RIBS AS THEY RACED down the stairs and through the main hall. Captain Alden and several members of the royal guard intercepted them.

"What happened?" Cora asked, though she expected she already knew the gist of it.

"Heavily armored soldiers are appearing within the perimeter wall," Alden said, her blue eyes wide with terror. "Two dozen at a time, surrounding the castle. I've sent archers to the wall, but the invading army hasn't attacked. They're waiting beneath a shield wall."

Cora's stomach turned. Darius was here. He wasn't going to wait for the border meeting after all. She breathed past her fear, reminding herself that they were prepared for this scenario. Even her guards were ready, as demonstrated by the clothing, weapons, and armor they carried. One guard passed Cora a pair of trousers, a leather gambeson, and a breastplate while another handed similar items to Teryn. With no time for modesty, Cora and Teryn dressed in the proffered raiment with haste, then donned their weapons—Teryn's sword and Cora's dagger.

After they were fully dressed, the party proceeded to the nearest battlement. Once at the parapet, Cora glanced down at the castle grounds. Just like Captain Alden had explained, soldiers gathered in clusters of two dozen all around the castle.

"Seven devils," Teryn cursed from beside her, his hands gripping the edge of the crenellated wall so hard his knuckles turned white.

"There's at least one hundred soldiers," Captain Alden said under her breath. Then, "No, one hundred and fifty. And more keep appearing."

Cora swallowed hard. Their garrison boasted three hundred, but that wasn't enough when the enemy was already inside the gates. Darius had memorized locations inside the keep itself; soldiers could already be surging through the halls...

Despite the fear tightening her chest, she anchored her soles to the floor, flooded her nostrils with cold night air, and connected to the elements. Earth beneath her feet. Breath in her lungs. The mist in the air. The light of the moon. The fire of her rage. Then, lowering her shields, she sought a specific strain of energy.

It sparked in her periphery, on the distant ground, then was gone the next moment. She whirled toward where she'd sensed him and saw a group of soldiers where there had been none a moment ago.

Then his energy returned, closer this time.

Then closer again.

She and Teryn turned away from the parapet just in time to see Darius appear on the battlement.

"There you are," Darius said with a smirk. He was

dressed in his same dark military-style ensemble as before, his gray hair swept back from his severe brow, but with a cuirass and gauntlets.

Captain Alden raised her sword, as did the rest of the royal guard, but Darius disappeared in the next breath. His absence did nothing to relieve Cora's fear, and in another heartbeat, Darius was back, a dozen soldiers behind him. His arms were linked with two of his soldiers, and theirs were linked to their comrades, forming a clustered chain of sorts. Cora's eyes widened at the sight. He could travel with that many companions simply by linking a group together and only making physical contact with two of them.

Darius' soldiers dropped each other's arms and withdrew their swords, taking up defensive stances.

"Majesty," Alden said, her eyes narrowed on Darius. "Orders?"

"Hold positions," Cora said, infusing her voice with as much calm as she could muster. Her fingers begged to unsheathe her dagger, yearned to flinch toward the bow and quiver that weren't there. Yet she kept her arms at her sides as she and Teryn stepped forward, flanked by Alden and another guard. Darius' men held their positions while their king mirrored the step toward the other party. He stood tall, his sword fully sheathed at his hip, hands clasped behind his back as if he had no reason to fear the blades pointed at him.

Why should he fear when he could worldwalk out of harm's way in the blink of an eye?

"What is the meaning of this?" Teryn asked. Cora could feel the fear rippling off her husband, but he too was putting on a good show of keeping his composure. "You agreed to give us three weeks to make our decision—"

"Yes, but that was before my reinforcements were

stalled." Darius narrowed his eyes. "Did you have anything to do with that? Aiding your friends in Tomas?"

"We were not involved," Cora said, holding his gaze without falter.

"Ah, but you knew about it, didn't you? When you asked for more time to consider my offer, you knew about the rebellion, right?"

"You threatened us with war. Why wouldn't I use any advantage to protect my kingdom? You're the one who broke my trust. You assured me you'd prove your merit—"

"Don't bother with that," Darius said, a dark chuckle coloring his words. "You never intended to consider my offer of alliance, did you?"

"I suppose you'll never know now. What you're doing—showing up at my castle with an army—is unforgivable."

He took another step forward, pausing only when Cora's guards did the same. Still, he kept his gaze locked on Cora's. "I told you my threats weren't empty, and I was tired of waiting while I knew I was being toyed with. You seem to have forgotten what I said about Ridine. That I could and would take it in a single night, should you give me a reason to."

"So you're here to fight us?" Teryn asked.

"I'm here," Darius said, "to give you one last chance to make a reasonable choice. You've forfeited your option of alliance, but I will still accept surrender. Take me to the tear at once, or Ridine is mine."

53

Cora didn't bother trying to mask the pound of her heart. Let him hear it. Let him think she was afraid. So long as he couldn't distinguish the cadence of fear from the pound of anticipation, it didn't matter if he noticed the spike in her pulse.

The key was masking her eagerness.

"How do you know I'm even apprised of the tear's location?"

He gave her a withering look. "I know, trust me. And don't bother deceiving me. I learned enough during my few jaunts to Ridine to understand the general location. Somewhere west of Lake Sarrolin, am I right? On the coast?"

Cora pursed her lips. Yet another reaction she didn't have to hide. She never should have let Mareleau send letters to Larylis through her and Berol without looking over them first. Then again, back when Mareleau had penned the letter, they'd had no reason to believe there was a spy freely wandering Ridine. The intel had only made it back to the castle because Larylis had shared it with Teryn. Darius must have either overheard one of Teryn's meetings with their trusted few allies or snuck into the royal study and found his correspondence.

Either way, Darius would not be fooled by taking him far from where he expected her to.

Thank the Mother Goddess she had no plans to.

Darius' expression darkened. "It isn't up for debate. You will take me to the tear. If you comply, I will accept your surrender and return to remove my soldiers from your premises. If you deceive or fail me in any way, my men will take Ridine. You have ten minutes before they will act on their own. We can spend that time debating and end this chat in bloodshed, or you can take me to the tear and save your castle. You may have forfeited an alliance with me, but we can still forge favorable terms for your surrender."

Cora and Teryn exchanged a glance. Her husband's throat bobbed, worry etched in his expression. He didn't have to feign that. They may have a plan, but that didn't mean it was infallible. So much could go wrong.

Teryn reached for her hand and squeezed her fingertips. She squeezed his back in wordless reassurance.

Darius' sharp tone invaded their moment. "What's it going to be?"

Cora stepped forward, releasing Teryn's hand with great reluctance. She burned Darius with a glare and spoke through her teeth. "I'll take you."

"Good," he said, voice tight. He extended his arm. "You can travel with a companion, I presume?"

"I can." Her gaze dipped to the proffered arm, hating that she had to touch him at all. But touch him she must, if she wanted to take him where he was meant to go. With a deep breath, she closed the distance between them, linked her arm through his, and closed her eyes.

She pictured a cliff's edge, waves battering the beach far

below. She imagined salty wind against her cheeks, the soft give of the grass beneath her feet.

Then she took a step.

And planted her feet in their destination.

She released Darius' arm at once and leaped a step back. One hand remained open at her side, ready to unsheathe her dagger should he round on her. "Well?" she said, raising her voice over the crash of waves far below and the rioting wind tearing loose tendrils of hair from her braid. "We're here. I've done what you asked, now remove your men from my castle."

He assessed her through slitted lids. "How do I know you took me to the correct location?"

Her lips peeled into a sneer. "I thought you could sense the tear, being the *mora's* rightful ruler and all. Oh...can you not? Ailan could."

A tic pulsed at the corner of his jaw. "Show me where it is."

Cora scoffed. "That's a bad idea. You'll be torn to shreds as soon as you enter."

"Then you have nothing to fear. Show me."

She uttered curses under her breath. "If you insist." She kept her gaze on him as she skirted past toward the edge of the cliff. The sound of waves grew louder. She halted just before the edge. "I won't turn my back on you until you provide me some space."

"You think I'm going to shove you off the edge?"

"Yes, and I'd rather you didn't."

He bared his teeth to show his displeasure but extended his arms and walked backward. She waited until he was several feet away before she turned her back to him. Her shields, however, remained down. Sensing.

Extending a hand, she stepped closer to the cliff's edge

and reached into the air like Ailan had done when she'd searched for the tear. Cora shifted her feet to the side, reached farther ahead.

Then she closed her eyes.

Pictured her destination in her mind.

And stepped off the edge of the cliff.

FOR THE SECOND TIME IN TWO WEEKS, TERYN WAS FORCED TO watch the woman he loved disappear with his enemy. He let every ounce of his rage show as he eyed the soldiers Darius had left on the battlement. They wore full armor and helms, obscuring their features. He couldn't make out their expressions, see if they were terrified or angry, determine whether they were acting out of fierce loyalty or magical compulsion like many of Morkai's men had.

It didn't matter, though.

Whether they were wicked enemies or innocent souls with families and loved ones, they'd come to his castle. Threatened his home. His kingdom. His wife.

Soldiers were essential tools for war.

But Darius' men would die tonight.

Teryn turned away from the enemy squad.

"Don't move," called one of the men.

Teryn paused but didn't bother turning around. "Your king has my wife. You think I'm going to act against him now? Besides, he didn't leave any orders for me. What harm can I do?"

Only silence answered, so he proceeded once more, past his guards who remained at the ready, swords drawn, eyes locked on the other squad. He stopped only once he reached the wall. Moonlight glinted off the shields hiding the hundreds of bodies filling the castle grounds, illuminating the archers who stood on the wall, awaiting orders to defend or attack.

He breathed deeply and unsheathed the dagger at his hip. Shuffling footsteps and the creak of armor sounded behind him, followed by one of the enemy soldier's voices. "What is he doing?"

Teryn brought the blade to his palm, laying the flat of it over its center.

"I have the means to signal our attack," the same man said. "We don't need to wait the full ten minutes for our king to return. One wrong move, and you'll lose any chance at escaping this alive."

"Your king isn't returning," Teryn said. Even if Darius did, even if everything went wrong and the King of Syrus returned triumphant, Teryn was determined to greet him with a massacre. A tableau of death.

"Is that a threat?" the soldier said. "Or do you not trust His Majesty to honor his word?"

"It doesn't matter if he honors his word. My wife won't be honoring hers." He angled his head over his shoulder, his lips peeling into a wicked grin.

The soldier huffed a dark laugh. "If that proves true, your reign is at an end."

"We'll see." With that, Teryn turned the blade, slashed its edge over his palm, and closed his fist. Blood dripped from his hand as he thrust his fist toward the wall and the grounds beyond. Then, with a whisper, he said, "My blood. My command. Your final fight begins."

54

Cora's steps were more precise than any dance.

She left the cliff's edge and planted her feet on soil. The sound of waves was muted by half, though Darius remained in sight. She was behind him now, at the edge of the woods that lined the coastal road. It was as similar a location to the real tear as she could get without positioning him too close to it.

Her hands moved with practiced ease. Even in the dark, in the shadows of the trees that stood behind her, she knew what to do. She kept her eyes locked on her target—Darius standing at the edge of the cliff, in the space Cora had vacated, feeling through the air as Cora had done—as she reached into the underbrush and extracted her bow and quiver. She didn't bother shouldering her quiver, simply plucked out an arrow, nocked it in place, and pulled the bowstring to her cheek.

She'd practiced this shot numerous times over the past week.

Practiced shooting from this distance.

Imagined her enemy standing exactly where he stood now.

She released the arrow, watched it soar straight for Darius' neck, just above the back of his cuirass—

Before the arrow could meet its mark, Darius stepped to the side and whirled toward her. The arrow whizzed past him, over the cliff's edge, and to the beach beyond. A small, winged silhouette shot into the sky, as if startled by the rogue arrow, and flew away.

Cora forced herself not to follow the shadow with her eyes lest she give away Berol's importance. She couldn't let Darius see the place the falcon now dove to, at another cliff's edge much like this one, far in the distance where the coastline curved toward the east.

Darius, oblivious or uncaring of the startled bird, took a step forward. In the next breath, he was before her, tearing her bow from her grip. She took a breath, a step, and used her abilities to travel several feet away, to the center of the road. Unsheathing her dagger, she brandished it at him, ready to strike should he get too close.

But he didn't draw his sword, nor did he close more than a few feet of space between them. The unveiled disdain in his eyes was sharp enough. "Did you think the crashing waves would be loud enough to mask your presence? To stifle the sound of your bowstring? You tried to fool me, and you failed. That makes you the fool."

She said nothing. Perhaps she should look more disappointed. In truth she was, though she'd never counted on her arrow reaching its target. It would have been satisfying, but Ailan had told her how difficult he was to kill. How he could heal from many wounds a regular human could not. Not only that, but he could worldwalk while injured, flee to safety until he healed.

There was only one weapon that could stop him long enough to land a fatal blow, and Cora was not in possession of it.

Darius stepped to the side, and Cora did the same until they were circling each other. He shook his head. "You've truly disappointed me, Aveline. I respected you as my kin. Admired you as a fellow witch and worldwalker. You've made a terrible blunder in trying to deceive me. Ridine is now mine. My men will attack and everyone in your castle will suffer for it. I'll torture those most loyal to you. Strip their flesh from their bones. Place everyone else's head on a pike."

He said those chilling words with a calm that made them that much more terrifying. All she had to counter her fear was a hope that Teryn's plan would work. That his wraiths were enough to protect Ridine.

Darius halted his circling and narrowed his eyes. "I hear the others too. How many are there in the woods? Fifty? One hundred? I take it this is an ambush. What are they waiting for?"

"I haven't a clue what you mean," she said flatly.

He *tsk*ed. "Did you think you could isolate me here? That I wouldn't stand a chance against your little soldiers? What you fail to realize is I don't have to stay to watch this pathetic ambush unfold. I have better uses for my time—"

He snapped his mouth shut, hearing the wingbeats before she did. It was the hulking shadow darkening the sky that had first alerted Cora that the time had come. Now the pound of Uziel's wings rose over the crash of waves.

Darius whirled around.

Uziel landed on the coastal road, a red glow burning deep in this onyx throat. Upon his back, at the base of his shoulders, sat Ailan.

With a huff of laughter, Darius drew his sword. "I see. I have a reason to stay after all."

Uziel lowered his head, and Ailan climbed down his leg, as easily as if she were exiting a coach. She was dressed in form-fitting trousers, a knee-length robe, and scaled armor over her chest, shoulders, and forearms. She unsheathed a sword with one hand and raised a double-bladed weapon in the other.

Only it wasn't a double-bladed weapon. Not exactly. It was the collar. The one thing that could stop Darius from worldwalking away.

"It's been a long time, sister dear," Darius said, tone mocking.

"Face me," Ailan said through her teeth, "and we can end this rivalry of ours at last."

"I'll face you, but I'd prefer to even the odds first." In the next blink, he disappeared.

Cora used that moment to focus on the space beside Ailan. She stepped across the distance, appearing at the Elvyn's side. "Has Mareleau been alerted that the battle has begun?"

"I sent Ferrah to her as soon as Berol entered the tear," Ailan said. "She'll be prepared for the worst-case scenario."

Cora hated that there even was a worst-case scenario. Which was why her role was so important. She needed to ensure the Elvyn could seal the tear before Darius discovered its location. "Are your wardweavers ready?"

"Yes. They await within the tear. They will weave as soon as the *mora* surges back to El'Ara and their powers strengthen."

Just then, two dozen soldiers appeared, the same way they had at Ridine. These men, however, weren't waiting under their shields. Instead, they surged forward at once.

"Now!" Ailan shouted.

Uziel opened his maw and shot a volley of flame at the men. Those who acted fast enough raised their shields, but at least half screamed as they fell to the blaze.

Another group of soldiers appeared. Then another. Luckily, Uziel's flame wasn't their sole defense. The flash of light had triggered motion from the woods. Now human and Elvyn soldiers ran forth to meet the enemy forces, even as they grew in number. Uziel roared and snapped but could no longer risk his blasts of fire, lest he harm their allies. The allied troops kept the space around Ailan, Uziel, and Cora clear, funneling the enemy soldiers away. Yet Darius made no attempt to drop his fighters near them. He wanted to face Ailan alone.

The sound of steel against steel drowned out the waves, rose above the wind. Would Darius ever stop bringing his soldiers? Had Cora been wrong—

Darius appeared before them, far too close for comfort. Uziel growled, but he couldn't blast Darius without risking harm to Ailan and Cora. He curved his body around them, but Darius only worldwalked to the side, keeping Ailan in view.

"Go," Ailan muttered to Cora as Uziel tried to hide them again.

Cora blew out a shaky breath. As much as she wanted to ensure her allies weren't outnumbered, that they truly could defeat their enemies, she'd already done her part here. She'd lured Darius, and now he'd fight Ailan.

Meanwhile, Cora had another mission to complete.

Ailan stepped forward, leaving the safety of Uziel's proximity.

With a grin, Darius disappeared and reappeared directly behind her.

Cora's heart leaped into her throat—

Ailan parried his sword just in time, moving as swift and as smooth as the night breeze.

Never had Ailan looked so unlike the elderly Nalia Cora had known.

She could trust this warrior to hold her own.

Cora had a job to do. People to protect. And an entire world to seal away.

With a deep breath, she closed her eyes and left the fray behind.

THE HAIR ROSE ON THE BACK OF LARYLIS' NECK as sounds of battle clashed farther down the coast. The clang of steel was too loud, too near the most precious location of all. The hidden tear just north of his post. Mere minutes ago, he'd witnessed an enormous black dragon—the same that had attacked Ridine—appear out of nowhere at the edge of the cliff with a rider on his back.

The blond-haired Elvyn stationed at Larylis' side had tensed at the pair's appearance, his fingers curling around the hilt of his sword. Not in fear of the dragon or its rider but yearning. Frustration. Impatience.

Fanon wanted to defend that rider. Ailan. The Elvyn who was his consort.

Though Larylis and Fanon could communicate, courtesy of the charm hanging from one of his gauntleted wrists, the Elvyn had said very little to Larylis since they'd taken their positions. Yet even without words, Larylis understood him, could read the terror etched on his face as he watched Ailan in the distance. She and the gray-haired man had been locked in combat for several minutes now, the latter's moves impossibly fast. Fanon's tense posture mirrored Larylis' own. They both wished they could be elsewhere—Fanon defending Ailan, Larylis defending Mareleau—yet both had taken up the duty to protect the location of the tear and intercept anyone who got too close.

Already the battle was creeping this way.

Soon they would need to act. Fight. Protect.

Larylis could hardly believe this was happening. No textbook had ever described anything close to this. There were no kings he could emulate, no warriors he could try to embody. Never had he read about a bastard who'd become king, only to relinquish his crown to save two worlds and be with the people he loved. Never had humans fought alongside Elvyn warriors to protect fae magic.

The nearest fighters continued to clash, though the enemy troops soon outnumbered the allies. Larylis' squad could no longer remain in waiting, nor could Fanon's.

"We join," Fanon said, his words translated through the charm.

Larylis tightened his jaw and forgot every great king he'd ever admired. Every line of text he'd ever used to construct an ideal version of himself—a standard he could never reach. Instead, he thought of Mareleau, Noah, and everything he held dear.

All he could be was himself.

That was enough.

Larylis Alante, battle on Khero's western coast, Year 171 of the Dragon. Loved his family more than life. Destroyed their enemies until victory was his.

He lifted his hand and signaled his soldiers to charge.

55

Cora returned to the battlement she'd left not long ago, though now it stood empty. Teryn, his guards, and the enemy squad were nowhere to be seen. Yet sounds of fighting blared all around; she'd traded one active battlefield for another. Even though her destination lay at Centerpointe Rock, she needed to ensure Ridine was safe. That, and she'd promised to take Teryn with her when the time came to push the *mora* from the human world. It could be too dangerous for her to attempt the feat alone. If anything went sideways, if the *mora* overwhelmed her or she began to harness it when she was supposed to push it back, she could depend on Teryn to anchor her.

She peered over the parapet to find a sea of mist and blood. The mist came from the hazy figures of the warrior wraiths that swarmed the grounds, hacking down Darius' fighters, their semi-transparent weapons making muted thuds against their opponents' swords and armor.

Her archers shot arrows into the melee, picking off more of the enemy fighters one by one. The vicious, bloody fight turned her stomach, but she couldn't bring herself to feel remorse. Not when the tides were in her favor.

Not when the win was hers.

Teryn had made the right call in choosing this battle as the wraiths' final fight. With Darius' men already inside the castle walls, Khero's chances of victory would have been slim without them.

She hurried away from the parapet and entered the stairwell leading down from the battlement. Opening her senses, she sought Teryn's location. To her relief, his energy pulsed back, not too far from where she was now. As she exited the stairwell, the clang of steel met her ears. She unsheathed her dagger—the only weapon on her person now that Darius had wrested her bow from her—and crept toward Teryn's energy as well as the sounds of conflict.

She fled down the hall, noting bodies strewn here and there. Most of them belonged to the enemy squad, but one corpse at the end of the hall was a member of her royal guard.

Her heart clenched.

She rounded the corner at the end of the next corridor and finally caught sight of motion. Captain Alden was engaged in combat with one of Darius' men, as were several more of her guards. Another bout took place down the next stairwell, the only sign being the clash of blades and the sway of the fighters' shadows against the stone wall, cast by the light burning in the sconces.

Teryn's energy pulsed from that direction.

Cora's heart thundered as she rushed toward the stairwell, keeping close to the wall to evade the notice of the other fighters. Not that any were unoccupied enough to pay her much heed. She reached the top of the stairs, her dagger at the ready, and proceeded down on quick feet. She pulled up short at the sight of Teryn. He and one of Darius' men were locked in armed combat. Blood covered one of Teryn's shoulders, his gambeson split open to reveal crimson soaking the linen of his shirt. His left hand was wrapped in what looked like a torn piece of cloth.

Yet the enemy soldier bore wounds too. One eye was slashed and swollen, a gash on his cheek just beneath it. His helm was gone, as were several other pieces of his armor, but he fought relentlessly. Teryn had the high ground and pursued the man farther and farther down the stairs, but with Teryn standing between her and his opponent, his back facing her, there was nothing she could do to help—

No, that wasn't true at all.

She released a slow breath, anchored her feet on the stone beneath her, and poured her focus onto the blood-splattered stair behind the enemy. Without even bothering to close her eyes, she lifted a foot, leaned forward...

And planted her soles on the intended step.

Teryn's eyes widened slightly when he spotted her, but he didn't falter. He kept the man's full attention as Cora swiped out with her dagger and slashed the backs of the man's knees. With a grunt, his legs buckled. Cora retreated down a few steps and Teryn plunged his sword into the man's throat.

Cora's chest heaved as she watched the tip of the blade protrude from the back of the man's neck. Teryn withdrew his sword, and the enemy crumpled onto the stairwell. Cora kept her eyes locked on Teryn, not the dying man or the pool of blood quickly slicking the stairs. Instead, she took in his face, the spatter of blood flecked over his skin, the wounds he'd sustained on his arms.

She sagged with relief to see him devoid of life-threatening injuries.

He assessed her with the same relieved intensity. Her name left his lips as he sheathed his sword. "Cora."

She ran the rest of the way up the stairs to him, skirting around the man and the blood, until she collided with his chest, his arms around her. The discomfort of his hard breastplate against her cheek didn't matter. Only he did.

He pressed a kiss to the top of her head and spoke into her hair. "This is the last of the soldiers who got inside the halls."

She pulled away, knowing they didn't have much time to waste. "The ambush has begun."

"Majesty." Alden appeared at the top of the stairs, followed by more of the royal guard.

It was then Cora heard the relative silence. The conflicts in the hallway above had ceased.

Alden gave her a knowing look. "Is it time?"

Captain Alden and the royal guard knew what came next. Knew what Cora had promised to do. Cora gave her a solemn nod. As much as Cora wanted to wait until every enemy fighter was felled, she couldn't linger. Not if she wanted to fulfill her vow to Ailan and lock Darius out of El'Ara.

"Our victory is secure," Alden said, tone brimming with confidence. "We will finish this."

Teryn and Cora exchanged a glance. If they left now, Teryn would need to call off the wraiths. They couldn't risk leaving them to fight without Teryn's guidance. When they'd served Morkai, they hadn't seemed to care who they killed, only that they fought.

"You can depend on us," Alden said.

"Let's go, then." Teryn sheathed his sword and extended his uninjured palm toward Cora.

She grasped his hand, gave it a squeeze, and worldwalked them back to the battlement. The conflict was quieter now, and as they looked over the wall at the castle grounds, they found only a few groups engaged in combat, some with soldiers from the garrison, others with the wraiths. Misty white continued to fill the field, but most of the wraiths had ceased fighting. Those who'd already been felled were unable to reanimate and had returned to their mindless meandering.

Regardless, Alden was right. The victory was already theirs; Cora could trust her soldiers to end this.

Teryn stepped closer to the parapet and unwrapped the bandage from around his palm. An angry red line marred his skin, but it wasn't actively bleeding. He held his hand out, palm to the air, and whispered, "At ease. Your battle is won. Your vengeance secure."

The wraiths stilled on the field. Some disappeared at once, while others simply lost their bloodlust and proceeded to slowly wander.

"When I call you next," Teryn said, "it will be to send you home."

He faced her then, nodding. This was all they could do for Ridine right now. Their next task lay at Centerpointe Rock.

Again, Cora took his hand. Closing her eyes, she pictured a large flat stone amidst a sea of green.

EVEN AFTER FIVE HUNDRED YEARS, AILAN'S BODY REMEMBERED how to fight. Her limbs moved in fluid motions, even as her muscles screamed. The rhythm of battle was ingrained in her bones, and with the return of her youth and memories came everything she'd ever learned long ago.

Warfare and violence weren't the most treasured arts amongst the Elvyn, but they were necessary for a future Morkara to learn. And learn she did, her training thorough. It had come to good use during the war with her brother so many centuries ago.

Unfortunately, what was true for her was true for Darius too.

He fought like death incarnate, with the advantage of unfamiliar human combat techniques paired with his worldwalking abilities. He was always escaping the swing of her sword, evading lethal blows and exchanging them for shallow wounds, if any. His lips remained peeled in a taunting grin as they dueled, his attacks unwavering.

But she didn't give up, even as her body grew weary. She kept her mind sharp, attuned to the whispers of her weavings. While she'd waited inside the Veil for the signal that Darius had arrived, she'd constructed a truthweaving, seeking guidance for success.

She hadn't heard a thing in response until the battle with Darius had begun.

Now they whispered to her.

Told her where to turn.

Alerted her of Darius' next move.

Even so, the battle felt endless.

When would her whispers guide her to land a killing blow? When would they shout, teasing out a weakness in Darius' defenses? When would she have the ideal opportunity to end him?

Sweat slicked her brow and dripped into her eyes as the softest, quietest whisper answered her question.

You won't.

You won't.

You won't.

It should have filled her with dread. It should have frozen her under a blanket of foreboding.

But it didn't.

She'd suspected for a while now that she wasn't meant to be the hero in this war with Darius. The prophecy had said so little about her, after all, and every truthweaving she'd cast about El'Ara's future had been about other people.

Noah, the Morkara.

Mareleau, the Edel Morkara'Elle.

She may not be the hero, but she was meant to fight. Destined to face her brother like this.

Gritting her teeth, she sliced out with her sword, thrust with the talons of the collar that she wielded like a dagger. One of the claws hooked into Darius' inner elbow, just above his gauntlet. He stumbled, his eyes going wide as he realized he couldn't worldwalk away.

This was her chance.

She lunged back and swung with her sword. He arched away in time to avoid a deeper cut, earning only a thin slash across his throat. It was too shallow of a wound to slow him down. Her only reward was the sight of his blood running down his throat. Still, she didn't give up. She shifted her stance, swiveled her arms, and slammed the edge of her blade against his abdomen. He released a grunt as the metal armor crumpled inward, her blade sinking into his skin. But at the same time, he tore the talon from his inner elbow and tossed it aside. Ailan ducked and rolled toward it, gathering it in her hand before leaping to her feet.

Darius now stood several feet away, blood trailing from the corner of his lips as he fiddled with the buckles and straps securing the front of his cuirass.

She gave him a wicked grin.

He may have the advantage of iron weapons, which delivered excruciating pain to pureblood fae, but his armor was human-made. Nothing better than garbage compared to the strength of Elvyn craftsmanship and armor harvested from the shedded scales of dragons.

Darius sneered back at her as he loosened a buckle.

Uziel took the chance to blast him with a ball of red flame.

Darius worldwalked away just in time and reappeared closer to Ailan—too near for Uziel to risk using his flame. He released the final buckle and tore his ruined cuirass off his chest. Blood seeped from his wound, but Ailan knew better than to expect enough blood loss to end his life. No, that blow hadn't been a fatal one.

But it had made his vital organs more vulnerable.

As if the blow had been nothing more than an inconvenient jab, he charged for her, swinging his sword. She dodged. Parried. He disappeared.

Her whispers guided her to the left.

She turned.

Met his blade.

Again.

Again.

It was never-ending, and the sounds of battle around them didn't cease either.

She needed the upper hand.

Needed to find his weakness.

She parried his blade, slashed out, and pivoted in time to meet his next blow. Her eyes dipped to the symbol at his lapels: a dragon encircled in a ball of flame.

She smirked. "Interesting sigil, considering no dragon would have you."

He bared his teeth in a dark grin. "Every dragon in

El'Ara will heed my commands once I'm Morkaius. They won't be subject to the prejudices of their former masters."

"The fact that you call a dragon's bonded counterpart their *master* shows just how little you know about dragons in the first place. They would never respect you."

He disappeared.

Reappeared to her right. She met his blade with hers.

"Because I'm impure?" he said through his teeth. "A half-blood? An imperfect specimen, a stain on your precious, stagnant way of life?"

"No," Ailan said with a smirk. "Turns out, dragons don't have a problem with humans."

His expression faltered.

She swung her blade, feinted left, then thrust with one of the talons.

He disappeared before it could do more than slice his torso.

Ailan whirled around just as he reappeared behind her. They exchanged blows, their swords clanging, the sound ringing through her ears.

"They've accepted her," she said, her smirk widening, darkening. "She has already succeeded at more than you ever have. More than you ever could."

He scoffed. "Are you talking about the human mother?"

"You complain about being judged for your human blood, but do you even hear the way you speak about your own kind? You don't respect humans any more than most of the Elvyn do. How does it feel to hate everything you are? To hate both sides of your bloodline so fiercely?"

"It feels like power," he said, slashing his sword against her breastplate.

Unlike his, her armor didn't crumple. It did, however,

make her stumble back at the force. She regained her footing and took up a defensive stance.

He spoke again. "I am better than both sides of my bloodline. I am the future of two worlds. Do not mistake my confidence for self-hatred, for I know my worth. You're the one who has always underestimated me. Undervalued me."

"You never once gave me a reason to hold in you any regard."

"And that shall be your downfall. You say the human mother has bonded a dragon?"

Ailan pursed her lips. Mareleau hadn't exactly *bonded* a dragon yet, but she had earned Ferrah's respect. Not that Darius needed to know that.

He chuckled. "I know she's safe behind the Veil with her son—my true enemy, second to you. And if I'm not mistaken..." His eyes narrowed to slits as he inched closer. Ailan stepped back, maintaining a safe distance from him, matching his steps as he began to circle her. "I'll find them in the dragon caves, then?"

Ailan's heart leaped into her throat.

Darius nodded. "Your fear has confirmed it. As for the tear..."

Ailan charged for him as he cast his gaze to the north.

He met her eyes with a wicked grin before disappearing.

Her blade met only air.

56

Silence replaced the sounds of the waning battle as Cora and Teryn found themselves on Centerpointe Rock. The wide plane of weathered stone stood at the center of a vast valley. Outside the valley slumbered the silhouettes of hulking hillsides.

The night was even darker here than it had been at the castle. Cora blinked to adjust to the change in light. She had only a moment to orient herself before she was barraged with irritated relief that wasn't her own.

You're here! I can't believe you made me stay away. Valorre darted down one of the hills and onto the field, practically bowling her over as he leaped upon the rock.

"I'm sorry," she said, caressing his neck, not bothering to mention that he was the one who'd insisted he be at Centerpointe Rock when she attempted her feat.

Just like Teryn, Valorre had feared her being alone during this endeavor. Yet, without knowing exactly when the ambush would begin, it would have been impossible to guarantee Cora could reconvene with Valorre before world-walking to the rock. So they'd decided he'd come here and wait for her as soon as he'd accomplished his important duties.

"Are your brethren safely back home now?" she asked.

He tossed his mane, radiating arrogance. *Of course they are. I'm highly capable. I guided the last pair of unicorns through the Veil yesterday morning. I've been waiting ever since. Do you know how worried I was about you?*

"I have some idea," she said, giving his neck a final pat. As much as she wanted to enjoy her reunion with her companion, she didn't have time to waste.

Teryn squeezed her hand. "Are you ready?"

"I have to be," she whispered back. With a trembling breath, she sank to her knees and pressed her hands to the surface of the rock. Her *insigmora* thrummed from her palms to her biceps, tingling every line of ink. Her magic rose like a tide in her blood, echoing the pound of fae magic that sang back.

She felt the *mora* pouring from the rock, sensed the well of magic that was available to her.

It was vast.

Terrifying.

Everything inside her told her this magic could destroy her. Could flay the skin from her bones should she try to harness it.

When last she was here, during the battle, she hadn't sensed anything like this. But she hadn't been Queen of Lela then. Now she was.

She swallowed hard, feeling deeper and deeper into that magic.

A gentle hand fell on her shoulder. Teryn crouched beside her. "I may not have the kind of magic you do, but use me."

"What do you mean?"

"Let me anchor you. Let me help. You are Queen of Lela and I am its king. I may not have what it takes to push the *mora* back, but I too have fulfilled every qualification necessary to be King of Magic. We can do this together."

She nibbled her lip, hating the thought of involving Teryn in this.

I may not be a Roizan, Valorre said, scraping a hoof on the rock, *so I cannot act as a vessel to harness the* mora. *But use me too. If it feels like too much, send at least some to me. Let me take some of the burden while you work.*

Between the warmth of Teryn's palm and her connection with Valorre, some of her terror eased. The strength of the *mora* felt less like a thrashing, cresting wave, and more like an unfathomable yet tepid sea. She could do this. She could lean on those she loved.

"All right," she said.

Then, refocusing on the thrum of magic against her palms, she spoke to the *mora*. "I am Aveline Corasande Caelan, Queen of Lela, Queen of Magic. Heed my edict. Move at my command."

∼

AILAN WHIRLED THIS WAY AND THAT, WAITING FOR DARIUS TO reappear.

He didn't.

Her stomach sank, telling her everything she needed to know before her whispers confirmed it.

North.

Look north.

There he was, the lone figure upon the farthest cliff she could see. Fanon's squad had kept the fighting relegated south of that point, as was his directive. With his abilities as a skyweaver—giving shape, form, and pressure to air—he could forcibly push back anyone who tried to get too close. Yet she couldn't see any sign of her consort in the fray, and now the one person they needed to keep off that cliff was there.

Alone.

His stillness told her he was waiting for her.

With no other option, she gestured for Uziel and climbed back upon his shoulders. She didn't take her eyes off her brother as her dragon flew her to him, landing on the coastal road not far from the nearest skirmish. From the buzz of *mora* humming through her, she knew Cora had yet to send the magic back through the Veil. However, she sensed...something. The *mora* wasn't moving in reverse yet, but it was reacting.

She had to keep her brother distracted long enough.

She dismounted her dragon, chest heaving with rage, and closed the distance between her and Darius.

He met her blade with a speed and fury he'd kept at bay until now. "Always, you underestimate me. Did you truly believe I couldn't sense the *mora*? You think you're that much stronger than me? You've always thought too highly of yourself."

It took all her strength to parry his strikes, to knock back his blade, to whirl to face him whenever he moved through space. Even with the tear so close, even with the tingle of the *mora* fueling her, fatigue was settling into her bones.

Or was it the crushing whisper that foretold of her defeat?

She pushed through the heaviness in her limbs, the tightness in her chest. She'd succeeded in getting under Darius' skin with her comment about Mareleau and Ferrah. Before that, her blow to his breastplate had made him vulnerable. All she needed was one chance. Just a moment to plunge one of the collar's talons into his skin and sever his head from his neck.

That was all it would take.

Then it would be over.

She would win.

You won't.

You won't.

You won't.

Her whispers didn't taunt, they caressed. Like a mother laying a child to sleep.

She swung her blade.

Darius disappeared.

Reappeared behind her.

But she was too slow.

His blade slashed open her thigh.

She cried out as she lost her footing. With a weapon in both hands, she struggled to catch herself as she fell to the slick grass. She planted her good leg beneath her, fought to rise to her feet, but Darius was there.

His blade soaring toward her throat—

It stopped mere inches away.

Ailan's gaze darted to the most welcome face she could ever hope to see.

Fanon.

Her consort.

The love of her life.

Fury twisted his features as he marched toward them, his invisible restraints freezing Darius in place.

But her brother's surprise wouldn't last long. He could worldwalk free in the blink of an eye.

Ailan took her chance and threw herself at her brother,

hooking one edge of the talon into his calf before closing the collar on its hinge.

Darius' eyes went wide. He blinked. Once. Twice.

With a thrust of her sword, she pierced Darius' abdomen, pulling it free just as Fanon dropped his skyweaving in exchange for a swing of his own blade. It arced toward Darius' neck, aiming for a clean and decisive beheading...

Freed from Fanon's restraints, Darius could now reach for the collar.

It didn't matter, for it would be too late.

Fanon's blade would strike before Darius' fingers even met the tines...

Yet it wasn't the tines of the collar Darius sought. Instead, he whirled around, closing the distance between him and Fanon. He pivoted, swung his blade...

And cut Fanon's hands off at the wrists.

His blade fell impotent to the grass below.

Ailan called out her consort's name, the agony in her voice like razors in her throat.

She was too distraught.

Too distracted.

Too haunted by the blood pouring from the ends of her consort's blunted wrists...

That she didn't see when Darius removed the collar from his calf.

Didn't see when he disappeared.

Or sense when he reappeared, just behind her.

She didn't even feel the slice of his blade.

Her whispers soothed her with a final caress.

Last Breath has come at last.

57

The *mora* surged toward Cora, the force of it nearly pushing her off the rock. It washed over her, through her, fluttering past. She sensed its journey then, the way it flowed through the Veil on unseen, underground webs of magic, bypassing the wardweaving that stopped everything else. Everything weaker. The strongest vein pulsed from a singular direction to the northwest—the tear. The *mora* was concentrated there, flowing faster, easier. All the lines met beneath her palms, flooding the rock, filling it, and then spilling over the top of the land like an invisible spring.

Now she fully understood why the *mora* couldn't return to El'Ara. She'd understood it intellectually before, after Garot had explained the Blight, but this time she could *feel* it. The way it flowed so confidently toward the rock before stalling and drifting outward in haphazard, sometimes violent waves. Its exit was unhampered by the Veil, but its return wasn't. The *mora* sought direction here at the junction of those veins, but it had no guidance, and it was lost without it. *This* was the importance of the Morkara's duties.

A duty she could mimic now.

As Queen of Magic, the *mora* saw her as someone it could obey.

Whether it *would* was the question.

Like an unruly child, the magic surged again, as if testing her resolve, her strength. It seared her palms, sent chills down her spine.

She focused on the coolness of the stone beneath her hands, the air in her lungs, the dew drops dotting the field, the moonlight streaming overhead. The elements were hers, reflecting the similar-yet-different ones that made up fae *mora*. The magic surged once more, battering her body inside and out. She focused on Teryn's steady touch, Valorre's comforting presence.

Her loved ones.

Her anchors.

She sent her intention back to the *mora*. It funneled from her heart, down her arms, into her palms, flooding the rock beneath her. It spoke to the pulsing *mora* in a silent demand.

Reverse.

Reverse.

Reverse.

The *mora* stilled. Its flow grew calm. And it opened itself to her will.

Possibilities spread before her as she felt the weight of *mora* settle over her. Its strength was somehow crushing and uplifting at the same time. A blanket of lead and light. A blazing, deadly inferno and a gentle ray of sunshine.

It was both. It offered everything. Nothing.

It was unyielding. It was pliant.

She could shape it in her hands even as it burned her.

Yes...she could shape it.

Visions flooded her mind, of all the *mora* offered. The

power it could give her. The enemies it could vanquish. The wars it could end. The curses it could break...

Curses.

She was still cursed to die childless, wasn't she? She never had found a way to rid herself of Morkai's most wretched punishment.

Darkness filled her heart, a companion she no longer tried to hide. Yet now that it was here...

It would be a shame not to use the *mora*. At least a little. She could use it without harnessing it. She could keep some for herself, couldn't she? Why shouldn't she be rewarded for all her hard work? Why shouldn't she wield what was freely offered? Why should she send the *mora* back at all? She could be Queen of Lela, Queen of Magic, and do *anything* in this world. She could stitch the tear from here and keep the flow of magic exactly as it was, keep siphoning all of El'Ara's power, lock the fae away and let the Blight take them while she used the magic as she saw fit. She could end Darius in a single flick of her wrist and ensure none of her people ever had to suffer. She could obliterate enemy forces without risking any of her soldiers. She could fortify her body, her soul, and—

"Cora!"

The voice tore through her raging, swirling thoughts.

Then another. *Cora!*

The two voices called her name, one inside her mind, the other ringing through her ears.

She was aware of Teryn's touch then, the hands that framed her shoulders, bracing her like she might drift away. Then she noticed the soft muzzle that bumped her cheek, the breath that blew across her face.

She forced her attention to narrow on that warm breath, those warm hands.

Only then did she realize her palms were no longer pressed to the rock. Instead, she'd risen to her knees, her spine rigid, her head tipped back. The *mora* radiated through her, howling in her veins like a vicious storm.

"You don't need it, my love," Teryn said, his hand moving to her cheek.

She opened her eyes. Her vision was blurry at first, but soon it cleared to show his face. He was pale, expression twisted with worry. Valorre's head was lowered beside him, staring at her with his wide russet eyes.

Teryn spoke again. "You don't need to harness it. You are enough as you are."

She sagged at his words. Fatigue tugged her bones, and she was desperate to collapse. To sleep. But she couldn't quit yet. Her duty had only just begun.

With a trembling sigh, she settled back into the feel of Teryn's hands and the vibrant energy that was Valorre's presence. That's right. She could lean on them. Turn over some of the burden.

"Cora." Teryn stroked her cheek with his thumb, his voice pitched with worry.

"I'm all right," she managed to croak. "I wasn't prepared for the temptation to harness it. I...I'm ready now. This time I'll rely on the two of you."

Teryn nodded. "Don't do this alone. You don't need to."

He was right. She wasn't alone. She could share this.

Teryn moved aside, giving her space to press her palms to the stone again. He moved his hands to her back, his touch both firm and comforting. Valorre kept his muzzle near her shoulder, bumping her with it, blowing hot breaths against her cheek again.

She wouldn't forget them this time.

Gritting her teeth, she faced the *mora* again, but she

didn't turn herself over to it. *Reverse*, she demanded, pushing back with her resolve. Fighting its flow. Urging it back underground.

Are you certain? it asked. It pulsed through her, infusing her mind with visions again.

Yes. Cora breathed the temptation away, let the *mora* swirl around her, through her, and into her companions, taking some of the weight off her chest.

You wouldn't rather wield it? Harness it? Take it?

NO. She pushed back even harder, shared more of her burden with Teryn and Valorre. *I am Queen of Lela, Queen of Magic. You yield when I tell you to yield. You move when I tell you to move. Now GO! RETURN.*

Teryn held her tighter.

Valorre's presence grew warmer.

The *mora* cycled through the three figures, then radiated down Cora's hands.

Through her palms.

Back into the rock.

And finally, its flow reversed.

～

MARELEAU HAD PRACTICED THE WARDING GESTURE AILAN HAD taught her dozens of times by now, and she still wasn't certain if it worked. Noah lay on her bed, wrapped in lavender silk swaddling embroidered with a gold dragon-scale pattern. She sat beside him and performed every move that her hands had already memorized. She pressed her thumbs to her ring fingers, angled her wrists, then linked her fingers together. Another turn of her wrists, and she pressed the tips of her remaining fingers together. She held the gesture for a few breaths, then laced all fingers before spreading them over Noah like she was covering him in an invisible blanket.

She stared down at her results. Like always she could see nothing out of the ordinary. How could she ever know it worked?

Remembering what Ailan had told her about practicing on herself first, she strode to the mirror and repeated the same gesture but for her own body. She tried to perceive *something*, some clue that it had worked, but neither her eyes nor her claircognizance told her a damn thing. Clenching her jaw, she whirled away from the mirror. She didn't have time to practice or wonder. Ferrah had returned from the tear not long ago, which was the signal that the ambush had begun.

How long ago had that been? Ten minutes? Twenty? Was it evening on the other side of the Veil, or daytime like it was here? She tried to estimate the hour, but math had never been her strength. Besides, the discrepancy of time between the two realms was an estimate, not an exact science.

Still, it chilled her to think that even though it had only been minutes for her, hours of battle may have already passed. Hours that Larylis could be fighting. Struggling. Or...

No, she wouldn't think of anything worse than that.

A knock sounded at her door, and Garot entered without waiting for her to answer. "Are you ready? We must make haste to the dragon caves as a precaution."

Mareleau wasn't overly fond of the idea of hiding in dark caves with a horde of feisty dragons, but Ailan had assured her it would be the safest place for her and Noah. That the dragons would protect them if the worst happened.

"I'm as ready as I'll ever be, I suppose." She returned to the bed and scooped up her son, cradling him close to her.

She shouldered his carrying sling as well in case she needed it. She'd come to rely on the convenient item and couldn't imagine these early days of motherhood without it.

She joined Garot outside her bedroom and found Etrix in the hall. Both had stayed behind to guard her and Noah. Garot led the way, though not with his swirling tunnel. Instead, they made haste through the halls on foot. The cheery sunlight streaming through the arched windows made it hard to imagine a deadly battle was taking place at that very moment.

They reached the stairwell that led down to the next floor—

Mareleau sucked in a sharp breath as threads of invisible energy poured over her, tingling her scalp, filling her throat, her chest, her stomach. Garot, already a step down, whirled to face her, brow raised in question.

Etrix placed a hand on her shoulder. "Are you all right?"

She opened her mouth but no words came out. The tingling force continued to wash through her, an ice-cold thrum so soft and foreign she couldn't make sense of it. Her mind spun, eyelashes fluttering as the energy flowed down her legs, her feet, then rose again.

Noah stirred in her arms, and the tingle lessened by half.

The sensation remained, but it was subtler now. Quieter. And it was pulsing between her and Noah.

"What..." She swallowed the dryness in her throat. "What was that? Did you feel it?"

Etrix furrowed his brow, head tilting to the side.

"We must—" Garot's words cut off as he reached into the pocket of his teal robe. He extracted a strange green orb, one that glowed with a pulsing emerald light. His tan, freckled face paled, his eyes shooting wide. "No."

Etrix rounded on the Elvyn. "One of the triggers was tripped? Where?"

"Not just one," Garot muttered as he reached for the top of the glowing orb with his thumb and forefinger. Gingerly, he tugged until something like a petal spread down. He peeled another, then another, until the orb flattened out into what looked like a multilayered map. If a map could be made from an unusual flower bud. She could hardly comprehend what she was seeing as Garot lifted one petal, then the other, flipping them and rearranging them like pages in the most oddly constructed book in existence. Finally, he paused on one petal. Darker green veins patterned its surface, which Mareleau soon realized weren't random or organic markings, but shapes of landmarks— lakes, forests, and mountains. It really was a map. And beneath one of the mountains marking the petal pulsed a small red light.

"The dragon caves in Bel'Dawn," Etrix said, brow knitting deeper.

Just as quickly as the red light flashed, it disappeared. Garot flipped through the petals with haste until he found the light again. "Now the Lo'Sel Mountains."

"What's happening?" Mareleau asked, her voice strained. She understood enough to know this map must be what alerted the Elvyn of non-fae trespassers. It was how they'd found Cora the first time she'd worldwalked here, as well as how they'd reached Mareleau's group when they'd arrived with Ailan.

Etrix and Garot exchanged a weighted glance.

Etrix's throat bobbed. "He's here. And he's worldwalking from cave to cave, locations he recalls from when he lived in El'Ara. He's figured out where they'll be hiding."

"That can only mean..." Garot's shoulders visibly

shrank, his expression empty as his lips flattened into a tight line. Mareleau had never seen him without a jovial smile on his face. Never heard him at a loss for words. Even Etrix, who always maintained a neutral, stoic air, crumpled, his eyes glazing with tears as he flung his palm over his heart, as if smothering a piercing ache.

Even without their reactions, she understood what had happened. It had been written in that strange tingle of energy she'd felt. The energy that continued to pulse between her and Noah even now.

Ailan was dead.

Mareleau was regent.

And Darius was coming for her and her son.

58

Larylis had witnessed the death of hope and hadn't been able to stop it. He'd been locked in combat with his own opponent, but the glimpses he'd stolen had shown Fanon and Ailan securing their win.

Yet by the time Larylis had pulled his sword from his opponent's belly, Darius was gone. And Ailan and Fanon...

He ran to them now, his heart in his throat. Both lay on the ground, Ailan motionless and Fanon half crawling, half dragging himself toward his consort on his elbows.

Because his hands.

Gods, his hands.

They were gone.

The black dragon roared and thrashed, a piercing, keening cry rumbling in his throat. He circled the two figures, wings splayed, a red glow burning behind the scales of his neck.

Larylis slowed his approach as he neared, which gave him just enough time to roll out of the way of the dragon's sudden blast of flame. The creature snapped his teeth, then charged—

"Uziel, stop!" The male voice was an agonized rasp, but the dragon obeyed nonetheless. "Drop your sword and bow to him, human fool!"

It took Larylis a moment to realize Fanon was speaking to him, but he did as told, dropping his sword to the ground and folding into a bow. Uziel released a hiss, then an agitated rumble, but from the corner of Larylis' eye, he watched the dragon take a grudging step back.

"Leave him be, Uziel." Fanon's voice was even weaker now.

Larylis risked rising from his bow. He cast a wary look at the dragon, who continued to hiss at him but made no move to roast him alive. Taking that as permission, he jogged the rest of the way to Fanon and Ailan. The latter was motionless, her neck severed, the sight too gruesome for Larylis to study. He turned his attention to Fanon, who was at least still alive, though losing blood quickly. He'd ceased dragging himself across the grass and now lay supine beside his consort at a haphazard angle.

Larylis crouched before him. "I'll tie a tourniquet—"

"I can't understand you," Fanon said through his teeth. Seven devils, of course he couldn't. He'd had the same translation charm around his wrist that Larylis wore now. A charm that had obviously been lost with his hands. Steeling his nerve, he sought any sign of the missing appendages, but Fanon halted him with a stern tone. "Don't you dare tend to me. Take the collar and go."

Larylis returned his gaze to Fanon. The Elvyn jerked his chin toward the other side of Ailan's body. Larylis saw nothing in the grass but heavy gouges and pools of blood—

No, there was something. Half hidden in the blood-soaked grass was a talon. Larylis rushed to retrieve it and found not one talon but two. It was the collar that had once adorned his wife's neck.

"Take it and enter the tear," Fanon said. "He's already inside."

Larylis' blood went cold. Darius...had entered the tear?

Fanon spoke again. "Uziel, take him."

"What do you mean, take me?" Larylis asked, but the sound was drowned out by Uziel's roar. The dragon slammed his tail on the ground in protest, setting the cliff rattling.

"Do you want to avenge her?" Fanon's voice was growing weaker by the second.

Uziel ceased thrashing and released a series of piercing chirps. Larylis didn't need to understand the language of dragons to know the creature was grieving.

"Then take him to the Edel Morkara'Elle. She and our Morkara are all we have left of Ailan. Do you understand? Do not fail her, Uziel."

Uziel swiveled his head and pinned Larylis with a forbidding look. He gnashed his teeth, his tongue flicking outward, sending small licks of flame into the air.

"And you, human," Fanon said. He closed his eyes, his chest pulsing with shallow breaths. "Do you want to save the woman you love? Do you want to succeed where I have failed?"

Larylis tightened his fist around the collar. "With everything I have."

"Mount the dragon," Fanon said, understanding his conviction even without a translation. "Enter the tear. Stop him before it's too late."

❧

Tears of fear and grief and rage stung Mareleau's eyes as she, Etrix, and Garot rushed from the palace toward the dragon caves. They'd accumulated a squad of guards who now brought up the rear. She wove her arms protectively around her son as she hurried along the same path Ailan had taken her down two days ago.

Ailan.

She was...gone.

Mareleau hadn't fully warmed to the woman, but it would be a lie to say she hadn't grown at least somewhat comfortable with her. Ailan may have stolen her and her son from the lives they'd known and loved...

But she'd treated Mareleau with respect. Fought to position her as a person of high esteem amongst the Elvyn, despite her human blood. She'd taught her the motions for wardweaving and encouraged her to work with the magic she already possessed without undermining her goals.

Just like that, she was gone.

Mareleau would never get to say goodbye.

Could never rely on the woman to protect and advocate for her.

Ailan had been their greatest hope in defeating Darius, and she was gone. Darius was coming for Mareleau and Noah next. Would they die just as easily? Would everything she and her friends and allies had fought for come to nothing?

A tremor ran through her, but it wasn't one of fear. Instead, fury burned her blood, weighing down her feet with every inch she closed toward the caves. The fire blossomed and grew into a wrath so hungry it begged her to fight. *Fight*, not hide.

But what the hell could she do? She wasn't a warrior. She couldn't even weave a damn protection ward. She was a selfish beast, born and raised, and now she was paying the price. There was only one thing she excelled at, and that was looking out for herself. Hiding was all she could do.

If only she weren't a narcuss. If only her magic were better, stronger. If only *she* were better and stronger.

No matter what you find in those shadows, came a voice from memory, *it is important that you love yourself.*

Salinda had said those words when Mareleau had sunk into self-hatred after discovering what she was. Well, a lot of good that did her now. She needed to protect others, not herself. What did *she* matter when she had someone so important to protect?

Is it easy to be selfish? This time it was Ailan's voice that rang in her head. *To me, it looks like your resistance to focusing on yourself is stronger.*

Yes, well...she'd been right.

Mareleau hadn't been able to shift her attention to her own well-being. Every time she'd practiced warding on herself or on her and Noah together, she'd burn with impatience. It had seemed like such a waste of time and magic when she'd rather grow her abilities for others. She needed to overcome her insipid magic challenge already so she could...

Her mind emptied.

Again, Ailan's voice spoke from memory.

You can't challenge your magic; you must wait for it to challenge you.

Calm knowing settled over her as a new awareness began to bloom, rising alongside the furious fire that still burned within. She didn't fully understand it yet, but something was starting to take shape.

The mouth of the cave came into view at last, the afternoon sun dimmed by the towering heights of the palace above. Ferrah was just outside the cave, slithering in anxious circles, then shifting from foot to foot, her feathered wings bristled. As soon as they approached the cave mouth, Ferrah slithered inside. The guards fanned out, creating a half circle around the entrance. Garot gestured for Mareleau to follow the dragon. Just as she was about to enter the dark maw, wingbeats sounded overhead.

The guards' hands flew to the hilts of their swords, but they didn't draw them. For the creature that descended was a familiar one. Uziel landed just beyond the ring of guards, bellowing a string of high-pitched chirps, too eerie to be sounds of joy. No, they were sounds of lament.

If that was the case, who was the rider on his—

Her heart nearly tumbled from her chest as the figure all but leaped off the beast's shoulders and raced for her. A sob broke out of her throat as his arms went around her from the side, careful of their son between them.

"Thank the gods," Larylis whispered into her hair. "You're here. You're safe."

She pulled back and assessed her husband through glazed eyes. His dark copper-tinged hair was mussed, his face splattered with dirt and blood. His armor was dented in places, his padded leather jacket ripped open and dripping blood. But he was alive. He was here and alive and that was all that mattered.

"You must be our Morkara's father," Etrix said, his tone flat. Worry and grief still dominated his expression.

"We can't dally," Garot said, his eyes on his petal-map. Where before only one red light flashed, now there were two.

Some small part of her had hoped Larylis' sudden arrival meant he'd been the one to trigger the alert, but that had been too much to wish for.

Garot spoke again. "We must get inside. Darius is moving from cave to cave, starting with those surrounding the Blight. We built Alles'Taria Palace over an existing cave system. He may not know the palace exists, but he may remember these caves. Even if he doesn't, he could find other fae to torture information from. If he comes across any Faeryn...with the discord between our two races, they may not hesitate to share intel."

Larylis angled slightly away from Mareleau and reached for something tucked under his jacket. He withdrew the two-taloned collar. "I'll fight him. I have this."

Etrix' eyes widened. "If you have that, then Ailan truly is..."

"I'm sorry," Larylis said. He may not have met Etrix before but even he could tell Ailan had been important to him. Now whatever frail hope Etrix had clung to was gone.

Gods, Mareleau couldn't imagine the depths of his grief.

"Fanon urged Uziel to take me here," Larylis said, "and for me to bring the collar."

"What of the soldiers inside the tear?" Garot asked. "The wardweavers?"

Larylis' face paled. "All I saw upon entering were bodies."

Etrix uttered a string of words the charm on her bracelet failed to translate. He faced Garot. "He's probably killed the wardweavers. There's no one to seal the tear once the human queen sends the *mora* back to us."

"*If* she sends it back," Garot said.

There was no condemnation in his tone, but Mareleau bristled nevertheless. "She will send it back. She's probably already trying. But if there's no one at the tear to seal it, she can't complete her mission, right? She can't simply push it back forever with nothing to contain it."

"She's right," Etrix said, already retreating. "I'll take Uziel back to the tear with three more wardweavers. We can't lose this chance."

He strode toward the black dragon, who continued to keen and bellow. Uziel gnashed his teeth at the dark-haired Elvyn but let him mount him anyway. Then, in a matter of several pulses of those leathery wings, they were high in the sky.

"Will he get there in time?" Mareleau asked.

"Faster than I would," Garot said, his eyes still fixed on the map. "My pathweaving doesn't work in the Blight, but Uziel can reach the tear quickly. If he'll listen to Etrix, that is."

Noah began to fuss and squirm, reflecting the panic tightening Mareleau's chest. She hushed and soothed him, bouncing him in her arms. He probably needed to be nursed or changed, but this wasn't the best time. They still needed to hide.

A sharp tapping echoed from behind her, and she spun to find Ferrah waiting inside the cave, her talons beating impatiently on the stone beneath her.

"On we go," Garot said. "Our best hope is to hide deep in these caves. Darius can worldwalk to this location if he has any memories of it, but unless he has distinct recollections of the cave interior, he'll need to traverse the tunnels on foot. And I don't suspect he's alone. My map doesn't show how many people set off the triggers if they are together in a group, and I doubt he'd be foolish enough to enter dragon caves by himself."

Larylis nodded. "I'll wait outside with the guards and halt him with this." He lifted the collar again.

Garot shook his head. "We should give it to your wife to use as a last resort. If Ailan wasn't able to stop him with it, I doubt a human like you could. No offense. If Etrix succeeds at bringing a new trio of wardweavers to the tear, and your friend succeeds at pushing the *mora* to us, we can hope to trick Darius into worldwalking back to the human world. He'll need reinforcements to take down our guards, won't he? If he leaves after the tear is sealed, we'll be safe from him."

Mareleau frowned. "You mean...lock him out and leave him as a problem for the human world."

"Better there than here." His tone was so empty. So tired.

Mareleau understood his apathy in the face of such grave odds, yet she couldn't stand the thought of hiding when their goal was to leave Darius in Lela. For Cora and Teryn to deal with. *If* they could deal with him.

It wasn't that she didn't trust their abilities.

Hell, they were all stronger and more capable than she was.

It was more that she railed at the thought of passing this off on them. Staying safe. Small. Hiding. While they continued to fight for their lives.

"Protect our Morkara," Garot said, his gaze locked on the red light on his map as it disappeared and reappeared on a different petal. "That is your strength and your duty as Edel Morkara'Elle."

All this time, she'd wanted to believe exactly that. That protecting Noah was her strength. Her duty. Her guiding light. That her magic would bloom and unfurl once she'd learned how to use it the way she yearned to.

Yet that fury continued to burn in her chest. Wrath, rage, and rebellion in one.

Was it her selfish side that hated being told what to do?

Was it her prideful side that always wanted to prove

others wrong when they claimed to know who she was? What she was meant for? What she was worth?

Yes. Yes, it was. And the confession came as such a relief that she nearly wept.

She understood her challenge now. It wasn't figuring out how to protect Noah. It wasn't refusing to leave his side. It certainly wasn't turning away from herself. It was *trusting* herself. Putting all her faith in her own abilities. Not the abilities she wanted to have, but the ones she already possessed. She didn't need to go against her nature; she needed to dig deeper into it and use it for all it was worth. Salinda and Ailan had been right all along, but only now did she see the truth.

Mareleau was a scheming liar.

A breaker of hearts.

A destroyer of men.

She'd pull off her greatest, most devastating lie yet.

She dropped her gaze to the collar in Larylis' hand. Placing her fingers over his, she squeezed his palm. Wordlessly, he released the collar into her care.

She held his gaze and asked, "Do you trust me?"

His eyes searched hers, swimming with fear. Then he steeled his expression and gave her a nod. "With my life, my death, and everything in between."

Her throat tightened. "Do you trust me with *my* life, death, and everything in between?"

Another flash of fear. Then a sheen of sorrow. But again, he gave her a solemn nod. "Yes."

59

Larylis didn't know the full details of what his wife was planning, but he had to trust her. He did, with his whole heart, even as he feared where that trust would lead. Despite his reservations, this was not the time to balk. Their enemy was near. He could arrive at any second. If Mareleau knew how to stop Darius, who was he to doubt her? Who was he but the other half of her heart? They would beat in tandem until the end.

He stood inside the cave, not far from its entrance, where the only light came from the blue-green luminescence coating the walls. Mareleau was deeper inside the cave system, and her distance somehow felt too near and too far at once. There wasn't a depth she could go to that would ease his worry over her safety. Yet he hated that he wasn't by her side. He hoped the semi-darkness would hamper Darius' ability to visualize locations ahead to worldwalk to, but that was only a gamble. Did Darius' half-Elvyn heritage give him better eyesight? The communications Larylis had received from Teryn and Cora detailed his keen hearing.

Larylis rolled his shoulders and his neck, his muscles

screaming in protest. Now that he was standing still, every wound and strain blared, every limb begged to lock up. He shifted his feet and splayed his hands, one then the other, refusing to succumb to inertia.

Then the shouts began.

From just outside the mouth of the cave, a clash of steel rang out. Garot had been right. Darius hadn't come alone. Larylis unsheathed his sword, his pulse quickening. In his mind, he began to recite famous kings of history who'd found victory during great fatigue, but he stopped himself. He didn't need to rely on those great kings anymore. He had himself. He had this moment. He would do this.

Larylis, the bastard.

Larylis, the crownless king.

Larylis, the husband and father.

Larylis, the man who preferred silence and books over parties and warfare.

He would do this.

He would help take down a tyrant.

The sounds of fighting cut off by half, but they continued to ring from outside. Then came footsteps. The aqua glow dappling the walls reflected off a trio of figures approaching. At the center was Darius, whom he'd only seen from afar until now. Even though his form was cast in shades of teal and shadow, Larylis could tell he was coated in blood. It slicked his hair, dripped from the cut on his cheek, painted his clothing and what little remained of his armor.

Yet despite the wounds he'd sustained, Darius was still standing. Still walking with ease and poise.

His fae healing was enviable.

Darius' expression darkened as he spotted Larylis. He motioned for his two guards to charge forward. They were much worse for wear than their master, both devoid of helms. One had a cut across his forehead while the other had use of only one eye, the other swollen shut. They charged past Darius, but before they could reach Larylis, a yellow dragon—half the size of Ferrah—slithered from a cavity in the wall and blasted a ball of golden flame at their legs. Two more dragons, these ones merely the size of large canines, climbed down the stalactites, gnashing their small yet terrifying teeth. Thankfully, none had eyes for Larylis, just the three intruders.

Or...not three.

Only two.

Larylis whirled around to see Darius already several steps ahead. There went Larylis' hope that he wouldn't be able to see well enough to worldwalk. He paid no heed to Larylis, as if he wasn't worth his time. Larylis clenched his jaw and charged after him.

"Stay away from my wife and child."

That got his attention. Darius halted and pivoted on his heel. "Your wife and child, you say? You must be the father of the great infant Morkara."

Larylis crept closer, sword raised.

Darius held his own sword, but its tip was lowered. He still didn't see Larylis as a worthy opponent. From the way he'd abandoned his soldiers to fight the dragons, he didn't value his own men much either.

"Fight me," Larylis said through his teeth.

"Why fight at all? What have I done to deserve your ire?"

"Do you truly need to ask? You seek to end the lives of my wife and son."

Darius ran a hand over his face, wincing at the still-bleeding cut on his cheek. He frowned, as if he hadn't expected the wound to be there. Was his rate of healing slowing down? Was there an end to his power? Was fatigue finally fraying his magic?

"It doesn't have to be that way," Darius said, tone clipped with impatience. His easy arrogance was gone. He *was* worried about something. "You and your wife can surrender to me."

Larylis scoffed. "And sacrifice our son?"

"No. Your wife can relinquish her role as regent and turn it over to me. I will oversee the boy's reign as Morkara and give you and his mother positions in my new government. You will be like a duke and duchess of the human world, second only to me and your son. It's better than any treatment you'll get from the Elvyn."

Larylis said nothing, simply appraised Darius through slitted lids.

"You know I'm right," Darius said.

"I know I can't trust you." Larylis' gaze flicked deeper down the tunnel where slithering motion approached. An orange light began to grow, shifting the aqua hues around them. Larylis pressed himself close to the cave wall just as the dragon released a blast of flame toward Darius. Larylis squeezed his eyes shut as heat seared his face.

The flame cut off.

Larylis opened his eyes to find Darius down the tunnel, his sword dripping blood. The dragon's body slumped to the cave floor, his detached head a few feet away. Tiny dragons crawled up and down the walls, hissing and screeching, but they made no move to get any closer to Darius.

"That's unfortunate," Darius muttered. "I have no intention of making an enemy of the dragons, as I'll soon be their master. I doubt the Morkara's mother wants to see me kill more of them either." He raised his voice at the last part, letting it carry down the tunnels.

Larylis pushed off the wall and charged forward—

Darius disappeared.

Then his voice, too close to Larylis.

"I'll have to try something else," Darius said from behind him. He sliced open Larylis' forearm, forcing him to drop his sword. Before he could retrieve it or launch away, Darius' blade came to Larylis' throat. Still behind him, Darius gripped his shoulder tightly. "Don't move."

Larylis froze.

One of Darius' soldiers emerged from the rear tunnel—the man with the swollen eye. He now had a singed left arm and burns up one side of his neck. Yet his other arm still held a sword. He exchanged a stiff nod with his master.

"Walk," Darius demanded of Larylis.

Larylis kept his upper body still as the three started off. They took only a few steps before their surroundings changed slightly. In a single heartbeat, they were farther down the tunnel, the aqua bioluminescence brighter and more condensed.

"I have your husband, Queen Mareleau," Darius said. There was a slight quaver in his voice that suggested Larylis had been right. His strength was waning. He was growing desperate. "I will give your husband just a few more breaths before I cleave his head from his body. After that, I'll do the same to every dragon in these godsforsaken caves—"

"Don't!" Mareleau's voice rang out from a short distance away. The panic in her tone was like a knife to Larylis' heart. "Don't hurt him, please!"

Darius and the soldier exchanged another nod, and the other man took Darius' place as Larylis' captor. It took all Larylis' restraint not to act. Not to tilt his head and slam it into the soldier's nose before taking his sword. The man was wounded enough to give Larylis a fighting chance.

But that hadn't been part of Mareleau's plan. Not that getting captured had been either...

"Then come to me now," Darius said. "Surrender to me and you, your husband, and your son can live."

"Don't believe him!" Larylis ground out.

Silence echoed back. Then footsteps. They grew nearer and nearer with every thundering beat of Larylis' heart.

"Don't, Mare," Larylis called. "Go back!"

She didn't pay his words any heed. Instead, she emerged from the cavern just ahead, Ferrah behind her, their son in her arms. She trembled from head to toe. "I surrender."

TEARS POURED DOWN MARELEAU'S CHEEKS AS SHE approached her enemy. She'd never seen him before, but she knew the gray-haired man was Darius. Her nemesis. Larylis was at the mercy of another man's blade.

Her shoulders quivered, arms convulsing as she wrapped them tighter around Noah's sling. A sob broke from her lips. "Don't hurt him, please! I'll do anything."

Darius' face broke into a grin that bore equal parts cruelty and amusement. She was everything he'd expected her to be. Weak. Trembling. Embarrassingly feeble.

It was exactly how Mareleau wanted to be seen right now.

Pride flared inside her, but she didn't let it show. She kept it burning in her heart and poured more and more of her intent, her *knowing*, into her glamour.

Her trusty, unfailing magic trick.

She'd never felt stronger. Never been more certain of her abilities.

Even before she'd laid her eyes on Darius, she'd understood his character. What he wanted to see in her and what he most feared to see. That impression grew now as she met his gaze. Despite his belief that the Elvyn hated him for his human blood, he didn't think any better of his bloodline. He considered everyone to be beneath him. He certainly had no respect for a pampered princess-turned-queen who'd been given a life of luxury.

Now he saw what he'd expected all along, and she played into that.

She wore a mask of frail obedience as she stepped closer and closer to him.

"Stop," he said. "Order the dragon to stay back."

Of course he would make that demand. So long as Ferrah kept her distance, she couldn't harm Darius without risking Mareleau and Noah too. With a sniffle, she faced the opalescent dragon. "It's all right," she said, tone simpering. "Stay where you are."

Ferrah splayed her wings but obeyed.

Good. That meant the dragon would listen to her after all.

You understand the next part too, right? she conveyed, but she received no answer. She and Ferrah weren't bonded like Cora and Valorre. Even though she'd explained what she needed Ferrah to do for her, she could only hope her instructions had made it through.

Darius' lips spread wider as Mareleau proceeded closer to him. She was halfway there when she stopped, her knees trembling. His expression darkened. "Come the rest of the way. Give me the child and relinquish your role as regent."

She fell to her knees, unable to hold herself up anymore.

At least, that was what her glamour displayed. Gods, for once in her life it felt good to be underestimated.

Weak. She poured her intent into her glamour. *Feeble. No one to fear. The most pathetic creature you've ever seen.*

"Give me the child." His voice was chillingly gentle.

She heaved another body-shaking sob and extended an empty, pleading hand.

Slowly, he closed the distance between them, then crouched before her. She cradled Noah's sling tighter to her as she met Darius' eyes. A soft smile lifted his lips but it didn't meet his eyes. "Hush, hush, Your Majesty. It will be all right."

More tears gushed from her eyes. Her empty hand found his coat collar. She grasped it like a woman devoured by grief, seeking anything to steady her. He extended his hands toward the bundle she cradled so tightly, so lovingly.

Her lower lip wobbled, eyes turned down at the corners as she held his gaze with a pleading look. "Promise me," she whispered.

He nodded, impatience tightening his false smile. "Anything," he said through his teeth, one hand clawing at the lavender swaddling inside the sling.

"Promise me..." she said again as she aided his efforts, lifting the bundle from inside.

Her fingers clenched his collar tighter while her other hand emerged from the sling. With her fist wrapped tightly around one of the hidden talons, she plunged the weapon into his gut. His eyes went wide as the tine sank into his flesh. She pushed harder, deeper. He finally had the sense to try to dislodge her, but she clung with all her might to his coat, their bodies almost flush.

"Promise me," she said, her glamour falling away, her sorrow twisting into monstrous, bottomless, victorious rage, "that my face will be the only thing you see when you rot in eternal hell, you arrogant piece of shit."

She twisted the talon, then shouted her final command. "Ferrah!"

With a piercing screech, heat encircled them in a violet blaze. Mareleau kept her eyes open, drinking in the terror that contorted the face before her. It was a beautiful sight, in all its repulsive, savage glory.

If this was the last thing she ever saw, she'd be satisfied with that.

She watched his skin boil and char, his eyes melt from their sockets. Until the purple flame pulsed too bright. Too hot. Until her mind grew hazy, her breaths short and sharp.

Only then did she release her enemy.

Only then did she succumb to death.

60

Death hurt a lot more than Mareleau had expected.

It was louder too. So loud.

She tried to ignore the sounds, waited for the pain to end. Soon she'd find herself in the otherlife, whatever that meant. Would she find a field of flowers? A tranquil ocean? An eternal banquet with an endless supply of chocolate? How long would she have to wait for everyone else she loved to join her? Hopefully a good long while.

She tried to envision what kinds of chocolate the otherlife might provide, but even as she pictured the most decadent truffles and a cake with ten tiers, that nagging sound interrupted her. It was...a word. No...a chirp? A screech? Why was death so godsdamned loud? Surely her heroic final act had earned her peace and not one of the seven hells instead. Well, if the latter was the case, she'd have to hunt down Darius and plague him in death. She wasn't above becoming a devil if that was her best option.

But no, she wanted chocolate cake, not—

There was that sound again. Why was there sound? Why was it so sharp and loud when she just wanted to sleep?

Sleep.

"Just let me sleep."

"She's alive. Gods, she's alive." The voice was even louder now, but it no longer grated on her nerves. It was familiar to her. Treasured. Why would she ever choose chocolate cake over *that*? Only now did she realize what the sound had been. Her name. Over and over. The word left Larylis' lips yet again, like a chant meant to tether her to the plane of the living.

Another sound shattered the haze in her mind. A sweet small cry.

Her heart pulsed in response, warming, spreading. She jolted, and pain shot through every inch of her.

Oh, right. Death was painful.

No, not death.

Life.

Life was...gods, it was agonizing.

Again that tiny cry reached her ears, and she opened her eyes. Smoke clouded her vision, but she blinked it away. Two faces stared down at her, one bronze, the other...

"Lare." Her voice came out a tired rasp. His cheeks were wet with tears and soot.

She tried to sit but every part of her revolted at the motion.

"Don't try to move," Larylis said. "You're hurt."

"But she's healing." Garot stared down at her with wide eyes. That was when she noticed him bouncing a still-crying Noah in his arms. Noah was no longer wrapped in his lavender swaddling, but the lighter linen layer he'd worn underneath. She'd turned her son's protection over to Garot before her confrontation with Darius. Now all she wanted was to hold her baby.

If only her arms would let her. They remained limp and aching at her sides. "What happened? Why aren't I dead?"

Larylis' eyes bulged. "You intended to die with that gambit?"

"Well, I hoped I wouldn't, but..." She winced, the corners of her lips cracking and stinging.

"You warded yourself today, didn't you?" Garot asked.

"Yes," she said, recalling how she'd cast the wardweaving before her bedroom mirror earlier. Even though she'd hoped the ward had worked, she hadn't been certain. Nor could she have known it would stop dragon flame.

Her magic had felt stronger than ever when she'd faced Darius, but she hadn't been focusing on protective wards. Every ounce of her attention had been reserved for her glamour. She'd been willing to do what needed to be done regardless of the result, even if it ended in death. Her intention hadn't been to undervalue herself to protect others like she had before. Instead, she'd performed her bold act because she knew without a shred of doubt that she'd succeed. That she was strong enough, clever enough, devious enough. Her death or survival simply hadn't factored into her plans.

"What about Darius?" she asked.

"He didn't fare nearly as well as you," Larylis said.

She needed to see for herself. Clenching her jaw, she tried to sit again, and this time she managed to lift herself on her forearms. Larylis braced her back and raised her to sitting. Several feet away, she found a charred husk that must be Darius. A sword lay between his shoulders and severed head.

"For good measure," Larylis explained.

Not far from the body, the soldier who'd held Larylis captive had also been relegated to a corpse, his sword stolen. She hadn't had to feign her terror at seeing Larylis with a sword at his throat. They hadn't anticipated him getting captured. They'd only discussed him holding back just enough to give Mareleau an opportunity to pretend to surrender. It could have gone wrong a thousand different ways, yet Larylis had played his role and she hers. She wasn't the only one who'd risked their life.

Mareleau shifted her attention from the dead to the living—herself. She stared down at her arms, finding them red and raw. Her robe's hem had been fully burned away and what little remained was charred. Every inch of flesh she could see was as red as her arms. Yet just like Garot had said, there were signs of healing too. She frowned. She didn't have fae blood, so she shouldn't be armed with rapid healing. Her glamour and protective wardweaving couldn't be responsible for the feat either.

In that case...

She turned her attention inward and felt the same tingle of magic she'd sensed after Ailan's death. It was stronger now, pulsing between her and Noah, who'd finally ceased crying in Garot's arms. "The *mora*," she said. "It's stronger now, isn't it?"

Garot nodded. "Even without using my pathweaving, I can feel my abilities have been fortified."

"Did the wardweavers make it to the tear?" Larylis asked. "Did they seal it?"

Garot had no answer. None of them could know for sure, not until Etrix returned. But Mareleau didn't want to wait. With a pained groan, she attempted to stand. Larylis aided her efforts, though his expression told her he'd rather she kept still. Someone else helped her rise—a solid force that nudged her other side, as if to help her keep her balance while she clung to Larylis.

Brow furrowed, Mareleau glanced beside her. An enormous head of white feathers and scales braced her ribcage. She bit back a yelp but managed to keep from flinching away.

Ferrah, however, seemed to sense her reaction. She pulled back slightly, her throat vibrating with a high-pitched chirp as she stared at Mareleau with slitted purple eyes. Wait...that chirping. Was it one of the sounds that had awoken her? It made more sense that she would have been perturbed by the strange hum of chirps than her husband's voice.

"She's been like that ever since she cut off her flame," Garot said.

"You mean, you didn't enjoy trying to burn me to a crisp?" Mareleau muttered. "I thought you'd be pleased."

Ferrah flicked her tongue and nudged Mareleau's shoulder, bumping her tender flesh with far more force than necessary. She made to push the creature away, but Ferrah nuzzled her palm, eyes closed, her humming chirps softening to a slightly more melodic tune.

"Oh," Garot said, pulling his head back. He blinked a few times. "Ooooh. Interesting."

"What's interesting?" Mareleau wasn't sure whether to try to push the dragon away again or if she should hold still lest Ferrah chomp her wrist.

"She's bonded to you."

"Bonded," Mareleau and Larylis echoed in unison.

Mareleau reassessed the dragon, who continued to nuzzle her hand, with new eyes. "You mean...nearly killing me endeared me to you?"

Sorry. The word entered her awareness. Not through

sound but *knowing*. Mareleau sucked in a sharp breath, not daring to believe that word had come from Ferrah. *You insult me. You think I wanted to burn you? I trusted you to cast a better wardweaving. I didn't think you'd get hurt.*

With every word, the voice grew clearer in her mind, taking on a feminine lilt with an unmistakable edge of chagrin.

Ferrah finally pulled away and removed her face from Mareleau's palm. *I expect better of my mistress and her magic in the future.* With that, Ferrah slithered down the cave and out of sight.

Mareleau stared after her, dumbstruck. After a few bewildered moments, she recalled why she'd wanted to stand in the first place. "We should get to the tear at once and confirm that it's been sealed. Garot, will you weave us —"

"Not *us*," Garot said. He passed Noah to Larylis, who in turn cradled his son against his chest with the tenderest care. "I will go myself. You're regent now, and I'll not have you making such a poor spectacle of yourself until you've healed, washed, changed, and...and done something about your hair."

Her pulse quickened at the last part. She reached for her shoulders, then her neck. It wasn't until she touched her nape that she felt even a hint of singed tresses. Her throat tightened, and she wasn't ashamed of the sorrow that filled her. Maybe it was vain to mourn her long pale locks, but she was only a hero, not a saint. And she wasn't even a real hero. Real heroes wouldn't relish watching their enemy burn.

"Fine," she said, voice quavering. "Please see that the wardweavers have succeeded and report back at once."

Garot gave her a tired smile, looking almost like his carefree self again. "You didn't waste any time settling into your new position, did you?"

She gave him a haughty shrug, ignoring the scream of her muscles. She didn't exactly delight in her role as regent, for it had come at the cost of many lives. Most of all, Ailan's. And many more goodbyes would soon follow. But Mareleau was born to be queen. Born to rule. Born to scheme and lie and deceive. She'd convince this world she was the best regent, the best Edel Morkara'Elle, they'd ever know. She'd make a life for herself, her husband, and her son. Not just any life. A happy one. A fulfilling one.

She wouldn't settle for anything less.

Cora didn't know how much time had passed. She sank into a trance as she, Teryn, and Valorre continued to urge the *mora* back. At first, Cora could tell there was something wrong. She pushed and pushed and pushed, but there was no relief. Nothing to aid her efforts at their destination. The strongest vein of *mora* that led to and from the tear remained as strong as ever.

The wardweavers...

They were gone.

Her magic nearly faltered then, but she refused to crumple under the realization. She had to trust her allies. They would come through. They would do their part.

So she pushed. On and on, she fought the flow of *mora*, resisted the temptation to harness it. She shared the burden with her companions, leaned on them more when her strength began to wane, then took back control when she recovered. At times, the cycle seemed endless. Like decades had passed. Centuries. She was convinced she'd become one with the rock and no longer held a purpose or identity. When this happened, Teryn always seemed to know. He'd hold her tighter, speak her name, and call her back to reality, just like she'd done for him all those months ago when he'd fought death.

Just when she thought she might be at the end of her reserves, relief came to her. It was small at first, just a stitch in a gaping chasm, but little by little her efforts were aided. She could almost feel the closing of the tear as it slowly lightened her load.

Her mind sharpened.

She opened her eyes for what might have been the first time in hours. Dawn was on the horizon, just barely touching the tops of the hills around the valley. Her palms remained pressed to the rock, Valorre's soft muzzle beneath her chin, Teryn's arms wrapped around her middle, his face pressed to her shoulder. He whispered encouraging words as she pushed harder, keeping the magic at bay while the tear grew smaller and smaller. Now that her mind was beginning to clear, the process felt achingly slow. Whatever time was passing in El'Ara, it was crawling here. One minute there was several here.

Yet she'd hold out.

They were so close.

And then...

The *mora* cut off.

She sagged as the resistance disappeared. The magic no longer hummed beneath her hands, no longer called to her with tempting visions. Body stiff, she sat back on numb legs. Teryn rolled onto his back, his forearm thrown over his eyes. Valorre settled at the base of the rock, looking dazed.

Cora felt...empty.

She'd only commanded that well of magic for a brief

time, but in its wake was a hollow lightness. Glorious relief. She turned herself over to it, closed her eyes, and let sleep take her.

∼

Teryn woke to birdsong and midday sun blazing on the other side of his eyelids. Then a peck on his cheek. He pried his eyes open and found Berol's face backlit by the warm sunlight. His arm felt limp and heavy as he lifted it to scritch her feathers. She chirped and nipped his cheek again.

"I'm all right," he said. He was glad to see she was too. She'd fulfilled her mission at the tear, alerting the Elvyn of Darius' arrival. He wasn't sure if her presence meant the battle had ended or if she'd flown here immediately after. She may have been here the entire time he'd held onto Cora.

He rose to sitting, and there wasn't a part of his body that didn't ache from the movement. Berol immediately rose into the air to land on his shoulder—his uninjured one, thankfully. Her weight wasn't exactly welcome, what with the gash he'd sustained on the other side, not to mention his myriad of other wounds, but he didn't have the heart to brush her off.

He shifted to glance where Cora had last been on the rock. His heart stuttered to find her no longer beside him, but as he cast his gaze to the base of the rock, he found Valorre sleeping there, Cora curled up with him, her head propped on his belly.

He calmed at the sight. Their duties weren't exactly over. There were still the wraiths to set free, the aftermath of battle to deal with, both at Ridine and on the human side of the tear, and a final trip to El'Ara—a first trip for Teryn—to say goodbye to those they'd never see again.

Even though he was anxious to set everything to rights, he figured he'd let Cora and Valorre sleep a while longer. Instead, he focused on the one thing he could do alone.

Stepping away from Centerpointe Rock, he unsheathed his dagger and reopened the wound on his palm. Berol let out a string of anxious chirps. The lesion was already red and angry and certainly didn't like being opened again, but he needed fresh blood to call the wraiths to him. As soon as a crimson well filled his palm, he let it drip onto the grass. "Come. It's time to go home."

Silently, the field fell under a misty fog. The haze soon materialized into figures. The wraiths' forms undulated, their eyes empty and unseeing.

"You did well," Teryn whispered. "You helped thwart the man who once ordered you to fight and die for nothing. Instead, you fought for the future of the land you were left to wander in. As promised, I have not abandoned you. As promised, I offer you an end."

He held out his hand but didn't move. He wouldn't hunt the spirits down and force oblivion upon them. He'd let them crave it. Let them come to him for their final rest.

One of the nearest wraiths swept toward him and paused a few feet away.

Teryn kept his hand open, his arm relaxed.

The wraith's form rippled, as if deliberating. Then it closed the final distance, placed his hazy, wavering hand over Teryn's...

The wraith disappeared.

Hunger and yearning filled some of the next closest specters, as if the end they'd witnessed had filled them with craving. One by one, more came forward. One by one, Teryn set them free. One by one, as midday crept on and the sun moved toward the horizon, Teryn fulfilled his oath.

He was practically delirious yet again by the time the final wraith approached. But as his gaze took in the spirit before him, his mind sharpened.

It wasn't one of the warrior wraiths. It was Emylia.

She gave him a sad smile. "Did I do enough to deserve peace?"

He met her eyes with a solemn yet earnest look. "You don't have to do anything to earn your rest, Emylia. You never did. You chose to wander. You can choose to go home."

Her lower lip wobbled. "I don't feel like I did enough. All I did was cause trouble in my life, and in my death...I didn't trust you. I tried to stop you from summoning the wraiths, but you set them free. You didn't succumb to the allure of dark magic."

"Not yet." He let a corner of his mouth lift.

She sighed. "You won't. I know it now. You've become something new. A human with a type of magic I've never seen before. A reaper of souls. I was so afraid when I first realized what you were."

"And now?"

"I'm not afraid anymore, just...ashamed."

"You don't have to be ashamed," Teryn said. He wanted to reach out and comfort her, but he knew what his touch would do. Just like with the wraiths, he wouldn't force peace on her.

"Tell her I forgive her."

Teryn startled at the sound of Cora's voice. He turned and found her sitting on the rock, caressing Valorre's neck. He wasn't sure how long she'd been awake. Had she been watching him while he'd sent the wraiths home? She'd at least been present long enough to hear him say Emylia's name, and the rest of Teryn's side of their conversation.

Cora spoke again, tone gentle. "Tell her she has nothing left to atone for. She never did."

He faced Emylia once more. The spirit sagged, either with relief or sorrow. "I'm so sorry," she said. "Tell her that. Tell her I'm so sorry for what my words led Morkai to do."

"She knows," Teryn said, but he conveyed her message anyway.

Emylia spoke again, and this time her voice took on a fierce edge. "And tell her...tell her she's stronger than she knows. She's stronger than anyone who has ever underestimated her. She's stronger than everything that could ever seek to tie her, trap her, or smother her. She's stronger than any shadow, any darkness, any curse. Tell her that."

A chill ran down Teryn's spine. What did Emylia mean by that? That Cora was stronger than any curse? Was it merely wishful thinking, a desire to make things right, or was it a sign of Emylia's magic? She'd been a seer when she'd been alive. Had she seen an end to the curse Morkai had placed upon Cora?

He shook the questions from his mind. Her words sparked a beautiful hope, but that hope was theirs regardless of the outcome. For it mattered not whether they had children of their own bloodline or chose heirs from another. Whether they ruled like their predecessors or started a revolution. He and Cora would forge their own future together. Royal politics and outdated traditions could go to the seven hells. A witch and a reaper were Lela's queen and king. They were already breaking rules and starting anew.

Still, he conveyed Emylia's words to Cora.

Emylia heaved another sigh, and her form sharpened

slightly. Then, with a nod, she stepped closer to Teryn and held out her hand.

"I'm ready to go home," she said, voice quavering.

Teryn's chest tightened. He and Emylia hadn't always seen eye to eye, but she'd helped him through one of the greatest challenges he'd faced. Taught him how to fight Morkai and reclaim his body.

She'd died for love. Fought for love. Grieved for love.

She deserved so much better.

He didn't know a damn thing about the otherlife. Who could truly claim to know? But he hoped it would treat her well. Hoped she'd find the rest her soul so deeply deserved.

He reached for her hand. "Thank you, friend."

She grasped his palm in a handshake he couldn't feel.

Her soul disappeared.

61

It was surreal to stand at the center of the Blight without a wall of mist anywhere to be seen. The colorless earth warped and puckered in a spiral pattern, meeting at a distinct point. Mareleau shuddered at the pulse of *mora* that flowed from that point, moving through the land, through her body. A tether of magic remained forever between her and Noah, a circuit she sensed no matter where he was. Larylis held him, several feet from where Mareleau stood, and still the pulse connected them as strongly as if he was in her arms. She supposed she'd feel it until the day Noah came of age and her role as regent became obsolete.

It was a bittersweet prospect. The day her child would no longer need her. She hoped she wouldn't be too disappointed to give up this power when the time came.

Etrix came up beside her. "We'll need to build a temporary shelter here until an official palace can be constructed. And you'll need to train in how to move the *mora* at once. Our priority is healing the Blight."

She met his ruby-brown eyes and found lines of fatigue on his ageless face. Even though he spoke in a diplomatic tone, he was grieving. His daughter had died only yesterday. It didn't matter that they'd been separated for decades, or that Etrix hadn't even known if she'd been alive in the human world before they'd recently reunited. A loss was a loss, and his was still fresh. A full week had passed in the human world, but here it had only been a day. Luckily, Cora had retrieved Ailan's body and brought it back, along with all the other Elvyn soldiers—the hale, the dead, and the wounded alike.

It must have been exhausting work for Cora, constantly worldwalking back and forth over the past week, often with multiple companions in tow. With the tear fully sealed, the only way Cora could enter El'Ara was with Valorre. Cora had sent word an hour ago—El'Ara time—that her mission was complete. All that remained was escorting Helena to El'Ara.

After that...

Mareleau would never see Cora again. She'd worldwalk away for the last time. Her throat constricted just thinking about it.

Making friends, losing friends.

Yet another bittersweet eventuality.

If you're building a new palace, came a voice in her mind, *I demand ample caves nearby.*

Mareleau glanced skyward and found the opalescent creature soaring overhead. She still wasn't used to her bonded dragon. Especially since Ferrah wasn't the warmest companion. She'd demonstrated a few short-lived bouts of neediness, approaching Mareleau at random times to head-butt her hand with the vigor of a beast who didn't understand her own strength. Ferrah otherwise remained cold and independent.

Like a cat, Mareleau supposed.

I resent that. I don't know what that is.

You don't have felines here? Mareleau thought back. She was amazed that that was all it took to communicate with her. *Small bodies, pointed ears, soft fur.*

You mean the Elvyn?

I said soft fur.

Isn't that what's on their heads? I suppose you wouldn't know. Ferrah said the last part with what Mareleau imagined was a smirk, before flying off and out of sight.

Mareleau touched the ends of her chin-length hair. She'd cried when she'd seen her reflection in the mirror yesterday, but today she wasn't feeling nearly as self-conscious. Her short locks suited her fine, now that one of her maids had taken a pair of shears to them and styled them in loose waves. It left her with nothing to braid when she was anxious, but that was probably a habit she should discard already. She was regent of El'Ara, after all.

"So...this will one day be our home?" Larylis said, coming up beside her with Noah in his arms. She frowned, puzzled by his words until she realized he was referring to the palace Etrix had mentioned. The Elvyn now stood several yards away, staring up at the sky as if mentally constructing their future palace. Mareleau imagined they had Elvyn specialists who designed and constructed their impressive feats of architecture, but if it distracted Etrix from the loss of his daughter, who was she to judge?

"Yes," Mareleau said, meeting his lips with a soft kiss before placing an even softer one on her sleeping son's forehead. She met her husband's eyes again. "Are you all right with all this? I know it's happening so fast. Everything we thought we knew about our lives and our roles has changed."

"I admit, this is nothing like the future I imagined for

us," he said, his gaze scanning the barren landscape of the Blight.

Her heart sank. Gods, he'd lost so much. Before she could open her mouth to apologize, he pinned her with a knowing look.

"Don't you dare, Mare." His tone was gentle, his lips tilted in a smile. "Don't tell me I've lost everything, because it's far from the truth. I will ache for the human world and the people we'll have to leave behind. But don't forget who I am at my heart. I wasn't born to be a king, but a lover and a scholar. I have my wife and child. And now I have an entire world to satisfy my intellectual curiosity. This place is a storybook legend come to life."

That was so like him, and it lifted her heart to the heavens. She wasn't sure how much of his words were meant to placate her, but they served to remind her that they could thrive here. They *would*. And they would do it together.

She pressed her lips to his again, and as she pulled away, movement caught her eye. She and Larylis turned to find the colorless landscape warping and swirling midair not too far away. Mareleau's heart leaped in anticipation. Etrix turned toward the vortex too. It spread wider to create a large opening.

Garot stepped out first. "Look how brilliantly the *mora* has improved my abilities! My Path works through the Blight now."

Fanon followed next, far less jovial. His complexion was wan, and dark circles shadowed his eyes. Mareleau's gaze dropped to the silk bandages wrapping his blunted wrists. She'd heard about the injuries he'd sustained, heard he might not even recover. But there he was. She wasn't his greatest fan, but he'd supported Ailan's wishes where Mareleau and Noah were concerned. So long as his loyalty outlasted his consort's life, Fanon might be an essential advocate in the coming days, second only to Etrix. She needed their support and influence on the tribunal to ensure the Elvyn continued to honor their vows.

Garot and Fanon stepped aside, revealing the faces of those Mareleau had been most excited to see: Cora, Teryn, Valorre, and...

"Mother!" Mareleau took off running. She hadn't expected to feel this relief, this sharp piercing love, this overwhelming comfort. Not for Helena.

But she did, and as she collided into her mother's arms, she knew Helena felt it too. Cora had been right to include Helena in her terms for the alliance. Mareleau needed her mother. Sure, they would likely fight again like they used to, and they would certainly say cruel things to each other when at their wit's end. But they'd mended a gap between them that neither would ever dare widen again.

CORA WATCHED THE REUNION WITH TEARY EYES. LARYLIS AND Teryn met next, bracing each other's forearms. She gave them a few long moments alone before approaching them and addressing Larylis. "I'm sorry I couldn't bring your mother or brothers."

"It's all right," Larylis said, and there seemed to be only a hint of regret in his tone. He may not be close to Annabel Seralla or his young half brothers, but it must have hurt at least somewhat to know he'd never see them again. Regardless, the Elvyn wouldn't permit it, as it hadn't been part of Ailan's negotiations with the tribunal. Ailan had secured a binding vow from them, granting Larylis and Helena protection, respect, and citizenship in exchange for the terms Cora had promised.

She'd fulfilled every term of her end over the past week, worldwalking the Elvyn soldiers who'd fought alongside the humans. The battle near the tear had been close, but as soon as Darius had disappeared beyond the Veil, many of his soldiers thought him defeated. The tide had turned after that, and the human-Elvyn alliance ended victorious. Still, there had been many casualties. Yet more lives Cora would mourn as queen. More deaths she bore the weight of.

Meanwhile, Teryn had overseen the aftermath of the battle at Ridine, which had far fewer casualties on their side. The wraiths had truly saved them that night. Shortly after Cora and Teryn had left for Centerpointe Rock, the battle had ended. The survivors had surrendered or fled. Captain Alden had chosen not to give chase to those who ran, and Cora agreed with that decision. Let them run. Let them tell the tale of terror that had befallen them. Let them strike fear into the hearts of anyone who would seek to come for Lela next.

"Thank you for everything you've done," Larylis said, bringing her back to the present. "For ensuring my place here."

"You're welcome," Cora said, then glanced down at Noah. She hadn't paid him much attention since birth, hadn't ever asked to hold him or rock him. Now she knew why—she'd been afraid. Too afraid that the bitterness that had clogged her heart would rear its head and force her to confront it. But she had confronted it. She cast a questioning look at Larylis. "Can...can I hold him?"

"Of course." His answer came so easily. He had no idea how hard it had been for her to utter those words.

Her heart beat a little heavier as he passed the child to

her. She looked down at the sleepy, pudgy-cheeked baby, her senses open to whatever reaction she might have. If she felt a bitter pang, she'd accept it. If she felt hurt, or rage, or tears, she'd let it come. And yet...only warmth filled her heart as she held the child for the first and last time. "I wish I could watch you grow up, little nephew," she said, and she meant every word.

"I wish you could too." Mareleau stood before her now, her eyes red from crying during her reunion with her mother.

Cora pressed a gentle kiss to Noah's downy head and passed him back to Larylis. Then she and Mareleau collided in a hug. More warmth filled her, every ounce of resentment gone. Free. She fully sank into the sorrow of the moment, the beauty of this goodbye. She'd hated Mareleau when they'd first met, considered her a rival. The kind of woman Cora could never get along with.

But they'd found camaraderie in darkness. They were different in many ways, but similar too. Stubborn. Bold. Unafraid of violence and cunning if it helped them reach their goals. They both railed against the societal standards that demeaned them.

Two queens.

Two friends.

Two women who would do whatever they could to influence their two separate worlds for the better.

They pulled apart, their cheeks glistening with tears.

"Goodbye, Cora," Mareleau said, voice trembling.

"Goodbye, Mare."

Cora and Teryn stepped back, and Mareleau, Larylis, and Helena huddled close. Valorre nudged Cora's shoulder. It was time for them to go home. Cora took Teryn's hand in hers and placed her free palm on Valorre's neck. She gave one last smile to the people she loved—

"Come, unicorn," Garot said, tone jovial. "I know you'll miss your friend, but it's time for them to leave."

The blood drained from Cora's face, and she sensed the same shock radiating from Valorre. "What are you..."

Mother Goddess, it all became so sorrowfully clear. The Elvyn intended for Valorre to stay behind.

"He's a fae creature," Etrix said. "He belongs here with his own kind. There is no more fae magic in the human world. If he returns to Lela, he will eventually lose his magic."

"He'll become a horse," Garot said. "That's what you call a hornless unicorn in your world, isn't it?"

Cora blinked, struck silent. Even Valorre was mute for once. "No," she finally managed to say. "He...he's my friend. My familiar."

"What they say is true," Fanon said. His tone lacked all the sharpness it used to contain. Instead, it was deeper, laced with grief and exhaustion. "Even more pressing is that we made a binding vow to Ailan. Everyone on the tribunal did, and it outlasts her death. We would accept these few humans as citizens in El'Ara, but none of our kind will be left in Lela."

Ailan had told her as much, but she'd imagined the Elvyn soldiers, not Valorre. Yet...a part of her had understood those terms extended to the unicorns. It was why Valorre had worked so hard to escort his brethren through the Veil before she pushed the *mora* back.

Even so, not once had she imagined Valorre being left in El'Ara when all was said and done.

"We cannot let you leave with him," Fanon said, tone surprisingly gentle. "Doing so would break our oath. And if you leave with him against our will, your actions will void what we agreed to. The tribunal will no longer be beholden to keep their vows."

Cora's stomach turned. She could imagine what that would mean. They could take it out on Mareleau, Larylis, and Helena.

He's right. Valorre spoke into her mind, his tone resigned. *I cannot leave with you if you want your friends to stay safe.*

Cora's heart cracked.

Then his voice took on a cheery tone. *So I'll just come back to you later!*

What do you mean? Her heart thudded with hope. Did she dare hope?

You heard him, Valorre said. *They cannot let you leave with me, nor can you take me with you against their will. But there's nothing in their vow that forbids me from leaving El'Ara of my own accord later for a fully unrelated reason.*

She puzzled over his words. *Your horn may have the ability to pierce the Veil, but our worlds are no longer connected in such a tangible way. The Veil is invisible now. There's no wall of mist to walk through.*

Our worlds still rest side by side. I'll find a way.

You're no worldwalker.

But you are, and we're connected. We always will be.

He was so confident, so assured. She wanted to believe him, but...

Do not doubt me, he said, tossing his mane. *I am a superior being among my kind. No unicorn has bonded a human before and none will ever again. I am the smartest and handsomest of all fae creatures. Surely I can find my way to your world.*

She couldn't help but smile at that. *Even if it means losing your magic and becoming a horse?*

He internally scoffed. *I'll still be the largest, fastest, and smartest horse on your planet. Don't lump me in with those brainless fornicators.*

Tears rolled down her cheeks, but her heart felt lighter. It was still breaking, and maybe it would never heal. She couldn't rely on the future he hoped for, but she could share his dream.

Maybe someday they'd meet again.

But for now...this was goodbye.

She pressed her face into his neck, memorizing the softness of his coat, the hum of his energy all around her. Teryn joined her, one hand on her shoulder, the other stroking Valorre's mane.

Tell Teryn not to look at a single horse while I'm gone, Valorre said, tone somber.

That's kind of a lot to ask.

Well, tell him not to look at a single one with affection. *He better keep those dazzling eyes to himself. And when he looks at his reflection and sees that stupid moonlight hair, he better think of me.*

Cora chuckled. *We both will. I promise.*

With her lungs still tight enough to burst, she forced herself to pull away from her unicorn companion, her best friend, and the creature who had set everything currently in her life into motion. He was the reason she'd left the Forest People. He was the reason she'd crossed paths with Teryn. He'd changed her life. She couldn't imagine the unbearable silence she'd endure once he was no longer in it.

I'll find you, he said, more certain than ever. *I'll cross worlds forever if I must. You'll see.*

See you soon, then.

She blinked tears from her eyes so she could memorize this final image. Mareleau, Larylis, Noah, and Helena huddled together. Etrix and Garot waving goodbye. Fanon offering a single nod of farewell. Valorre at the center, his head held high, sunlight glinting off his pale fur.

Teryn squeezed her hand, and she returned the gesture. Then she inhaled a deep breath and closed her eyes.

Took a step.

And left a piece of her behind.

EPILOGUE

ONE YEAR LATER – HUMAN REALM

The Reaper King and the Witch Queen lorded over Lela in a bloody iron-fisted reign, striking terror into the hearts of all.

At least, that was what some stories claimed, as told by their enemies. Not that they had many now. A year had passed since the fateful battle, and not once had Norun renewed hostility toward Khero. The kingdom had plenty to deal with after fighting a six-month-long rebellion before ceding Haldor and Sparda back to their former kings. Now Khero had two more allies standing between them and a much smaller enemy kingdom. Cora was certain she could eventually convince King Isvius to forge an official peace pact between Norun and Lela.

Syrus had been more than eager to do so. Once Darius' heir—a wealthy duke who'd boasted the highest merit rating on the island kingdom—took his new post as king, he was quick to disassociate himself from the former king's actions. It was a smart choice on his part, considering Syrus bore the responsibility for the deaths of King Larylis and Queen Mareleau.

The lie grated on Cora's nerves—and her heart—but it was essential. Hardly anyone would believe the truth. She may have claimed rule over the land by right of magic, but if she wanted to keep her crown in the eyes of the people, it was best she didn't spout tales of faerie portals and wars with ancient Elvyn princes. As much as she hated pretending her dear friends were deceased, it was much more believable than them living in a parallel realm inhabited by fae.

Besides, the lie had encouraged peace with Syrus' new king. Cora burned with curiosity to discover what would come of the kingdom without their ageless, five-hundred-year-old king. Would his meritocracy last? Or crumble?

Only time would tell—

"Are you thinking about work, my love?"

Cora shook her head and lifted her gaze to Teryn's. Her cheeks heated, giving her away. Damn. She'd been caught.

"Perhaps," she said sheepishly.

Teryn was half reclined on the blanket they'd laid out in the shade of a cherry tree. His silver hair was longer now, falling just below his shoulders. He was dressed in trousers, a linen shirt, and an open black waistcoat. It was a warm spring day, perfect for a picnic under pink blossoms that drifted from the branches like snow. They had a spread of bread, fruit, and tea sandwiches before them. The sun was bright, the air was fresh, and this was one of their first calm days to themselves in an entire year...

And here Cora was thinking about work and politics. Again.

"We do deserve a day off, you know," Teryn said, lips quirked in a sideways grin.

He was right. After everything they'd worked toward this past year—forging peace, merging Vera with Khero, strengthening their position as king and queen, recovering from physical and emotional wounds—they truly did deserve some time to just be themselves. Teryn and Cora. The reaper and the witch. Two young people in love.

She scooted closer to Teryn, and he fully reclined the rest of the way, angling his body until he was resting his head in her lap. She adjusted the skirts of her cream day dress, arranging it in pools of lace around them. "I'm sorry," she said with a wry grin. "I'll pay attention to you now. I promise."

He grinned up at her, his face dappled by sunlight and the shadows of the cherry blossoms. Cora tilted her head back and found Berol on one of the branches, preening. A gust of wind rattled the blossoms, forcing Berol to splay her wings. In its wake, a flurry of pink petals rained down over them. Cora grinned wide and extended her hand, trying to catch them as they fell. She managed to snatch three before the flurry settled. She opened her tattooed palm and let the petals drift onto their picnic blanket.

Her attention then drifted to her *insigmora*. Her tattoos had ceased growing on their own. It truly must have been the influence of fae *mora* that had made them take on a life of their own in the first place. Still, she didn't need them to grow or change. She treasured her tattoos exactly as they were, a symbol of what she was. A memory of everything she'd experienced, inked on her body.

At least the absence of *mora* hadn't hampered her witch magic. Her abilities continued to grow with every day. Six months ago, she'd managed to dissolve Morkai's previously indestructible book. With a single touch, it had melted to ash. The last visible trace of him was gone.

Teryn's magic remained unchanged. He'd grown used to seeing spirits and would give final rest to the rare few souls who sought him out for it. They hadn't come across any dangerous entities yet, but if they ever did, Teryn was prepared to dispose of them by force.

Teryn's fingertips brushed her cheek, and she shifted her gaze back to him. He grinned up at her from her lap. She ran a hand through his pale tresses, brushing a few errant strands from his brow.

His lashes fluttered shut. "I like the location you chose for our picnic."

"Did you only just now notice?"

"No, I noticed from the start. What a sentimental woman you are."

She snorted a laugh. Though he was right. She'd chosen their location with great fondness. The tree they sat under now was the very same Cora had once shot an arrow into the day she met Teryn. The stream rushed by their blanket in a soothing rhythm.

Teryn wasn't the only person this location reminded her of.

It reminded her of Valorre too.

A heavy sensation struck her chest, and she winced.

Teryn's eyes flew open, brows furrowed. "What's wrong?"

Cora rubbed her breastbone, but the pressure remained. "It's...I don't know. I keep feeling this...ache. Almost like my lungs are inflating, but not my actual lungs. More like...a flare of magic?"

Teryn lifted himself from her lap and faced her. "You don't think something's wrong?"

The sensation passed, and she donned a reassuring grin. "I'm fine. It's probably just my magic growing in a new way."

He didn't look convinced so she leaned forward and pressed a kiss to his lips. He returned it with tender care.

The ache sparked in her chest again.

She pulled back with a grimace she couldn't hide. This time there was more than that heavy feeling. There was a tingle of energy with it, a familiar strain...

A chill ran through her.

It couldn't be.

The energy grew closer, brighter, almost painful in its resonance. Emotions that were hers—yet somehow not hers—flooded her. Anticipation, anxiety, impatience, excitement. It was so overwhelming, it sparked tears in her eyes.

She rose to her feet before she realized she'd moved—

Just as a flash of white emerged from the dense foliage downstream.

A gasp left Cora's lips.

The white unicorn froze in place, ears erect, muscles quivering. Then all three were moving—Teryn, Cora, and Valorre.

I found you! Valorre's voice filled Cora's mind, the most welcome sound she could imagine. *I found you! Do you know how long I've been looking?*

Valorre could hardly hold still as Cora reached him and threw her arms around his thick neck. He tossed his mane, kicked his hooves, and nuzzled Cora with almost enough force to knock her over. She didn't care. Laughter left her lips as happy tears streamed down her cheeks. Even Teryn was moved, his eyes glazed and crinkled at the corners as he patted the unicorn from the other side. Berol must have flown with them when they ran, for she now perched on Teryn's shoulder, chirping and attempting to nip Valorre while Teryn petted him.

Once their excitement cooled to a simmer, allowing

Cora to form words, she asked, "How did you manage it? How did you find us?"

I don't know, he said, equal parts innocent and excited. *I followed my heart and thoughts of you. And Teryn too! I tried to do the same thing we did when we worldwalked together. It was much harder without you, but...*

He tossed his mane, and his tone changed at once.

But I am exceedingly capable, as you well know. I had no doubts that I would figure it out, and I did. Looks like I can use your magic just fine.

Was that what that strange sensation had been? Valorre using her magic? She'd begun feeling it more and more the past week. She pressed her face to his soft coat. "I never doubted you."

I've seen some very strange things, Valorre said, abandoning his boastful demeanor. *I saw a world without trees, only tall rectangular castles and horseless metal carriages that swarmed the ground. Humans cluttered the naked, treeless streets. Then I saw a world inhabited only by dragons. That was my least favorite. I also saw a world of eternal snow and a world of eternal night. I rather liked the world of eternal spring. There were these tasty apples...but they did something strange to me. I think I walked on a rainbow? And maybe I frolicked around a bonfire with wolves? The next day, I couldn't feel my tongue or my legs.*

Cora could hardly comprehend his words. He'd traveled to multiple worlds on the way here? And was poisoned by an apple? That was troubling. Mother Goddess, he was lucky to be alive.

She refused to let panic overwhelm her and took comfort in his presence. He was here. He was safe.

"Well, aren't you the world traveler," she said. "Or...

multi-world traveler? Whatever the case, will you stay now that you've found us?"

He huffed a breath. *Obviously.*

She wrapped her arms around him again. "I'm really glad you're home."

I am too. A sweet silence fell between them until it was broken by, *Is Teryn glad I'm home?*

With a roll of her eyes, she pulled away from Valorre and conveyed the question to Teryn.

Teryn spoke with unwavering sincerity. "Val, I couldn't be happier."

Valorre tossed his mane with finesse, ensuring it rippled extra elegantly for Teryn's sake.

Teryn extended his hand toward their picnic blanket under the cherry tree. "Would you like to join us?"

Oh, a food blanket!

"A picnic," Cora corrected.

Are there apples?

"You want apples after everything that happened in... where was it? Eternal spring?"

Teryn frowned. "What's this about eternal spring?"

"I'll fill you in," Cora muttered.

At the same time, Valorre gleefully conveyed, *I always want apples!*

They reached the blanket, which sure enough had three very non-poisonous apples, one of which Teryn handed to Valorre.

Valorre internally sighed, then took the apple from Teryn's palm, munching away at once. *He really is the best of men, isn't he?*

Cora chuckled as she and Teryn settled back onto the blanket. "All right, Valorre. You've got some explaining to do. Tell us more about your travels."

SEVEN YEARS LATER – FAE REALM

Once upon a time, Mareleau had considered herself to be a woman without a heart. Or, if she'd had one at all, it was surely a shriveled thing, smothered by brambles and thorns. She now knew that had never been the case. She'd always had a heart; she'd simply kept it closed off for too many years. But love had helped break down her walls, and not just love for her husband. He'd been the first to breach them, but even Teryn had helped weaken them when she accepted him as her brother. Cora had shattered them the rest of the way, barreling into her heart despite neither of them wanting her to be there.

After that, it had been easy to love. Or...*easier*.

She'd repaired the burned bridges between her and her mother.

And she became a mother herself.

Now she knew what it was like to have a piece of her heart exist outside her body. First, it had cried, then it had crawled. It was most frightening when the piece of her heart had learned to toddle. She'd soothed many bruises and falls then, but just like the organ that beat in her chest, the child that represented her external heart recovered from every spill.

Noah was seven years old now, perched on a stool beside his father. Mareleau grinned as she watched the pair peering into a crystal cylinder that gave them a view of the stars overhead. They were outside on the rooftop terrace above their suite at Ailana'Auro Palace. The grand home of the Morkara had finished construction a year after the tear was sealed. Mareleau reclined on a cushioned divan, sipping

Faeryn honey wine, while Ferrah dozed peacefully beside her, taking up a good half of the terrace.

The night was dark yet the stars glittered like rainbow shards, more brilliantly than they ever did in the human world. Larylis pointed out a constellation, conveying lore and facts about the stars that comprised it. Her husband had been right; El'Ara had provided ample interest for him. He relished learning all he could about the world. He'd become fluent in the fae language a year before she had, and now worked with Garot to record human history. Or as much of it that Larylis knew and could recall. Which was substantial, to be honest. Garot still served as the chief path-weaver in service of the Morkara, but his work with Larylis allowed him to explore his love for stories. Even taboo ones, like human history.

Mareleau took another sip of wine and turned her gaze to the heavens. The stars looked so different from how they had back home. Well, back at her previous home. This was her home now, and she, Noah, and Larylis had important roles here. Even Helena had adapted, and was now a member of Elvyn high society, mingling with the other esteemed mothers.

Regardless, the differences between El'Ara and the human world begged the questions...what exactly were parallel worlds? Were the two realms on different planets? Different planes of existence? Several prominent truth-weavers had their own theories, but it seemed not all of them agreed. The whispers of their weavings often conveyed ideas that conflicted with one another's findings.

Those conversations always made Mareleau smile. She knew firsthand just how flawed prophecies and truthweav-ings could be. The prophecy that had tangled her life had made it seem like her son would be front and center, a chosen one born to battle darkness and save the world. In truth, Mareleau and Cora had played the most significant roles. Yes, Noah's birth had set everything into motion, but he hadn't physically performed any of the feats the prophecy had spoken of.

Which was exactly what had brought the prophecy to fruition.

Mareleau and Cora, two women Darius had underestimated, had defeated him in different ways. Cora took control of Lela using intel he'd given her. Mareleau took his life.

Mareleau's sense of victory, however, was always clouded with a pang of longing. She missed her friend terribly.

Noah giggled at something Larylis had said, then turned the crystal cylinder for a change of view. Their son was aging as normal human children aged, which was supposedly somewhat faster than the Elvyn did. He was growing so quickly, his looks already taking after Larylis'. His hair was several shades lighter than his father's, a rosy gold to Larylis' dark copper. Meanwhile, Larylis' tresses reached his nape in loose waves and a short beard graced his chin. It suited him well, giving him a roguish-yet-scholarly look.

Noah averted his gaze from the cylinder, and his shoulders sank. Mareleau was immediately on alert, attuned to his moods like the admittedly overprotective mother she was.

Larylis noticed too, pushing the cylinder aside to face his son. "What's wrong?"

Noah glanced from Larylis to Mareleau.

She was already on her feet and tried her best to keep her composure as she closed the distance between them. Crouching beside them with a gentle smile, she asked, "What is it, my love?"

Noah dropped his blue-green eyes. "Aribella told me that I'm...I'm a witch, an Elvyn, and a human all in one."

Mareleau clenched her jaw. Aribella was a spoiled brat. Yet she was also the daughter of one of the most respected tribunal members and one of Noah's classmates. Keeping her tone even, she said, "Yes, that's true. You know this, darling."

"Yes, but..." He met her gaze. "She said I'm destined to be evil. That the last person like me tried to destroy the world."

She forced her lips into a reassuring smile. "Noah, I too have the blood of witches, humans, and Elvyn. Do you think I'm evil?"

"You can be scary sometimes, Mum," he said with unabashed candor.

It was all she could do not to laugh. "Yes, well, being scary isn't exactly evil, is it?"

He shifted from foot to foot. "What if I become like him? What if, once I'm old enough that you're not regent anymore, I...do bad things with the *mora*?"

Her first instinct was to insist that would never happen. In her heart of hearts, she knew it was true. But she wouldn't be like Satsara. She wouldn't brush aside serious topics and put her son on a pedestal.

"Here's the thing," she said. "Every person, whether human or fae, has aspects of darkness and light. I was once afraid of my darkest side, afraid of what it meant to be a narcuss. And it's true that all forms of magic require respect and temperance. But you can notice shadows in your heart without letting them take over."

"How can I be sure I don't let them take over?"

"A very wise woman once told me," she said, recalling her conversation with Salinda so many years ago, "that it's a choice to follow the path of hope and love, even when you have dark feelings. Strength isn't being good or perfect but meeting your darkness face to face and moving forward instead of sinking into it. No matter what you find in those shadows, it is important that you love yourself."

Gently, she tapped his chest, right over his heart.

He puckered his lips, shifting them side to side as he pondered her words. "I don't get it."

She and Larylis laughed in unison. Larylis ruffled Noah's hair. "You don't have to understand it yet, but do remember your mother's words. She's a very intelligent woman."

Noah turned a wide-eyed look to Mareleau. "I thought Pa was the smart one."

Gods, even his unintentional insults were adorable. "He is, but I'm quite smart too. And so are you. Thank you for coming to us with such a heavy question." She hugged her son tight. "And if Aribella ever says something like that again, you tell her I'll—"

"Let's not threaten his classmates, love," Larylis said with a laugh.

"I told you," Noah said as Mareleau released him from her embrace. "Everyone says she's scary."

"I'll take that as a compliment," she mumbled.

You know, came Ferrah's lazy voice in her mind, *I could always create a...little accident for this small rude Elvyn who has filled our dear Morkara's head with such somber thoughts. If necessary.*

Mareleau shot her gaze toward the creature and found the dragon still dozing on the terrace. Or pretending to doze. *We are not murdering children. Not even brats like Aribella.*

Just a scare.

Mareleau glared at the dragon until the creature cracked

open one violet eye. She understood Ferrah's teasing mirth then. *You're a real feisty beast, you know that?*

Likewise. Ferrah closed her eye and settled back into slumber.

Mareleau shook her head, lips stretched in a wide grin, and settled in between the two loves of her life. With one arm wrapped around each of them, she said, "Show your scary mum your favorite constellation."

WANT MORE EPIC ROMANTIC FANTASY?

Keep the magic alive! The *Prophecy of the Forgotten Fae* trilogy is now complete, but I have more fantasy stories for you to enjoy! I hinted at my other book worlds in the epilogue. Wondering about the other "worlds" Valorre journeyed through when he was looking for Cora? You'll learn all about my different fae courts in my Faerwyvae books!

If you're craving more epic fantasy with angsty romance, *The Fair Isle Trilogy* is for you! It features a feisty heroine and a cruel fae king (he has antlers!) in an enemies-to-lovers romance you won't want to miss. It's set in a Victorian-inspired world where fae and humans clash. Start with *To Carve a Fae Heart*.

If you're craving something lighter and fluffier, try my *Entangled with Fae* series! These standalone new adult fairy-tale retellings are full of banter, swoon, and happily ever afters. They can be read in any order, but if you don't know where you want to start, try *Curse of the Wolf King: A Beauty and the Beast Retelling*.

ACKNOWLEDGMENTS

My goodness, this book was a challenge! It's been a few years since I've finished a trilogy, and this one was such a complex story to wrap up. Even though *A Fate of Flame* is based on an older, unpublished version of the story, "rewriting" it wasn't any easier than creating it from scratch. Having the old version lingering in my head often hindered my process, as I found myself with story threads I no longer needed and brand new unforeseen possibilities to explore. So it required a lot of work and creativity! But I am so proud of the end result and that I've given this trilogy the final shape, style, and emotion it has always deserved. These characters mean the world to me, and expressing their stories, journeys, and growth has been so satisfying. I have so many people to thank who fueled that process!

To my readers, of course. I am honored that you've read this trilogy, whether you've been a fan since its first iteration as the *Lela Trilogy*, or if *Prophecy of the Forgotten Fae* was your introduction to the land of Lela or even my work in general. I am thrilled that you've joined me on this journey!

To my husband, daughter, and all my pets (the latter of which I now have four). I love you! The human ones give me verbal encouragement that truly lifts my heart while the soft ones calm my anxiety when I just need to swamp around and touch something fluffy.

Thank you to my editor, Kristen, at Your Editing Lounge. You are amazing!!!

Thank you to my typo hunters and proofreaders, Claire, Emily, and Bianca. Y'all are the best.

Thank you to my PA, Emily and Luna Blooms PA Services. You take loads of stress off my plate!

Thank you to author pals Valia Lind, Hanna Sandvig, and Kay L. Moody who encouraged me through bouts of self-doubt, stress, and just writerly problems on a weekly basis while I wrote this book. You guys helped me push through!

And thank you to all the other Queens of the Quill who always encourage my author journey: Joanna Reeder, Rose Garcia, Stacey Trombley, Charlie N. Holmberg, K.C. Cordell, Clarissa Gosling, Abby J. Reed, Kristin J. Dawson, and Alison Ingleby.

Thank you Alisha Klapheke, my critique partner! Knowing someone is reading my early draft and assuring me it isn't hot garbage is enough to keep me sane.

I have so much gratitude for the author and reader community at large and all the amazing authors, influencers, and readers who encourage me or engage with me on social media. Writing can be lonely work but your interactions with me make me feel like I have a million friends!

Thank you always and happy reading,

—Tessonja

ALSO BY TESSONJA ODETTE

ABOUT THE AUTHOR

Tessonja Odette is a fantasy author living in Seattle with her family, her pets, and ample amounts of chocolate. When she isn't writing, she's watching cat videos, petting dogs, having dance parties in the kitchen with her daughter, or pursuing her many creative hobbies. Read more about Tessonja at www.tessonjaodette.com

instagram.com/tessonja
facebook.com/tessonjaodette
tiktok.com/@tessonja
x.com/tessonjaodette

Made in the USA
Coppell, TX
01 March 2024